DUST

SPECIAL EDITION

T. NELSON TAYLOR

CineCapture
Press

CineCapture LLC
PO Box 263701
Tampa, FL 33685

Please visit www.tnelsontaylor.com

First Printing: June 2009
First Electronic Edition: March 2010
Second Edition: August 2014
Third Edition as
Special Edition: September 2022

ISBN 979-8-9866787-3-3

Chapters

For <u>us</u>.

The most exciting phrase to hear in science, the one that heralds the most discoveries, is not "Eureka!" but "That's funny . . ."

~Isaac Asimov

Awakening

The cruelest clap of thunder reverberated through Cupertino's western foothills. Once distant grumblings became enraged outbursts. Emily's callow blue eyes danced underneath their lids without interruption, squinting only when the vivid flashes painted her bedroom's walls. A furious pounding erupted upon her door, but she did not hear her father's angry voice accompanying it. Instead, a crazed laughter pierced through the concussions. It was the distortion of a prize won by her mother at their church's annual fair. Xeno. He demanded entry and was about to have it.

At a blissful pixel in time not long ago, the Miller family echoed the Silicon Valley suburban archetype. Suzanne—a comely athletic Californian with sun-bleached hair and an unquenchable thirst for the outdoors—recently returned to Santa Clara General to complete her internship now that Emily was encapsulated by everything Fourth Grade. It was time; there would be no siblings.

Suzanne's high school sweetheart, a tall and fit Valley boy named Chris, was on his sixth year as a senior biomechanical researcher for Amerimem Industries. He never quite matured from adolescent geekdom, which meant Suzanne endured her husband's predictable moments of awkwardness, and tendencies to ramble on about technological advances. Yet every once and a while, Suzanne would rave about some off-the-wall breakthrough she read that morning, and invariably her coworkers diagnosed her with terminal osmosis. Incurable they said, then proceeded to prescribe several nearby treatment clinics featuring the finest sommeliers in residency.

Chris and Suzanne were in their late twenties and full of youthful energy, meaning their evenings were rarely idle. St. Luke's Annual Fair was one of their favorite diversions to spend some of that energy, and they couldn't resist the carnival food trailers scattered about the grounds—their professed annual health rebellion.

Suzanne placed a hot wand of cotton candy in Emily's hand, knowing full well that it meant scrubbing her blue-dyed face moments later.

She nudged Chris' arm and pointed towards the games area. "Let's go win something!"

"Win what?" Chris' attention changed from the myriad of blinking lights before him to the face of his daughter. Eyes rolled.

Suzanne shrugged. "I dunno—anything. You can't go to a fair without winning something."

She noticed a departing young family whose boy was toiling to shoulder a plush tiger twice larger than him.

Chris saw the boy and responded flatly, "True."

Emily pacified herself with another sizeable clump of sugar, managing to scarf down the sticky blue patch previously dangling from her mouth. She pointed towards the squirt gun races, eyes wide. "That one!"

Suzanne sighed and plucked a moist wipe from a small plastic pouch in her purse. Their walking pace quickened towards a game trailer that exhibited a wide variety of stuffed animals dangling from the ceiling and down the walls. A monstrous snake stretched across the entire back wall. Below it were bunched monkeys, a horse or two, baskets of puppies, a panda bear, a big fat crocodile, and the requisite cartoon characters du jour.

A race just finished when a large bell decimated everyone's ears. A shrill announcement blasted from in front of the targets. "Lane 3's a winner!"

Smug in his triumph, a middle-aged braggadocio wearing overtly large horn-rimmed glasses gave all the youngsters aiming advice while collecting his second largest prize of the evening—a two-foot-tall blue capuchin monkey.

"That should keep Rocco busy for a week," he said. "I must acquire another for Tulip."

Chris absorbed the man's hubris in stride. It was nothing but trash talk. "All three of us," he said to a rather darkly-baked carny sporting a sun-bleached ponytail slipped through the rear of a farm machinery company's logo ball cap. The stench of ashtray and sweat radiated from his clothing. It wasn't the obligatory ashtray occasionally used for visiting guests on your back patio; it was more reminiscent of those forgotten in the back corner of a dreary pool hall at the end of a long night—overstuffed and dowsed with light beer.

"Me too, fella." The man said, his new monkey wrapped around his neck.

"One for five, two for eight, three for ten. Gotta have five to race," the carny bellowed. "One more to race folks! Bring two and someone goes home with a jumbo!"

Chris handed him a twenty and collected his change. Everyone waited in anxious anticipation. The Monkey Man, seated on the other side of Chris, paid next. The carny continued down the line to collect entry fees from several newcomers. All twelve shooting lanes filled, decreasing the Miller's odds for success. Chris naively believed skill had everything to do with it. He knew his family would win. Odds and probabilities raced in his mind. His wife always won, but if not her, surely he would take it. Suzanne readied Emily's aim, and then lined up her own nozzle, as did Chris. Their total concentration had a wolf's focus during a hunt. The Monkey Man glanced towards them and silently chuckled.

The bell's deafening clang made Emily jump. She let out a quick squeak then managed to coax her stream of water close to the target—ye olde mouth of clown. Chris was in the running, having centered his stream after a miniscule adjustment. The Monkey Man was nonetheless in the lead again. His lane seemed to have an edge, Chris wondered. A *difference in water pressure? Non-uniform droplets due to minute differences in the nozzles?* Chris couldn't help the noise of critical thought.

The bell's shrill alarm startled Emily once more.

"Woohoo!" Suzanne shouted, high-fiving Chris and Emily.

The monkey man sulked in disbelief. Chris leaned over and proudly murmured in his ear, "She *always* does that. Always. Scary, huh?"

The Monkey Man grinned at Chris while reaching for his wallet. "Tulip can wait."

"Big winner in Lane Six! Pick your prize, anything on the wall!" yelled the carny.

Suzanne bent down and smiled to Emily. "Go ahead, Em."

"Me?"

"Yep, anything you see up there. Whatever you want."

Emily studied the wall for over a minute before pointing towards the lower-left corner.

"Him!" She yelped less than modestly.

After the carny poked around in the corner, repeatedly selecting the wrong toy, he finally produced the only plush clown doll in the trailer. "This one?"

Emily nodded. "Uh-huh."

"Well, he *appears* happy, but I don't trust clowns." Her father joked.

"Clowns get a bad rap, you know," said the Monkey Man. "Blame the movies."

The Millers stepped away, heading for every carnival's torture—an emetic called The Bullet. It featured two massive steel 40-foot arms, rotating vertically with counterweighted egg-shaped rider cars at one end. Each car contained four seats facing back-to-back, and the cars themselves would roll in either direction. Chris had already planned ahead by popping two Bonine tablets an hour earlier, and they seemed to be effective until he noticed a dripping water hose nozzle hooked vigilantly on a railing near The Bullet's debarkation point.

"Oh no," he choked.

"What's his name, twinkles?" Suzanne asked.

Emily searched the clown for a nametag. "I dunno."

"Well, you have to give them a name or else they don't have a soul."

Chris laughed, "That's why nobody names livestock. I bet you wouldn't eat anything named Curly."

"Ewww!" Both girls gagged.

Suzanne put her hand in front of her mouth. "Chris, that's disgusting. Probably true, but disgusting."

"Ex-eno," Emily blurted, reading from a small tag found on a seam at the clown's hip.

Suzanne looked down at her. "Who?"

Emily cried, "Exennnnoooo!"

"Huh?"

"Here Mommy, look—on the tag. X-e-n-o."

"Oh, twinkles," she laughed, "The X is pronounced like a Z, so it's Xeno."

"Xeno? Xeno?" Chris mumbled. "What a delightful moniker."

"Shh!" Suzanne whispered.

Every hammering salvo from Xeno became unbearable and progressively more percussive. With each blow, the bedroom's wooded doorframe began to weaken—creaking, cracking, splitting the nerves at Emily's core.

She mashed the palms of her hands as tight as she could against her ears, sobbing from the torture. "Mom!"

A bolt of lightning sizzled just outside her window, creating a tremendous explosion in the air, as if a grenade had detonated in the same room.

Emily abruptly sat up and screamed, "MOM!"

Nothing. With one tremendous blast, Xeno destroyed the doorway and slowly made his way toward Emily's bed. His mouth dripped with the fleshy parts and blood of an unknown victim, his oil-painted smile was an expression of hideous pleasure, and his eyes reeked the color of dark urine. His once perfectly-clean harlequinade garb was now a grungy mess, as if he rolled around in some city sewer and absorbed its foulest contaminants. He loomed before Emily, one hand clenched in a tight fist, the other pointed directly between her eyes.

"You can't run from *me*," he gurgled.

He jumped towards her bed with an unbelievable burst of speed and grabbed the control unit of the tiny, white music player that Emily fell asleep wearing each night. The churning fire within Xeno's hands immediately melted the little plastic device, and the wires leading to her ears began to glow white-hot. Melted plastic insulation dripped onto her legs, and her earbuds exploded in small balls of flame. The sides of Emily's skull began to fry, bubbling her earlobes as they turned black—crackling and smoking from the loss of fluid. In shock and convulsing violently, her hands began to sever at the palms after grabbing onto the heated wires. Xeno yanked the wires tight, bringing the screaming and shivering small girl within inches of his decrepit face. In his jagged deep voice, he growled, "Hear no evil."

Emily screamed at the top of her lungs, "MOMMY!" then awakened in her father's tight embrace.

"It's just a bad dream, honey. . . just another bad dream," he whispered, also weeping.

As Emily sobbed, Chris sniffled and stared at the heavy rainfall pelting her bedroom window. He cringed at the silhouette of Xeno perched on the dresser in front of that window—the pain of remembering one of his family's happiest moments. The doll just sat and smiled as it always did.

After several minutes, Chris relinquished Emily back to her pillow. "It's okay, honey. It's over now; get back to sleep."

Emily nodded as he tucked her in. She agonized at the window and at Xeno, whose dark outline blinked with every flicker from the retreating storm.

"Dad?"

Chris had returned to his room.

"Dad!" Emily shouted.

Chris slowly reappeared at her doorway with folded arms. "What?"

"Daddy, come here."

He sat beside her, wiped a few strands of hair from her face, and in a lower tone, repeated, "What is it?"

"I love Xeno, but right now he scares me." Emily pointed towards the dresser. Chris snatched Xeno from it, kissed Emily goodnight, and disappeared back down the hallway.

It hadn't been long since the wreck, Chris thought. She just completed her fourth twelve-hour shift at the hospital that week and was on her way home. A sheetrock contractor was also headed home, but only after hanging with a couple of his subcontracted helpers and their case of Finelager. In a half-conscious stupor, the contractor slumped upon the steering wheel, sending his 1-ton pickup onto the road's right shoulder. He yanked on the wheel too hard, lost control, and swerved into the opposite lane, crashing head-on into Suzanne. With all the modern safety features in her car, it was no match for the massive truck and its heavy frame. Even so, both died instantly. The contractor neglected to wear a seatbelt, and the emergency workers found most of him fifty yards off the asphalt, tangled in a barbwire cattle fence.

Chris' jaws oscillated at a swift pace. His rage over the senseless loss rushed back. The grinding slowly changed to tears once again as he fell against his pillow and whimpered, "Oh God, Suzy . . . God, I miss you."

Nothing much changed in the two years since that night. There was an abundance of help from friends and family at the beginning. After a few months they wanted a return to normalcy. Jennifer Smiley's daughter, Patricia, has been Emily's closest friend since they were toddlers, and the Smiley's looked after Emily as though she was their own, particularly during the school year. While taking care of Emily had become an easier routine, maintenance of the Miller household, particularly Chris himself, had become a nonstarter. Household projects were piling up and redecorating long overdue. It wasn't so much a measure of Chris' availability to do the work, but more a test of willpower. He resisted change. He didn't want to lose the sense that, perhaps somehow, Suzanne would walk back through the door, and everything would reset. All of her pictures were still on the refrigerator. All of her internship papers were still in the office. All of her soaps were still in the bathroom, and all of her clothes still hung in the closet. *She could just walk right in, and everything would be all right.* Chris cried himself to sleep, clutching Xeno tightly.

He awakened the following morning to the ding-dong chimes of his ordinary doorbell. He peered through the nearest window. It was still dark outside, but his old Panasonic flip clock read 7:20 a.m. Time to get Emily away to school. He haphazardly threw on his robe and reading glasses then headed downstairs. Much to his surprise, Emily had already dressed herself and was ready to go. Chris answered the door and immediately started apologizing about their tardiness to Jennifer Smiley. She turned to avert her eyes, pointing downward, clearing her throat with exaggeration. He looked down and came to a shocking realization, frantically closing his half-opened robe.

"Daddy!" Emily shrieked.

"Damn! Sorry, Jen."

Jennifer winked with a laugh, "Nothing to be sorry about, sweetie."

Chris blushed as he kissed Emily goodbye. "I won't mention that to Jim."

"Damn right you won't," laughed Jennifer as she turned to walk away.

Chris guessed that Jennifer was just trying to make him feel better any way she could. It was part of a surrogacy until he could move on.

By that time of the morning, Chris usually headed off to work. After realizing that he hadn't bathed or properly dressed, he made a mad dash for the bathroom. A quick shave, a rinse of the face, and a brief combing was all he had time to complete before donning the khaki and oxford uniform. Then came a near-tumble down the stairs. He rifled through the kitchen, plucking an apple from their fruit bowl. Breakfast. Chris bolted for the garage where his second true love awaited —a fully-restored, brown, 1978 Volkswagen Rabbit Diesel, a gift from his parents to commemorate his first day at engineering school. A trace of vapor escaped his exhale. *Chilly*, he thought. Chris waited for a few seconds while the old glowplug ignition system clicked, signaling it was warm enough to start. A few more seconds elapsed. Chris pulled the choke, turned the key, and the engine kicked over with its typical puff of black smoke and loud, pinging gurgle. Today was an important day at his laboratory; punctuality was paramount.

Amerimem Industries

His tremulous diesel was nimble as ever—when it ran downhill. Flat roads and steep uphill grades were another matter. Chris knew about the Energy Crisis of the late 1970s, when engineers made deep sacrifices for sensational fuel economy. The Volkswagen's 49 horsepower rating when new fomented Chris' suspicions that several of his horses had escaped over the years, and observing minimum speed limits when clawing up long grades required expert planning.

He pulled up to a stoplight and became marginally irritated by yet another pontificating battery driver, holding their nose and waving off the caustic diesel smoke. Chris endured at least one of these occurrences every day, and it wasn't long before he lost count. Unfazed, he revved the engine just before the light turned green, leaving the ass in a choking carbon cloud.

Better than a finger, he thought.

Naturally, Chris was forgetful that his dreadfully underpowered grocery cart had difficulty outrunning the neighborhood dog, let alone an electrified sedan—a fact painfully remembered as he received that dreaded finger while being overtaken.

Several moments on, Chris arrived at the employee entrance to Amerimem Industries' vast campus, housing the largest semiconductor developer and foundry in the United States. Cruising up to the security terminal, he swiped his card, entered his PIN, and posed for the security guard's camera.

"Good morning, Doctor Miller. Enjoy your day," said an attractive female voice from the console.

The gate rose and the unidirectional tire shredder recoiled into its concrete bunker. Chris nodded towards the lens. "Morning Julie. Thanks," he said, rattling off towards the parking garage.

There were several main buildings within the Amerimem complex. Three years ago, the original manufacturing and office facilities underwent conversion into a museum, and Corporate's shiny new administrations annex emerged next door. Behind those buildings were the foundries and an ultra-modern Research and Development facility. All of the building designs were soullessly efficient glass and concrete boxes. Their character came from within. Chris made his way into the secured garage section reserved for Amerimem's top engineers. He found his favorite space unoccupied near the elevator, parked, and went inside. At the main lobby, he met his director, Jack Kattner, the company's Chief Technical Officer.

Kattner was a boisterous executive at the power apex of his career. He was in his early fifties, reasonably fit for a man of average height, dressed conspicuously better than most of his colleagues, and kept his bristle brush salt-and-pepper hair perfectly leveled at all times. Even though the corporate offices were in DC, Kattner was the top executive of R&D—always hands-on. Everybody knew Jack on sight, but they often recognized his booming and authoritative voice long before he arrived at anyone's office door. Intimidating for some, but for the most part, he was a respected leader and well-liked.

Kattner was fond of using last names to elevate his perception of command, but not necessarily on first introductions. "'Morning, Miller. I'd like you to meet your new team member, Matthew Jacobson. He's a Yale man."

Jacobson shook Chris' hand. "Pleasure to finally make your acquaintance, Doctor Miller. Your journals in tissue assimilation are legend."

Chris blushed as he pushed his glasses back upon the bridge of his nose. "Oh, huh. Well, I've been able to keep it sustained, but as soon as I get it to—"

"Gentlemen," interrupted Kattner, wise to the fact they were still at the front lobby. "We'd better finish the introductions in my office."

"*Right*," said Chris with tinge of sarcasm, gesturing with some sort of spooky hand-waving motion that obtained a smirk from his new team member.

"You prefer Matthew or Matt?" Chris asked.

"Either's fine."

The three made their way to Kattner's suite on the sixth floor. Kattner swiped his card and entered a sequence on the code panel.

"Whatever happened to trust?" he said.

They entered and exchanged greetings with Kattner's exotically slender yet voluptuous and fashion-calculated assistant, Rebecca Morningwood.

She examined Matthew, feet to forehead. Not the typical physique of a desk-bound nerd, she thought.

"Mornin' Chris. Who's the new guy?"

Jack Kattner broke in before Chris could answer. "This is Jacobson, a new research team member for Miller. This way, gentlemen."

Kattner rushed them into his office and shut the door. He straightened his Italian silk tie and plopped into his rather overstated leather chair. "Chris, where are we with Project Tumor?"

"Tumor?" Matthew asked.

Chris cleared his throat. "In an evolutionary step regarding tissue assimilation, Tumor is somewhat of a facetious title for a project in which active human brain tissue is suspended in a platform designed to exploit its ultra-dense memory array. We've gone just about as far as we can go in silicon reduction, and we can't take it below 1.2 nanometers because of the residual quantum tunneling effects. It will just mean more stacking . . ."

Matthew raised his finger. "And more heat."

"Exactly. Point being, Moore's Law is unsustainable at the present trajectory. Sure, there are other avenues, and I don't believe in size constraints. It'll be picometers within six years—trigate transistors, inexpensive super cooling, memristors . . . suffice to mention the quantum fields—qubit states and so forth, the catty stuff I'm sure you already know. Those will come to market and undergo programmed expansion within the next few years, concurrent with our petabyte-IOPS SSDs. Well, when error-correction algos improve another five percent, that is."

"Then what?"

"Exactly how familiar with the human encephalon are you?"

Matthew cocked a brow.

Chris pointed at a framed poster of a modern processor on Kattner's office wall. "Think of this current wafer. Our largest multicore architecture includes 50 billion binary transistors, give or take. Each of which only indicate two states, on or off—yes or no. In contrast, our brains average 100 billion neurons and each one of those has synaptic connections to 10,000 other neurons. One quadrillion connections. Each of those neurons, depending on type, transmit multiple states, not just binary. Neurotransmission outperforms anything current technology could possibly manufacture over the next twenty years, and it does so with minimal cooling. We believe that the long-term memory sections in humans contain the area densest with stable neurons."

"Stable?"

"Yes. Short-term memory populates and exits by routine, as do certain other forms of memory. We're not one hundred percent sure it's due to routing or exact chemical arrangement of the neurons. Some of us also suspect plasticity effects."

"Ok, busted. Explain."

Chris glanced towards Jack before continuing. "You may recall some miracle stories over the years—patients with severe brain trauma slowly recovering lost memories."

Matthew cautiously looked at Kattner before answering. "Sure."

"Neuroplasticity occurs when the brain reacts to the damage and adapts by conjuring from other points of reference. It just happens that the long-term memory areas, or excuse me, the areas traditionally attributed to long-term memory—I want to be correct here—are the most suitable for this project. The others have insufficiently high anomaly rates. Ever experienced déjà vu?"

"Who hasn't?" Matt stole a glimpse through a glass wall towards Rebecca, who was administering a lab technician.

Chris paid it little attention. "Temporal lobe anomalies. It's a simple matter of your neurological 'food' going down the wrong pipe. You witness something and, instead of going to short-term memory, it routes to long-term and *then* terminates at your 'working cache' memory—spoofing that memory as a past experience. You can't differentiate it. The problem is that the memory has no time or date stamp. Without a corroborative reference, simple doubt foments at the recognition level. At least, for most of us, it's a basic doubt. Others might swear on their mother's grave."

Matthew snapped his head around and folded his arms. "I don't believe it."

"I guess he's one of the 'others'." Kattner laughed, rolling his eyes.

Chris straightened his glasses. "It's as simple as that. Since it came from long-term memory, people ultimately conclude that it was an unexplained phenomenon."

Kattner smirked again, "Déjà-vu", and then coughed as he choked on a jellybean. "Science will explain everything one day—*everything*. People don't want facts or truth; they just want to hear something that makes them feel special, virtuous, and entitled—as if they have superpowers. Sorry, Miller. Go ahead."

After a brief, incredulous glare towards his boss, Chris continued. "Anyway, as you know, we are now able to support a stable atmosphere to cradle the tissue. And, we've been working towards interfacing.

"You and everyone else has been working on interfacing." Matthew quipped.

"Sure—sensory and motor. Basics. We're into the higher functions and memory, now. So far, we're able to initiate a basic neural connection algorithm—basic storage and recall functions too. As you can imagine, over a trillion connections can't be executed manually, and we've yet to determine the exact synaptic coding. We're *very* close, however."

"My God!" Matthew gasped. "You *do* realize the other potential implementations, right? People will want you to jack right into their cortexes, or worse, demand some cliché immortality service. Watch!"

Kattner rocked his chair back, folding his hands behind his head. "We aren't interested in anything like that—just the blank storage potential."

Chris pursed his lips. "Besides, the quantum processing required to handle the entire function of a human brain is at least a decade out, and even then, it won't handle full capacity of single section of long-term human memory. These are the baby steps. First, a stable synaptic connection to the neural net, which we call Axon Terminalization, then the decoding of the neurons themselves. Once we achieve those connections, we'll assess the chaining of more than one tissue section and so forth."

Kattner looked over towards a slack-jawed Matthew. "Ready to get to work, Jacobson?"

"Absolutely."

"Okay Miller, why don't you show him around our little funhouse."

"Um, sure Jack. No problem." Chris turned to Matthew. "If you have to use the restroom *Matthew*, now's the time."

"Chris, on second thought—just use Matt."

Chris closed Kattner's office door behind as they strode briskly down a long corridor towards the elevators. From the lobby, two agents escorted them down another hallway to a high-security area. Chris and Matt's credentials underwent additional scrutiny via card swipe and PIN entry. The agents then brought them to another set of elevators. After a brief wait, Chris and Matt stepped inside. Matt searched for a control panel before Chris looked up at a camera in the corner and in a clear voice said "B-9". The doors closed and they descended.

Chris turned to Matt, who was desperately fighting a smirk. "There are eleven floors down from the lobby. Santa Clara doesn't want to compete with San Jose's skyline and there's less chance of contamination. The entire building has a float-ing foundation, so tremors aren't a factor. The clean room on B-9 is better than an ISO Class 1. Since we are dealing with biological matter, it must be perfect—or as close as possible to it."

Matt shrugged. "Oh man, I've gotten myself into *Andromeda Strain*."

"Funny—the name of the lab is Andromeda," Chris laughed. "But it's only a fifteen-minute entry procedure here, and you're going to love the bunny suits, trust me."

The elevator doors slid open, revealing another manned security checkpoint and staging kiosk.

"Gentlemen, please follow me to the Green Room," motioned one of the guards in the security detail.

Just down a hallway, the three men entered the first door on the right. "Doctor Miller is already familiar with the entry procedure, so I'll let him run you through it."

"Thanks Steve." Chris held open a locker door. "Okay, first we stash our clothes in one of these and continue into the next room for an air shower."

Both men were rather fit, but as Morningwood suspected, Matthew possessed the chiseled body of an Olympic gymnast. Chris was about 6'1", 190lbs and had short-cut dark hair parted on his left. Matt was slightly larger, had sandy brown hair—almost chestnut—and he kept it parted in the middle. Anyone made a crack about it, he'd just say, "Eighties retro" and that was it. Chris scrubbed his hands and exchanged his glasses for a pair of disposable contacts. He walked over towards the revolving door and pressed a large green button. A loud buzzer shrieked through the room as the airlock doors began to slowly rotate. The motors growled with a loud roar as Matt and Chris entered the air shower. For the next thirty seconds, the naked men endured a high-intensity blast that flowed from the ceiling to the grated floor beneath their feet. Another buzzer sounded and a rotating door on the other side of the room began slowly turning. Chris motioned and they passed through to enter the next area.

"I thought it would be cooler," said Matt.

After opening a drawer, Chris reached in, pulled out something the size of a candy bar, and threw it to Matt.

"Here, put this on."

Matt unraveled the slick, bouncy material. "Uh . . . what is this? There's only one hole."

"Body condom. The hole is for your face, but you stick your legs through there like this. Watch."

Chris picked his up. "Find the feet and stick your thumbs inside the face, rolling them inside all the way to the toes like this. Stretch the entire ring wide while you sit and wiggle your way in, feet first."

"Hey, wait. Won't you suffocate in that?"

"What, like in *Goldfinger* with the paint?" Chris laughed. "*MythBusters*. Great show. You should watch it."

Chris managed to make the act of donning the body condom appear effortless—inserting in his feet, stretching up the legs then torso, inserting one arm at a time, stretching the hands into place, then finally stretching the last part over his head, leaving only his eyes, nose, and mouth exposed. Next, he retrieved a disposable respirator mask and placed it over his mouth, stretching its elastic band over the back of his head.

In a muffled voice, Chris gestured, "Got it?"

Matt nodded, rolling the body condom up to the toes, and then placing both feet in—stretching the latex over his lower half.

"Hey, it's kinda squishy!"

"Yeah," Chris laughed. "It's a lubricating lotion similar to a topical hand sanitizer. It feels like that until you take the condom off. Once exposed to air, the lotion evaporates. Oh, and you won't need a bath!"

"*Kinky,*" said Matt as he wiggled the rest of his body into the sheath.

Chris fetched two bunny suits and handed one to Matt. The suits came complete with attached boots and hoods. Only the safety masks remained.

Matt pondered aloud, "Ever wonder why clean rooms and suits are always white?"

"I thought it was to show cleanliness . . . white gloves and all that. And if you soiled anything, you saw it. Or, perhaps that it helps with the lighting?"

"If you ever owned a dog, you know black is next to impossible."

Chris laughed, "That's ridiculous. The color of dog hair doesn't change the fact it's usually everywhere. Ready?"

"Of course!"

At the next revolving door, Chris depressed a large green button. Another loud buzzer sounded, and the large doors began to rotate. Once inside, the men found themselves at the front of a large project room. In the middle, several technicians surrounded what appeared to be a large hind quarter of an animal, perhaps a horse or mule. The leg had multitudes of wires and sensors dangling about. A yellow beacon began flashing and the technicians simultaneously stepped a few feet away from it. A bell rang loudly, initiating a five-second countdown. At zero, the leg articulated. Starting slowly, the hoof jerked backward then forward in a releasing motion. After a few repetitions, one of the technicians changed a potentiometer, increasing the repetition speed. The motion quickened as noticeable contractions in the upper thigh area became evident. In awe, Matt stared at the experiment through the double-paned observation windows.

Chris pointed at a doorway. "This is the first of the biomechanics labs."

"What's that? I thought you were working on brain tissue interfacing."

"This is a collateral result of our preliminary experiments. At first, we were looking for a simple, electro-impulsive link to organic tissue recognizing simple binary commands. If you recall, muscles contract when stimulated with electricity. We're discovering that muscle tissue will actuate with far less current, much the way synaptic impulses instruct your own muscles. Instantaneous electrochemical reactions."

"How do you keep it, um, healthy?"

"It's nourished with an IV fuel solution mixed with a synthetic circulant—a type of 'blood' per se. The signal testing helps keep the muscles toned in the interim, but before that, we primarily used electrotherapy, similar to using a typical TENS unit. Without regular exercise, the tissue deteriorates in atrophy."

"That's neat but, what are you going to *do* with it?"

"We hope to make a few patents off the process since our main competency is memory. When I first arrived, Jack shared a little corporate wisdom—said most of Amerimem's profits were derived from licensing, not from our actual product manufacturing. I imagine there are plenty of applications for low-consumption power, robotics, and of course, all of the human medical implementations—prosthetics and so forth. The brass loves licensing rights and, if it's a byproduct of our main research, why not?"

"Smart."

"Let's get to *my* area."

Just down the main corridor, lined with stainless walls and double Lexan casements, was another set of sliding doors like those of an elevator, but in the same style of the rooms on that floor. After entering, the doors closed behind them, encapsulating Chris and Matt within another small chamber. A yellow warning beacon rotated on the wall as another blast of air washed them.

"It's the final cross-contamination precaution," shouted Chris.

"Right!" Matt gave a thumb's up.

The beacon stopped, and the doors at the other end of the small room opened to a large, dark space. Chris walked through and flipped on the overhead lights, flooding the laboratory in the brightest pure-white luminescence. "Welcome to Andromeda," he announced with pride.

Immediately noticeable were the multiple workstations for individual experiments, most of which were simultaneously ongoing. The back wall featured an interactive blackboard, a few large flat-screen monitors, and a large projector screen.

Matt pointed at the wall. "Why so many displays?"

"Each experiment is based on different types of memory modes within a single neuron. We believe that some of the sections are dedicated to the senses themselves, not just the off/on binary like our current electrical models. Our cursory experiments used those simple binary store-and-recall types, and they're quite massive in storage ability, but we quickly realized nothing remotely close to the full potential. Visual and audio memories are the next research point, and that's where we will begin tomorrow."

Matt pointed towards the front corner of the lab. "What's over there?"

Chris turned on the lights in the coolers, illuminating several preserved human brain samples. Matt walked over to the coolers and strained to see through the condensation. One of the glass container labels caught his eye.

"*Abby?* Oh man, that's hilarious!"

"Yeah, a sense of humor is required around here. Tomorrow, we will implement the preliminary algorithm for axonal interfacing. I'll need your audio synthesis encoding/decoding station functional. That's located over there."

Chris walked over to a station on the right side of the lab. "This is the sustenance module for the tissue. I'll be here, running the algorithm and monitoring the visual information indicators for tagging. Once we get it connected and mapped, the battle's over." Chris took a long look around. "That's it for the tour. You ready to get out of here? Had enough of the slimy for today."

Matt wiggled. "I was just starting to like it!"

Chris killed the lights and hit the switch to open the wash chamber doors. Again, a blast of air rushed downward across their suits, the yellow beacon stopped, the blowers ceased, and the door on the opposite side opened. The entire entry sequence reversed until they returned to the Green Room.

There, they stripped off all their gear down to the latex body condoms.

Chris reached into a drawer, grabbed a small, flat piece of plastic, and sliced open his latex suit. "Don't try undressing, just cut it off. Much easier."

Matt took the blade and made short work of his suit, slicing it away and exposing his slathered body.

"It stills feels greasy."

"Count to fifteen."

"Alright."

Matt counted silently. "Awesome. It really *is* like a hand sanitizer. I never thought of using it everywhere, though." He ran a hand along his arms and legs, now perfectly clean, dry, and silky to the touch.

They slipped their clothes back on and headed for the elevator. Chris looked into the camera once again, ordered the ground floor, and turned to Matt.

"As I said, tomorrow we initiate the axon terminalization algorithm. Once the connections occur—hopefully, that is—I want you to process the initial acoustic signatures for a reference lock."

The doors swung open to Rebecca Morningwood's reception. "I've been instructed to bring you both back to Jack's office."

"Anything wrong?" Matt asked.

"They don't tell me anything, sweetie—only what they want me to do."

Upon arrival, Chris and Matt took their seats in front of Kattner's desk. From a doorway on the side of the office, he shuffled in at a swift pace.

"Gentlemen. Our network detectors revealed an attempted breach this morning. Nothing new; we're pinged by hundreds of hacks regularly. Most are just high school brats trying to show off. We catch competitors testing us from time to time, however. Nothing provable, but we know better. This last one came from an "undetermined". Our top people couldn't nail down the continent, let alone the country—peculiar if not disturbing. Anyway, I wanted to give you boys a heads-up. Until this is resolved, we have to go back to the old manual LAN backups instead of the central server. Miller, I understand you are beginning the first phase of the connection with your project tomorrow?"

"Yes."

"Excellent. I'll have it piped up here if you don't mind my looking over your shoulder."

Matt chimed in, "You sure you don't want to come down and get slick with the guys?"

"Matt!" Chris yelped.

Kattner laughed and turned towards Matt, "Did Miller tell you I came up with the idea for the lubricant? You should have been here when we used the old rubbers with that powder. I don't know which was worse—the constant sneezing or the surprise Brazilian."

Matt cringed.

Chris reclaimed Kattner's attention. "I don't have any problems with anyone looking over my shoulder, Chief. If everything proceeds as planned, we're in for a show."

"Great. See you both tomorrow."

They departed Kattner's office, exchanging pleasantries with Rebecca before heading downstairs towards the lobby's exit.

When they were partially alone, Matt turned around to Chris. "I need to get this off my chest—they told me about your wife before we were to meet . . . in case it ever came up. I'm very sorry."

At first, Chris looked astonished by the privacy intrusion—that a company would brief a newbie on such personal matters, but he quickly remembered Amerimem's manual delineating the need for psychological profile sharing, given emergency lab conditions when isolated.

"I guess you can tell I'm not quite over her."

Matt shook Chris' hand, "It's a huge mistake to think that moving on involves forgetting."

Chris smirked, "See you tomorrow."

Matt paused to grab a drink on the way out of the lobby while Chris made for the garage. Once there, he threw his briefcase on the Rabbit's passenger seat, climbed in, turned the key, and had no wait for the old diesel to start since the afternoon temperature was warm. Rumbling the brown bucket back into the Santa Clara sun, Chris pulled up to the exit gate, waved his card, and watched the gate swing upward while the tire-slashing barrier withdrew into the pavement. No PIN entries or friendly salutations from the guards. While entering the complex was a security labyrinth, departing was a hassle-free affair.

Soon, Chris would face his daily challenge—the climb up Stevens Hill with 49 horses, some surely missing. It was a straight ascent of about two miles, but the grade was usually too steep for the Rabbit's top gear. Chris built his speed to 63 MPH before hitting the first section.

"Okay, old gal," he said aloud, hoping to coax the old car. "Today we make the top before second."

Slowly and surely, the car began to decelerate. Chris planted the accelerator pedal to the floorboard, but eventually had to place the transmission into third. The engine's speed revved up immediately as he made a smooth shift, yet the grade quickly outmatched the powerless diesel. The hatch-back began to buffet and choke as its speed dipped too low for the gear ratio to maintain.

"Damn!" Chris begrudgingly shifted into second.

The car gradually gained momentum, but barely crept past 30 MPH. It was enough to get a horn blast and a "Get off the road!" on some days.

Chris mumbled, "What was it—speed? The shift? Conditions?" He despised not knowing the exact cause, and he grinded on it for several minutes, dismissing it as inconclusive. There would always be a next time.

After entering the gates of Sonno Dolce, Chris made his way to the Smiley's residence, located on a corner three blocks over. He heard the faint, throaty barking of Snickers at the top of their driveway. Chris recalled Jennifer naming him after a mishap with a chocolate bar. That was three years ago. He was about to ring the doorbell when the door swung open, revealing Emily and Patty, who grabbed his hands and dragged him to the kitchen table.

"Dad, come and see this!" Emily shouted.

She and Patricia pointed towards the table where a large jar held what looked like a human brain made from sculpted green sponges suspended in the middle of the water. Behind the exhibit was a poster board depiction of a brain and an explanation included below it.

Jennifer walked towards them. "The girls were inspired by your work, Chris."

"Nice job, you two!" Chris puzzled over the floating sponge brain. "How did you get it to remain in the middle of the jar?"

Patricia sat on the floor in front of him. "We glued a couple of ping pong balls in the middle and tied them to the bottom with a thin, black thread."

Chris smiled at the girls as they proudly displayed their completed science project. Jennifer finished stuffing Emily's backpack and then poked Chris in the arm.

"So you know, she came off the bus with a note from her teacher saying that if she catches her using any electronic devices during class again, she will confiscate it."

"Again?"

"Yep. Seems she spends more time with music than the books."

"I can't help it if they don't know how to multitask." Emily chided—to Jennifer's amusement.

Chris sighed, "Emily, you know that's not the point. Come on, grab your belongings and let's go home. Thanks Jen—and here." He handed Jennifer a folded hundred for the materials and for helping with the expense of keeping Emily.

Jennifer smiled, "Thanks. I know she's a handful, but you'll get through this." Then she turned to face the girls, "Emily? Don't forget you have to do a chapter for your reading class."

Emily, in a terribly thick Cockney accent, responded, "Are you 'idding me? That wizard boy book again, is it? Ugh. That's for the kids, isn't it then? I'll 'ave none of it, mum!"

"Get in the car, Miss Doolittle," Chris turned towards the door. "I happen to like him, thank you very much."

"Hey Chris, I was wondering when you might consider purchasing a cell phone for Emily. I could reach her directly in the morning and have less aggravation in the pickup line."

Naturally, Emily perked up for the answer, thanking Jennifer with her eyes.

"Wait—you think buying her a phone is the solution for her focus issues? Remember what happened with the social networking last year?"

"Yes, but—"

"Sorry—you know how I feel about those devices. Between the developmental health risks and wasted time, she'll have to wait. You can do what you want with Patty, but I won't let Emily have one of her own for now. She has too many toys as it is!"

Emily cringed, "Ugh!" then inserted her music player's earbuds. She paused, remembering the Xeno nightmare from the previous evening, then cranked the music anyway.

Chris fired up the Rabbit and started to back down the driveway. Jennifer jumped back from the dense black cloud of diesel exhaust and chokingly mumbled, "*He's* worried about health risks?"

Once home, Chris climbed out and said, "Emily . . . EMILY! Jesus, must you have those on all the time? Go get cleaned up and finish your homework, then we can watch a show."

"Like what?"

"Like . . . something scary?"

"As in really scary or wizard boy scary, which isn't really scary at all."

"Really scary."

"Okay," replied Emily. "I'll be right back."

"Homework!" Chris reminded her.

"Daddy!"

He withdrew to the master bedroom to take a short breather while Emily bathed and finished her studies. The phone rang. It was a vintage red desk phone—the boxy-looking 2500-style with the heavy handset, springy square number buttons, and a loud bell ringer.

"Hello?"

"Miller, it's Jack."

Chris wondered why his director was calling. "Um, hi Jack, what's up?"

"What did you think of Jacobson? Can you work with him? We've got a big day tomorrow and I need to make sure he's good enough to handle the audio portion for you."

"Well, yeah, sure. I mean, he has the credentials and he seemed to know what he was doing in the lab earlier today. Why? Something wrong?"

"No, nothing. He came highly recommended from DC, but they never tell me anything beyond anyone's dossier. If you think he'll do, then that's fine by me. I'll see you in the morning."

Chris stammered a little, still puzzled by the call. "No . . . no problem. See you then. Good evening to you."

He clicked off and mentally replayed Matt's introduction, attempting to pinpoint anything peculiar.

Emily suddenly pounced on his lap. "Okay Daddy, scare me!"

He gasped and sat straight up. "Give me a minute."

Chris switched on the bedroom television—a nice widescreen he purchased for Suzanne on their last anniversary. He thought he could spice things up by using the TV in certain ways to set a mood, and it worked quite well. Fortunately, Emily never stumbled on "the collection", but he knew it was about time he disposed of those things before an accident occurred. Too many memories lying around, he thought. Were they for him, or for Emily?

Chris grabbed the television's remote and scanned the On-Demand section briefly before settling on a terror classic.

"Ooh, perfect!"

The Evil Dead began to play. Emily started to laugh almost immediately, and in doing so, her father broke free of any residual depression in that moment.

A few more minutes passed. "It's *stupid!*" Emily declared.

"Exactly," Chris smiled.

The movie closed with Emily's squealing "EWWWWs!" Chris kissed her goodnight and sent her to bed. He pointed towards Xeno, "G'night, Em. Oh, don't you want to take your friend with you?"

Emily, laughing until that point, replied, "Um, okay, but he better not bother me again."

"You can always throw a sheet over him or something."

Emily made her way to her bedroom in a state of apprehension after enduring so much carnage. She looked upward from her window, out over the hilltops into the darkness, and exhaled at the sight of twinkling stars. Not a single cloud. She placed Xeno on her dresser facing towards the window. There would be no heavy weather that night. He smiled as always.

The Connection

Chris rubbed his eyes, yawned, and cracked several joints in an extended stretch. His ears suddenly detected the dulled rush of water from Emily's shower down the hallway. Impressive, yet the sound signaled that his self-starting daughter was more enthusiastic to face the day than her slacking fatherly role model. He glanced towards the dresser mirror in reprimand and heard Suzanne's whisper. *Do better.*

By coincidence, both Chris and Emily had important project presentations this morning. Chris cleared his haze with a favorite Italian espresso laced with three heaping spoonfuls of Mauian raw cane sugar. After which, he raced for an express shower to meet Emily's departure time. By competitive nature, she was already seated in the car, patiently waiting for her father with an impish grin.

Chris grabbed an apple on the way to the garage. He opened the driver's door and climbed inside.

"Big day, huh?"

Emily shrugged and removed her pulsating earbuds. "I'm sorry, did you say something, Mister *Second Place*?"

"Oh, ha ha! I bet you didn't—"

Before Chris could finish his sentence, Emily put her world back into her ears and bobbed to it, mouthing unintelligible lyrics while looking across at her father—her eyes mocking him all the way.

"Hey, you can't wear that!" Chris yelled.

Emily yanked her earbuds out. "What?"

"You can't wear that top and you know it. It shows your bellybutton!"

"Huh?" Emily acted as if she couldn't hear him.

"It's not even yours . . . I think. Where did you get it?"

Emily's brow furled. "Patty's, but she wears it all the time."

"Not to school she doesn't! Go upstairs, change out that top, and bring it with you when you come back."

Emily dropped her playful expression and moped back into the house with an indolent gait. Chris adjusted his seatbelt and reached for the key. His phone suddenly blasted the special ringtone assigned to his office. He muttered some expletives as his hand struggled with the lap belt covering the opening for his trousers' left-front pocket. This went on for several seconds until he was finally able to produce the handset and check the screen. *Kattner? This early?*

"Good morning, Jack." Chris opened.

"'Morning, Chris. It's Becky. I know it's early, but the techs are prepping this morning's run and they're wondering which container's going first."

"That's odd, Becky. The first container is already marked and staged at the front of the holding cooler."

"Well, they didn't know since you only wrote 'Abby' on it. They won't shut up about it."

"Ugh. Sorry. I suppose the lower label must have become loose and fallen off somehow. Probably in the bottom of the cooler where they can't see it. Regardless, Abby is correct. If we have to use a second sample, it's Control Number TM622."

"Okay. I'll let them know. Thanks, and pardon the early buzz."

"No worries."

Chris replaced the phone into his pocket while Emily dragged herself back downstairs. She climbed into the car—music blaring from her ears.

Chris smiled as he turned over the rumbly diesel. "Much better."

Emily shook her head and curled her body towards the right—away from authority.

Upon arrival at the Smiley's, Jennifer was standing in the driveway, panting after just having loaded the girl's science project into their minivan.

"'Morning Jen," said Chris. "Did you know the girls were exchanging clothes?"

"Yeah. They do it all the time. Why?"

"Emily tried to wear this to school today." Chris handed the short top to Jennifer.

"Ugh . . . That's Patricia's, and she knows she can't wear it to school. I'll have a word with them in a minute, but I don't want it to shadow their big day."

"Oh, no problem; that project's a winner!" Chris restarted the car, stuck his head outside the window, and yelled over the rattling engine. "Knock 'em dead, kids!"

Jennifer covered her nose and mouth, waving as Chris' trailing soot cloud dissipated towards Sonno Dolce's exit.

"'Morning Doctor Miller." Julie's familiar warmth greeted Chris at Amerimem's gate.

"'Morning." Chris looked up at the camera before swiping his access card.

"How many today?" Julie asked.

"How many what?"

"Espressos. I can smell them from here."

"Wait . . . No tailpipe joke? I'm disappointed." Chris smiled as the gate rose, "Just one today, Jules."

A sudden horn blast from behind startled Chris enough to make him jump and stall the Volkswagen. He became completely flustered as he fumbled for the ignition, Julie's laughter cackled from the loudspeaker. A voice from behind shouted, "Hey old man, if I wanted to inhale that much oil, I should have been a freight hauler!"

Chris tried getting his car back into gear, only to stall it again when the gate swung down just in front of his car, almost striking the hood. Julie was in hysterics.

"Sorry Chris, you know there's a ten second timer after you swipe." Her statement came with more comedic frustration as Chris started his car in a panic while retrieving his gate card.

Of course, this meant a second honking from Matt, leaving Chris no choice but to encapsulate him in a large cloud of black smoke—but not so dense that Matt couldn't see Chris' internationally-recognized *digitus impudicus*.

Julie was still cackling when Matt pulled up to the terminal. "And what do we seek today, brave knight?"

"We seek the Holy . . . Crap, I can't breathe!" He coughed uncontrollably, swiped his card, and passed through.

After parking and having a few laughs from the gate incident, Chris and Matt ventured inside, checked with security, and made for the elevators leading down to the lab.

Chris jokingly coughed and cleared his throat. "Geez, where've you been?"

"At a Bakersfield truck stop. Can't you tell?"

The elevator doors slid open, revealing Jack Kattner and Rebecca Morningwood in anticipation.

"Miller, I need to get us all on the same page. You and Jacobson step over with us to O-9, okay?"

Slightly hesitant, Chris mumbled, "Okay."

Once seated inside the small conference room, Kattner took a sip of chilled water and donned his readers.

"Today marks a momentous day for our particular science. I think we all know what the impacts are if we're successful. The research grants and company funding . . . I can't stress how important it is that we get this right on the first attempt. Jacobson? Green as you might be, I need you to relax—just be supportive. If you have any concerns or questions, go through Miller first."

"Yes, sir." Matt glanced toward Rebecca with contemplative eyes—not exactly subtle.

Kattner paused, then turned to Chris. "Go ahead with your briefing, Miller."

Chris cleared his throat again, trying desperately not to crack in coincidental thought.

"Hmhmm. Today is Connection Day, or at least, that's what I am calling it. As I mentioned yesterday, we are confident with our algorithm for making physical connections within the human synaptic sequence. So far, we've been able to painstakingly manufacture a few dozen in microsurgery and perform error checking on the fronts of capacity, integrity, and logic. As you know, Matt, some of your qualifying exams were based on those results. Essentially, we've taken months to develop our systems, producing the equivalent of a pre-silicon processor. It's a process of completing some backward steps in order to progress forward, except, instead of going down the decades' long road of silicon and Moore's Law, we intend to make a leopard's leap. Since the realization of manipulable neurons, we subsequently recognized that we had to engineer an efficient method for manufacturing dendritic connections en masse."

Kattner interrupted. "This is where our international research branches came into play."

"Right. You probably read of our acquisition of a nanotechnological firm in Shenyang, China. That much was public. We've teamed a special section for the development of a synthesized picobots that will create the connections automatically and at a rate astronomically faster than conventional robotics."

Kattner interrupted again, "Before you ask, Shenyang will *not* be monitoring the procedure. Security concerns from corporate in which I happen to agree. I don't care what anyone says, international communications are intrinsically insecure."

Completely absorbed by the conversation, Matt turned back towards Chris and asked, "Okay. I'll play along. How fast?"

"Twenty billion per second."

"Holy shit!"

"That may sound fast to you, but keep in mind that there are roughly one hundred billion neurons in an entire human encephalon with ten thousand synaptic connections each. The quadrillion. Do you hear Carl Sagan's voice yet? Point being, you can imagine why we are working with a much smaller sample—one that would take less than a minute to connect, yet yield more raw storage potential than the planet's largest single drive array . . . times a thousand. In cliché comparable terms, the current entire database of the Library of Congress on a single millimeter square of tissue. And before you ask why we simply don't emulate the tissue entirely by picobots, just think of the axonal connection process itself. Manufacturing one equivalent section would take too long."

"And this is where you really need to focus, Jacobson," said Kattner, testing that Matthew might be paying too much attention to his assistant. "Go ahead, Miller."

"Once the connections are intact and stable, you will run you're A/V logic and integrity tests from the station you previewed yesterday."

"Understood." Matt turned to Kattner. "When's the kick-off?"

Kattner set his drink down and said, "Right now," then stood up. "Let's go, Morningwood. I want to get a fresh cup upstairs before tee time. Good Luck, Gentlemen." He took his assistant by the arm winked towards Matthew. "*Ladies.*"

Chris and Matt entered Level B-9's staging area and repeated the decontamination process.

"Curious. Does the connection procedure make any actual noise?" Matt asked.

"None that I'm aware of. Dao told me it would be barely visible to the naked eye while the bots work. She didn't forward anything about audible sound. Good question."

"Dao? Wait a minute. Who's Dao?"

"She's the lead in Shenyang. We've been conferencing over the past few months, working out the programming details. Quite nice."

"Nice?"

"Well, I've only seen her on a monitor, but—hey. Why so interested?"

"No, no, I'm not . . . Trust me. I'm just wondering how much *you* pay attention since—"

Chris abruptly turned around. "That's my business, okay?"

"Yeah, sure man. Sorry."

They made their way down to the Green Room, undressed, and started prepping their body condoms. A few awkward moments passed.

"She's smart, athletic, definitely attractive—but not ostentatiously so." Chris said.

"You mean like Rebecca?"

"Not at all. And by the way, Jack noticed."

"Yeah, and I noticed that she noticed him noticing . . . and she liked it."

"I'm not going to comment on that, just be cautious, okay?"

"You've nothing to worry about with me, Doc. So anyway, what about your China girl . . ."

Chris looked at Matt with a hint of contempt. "Natural coworker. Agreeable and productivity-minded. Typical until disagrees with you. She can be rather cutting. She also gives me the feeling that if someone ever crossed her, she would destroy them. I mean, you can sense it. Something about the way she comes across—a confidence."

Matt laughed. "So, you like her, in other words."

Chris blushed, "Well, yeah, of course I like her, and I like to think it's mutual, but it's impossible. We consult frequently, but she's on the other side of the world immersed within a vastly different culture. Attraction aside, the only common ground we share is the science. Maybe that *is* the attraction, I don't know. Besides, I'm not sure I'm over Suzanne yet or if I will ever be."

Matt stretched the body condom's opening. "I could get to like this."

"What?" Chris asked.

"Nothing. Look, if I may, have you been with anybody else since?"

"Why do people ask if they can ask a question, then include the question in their question? Never mind. No, I've not been with anyone since. Some buddies dragged me off to Reno for the weekend and it didn't go well. I wasn't ready, and it's not the way I'm programmed. You?"

"Me? I can say I've had pretty good luck with rebounds. You don't have to forget the past, just move on and make sure everything still works, yanno? I've never been in your situation, though; I can't possibly know how I'd react."

"Do you have anyone around here?"

"No. They keep me moving around a good bit. I have a friend with perks back in Washington."

The buzzer shredded air as Chris walked through the outer airlock and onto the last air cleaning station before reaching Andromeda. Matt followed closely behind, both enjoying the fresh blasts of air before traversing the final lock. There were no technicians working on the muscular animation programs that day. Four of them were on their way out from the final staging of Project Tumor.

Chris and Matt arrived at their perspective stations and began preparations. After Matt completed sequencing his station and testing for connectivity, he walked over to Chris' area to have a look. With hundreds of optic fibers protruding from an open-topped cube that appeared to be made from obsidian, inside was a small square of cortex tissue, about the size of a postage stamp, floating on the special sustaining circulant. On the inside walls of the cube were tiny nozzles misting the tissue with the circulant to keep it moist. Sealed microelectronics also lined the inner walls with a notable fine edge left open, exposed just at the fluid level surrounding the tissue.

"That's it?"

Chris kept his head down and didn't notice Matt walking towards him at first. "Yeah. It's a little cumbersome now, but we're confident the final product can be reduced to about the size of a deck of cards, maybe less. The sandmen in the processor division were able to manufacture a neuron connector on the scale of two billion distinct nodes. Given the possible connections, we've been able to simulate those virtually and program the bots to connect accordingly."

Jack Kattner blared over their headsets. "Miller, we're all ready to go up here. What's the ETA?"

"About four minutes, Jack."

"Roger that."

Matt returned to his station. *I can't wait to see this.*

Chris loaded the robotic arm's clasp with a rather robust syringe containing a red fluid abounding with his army of microscopic engineers. The mass of bots remained too tiny for human eyes even though millions of them were swimming within the liquid. Upon introduction into the special suspension fluid, their programming activated, mimicking the reaction of human sperm forging their way to an egg. Chris triggered the robotic arm sequence, swinging it around and carefully lowering the tip of the needle down to just under the surface of the tissue's fluid.

He checked his screen. "Okay—starting the ten second countdown on my mark."

A loud buzzer blared outside the chambers of the lab and the yellow warning beacons flashed. Chris took his seat, observing the event just to his left while confirming results on his monitor. Carefully, he depressed the sequence activation switch on his screen and simultaneously yelled, "And—MARK!"

A female computer-generated voice was heard through all monitoring speakers, "Connection Sequence is activated. Ten . . . Nine . . . Eight . . ."

"I know that voice." Matt watched the module on the left of his three monitors in childlike anticipation. Chris also gazed at his own monitor, and even though the action was just a few feet away, he actually had a better view from a camera suspended just above the containment cube.

"Three . . . Two . . . One . . ." The robotic arm injected the picobots into the fluid. Almost immediately, a humming sound became audible, and it grew louder until an ear-piercing tearing noise erupted. The module violently oscillated, stressing the connecting fibers until a few broke, spewing green suspension fluid over the project area.

"Shut it down! Shut it down!" Kattner barked into the intercom.

Chris was stunned by the reaction—one he obviously didn't anticipate. Noticing that Chris wasn't moving, Matt jumped up and dashed over, yelling Chris' name.

"Chris, where is it?"

"What?" Chris remained glued to his monitor in disbelief.

"Where's the Emergency Shutdown?"

"Oh—damn!" Chris hit the large red button on the right side of his station. Immediately, a tube blasted the experiment with liquid helium, freezing the module hard as a block of steel in seconds.

Matt walked over and looked at it. "Jesus, what a mess!"

Chris sat back down and stared at the dripping project area, himself covered in bits of tissue and fluid residue. Panting, he half-whispered, "I don't understand."

"Oh man!" Matt cowered as he held his nose. The odor was hard to describe; it was something between burnt hair and a

well-worn elevator in a 1940s New York City tower—
electrical—except much stronger.

Kattner shouted into his microphone. "Miller, what the hell
happened?"

"I don't know. It had to be something involving the bot
environment's reaction to the fluid."

"Ya think? Get yourself a shower and come back up here. I
need to run this by Doctor Ming. If it's something minor, we
can try again later this afternoon. I'll send the crew down for a
reset. It will take a few hours." Kattner checked his watch.
"It's almost lunchtime. What do you say we get a bite and
diagnose this during a videoconference?"

"Yeah," Chris gulped.

The beacon lights extinguished as Matt and Chris entered
Decontamination and received the obligatory spray-down
before reentering the inner air lock of the lab. Once they were
back in the elevator on the way up to Kattner's office, Matt
blurted, "Amazing."

Before he inquired, Chris mumbled something under his
breath, "The most overused word by TV simpletons," before
speaking up. "Anyway, what?" he asked.

Matt didn't catch the first part. "Amazing that something so
small can make such a big mess."

"That was a few *million* little somethings."

"Yeah. I guess so. Still, it's incredible."

"Hopefully, Dao can figure this out. She had it perfectly
calculated—no faults—so I think maybe it's on *us*. Whatever
the reason, I just want to get back in there. I waited three
months to initiate that reaction and I need it to work this
time."

The elevator doors swung open, and they found their way
to Kattner's office after a few steps. A catering crew was in the
process of leaving when Chris and Matt arrived at Rebecca's
desk. She looked up, waved her finger as if to say "tisk-tisk",
and then led them back to Kattner's conference room. Inside

on the large table awaited a small buffet specially prepared just for the four of them.

Kattner was already seated at the head of the table. "I hope you don't mind the tilapia. I requested something light; it was a short notice."

They filled their plates, but Chris only gathered a light portion. His anxieties kept him too occupied to feel justifiably edacious. They dined in relative silence for the first few minutes until Kattner set his napkin upon the table and asked Rebecca to contact Dr. Ming. Moments later, Morningwood reentered the room clutching a fresh diet soda and picked up a remote control. A large rectangular screen lowered through a small opening in the ceiling close to the opposite wall at the far end of the room. The projector's laser blasted Amerimem's logo upon the screen. In the top right corner, "Establishing connection..." appeared.

"*Irony, you dick,*" Chris thought.

Dr. Dao Ming appeared on the screen from her office. Matt sat adjacent Chris, leaned over quickly and tapped him on the arm, whispering, "Exactly as you described."

Chris smiled and realized that Dao noticed Matt commenting about her, and that it must have been positive because she blushed. The brief interaction was enough for Kattner to clear his throat while glancing in Matt's direction.

"Doctor Ming, did you receive the brief from Miss Morningwood on our little glitch?"

After a slight pause due to satellite lag, she replied, "Yes, Mister Kattner. We are researching all possibilities. We are most confident our programming is correct for that sample. The slightest deviation in controls will change parameters, however, causing what may appear as an aggressive default state. Put differently, if a search parameter changes, the program may aggressively seek another substance. If we knew exactly what the project entailed, our team would build a context profile."

Kattner laughed. "Come on, Ming, you know we can't do that."

Dao continued with chiding eyes, "In any regard, our division is currently examining your report and expects a decisive solution in one hour."

"Thank you, Doctor Ming. Please transmit that report directly to Doctor Miller."

"You are welcome."

She bowed and smiled in Chris' direction as the connection terminated. He attempted to reciprocate, but the screen transitioned to the company logo before he could mouth anything.

"Okay folks, I've another meeting that will conclude in about two hours. Miller, the techs will have the second module ready by around 3 p.m. You people created a real mess down there, so you can imagine all the gripes, right? The boffins have their nightmares, too. You remember the first time our horse leg kicked, don't you, Miller? Anyway, let me know when you're ready."

"Thanks, Jack." They departed for Chris' office.

"That wasn't so bad." Matt closed the door behind him. "I thought he was going to rip our heads off for some reason."

"Jack doesn't work that way. Granted, I should have anticipated the potential for a catastrophe, but I simply didn't remember that individual size is not so important as mass."

"Always the excuse, right?"

Chris turned back, rolling his eyes.

After reviewing his own notes, Chris awaited the comparative report from Dr. Ming. As promised, he received her email within the hour and digested it immediately. "Oh, I have you now," he muttered.

Matt prairie-dogged from his cubicle. "What?"

"The fluid temp may have been off by two degrees. Dao, I mean, Doctor Ming's parameters for the sustaining fluid are quite narrow . . . within a degree of thirty-seven Celsius, in fact. If it's too cold, the bots may violently mass, generating enough heat necessary to stay within their own operating parameters."

"Thirty-seven—normothermia. Okay, what if it's too warm?"

"In that case, they don't move at all, supposedly. I bet we were too cold."

Chris located the test data sheet, scanned down the page and pointed, "Yes! It was three off, actually."

"So, the fluid was running around thirty-four?"

"Yep."

Chris picked up the phone and dialed his boss.

"Hi Chris," replied Rebecca. "Jack's still in that meeting. Did you find anything?"

"Yes, Becky. Tell Jack we found a problem with the temperature of the suspension fluid. The misters were causing intermediate temperature reductions, making the bots react violently. Tell him we'll be ready for another run today."

"Will do, Doctor Miller. Congratulations."

"Not yet!" Chris hung up. "Matt, I'm going down to the lab and implement a mister circulant temperature increase to compensate. I want you back down there no later than two-thirty."

"No problem. I can't wait."

Chris galloped down to the lab, underwent the decontamination sequence, and began working on the changes. In the initial design stages of Tumor, he determined that the temperature of the fluid emanating from the misters should be the same as the suspension fluid already in the module. One simple and reasonably mundane variable became lost when the fine mist of that fluid comingled with the lab's air temperature. Chris calculated that the mister fluid temp had to be an additional 6°C warmer to compensate. That particular suspension fluid was able to operate at the required temperature, so the only adjustment needed was in the mister's fluid reservoir. A relatively short twenty-minute wait ensued while the temperature reached its desired goal.

Ready!

Chris noticed that it was getting close to the time Matt should be arriving and, to his confirmation, Matt entered the lab at precisely 2:30 p.m.

"How do we look?"

Chris turned from his monitor. "Perfect. I've already tested the fluid temp—pre and post-mister—and it now maintains a perfect thirty-seven."

"Fanfreakintastic."

A few minutes later, Kattner cracked into their headsets. "Okay ladies—let's see some magic."

"Hey Jack, we'll be ready to go a few minutes early if you'd like."

"Sure Miller, no problem. How does the lab look? God knows I pay those guys enough. It better be spotless."

"I didn't see anything, Jack. It never happened."

"That's great. As far as I'm concerned, it didn't. Ready when you are."

Looking over towards Matt's cubicle, Chris asked, "Ready?"

Matt appeared distracted by something else on one of his monitors, but managed to say "All Go, here" before begging a repeat from Chris.

Once again, Chris took a pre-staged syringe from the temperature-controlled holding facility and placed it in the actuating holder of the robotic arm.

"Initiating insertion sequence" radiated through the headsets and in the monitoring area of Kattner's office. The robotic arm speedily swung back around and executed its careful penetration into the top layer of suspension fluid surrounding the second tissue sample. There was a signal in Chris' monitor, indicating the sequence was complete. Matt, Kattner, and Rebecca fixated on their monitors in anticipation.

"Ten second countdown on my mark."

Chris flipped open the safety latch on the activation switch. The yellow rotating beacon lights activated outside the lab, followed by a short series of loud buzzes, similar to those of a fire alarm.

"And—MARK!"

Chris slapped the activation button, and the countdown began. As a precaution, he monitored the screen displaying the inside of the module, while his right hand hovered over the emergency shutdown switch.

"Three . . . Two . . . One . . ." knelled from the computer in the headsets.

The actuator holder on the robotic arm injected the suspension fluid containing the picobots. Gradually, the humming sound returned, and it became somewhat louder, but not uncontrollably as before. The fluid surface also vibrated, but no more than tiny ripples in glass of water on a counter with a blender running nearby. Chris peered into his monitor as the syringe retracted, which was now devoid of its payload.

Starting from where the syringe was located, the liquid surface became more of a deep black solid, joining the outer walls of the module to the tissue, somewhat stretching it at the terminal area.

"Tone!" Matt excitedly watched his monitor's spreadsheet verify the axon connections. First, there was one million, and then a smattering of a few million more, and then the total rocketed exponentially.

"Chris, are you seeing this?"

Distracted by the extraordinary event growing in the module, Chris looked at his other monitor, awestruck as his sum of axon connections snowballed. His display hit a few million quickly, and then the number accelerated on a fantastic scale.

"Dear God," Chris muttered, not caring if everyone heard him.

The hum dissipated over the course of a few seconds, and the fluid inside the module now appeared as an obsidian-like crystalline material, somewhat matching the appearance of the module itself. The picobots completed their task, but the business of accounting all the connections lasted another two minutes. 9.256712^{12} blinked as the final result on the monitor.

"Axon Terminalization complete," echoed from the computer's intercom.

Astonished and mystified, Rebecca asked Kattner, "Jack, I don't recall my remedial math well, but isn't that number—"

Kattner jumped up from his desk, "Pack your bags Becky, we're going back to Oslo!" Then under his breath stated, "And this time not just for a Kavli."

Matt tapped on his microphone. "Chris, if I'm looking at this number right, that's almost ten *trillion* connections. We got the whole thing?"

"The area of tissue represents roughly a ten percent portion of the total usable mass of the subject encephalon's long-term area. We estimated that there are a possible one hundred trillion connections. So, yes, that looks acceptably close to ten percent to me."

"Oh, man, what a trip! Acceptably close, he says. Ha! Okay, let me know when you're ready to start analysis. I have a stable tone."

"Roger that. I need to wait about thirty minutes while I confirm the stability readings . . . see if anything changes."

"The stability of the stability rate. Got it."

Chris looked at the main monitoring camera, "So, Jack. How are we looking?"

"We're going back to Norway next spring, Miller, that's what I think. You?"

Chris carried a sly tone in his voice. "You'll have to make Doctor Ming sit and *watch* this time."

"Mmhmm. Can you give me anything on stability yet?"

"Nothing concrete. I noticed some slight changes cycling arbitrarily. The connections are oscillating on a minute scale, so I have to begin testing in a few minutes."

"Okay, let me know."

Kattner turned off the monitoring station. "Becky, inform Catering downstairs to get us a standard Celebration Package ready, but make sure they upgrade the champagne. They gave us a bottle of 'Cor-something' last time, I nearly fired the manager."

"Aren't you forgetting something?"

"What do you mean?"

Morningwood pointed to the monitor displaying Doctor Miller's station.

"Oh, damn. Right." Kattner stared at the screen. "Just add something you know he likes."

Matt noticed something peculiar after observing his monitor for several minutes.

"Chris, you're not going to believe this. I show stable connections across the board, yet the number continues to fluctuate. Only in the thousands mind you—less than one one-thousandth of a percent—but it's oscillating up and down every few seconds with no recognizable pattern."

"Yeah, I have the same readings over here. Jack and I just discussed it. Nothing major. Go ahead and begin your testing. I'll be doing the same."

Chris started a preliminary memory cycle on the tissue. He began with a few chunks, nothing more than a few megabytes each, testing for recall without creating a cooling issue. Matt did the same—testing each axon connection for audio data retention and recall. He loaded them in small sections, similar to loading a sound file player with a song, hitting play, then deleting the file. All tests returned positive, but not without quirks.

"Interesting, Chris," Matt said. "These readings I would dare consider as consistent with human function."

"What do you mean?"

"Digital information appears to be stored, retained, and recalled at an apparently nominal rate. If I inject analog synthesis, the digital information appears to be subject to additional interpretation, taking longer to absorb, so-to-speak. When recalled, I get significantly more raw data than what I inputted. I'm not sure what to make of the data, but I think it could be related to some other contextual relationship linked to the areas you are exploring."

"Hmm. I'm also receiving some similar data in the memory matrix. Raw information cycles quickly, yet information that is more complex—information involving primary sensorial types—is more difficult to get flowing, but not at a deviance greater than four percent. Visual information seems to run the fastest and smell the slowest, with smell also being the slowest to *unload.* I am also focusing on the connections that repeatedly cycle. Aha, that's it!"

"Well, don't keep us all in suspense, Dr. Frunkenschteen."

"*Stein*! Anyway, what I just discovered after a trace run is that a certain portion of memory transfers out of the closing connections just before they close, and redeposit through new connections in other cells. The process is constantly going at intervals seemingly arbitrary. Kind of like an elastic processor clock running as needed. I keep returning to the plasticity effect."

"Sounds fine to me Doc, but what's the bottom line here. Are we good?"

"Yes, I think so. Hold on. The full access test just finished. Yes, definitely. One hundred percent up and down—confirmed!"

Matt stood up, walked over to Chris' station, and gave him a slap on the back while grabbing for a handshake. "Well, you did it. Congratulations."

"Thanks."

Chris paged Kattner's office. "Oh Jaaack, I'm ready for that drink now. How about you?"

"One moment, Doctor Miller," replied Rebecca before Kattner bumped her aside.

"Great work, Miller . . . just . . . incredible. Put it in stasis and you two get up here."

Kattner turned to his assistant and said, "He's back. Don't worry about him, okay?"

"You're the boss." Morningwood said on her way out.

Chris activated the sleep mode program, which unloaded the tissue data and kept the misters running to sustain the air-exposed environment. At the same time, Matt downloaded his tests and shut down. As he made his way back over to Chris, he paused by the complex module and took a long look at the misted tissue. *Incredible. This is going to be fun!* He thought.

"Ready?" Matt was anxious to lose the bunny suit.

"Finishing up now. I'll be right in," said Chris.

On adrenalin highs, the two men breezed through the decontamination sequence and returned to the prep station, removing their suits and body condoms in fast order.

Matt was the first to enjoy the fresh sensation. "Ahhh, that never felt so good!"

"Better get used to long runs. We've a lot of application testing and redesign coming up."

"Right. I'll look at it as doing my part to save California's water supply."

Chris laughed as they headed up to Jack Kattner's office.

Kattner rotated a bottle of champagne in his hands, scanning the label.

"Morningwood! How in the hell did you pull *this* off?"

"Oh that; It's Cristal."

"Yes, I can see that, but *how* were you able to get it?"

"The catering manager remembered you. Once I told him my office was preparing for a small celebration and that it was sponsored by *you*, he did a double-take. He said to give him an extra thirty minutes and he would take care of it since A) he likes his job and, B) the company only stocks, as he called it, 'carbonated piss', because most of the champagne celebrations he caters are for line teams."

"Put him back on the Nice List and send a Thank You memo that includes a $50 gift certificate to a local restaurant."

"Yes sir." Rebecca turned and rolled her eyes. *$50! The guy sprints for a $600 bottle of champagne and gets a $50 card in return? What a cheapskate!*

The office's front door swung open. Chris and Matt stepped in.

"Hi boys. Jack is waiting for you. I'll be right behind."

"Thanks Rebecca." Chris smiled wide, as did Matt.

As soon as Jack's door opened, a loud pop startled both of them. Kattner began pouring the first glass of champagne. "Come in. Come in. Grab a seat. Here, Miller. Here you go, Jacobson."

"Thanks," replied both. Chris stared at his glass a few moments.

"Here." Kattner handed the last glass of champagne to Rebecca, then raised his own glass.

"Today is a momentous occasion. We enjoyed many celebrations in the past: The first sixteen and thirty-two-bit processors were developed here, as were most other major developments in high-volume static memory. The manufacturing achievements are ours, but *this*—" He paused for a sip of champagne. "This development marks a quantum shift in the way future memory will be designed, and it was us— really you, Doctor Miller, but as a team—us, that made it happen. I am very proud to have you all, and I look forward to our day in Oslo. Skål!"

The others raised their glasses. "Cheers!"

Chris pondered his for a moment longer than the others before partaking.

After a few gulps, Matt noticed a pleasant peculiarity. "What is *this*?"

"What—the champagne?" Kattner asked. "You can thank the catering manager for that one. I almost had him fired the last time he brought me the cheap stuff, so the rascal runs out this time and buys Cristal."

"Nice."

Morningwood rolled her eyes again. *$50 . . .*

Getting back to business, Kattner turned to Chris. "Miller, how soon before I can make a presentation? I need the folks in Washington to see this before someone leaks it."

"Hmm. Preliminary testing should only take a few days, and I already have a beta in development for the module, so five days. Six at most."

"Perfect. I'll get it set up. Morningwood?"

Kattner started to turn around and instruct her, but she said, "Already on it," before he ever had the chance.

The men drained their refilled flutes and soon departed the office. Matt smiled, licking his chops. "Man. *That* was some good drink."

"I suppose it was." Chris dug for his keys.

"You okay?" Matt asked.

"Yep." Chris said without a hint of a slur. "See you Monday, *partner*."

Matt winked. "Can't wait!

Notte Della Pizza

Chris stepped with a slight swagger into Amerimem's garage, opened the door to his beloved Rabbit, threw in his attaché case, and slid into the driver's seat. In short order, he fastened his seatbelt tightly, turned the key over, waited for the click, then rattled the engine to life. He checked his rearview mirrors, backed out of his parking space, and made for the exit. With a wave of his card, the complex's exit gate lifted, allowing an exuberant and vindicated scientist to triumphantly return home. Surely, his discovery would become one of the most significant in the world, he thought, but he couldn't tell a single soul about it—at least, not yet. For now, he basked in sequestered glory while relishing the work ahead. He never felt so confident.

Today, you're mine!

Chris raced up to the final intersection before the Stevens Hill run. With no one in front of him, he decided to take advantage of a rare opportunity. Anticipating the green light by watching the bisecting street's signal turn yellow, he revved the engine and popped the clutch, managing to coax a small chirp from the front tires of his ferocious rodent. He faced a half-mile straightaway before the steepest grade of the hill began, then up another mile to the top. Chris diligently ran through the gears, reaching fourth and 67 MPH just before the incline. As the car digested the grade, the engine waned, succumbing to gravity and the fact that his 49 horses (probably less) were better suited for a commercial washing machine. At 52 MPH, Chris made a rapid downshift to third.

He missed the shift's timing with the clutch pedal, causing its synchronizer to disengage, shredding his concentration with a deafening grind as he attempted to bully the stick. He panicked in disbelief, repeatedly grinding the stick downward, attempting to save his perfect run. His speed plummeted and, at 38 MPH, the transmission's synchronizer sarcastically allowed him into second. Chris pounded the steering wheel with his right fist. "You *had* it. You had it and *blew* it!"

Stevens Hill chalked up another win.

Chris passed through Sonno Dolce's entrance and brought the car to a halt on the curb in front of the Smiley's house. On cue, Snickers began barking furiously from within, and his fury crescendoed when his antagonist reached the front door. As Chris attempted to knock, the door wildly swung open, revealing Emily and Patricia proudly displaying their First-Place ribbon. Jennifer was right behind them, and Snickers swiftly poured out of the door and rammed his wet nose deep into Chris' crotch.

"Hey!"

Emily raised the ribbon in front of her. "Daddy, look!"

"I see that." Chris knelt and scratched Snickers behind the ears. "Great Work, girls. That's fantastic!" He then looked upwards beyond them. "Jen, would you all like to go out for some pizza? Later tonight, I mean . . . if you aren't busy. I feel like celebrating—could use the company, you know."

Of course, realizing that their favorite parlor also meant vying for prizes at its arcade, the girls immediately refocused jubilation on the next stop on their never-ending entertainment itinerary. Their undivided attention instantly turned to Jennifer, replete with all the "come on, pleases" parents typically endure before their inevitable capitulation.

"Jim should be home in about an hour, and I know he'll be ready for a beer, so yeah, sure. Make it about seven? I'll call you in a few minutes to confirm."

"Perfect."

The girls exchanged high-fives and fist pumps, declaring yet another win with a "Yes!" confidently hissed.

Emily turned toward Patricia before jumping into the Rabbit. "You keep the ribbon."

Chris climbed back into the driver's seat, adding, "And this is *my* treat, Jennifer, so tell Jim not to even try."

She laughed as he cranked the engine and drove away. Her laughs suddenly transgressed to hacking coughs.

"Jesus!"

Emily jumped out and scrambled up to her bedroom. Chris reminded her to keep an eye on the clock and to be ready in an hour. They had a little over an hour, but Chris learned long ago that when responsible for coordinating an appointment, it was typically prudent to overestimate the time needed. He made his way from the garage up to the kitchen, opened the refrigerator door, and grabbed a bottle of water. He stepped over to one of the kitchen drawers where he kept some buffered aspirin handy and popped two tablets. Chris spun the cap off the squared water bottle and took a few gulps to wash the pills down. He swallowed them with mild difficulty, having never been relaxed when taking pills. He removed his glasses and breathed deeply in anticipated relief.

I don't care if it is the finest champagne in the world— always headaches.

He remembered the promise he made to himself after Suzanne died—to not drink and drive. He knew he didn't consume nearly enough to be impaired or illegal, but just enough to induce an annoying throb in his temples. Chris headed to his room for a shower, and as he passed Emily's room, he could hear her singing along to the latest pop nonsense blaring over her shower's radio. He grinned wide; the bliss of happiness in his house had been a rarity.

The master bedroom's telephone rang just as he entered. A computer-synthesized voice from the phone's unit declared, "James Smil-e-ay," as it often mispronounced names. Even though he knew it was Jennifer by the caller ID, he still answered with hellos.

She started with a playful tone. "Chris—hey, it's Jen. We're good for seven, but Jim isn't pleased about you paying."

"A few suds will wash away any concerns your husband may have, Jen. You know I always take care of it when he hits the john for the third time."

Jennifer laughed. "Bingo! See you in a few."

Chris finished the last of his water, undressed, and climbed in the shower.

Several minutes later he emerged, sparkling and refreshed. He decided to dress ultra-casual for the restaurant by donning a newer T-shirt and a pair of khaki cargo shorts. The weather was certainly warm enough, and he never entertained formality unless for business or a date. He pondered this while sitting on the edge of his bed lacing his white tennis shoes.

The black ones make my legs look too white, he thought.

As he tied the second knot, he stared into the closet where Suzanne's clothes were still visible.

Loud music bounced off the hallway walls as Chris walked toward Emily's room to make sure she was getting ready. He overheard her talking on the phone with Patricia about what they were going to wear. He knocked on her door and waited for the volume to recede.

"Hold on," she whispered to Patricia. "Yes, Daddy?"

"Five minutes."

Chris continued walking down the hallway and down the stairs towards the kitchen. As he left, he overheard Emily back on the phone.

"We're leaving in five minutes, so I have to get ready. Bye." The music returned to its previous volume.

Emily eventually sashayed her way down to the kitchen where Chris awaited. He gave her a lengthy look and chuckled. "Uh-huh. I see you're determined to wear that top today no matter what."

Emily shrugged, "Yep!" She snapped in her earbuds and walked towards the garage.

"Em! This way." Chris pointed at the front entry.

Emily reluctantly removed her earbuds. "Do we have to?"

"Yes, we are not supposed to be there until seven. That's a few minutes from now, so we have a little time to kill. Walking's good for you."

"Ugh!" Emily trudged through the front entrance and replaced her earbuds.

Chris understood that the walk would also help alleviate his "microver"—what he called a micro-hangover. The throbbing eventually receded.

They shared a pleasant five-minute jaunt towards the front enclaves of Sonno Dolce, waving at a few neighbors as they passed. When Suzanne was alive, they regularly took the same stroll. Chris noticed a reverential look in some of the neighbors faces as they waved. They loved Suzanne because she frequently volunteered for many of the association's activities. Chris and Emily were frequently seen in their car by those neighbors, but this was their first walk since Suzanne's departure.

At 7 p.m. sharp, the Millers arrived at the front door of the Smiley's, catching Snickers off-guard. He erupted at the ring of the doorbell in a flurry of barking anger—that anyone could be on the grounds without his knowing, let alone at the front door, quickened the pace of his alarms.

"They're here. Let's roll!" Jim Smiley opened the front door to greet the Millers.

Chris recalled the resonance of his father's voice from decades past. *A handshake represents a goodwill gesture to an agreement, a greeting, or a sign of good sportsmanship*, he said. *It should be firm to show confidence and support—never the dead fish—but not too strong; that's a distasteful show of false dominance.*

James Smiley was a robust man who liked to work as hard as he played. As a residential housing contractor, he developed a noticeably strong grip from swinging a hammer over the years. His father also told him of dead fish, and because of that, Jim locked his hand with the high-pressured grip of a shop vise. Chris took this in consideration every time Jim's greetings crushed him. This time was no exception, although there was always this little smirk Jim made just before laying waste to his opponent's hand.

"What's up, *Doctor* Miller?" Jim always put the emphasis on the title, possibly due to a sense of inferiority. The title was no match for the handshake, and Chris struggled to respond without a perceptible change in the natural tone of his voice.

"Hey, Jim. Just another busy week at the lab. Ready for a cold one . . . You?"

Jim jerked his head back. "Really? My, this must be a special day."

He led Chris over to their minivan. The rest of the Smiley's, except Snickers, piled out of the home and into the lawn by the driveway. "Born ready! You and Em hop in."

The five of them settled into their seats as Jim drove towards Campbell's Mall and into the parking lot of The Forest – Fun and Adventure.

Chris once said the entertainment gods got it right with this place. Exceptional gourmet pizza, an in-house craft brewery, and one of the largest arcades in California was a remarkable feat. Throw in a mature section complete with classic arcade and sports games, pool tables, two dozen bowling lanes, and more importantly, a vast beverage selection on tap, the Forest was one of the busiest establishments in the valley.

Jennifer reminded the girls as they bolted towards the entrance, "Don't run off, we need to purchase your cards and place our order first."

The group walked inside where a pair of hosts greeted them, arranged dinner seating, and took entertainment orders. After conferring, Jim, Jennifer, and Chris decided that the girls would be adequately entertained with a Minor card each to start, so that's what they told the hostess before she walked away. Chris, forgetting, went to take out his wallet before being reminding himself that the final bill was all-inclusive. As soon as the server returned with two Minor Fun Cards loaded with 120 credits each, the girls ran for the games.

"Hey, I want you back in ten minutes, so only play a couple of games." Jennifer yelled. "What do you two want to drink?"

"I want a orange," replied Patricia, who warranted a quick correction from her mother.

"*An! An* orange."

Emily bashfully looked up at Jennifer. "Can I get a Doctor Pepper?"

"I'll ask the waitress, sweetie. Don't forget to wash your hands after you finish playing, okay?"

"Yes, Missus Smiley."

And with that, the two girls disappeared into the myriad of cabinets on the other side of The Forest's vast arcade.

"Missed your calling, Jen." Chris said.

"It's a curse, you know. Grammar. My mother's fault."

"Smart woman."

"Yes, she was, and now I catch myself mimicking her."

Unlike video arcade games, the ticket-dispensing variety attracted an innate sense of greed, as well as a challenge to ego. They all want to be *that* kid holding the most tickets at the end of the day. Emily was no exception. Immediately, she took issue with Skee Ball Alley. Patricia queued to test her skill with a basketball free throw machine. Both were lost in heaven.

Jim reviewed the selection of draughts while Chris ordered an extra-large New York style crust on the Waitron—a tabletop wireless electronic ordering and payment module.

"Hmm, I was thinking about some sort of ale. That okay with you, Chris?"

"Yeah. That's fine, but not too dark. Been a while, you know."

"How's about a pitcher of Altstädter?"

"There's always a first time, right?"

"Jen?"

"I'll have a glass of wine. Something light and juicy."

"They used to have a decent Sauvignon Blanc."

"As in blank out," Jim laughed, pointing towards his wife. "She doesn't take too well to that one for some reason."

"He's right, Chris. I prefer not to get tipsy, so if they have a Pinot Grigio, that'll work for me."

"Okay, they have two, and I know which one of those particular selections comes from downstate. I'll get you the alternate."

"Thanks."

Chris entered the order and pressed the submit button. "Okay, that should only take a minute."

Jim nodded. "So, Jen said you had a good day at the lab. Anything life-changing?"

"Hmm. Close, but you know how these things are, Jim. I can't really go into specifics. What I *can* tell you is that, yes, we had a tremendous day in the lab with a successful test of a new system. It will considerably change the way we use certain electronics, but that's about all I can safely say."

Within moments, a server arrived with a pitcher of Altstädter, two frozen mugs, and a chilled pinot.

"That good, huh? Well, I can't wait to see it. Here you go." Jim poured a mug of the ale until its head poured slightly over the top. He handed the pitcher to Chris, who poured his own.

"Thanks. I can't wait for the reveal either, but we have several weeks before any announcement."

Patricia and Emily returned, carrying a small bundle of tickets in their hands. Jennifer always made a good habit of checking on the girls who, in their excitement, typically forgot the inconvenient details.

"Did you both wash up?"

Patricia answered in the form of a question pretending ignorance to the consequences of noncompliance. "Um, no?"

"You two go wash your hands, pronto," said Jennifer. "The pizza will be here any minute."

It wasn't long before the girls returned from the restrooms and noticed that their food was already on the table. The five of them devoured the coal-fired pie in short order while savoring their beverages. Conversation was light. Emily intended to consume as much soda as possible, taking advantage of the fact Chris never bought it for her unless it was a special occasion—a carryover from her mother's rules. Realizing the girls were at the end of their meal, Chris ordered two Major Fun Cards from the Waitron. Next, he swiped his debit card through the unit's terminal.

"Hey!" Jim scowled. "Man, that's not cool! You never gave me a chance."

Jim swiped the Waitron from Chris' hands in a failed attempt to cancel the transaction. "Jen, I thought I told you to tell him I was paying this time."

Chris thought Jim's performance was as unconvincing as ever. Jennifer shrugged as she quaffed the last drop of her grigio. Patricia poked Emily and motioned for her to grab their tickets so they could continue gaming.

Emily hopped down from the booth. "Dad, we're going back."

"Okay, we'll come and get you when we're ready to leave, and I want to see four times that many tickets when I do!"

The adults walked over to the pool tables as the Terrible Two disappeared. A little over an hour later, Emily showed up at Chris' side, wrestling a large bundle of tickets.

He raised a brow. "Finished already? Where's Patricia?"

"She's still playing. Like, my card stopped working. I think it's empty. Look what I got!"

"Now *that's* a pile of tickets, Em. How many?"

"I dunno. Can we go get them counted?"

"Sure. Let Daddy finish his game and we'll have a look. Here, take my card. There are maybe thirty credits remaining. That should last you. Mister Smiley and I have some unfinished business."

Emily darted back to the machines while Chris refocused on the task at hand. He was more of a nine-ball fan, but Jim always insisted on maximizing his money by playing the full rack—Eight Ball.

Into his third consecutive shot, Jim miscued. "Damnit! Cheap sticks."

Chris sported a terribly thick Irish brogue as he reached for a small cube on the pool table's side rail. "Aye lad, but a wee bit of chalk never hurt nobody neither."

One by one, Chris' solids made their way home to the holding rack below; the table's green felt became more visible in their absence. Each time, he deliberately rechalked slowly while looking over at Jim in a taunting manner. He would never have the pleasure of equaling Jim's death grip, but this was enough of a payback.

Chris echoed an old talking pinball machine as he lined up his final shot. "Eight-ball . . . corner pocket."

Carefully, he ran the stick back and forth through his hand's open bridge, with the cue's tip stopping just short of the lower third of the cue ball. When he was confident, Chris jabbed the ball with a controlled stroke—just enough to transfer the correct force on the Eight ball to send it home while stopping the cue ball dead with the applied English.

It was a slow and painful death for Jim's ego. He jokingly cried on his wife's shoulder as she gazed in the amazement of Chris' skill. "I can't believe you ran the table on me. Where's the fun in that?" Jim asked.

"Misspent youth, Doctor Miller?" Jennifer laughed.

"That's right. Eight years of engineering school. And in that time, one might learn other useful life skills."

After replacing their cue sticks back on the racks, the parents waded into the arcade to rescue their kids. They found Emily in her usual spot—in front of a Skee Ball machine with a magnificent jumble of tickets. They spotted Patricia working off her orange soda high at a dance game.

Emily turned around after her final toss. "Daddy, I'm out. Can we go count these now?"

She placed her pile of tickets on top of the prize counter and waited for a clerk. While she waited, she examined all the prizes. Cheap plastic bugs, extra-large pencils, a row of stuffed animals on the back wall, yo-yos, radio-controlled cars, candies, telephones, radios, music players, pop-action figures and dolls. After servicing other customers, a Hispanic-looking clerk finally arrived. He collected Emily's tickets, dropped them in a small bucket, and then placed the bucket on a special scale. Immediately "1017" flashed on its display.

"Wow chica, that's a lot of tickets! I give you a few minutes to look around to see what you want, and I come back."

Emily nodded, but her eyes had already targeted something. She pointed it out to her father.

"You're kidding right? You want to spend almost everything on *that*? Are you sure?"

"Uh-huh."

It wasn't exactly what she wanted but if she couldn't have a cell phone, just maybe he wouldn't mind this monkey phone. "Can I have it?"

"I don't see why not." Chris motioned the clerk.

Jennifer's curiosity forced her to have a look at what Emily selected. "Oh, the monkey phone! How adorable."

Emily nodded in wide-smiled agreement.

Jennifer looked up at Chris. "You realize you're contributing to the natural delinquencies of a young girl, right?" She laughed then stepped over to the other end of the counter to help Patricia's count.

"Em, get a fifteen-ticket pencil and give the other two to Patty," said Chris. "You can take notes with your friends while you talk."

"Good idea!"

Chris mumbled under his breath as they headed over to Patricia's buying spree, "Yeah, one of these days I might become known for that."

Her 825-ticket tally would end up buying a deck of cards, a stuffed dolphin, three spiraled pencils, and a plastic spider.

Jennifer became a little overwhelmed by the long day—the commotion of the arcade, and a questionable glass of Pinot Grigio. "I'm ready to head home, how about you guys?"

After the relatively short ride back to the gates of Sonno Dolce, Jim spared the Millers a walk by taking them directly home.

Jennifer opened her window as they spilled out of the van. "Thanks for a fun evening, Mister Chris and Miss Emily!"

"Yep, our pleasure." Chris walked around to shake Jim's hand, quickly remembering that perhaps he should be spared retaliatory pain by opting for a cute salute instead.

As the Smileys backed down the driveway and pulled away, Emily, still excited about her fruitful trip to The Forest, yanked on her father's sleeve. "Dad, can you connect my phone so I can call Patty?"

"Can I, or *will* I?" Chris smiled. "It's too late to be calling anyone, Em. I will do it first thing in the morning."

"Aw man!" Emily sighed before remembering an important fact. "But I'm calling her cell phone and she puts it on quiet at night."

Chris paused for a moment. "Okay, but only because this isn't a school night. On those, you can only talk after you complete your homework, and you must be off of it by eight. Same rules as before, understand?"

Emily pumped her fist, "Yes!"

Chris connected the monkey phone to the wall socket in Emily's room, and she wasted no time dialing her best friend. Chris paused for a moment by the door to make sure the phone worked properly before continuing down the hallway towards his fortress of unwanted solitude.

Intelligent Design

The following week, Dr. Miller and Matthew Jacobson, along with several techs who floated between Andromeda's labs, diligently toiled to complete a functional demonstration unit before Kattner's DC presentation deadline. In addition to the primary test module, Chris developed two prototypes in collaboration with Amerimem's minimization department—a branch the execs lovingly nicknamed Shrink, Inc., and ran by engineers called "belittlers". The prototype module's full footprint was that of a mid-sized passenger sedan. Within the first few days, the dauntless belittlers—who'd reduce their mother's coffins if given the chance—miniaturized the memory module to the size of a half pack of chewing gum and just three sticks thin. This greatly surpassed Chris' expectations, and it allowed the surrounding interface to be considerably contracted. A titanium containment unit internally handled temperature control via the artificial circulant, which carried a lifespan of about twenty years. When left "unplugged" the unit defaulted into stasis mode, increasing the tissue life indefinitely. Even though the new unit's dimensions were similar to a laptop's solid-state drive, Chris resisted any derivative moniker for it.

"Matt, I'm torn."

"By what?"

Chris held up one of the newly minted memory modules. "What to name these. 'Soft Drives' or 'T-Drives', with the 'T' standing for tissue. Any idea?"

"Difficult. Tissue drive rings as something found near a toilet. What did the Shrinks say?"

"They wanted to call it Double Mint, but that's a lawsuit waiting to happen and why I bypassed it." Chris frowned. "So, 'T-Drive' then?"

"The kids will play with that one."

"Hmm. I suppose you're right. 'Soft Drive' it is."

Matt raised a brow as if to make additional comment, holding up a finger."

"What?" Chris asked.

"Nothing." Matt replied. "Someone will always find negativity if they're looking for it."

Chris placed the module next to a duplicate on his testing bench. He developed both machines for different presentations of the new drive, settling on two familiar and simplistic platforms. The first was a legacy laptop with its internal optical drive removed to make room for the module. For the second design, he utilized an even older seven-inch portable movie disc player modified to house the drive and output to its display.

Matt was busy completing his work on the interpretive audio synthesis portions of the programming for the housing units. The base of his programming was derived from the successful tests during the previous week, and the functionality tests completed during the last four days. The original module remained functional to assist with nominal parameter benchmarking.

Kattner abruptly broke the lab's silent rhythm, bellowing over the technician's earbud monitoring system with his graveled trombone of a voice. "Still on schedule?"

"Affirmative, Jack." Chris adjusted his microphone. "A few minor details yet with interfacing the video, and I expect to have those issues resolved by the end of Monday. Matt's completing his coding now. We'll need more testing, but our expectation is that you'll be on target for your presentation."

"Excellent. Let Rebecca know if you need anything. I'm headed over to Las Bajos for a quick nine and a Macallan."

"Thanks for rubbing it in, Jack!"

Andromeda became relatively quiet compared to the myriad of testing earlier in the week. It was Friday, late morning, and most of the support techs had already escaped to their families or the closest bar. There were no tests ongoing in the muscular biomechanics labs or elsewhere in Level 9. All the monitors, including the main viewing screens, were still active—albeit dark with a steadily blinking message in their top-left corners. "Awaiting Content..."

Matt kept a sharp focus on his monitor, confirming each keystroke of coding. His keyboard's neoprene protective cover muted any tapping noise as he churned away. His left temple developed an itch, and he unconsciously poked his finger under his safety goggles and behind the tight-fitting body condom covering his head. Satisfied, his hand returned to the keyboard without a second thought.

Chris continued simulations on his portable designs for the memory modules. He installed one of the new soft drives into the laptop prototype and booted the device. Even in complete silence, no individual function of the tiny computer was intelligible when it tasked the new soft drive—one of the primary benefits of near-noiseless solid-state architecture. A micro fan hummed at the very edge of audibility, then the boot sequence searched fruitlessly for media in an empty memory card slot until it wound its way towards the soft drive. A moment later, a familiar BIOS opening screen appeared, then the Linux desktop. Chris began a silent dance on the laptop screen's crystalline surface with his gloved hands.

A faint glow reflected on the outer rim of Chris' safety goggles. He lifted an eyebrow just as the glow exploded into bright white flashes that illuminated the entire laboratory.

Chris innately spun around to face the source—a deer in headlights. The large projector screen flickered in a sequence of static-filled white flashes. Matt jumped out of his chair and slowly paced towards Chris' station, both of them glued to the main screen.

A loud explosion boomed over their monitoring earbuds, followed by someone frantically yelling, "I'M HIT! I'M HIT!" Matt's eyes popped as the image of an apparent battle scene continued to come into focus. He never blinked. A tan Humvee crashed into an adobe wall as soldiers, wearing United States fatigues, scrambled to take cover. Explosions on every flank, close-proximity Kalashnikov rifles on full auto blasted over the lab's audio channel with their high-velocity 7.62mm jackets ricocheting off the walls. The viewpoint appeared in a first-person angle, as if someone had filmed this scene with a handheld camera, except the picture's movement quality seemed more intuitive than those stylized by flashy camera work. The scene abruptly shifted, appearing to peer down the length of a petite cement wall. Additional soldiers were pinned by gunfire in the foreground—mortar fragments rained on their headgear from rounds striking the top of the wall. A soldier grabbed his walkie-talkie and screamed, "GZFDC, GZFDC! Requesting immediate R3 at X-RAY TANGO—" The images and audio faded to static and white flashes, and then completely dropped out, with the "Awaiting Content..." default message vigilantly and silently blinking afterward.

Chris stared agape at the screen for a few moments before he turned towards Matt. "Did you see tha— Hey, what's the matter?"

Matt stood trembling, staring at the screen with a blank expression. Shaking uncontrollably, he whispered, "It's impossible."

"What, Matt? What's impossible? What was that?"

Matt sat down at the closest station and tried to breathe. Quivering with his goggles slightly fogged over from all the heavy breathing, he struggled for words.

"You can take your time Matt, but I'm going to go out on a limb here and speculate that this has something to do with you. What was it?"

"It's impossible!"

Chris grew more frustrated. "What?"

"That *was* me."

"Huh?"

"That was me, Chris, but it's impossible. I wasn't wearing any cameras or anything. Nobody did."

"What do you *mean* that was you?" Chris demanded.

Kattner never mentioned anything about a military history, and Matt never volunteered anything about it. As far as Chris knew, Matt was a standard issue Yale GenX tech, fifteen years removed.

"I mean—that was me several years ago. I was there! I went through that firefight, but it's impossible. Chris, nobody knew about that mission. It was classified, and there were definitely no cameras. It's as if it came from my own eyes and ears!"

Chris' took a step backward. "You have some explaining to do, and you better do it fast. I want to know who the hell you really are and exactly why you're in my lab!"

"Can't hear you." Matt pointed toward his earbuds.

The intercom system abruptly interrupted with Rebecca Morningwood's voice. "Chris, what was that?"

"Nothing Becky. Someone must have forgotten a DVD in one of the drives, and I triggered it to play by accident."

"A movie? In the lab?" Morningwood shrugged. "Okay— just seemed weird. The pipe was all quiet up here. That made me jump."

"Sorry; I imagine it would! Probably one of the afterhours cleanup guys. Big screen, you know. I've already removed it, so no worries."

Chris motioned Matt to walk over to his station and sit in a place obscured from the cameras. Once there, he signaled Matt to turn off his monitoring/intercom belt pack.

Chris adjusted his glasses. "Okay . . . not much time before someone wonders why we're so quiet, so spill it—what's going on?"

Matt took a deep breath and glanced around the room to make absolutely sure there wasn't any chance of eaves-dropping. "You're not going to like it, Doc. Kattner knows I'm under orders. Not sure those will stand after that. I really have no choice here." He looked Chris in the eyes. "I'm here for surveillance, to monitor your project."

"What? Who's 'they'?"

"Shh. Keep it down."

"Matt, we're nine floors below ground and the monitors are off; nobody's going to hear. Who's they?"

"Pentagon."

"Who?"

"Blue Ops. Look, I don't think I have time to fully explain. Just know it's part of the Air Force."

"I need more than that."

"Let's get one thing straight—needs are subjective and given to bias."

"No way. I can't unsee it, Matt."

"Right." Matt sighed. "Here's the deal: Boxwood keeps an eye on just about everything. If they get wind of something potentially useful, they want to be on top of it before anyone else takes a shot. Not such a tough concept, right? National security?"

"Oh, you've got to be kidding me. That's insane!"

"No, Chris, it's true. They're into everything. Hell, they've even got an operator down at General Mills while they develop some kind of ultra-energy paste for longer mission times."

Coming to the realization that Matt was truthful, Chris sat on the floor and tried to absorb the past few moments. A minute ago, he was completing the final prototypes for a presentation by Kattner, now this. He began to question the authority in infiltrating a corporation's inner sanctum.

"Okay, so hack or not, you're some goddamn plant and Kattner knows it? Explains a few things."

"Who do you think he's making a presentation to next week?"

"I thought he was taking it to our board in Washington. My God!"

"Chris, look, the military is one of the largest consumers of domestic technology. Jack will take it to the board, yes, but the protocol is that it goes through us first."

"And that's supposed to make me feel better?"

"No, but it's better than someone else. Our military wants— needs— to have everything first. And why shouldn't they? It's for our own protection."

"I've heard that before. Wasn't it MacArthur? 'Be there firstest with the mostest' or something?"

"Actually, it was a Confederate general that said it first. Not quite MacArthur's version, but close enough."

"Oh, *great*. That worked out real well for him now didn't it."

"Who? MacArthur?"

"No, the other guy."

"He was never actually defeated, but yeah, not so good."

"Well, forget that. What are we going to do about this?"

"What?"

"Matt, I don't know what to do about you, or if Kattner wants this after what just popped on the screen. You're here, fine, I should probably keep my mouth shut, not that I have much of a choice. What the hell was that on the screen, though? I mean, what the hell *caused* that?"

"Hey man, you got me, but I'm going to find out before my mission terminates, I promise you that!"

What caused a vision to appear from Matt's past? Chris wondered. He looked up at the screens then down to his station and the original testing module. "Matt, it's almost lunchtime. We'll come back and try to figure this out afterward. I'm pressed to get those testing units ready for Kattner too."

"Suits me."

Both men departed Andromeda through the biomechanics corridor, back through the air scrubbers, and out to the Green Room.

"I can't believe I didn't catch onto it all this time. I'm an idiot. A complete idiot," Chris muttered as he stripped off his bunny suit, mentally reviewing each lab technician and research assistant since he became Amerimem's top engineer.

"I'm still here for you, man. I'm not exactly proud about the whole deception game. Actually, this was my first assignment. Not such a great agent, huh?"

"I suppose not. What are they going to do to you if they find out?"

"I don't know. Probably reassign me. That or prison."

"You could have lied about it; said you didn't know."

"Would you have bought it?"

"Not for a second."

The two sat down upon arrival at Chris' regular sandwich shop across the street. He stared blankly at a toasted turkey basil on Italian, some plain potato chips, and a diet soda. Matt, nervously noshed on a meatball sub.

"And what about me?" Chris asked after an uncomfortably long silence.

Matt swallowed his last bite. "I don't know that either."

"So, this is all a covert operation, but if you're made, it's really no big deal. Reassignment?"

"Or prison."

"Well, I mean, there's no 'if I tell you, I have to kill you', stuff, right?"

"No," Matt laughed.

"Well, that's a relief, I suppose. Then what about Jack?"

"What about him?"

"Does he know what you do, exactly?"

"He's not supposed to, but I think he's a smart guy . . . knows the game. The important part is that he knows why." Matt gulped from his bottled water. "All he knows is that I came suggested through the board, and two from the board are, how should I put it, 'influenced'."

"And, who is that?"

"I can't tell you. I'd have to kill you." Matt kept a serious face.

"Oh—funny, ha ha!" Chris shortly realized that Matt was somewhat serious. "Really?"

Matt laughed, "No. But I really can't tell you *that*; I'm in enough hot water already."

The men finished and returned to Amerimem—back through all the security checks, down the elevator to B-9, past the last security checkpoint, through the first air blast, and into the Green Room. Chris reminded Matt to keep the monitors off for now. Once again, the two scrubbed down and suited up. Both entered the last air chamber when Chris noticed Matt doing something odd.

Realizing the potential hazard, Chris jumped in front of him. "Hey, you can't be doing that."

"What?"

"That!"

Chris pulled away Matt's finger, which under his protective eye shield. The air scrubber suddenly activated with a fierce blast of air, wildly flapping their bunny suits. Matt tried to respond, but the noise from the scrubber and the sheer force of its wind momentarily paralyzed the exchange.

After the scrubber completed its cycle, the yellow flashing beacons signaled them to enter the last revolving air lock.

"You didn't by any chance do that earlier, did you?" Chris asked.

With a guilty tone, Matt's head drooped. "Maybe. Problem?"

"Interesting." Chris flipped Andromeda's lights on and walked over to the original Tumor project. The misters continued their function, keeping the exposed tissue acclimatized. The module was still active on the monitoring system. Chris stared at the tissue then looked up at the screens, which maintained the same message, "Awaiting Content…"

"You're not—" Matt attempted to ask.

"Matt, the content recorders are queued, right? I mean, they should record anything that occurs on the monitor."

"Well, yeah. Sure. But only if we're in a test sequence."

"What about the lab security cameras. Can you access those?"

"You'd have to give me a minute, Boxwood slipped those codes to me, but it will take time."

"Do it."

Twenty-five agonizing minutes passed before Matt called Chris over to his station.

"Okay, I think I'm in. Here's the camera in the hallway coming into Andromeda, and here are the cameras for our stations."

Chris pointed at another spot on the monitor. "I need that one—the one showing the main screens on the back wall. Can you isolate it?"

"Yeah, hold on. There. Got it."

"Okay, good. Run it back slowly."

Matt rewound the video surveillance footage at a rate of one minute per second.

"Ah. There we are leaving, then the flashes and the scene. Go back further, at a slower rate."

Matt bumped up the rewind rate to five minutes per second.

"Okay, good." Chris never blinked while the footage reversed into the early a.m. hours. A split-second blip flashed by.

"Hold it! Go back to that."

"I didn't see anything."

"There was a flash. Remember, this is at five minutes per, so any anomaly wouldn't be more than a blink."

"Got it. This is around 2310 last night."

Matt cued the tape to just before the flashes. Similar to the first occurrence, the main screen on the back wall flickered slowly then played a brief scene. This time it was a woman undressing in a provocative manner while standing at the foot of a bed.

"Hey, all right!" Matt cheered.

Chris pointed at the screen. "I know her. I know her! She's one of the tech's girlfriends. I met her a few months ago at the company Christmas party. What the— Matt, back it up further with the same speed as before."

Still laughing, Matt placed the rewind speed again at one minute per second before toggling the transport. Twenty-seven seconds later, several personnel appeared on the monitor.

"You see. There he is prepping for today. Hang on a minute. Can you grab him from a different angle? His back is turned, and I can't see what he's doing."

"Yeah, hang on."

Matt reconfigured the camera view and rewound the video. The tech refreshed the circulant reservoir, and then paused for a moment. Appearing to do something with his hands, his back was still facing the camera. Chris became anxious. "Come on. Turn around."

The tech slowly turned around and revealed his hand inside his opened bunny suit on the backside of his neck, exposing a portion of his chest.

Matt jumped up. "Aha! Bingo!"

"You recognize the pattern?"

"Sure, but what do you think is actually happening?

"Obviously, some form of matter is being introduced into the original module, but I don't know in what exact form. Of course, a Class 1 clean room is only as clean as its inhabitants' discipline. Even if every procedure is followed to the letter, Class 1 is not Class Zero. Point being, it's not perfect."

"Do we have any flashlights around here?"

"There's one in the aid kit on the wall by the entrance."

Matt walked over to the front entrance and opened the station's emergency kit. On the right-hand side of the box was a standard Maglite torch. He killed the overhead lights inside Andromeda, leaving only the glow from the computer monitors. They provided just enough light for him not to bump into everything on the way over to the original Tumor experiment.

Chris stood up and joined him. "I think you're onto it."

"Yep, let's have a looksie."

Careful not to shine the powerful flashlight in their eyes, Matt flicked the beam on and began surveying around the room. Instead of looking at the room, Matt and Chris were intensely studying the beam itself.

"You see that?"

Chris looked at mostly empty airspace until he found a tiny particle strand floating precariously in the beam. "Yeah, there it is. That's the only one I see though."

"Me too." Matt followed the fiber around for a minute before unwittingly blasting Chris' eyes.

"Hey! Thanks a lot, jackass!" Chris squinted and threw his hands in front of his face.

"No problem!" Matt smiled. "I need to run a task."

Chris knew what was forthcoming and maintained his skepticism. "Be my guest, but you're going to have a hard time coaxing anything to land exactly where you want."

"Well, give me a hand and we'll blow it in there if we have to."

They walked over to the section housing the original Tumor project. The misters were still functioning properly, keeping the tissue sample's environment stable. Matt shined the flashlight across the top of the small, black opaque rectangle, revealing little droplets of mist as they swirled about in the air, making their way slowly down to the cranial tissue.

"Here." Matt handed the flashlight to Chris, "Hold this just over the module."

Matt loosened his protective goggles. He leaned over the module next, about a foot over its top, stretching the upper part of his body condom just over the hairline of his forehead. Waiting a few seconds for that to dry out, he fluffed his hair, releasing a few particles that danced in the beam of the flashlight.

"That's a lot, Matt. Don't move or you'll draw them away."

Slowly, the particles descended towards the module. A few aimlessly drifted away on the swirls emanating from Matt's miniscule nose breaths. Several particles remained unaffected. He followed them downward with the flashlight until they disappeared within the mist. Within seconds, the room lit up with bright white flashes from the main viewing monitors. The main projector screen also flickered. In rapid succession, some visuals flashed within the static and white flashes. Audio was mostly static too, but occasionally made noises reminiscent of tuning an old longwave radio. Alas, no unmitigated scenes rendered—only fractional blips.

"Incredible." Chris turned to Matt. "Probably too many."

"Too many?"

"Yes, too many. I think it tried to read them all at once. Either we have to find a method to get only one fragment in there at a time, or we'll have to find a method for the module to recognize and digitally separate each fragment."

"I like the second idea better, Chris. I'm not going to be chasing down one little fiber all over the lab with a flashlight and tweezers."

Chris laughed at the comedy potential. "Sure about that?"

"Um, yeah."

"Can we try that again; I want to be sure."

A voice from the other side of the headset resonated, "Did you copy that?"

"Yes."

"Opinion?"

"I am not sure."

"I *think* he may be interested."

"He is-a not interested in what you think, nor am I."

"Pardon me, but—"

"Reformat and courier it directly to me. Share this-a with no one. You have ten minutes, understand?"

"Yes."

A cassock-wearing man in his late thirties arose from his monitoring station located in a room with centuries-old wood floors and stone walls. Bells clanged in the background, along with the faint sounds of nautical traffic and the rhythmic chiming of multiple mast halyards striking their metallic chords at a nearby marina. Reaching into a cabinet, he selected a micro card from a stack of black micro cards, returned to his station, and downloaded a video copy of Andromeda's video logs. When the download completed, he removed the card from the reader, placed it in a small envelope, and sealed it with a wax emblem bearing a crucifix with the letter T at the top-left corner. Next, the man walked towards the chamber entrance where two robed guards attended the doorway.

"Take this to him, *subito*. No waiting, and report to me as-a soon as you return."

The young guard standing on the right produced his hands from within the sleeves of his cassock. He accepted the envelope, gestured, then disappeared down an ornate stoned hallway at a brisk pace. Upon reaching a similarly guarded archway, one of its sentries reached for the piece of communication, but the courier rejected him. Two robed men were conversing at the back of the resplendent chamber within view of the courier. One was a tall and middle-aged priest, standing and making pointed hand gestures with a raised voice. The man seated before him appeared much older and, whether he knew it or not, seemed near the end of his life. He took notice of the courier's arrival outside while ignoring the priest's tirade before him.

"*Direttamente*," stated the courier, as he showed the official seal on the back of the envelope.

One of the guards turned around, intending to enter the chamber to inform the elder man. No sooner than he did, the elder looked around the interrupted priest and motioned toward the courier, inviting him to come forward. The guards about-faced and allowed the courier through.

Visually irritated, the priest, a bishop named Narciso Esposito, halted his dispute to ask the courier, "What is it that is so important as to necessitate our interruption?" He then extended his hand so that the courier could kiss his rather ostentatious signet ring. The courier, hesitating momentarily to glance at the elder man, knelt before the expectant Esposito, and nervously kissed his ring.

"Pardon me, Your Grace. I have an urgent communication from Monsignor Trovarto for His Eminence."

The young courier knelt before the seated elder, extending an envelope from his right hand. Cardinal Vasco Tagliabue took the envelope and raised his bifocals to inspect its seal.

"*Grazie.*"

The courier stood and cowered before Bishop Esposito, who harbored a grimace. Once the courier vacated the chamber, Tagliabue motioned his sentinels to close the doors and remain outside. He turned towards to Esposito, and feebly raised a finger.

"You should not make such vain and archaic displays, Narciso. People take notice. They talk. Now, what do you make of this?"

Further annoyed that his interruption now included discipline, Esposito contemplated the fact that he was currently in no position to debate his superior.

"Yes, Your Eminence. The communique is from Monsignor Trovarto."

"Do me the favor of opening it."

Esposito walked across the room to an ancient-looking wooden desk and retrieved a letter opener. He broke the letter's vermilion seal and walked back over to Tagliabue. The cardinal looked up at Esposito as he handed over the envelope.

"*Grazie.*"

Replacing his glasses, the elder man inspected the contents of the letter.

"Hmmm," he mumbled. He then shook the envelope to let the rest of the contents drop into his palm.

Esposito bent down to see what was in Tagliabue's hand. "A memory card?"

With modest difficulty, Tagliabue stood up and handed the chip to Esposito. "Let us take it to the *Telemagine*. Trovarto seems to think it is important."

The two priests walked back behind Tagliabue's desk. The cardinal pressed a hidden button just underneath the desktop's cornice. A thin metallic dowel extended a meter upward from the front-left corner, and a similar dowel appeared through a slot traversing the width of the desk's top, perpendicularly intersecting the bottom of the vertical dowel. As soon as the dowels stopped moving, the intermittent intersections of thousands of micro laser refractions created an ultra-resolution, interactive, flat holographic image. Tagliabue retrieved a wafer-thin wireless keyboard from a drawer and unrolled it upon the desk. He inserted the tiny chip in a slot on the side of the keyboard. A feed from an observational camera played video from the recent events in Andromeda on the display. Several minutes passed until the video concluded.

"They never cease to amaze me, these scientists," Tagliabue sighed. He turned around to face Esposito. "Contact Washington. Instruct them to handle this affair in the most expedient and discreet manner. I do not want them to complicate matters as they did in '62." He looked away and thought to himself. *Damn sloppy.*

"Yes, Your Eminence."

Chris paced about. "I should tell Jack about this."

Matt abruptly turned around. "I don't know about that. Think about it for a second. God knows what the Pentagon would dream up with this kind of technology. It's too new. Too, I don't know, invasive."

"I don't understand."

"Chris, my imagination is running wild. I think they will put us to sleep, tap into the old noggin, and float whatever they want us to think about at night. Heck, maybe even do it while we're going down the road!"

"That's crazy."

"Oh? Mengele ring any bells? How about Oppenheimer? They knew what they were doing, but did they stop? No! You know Boston's already working on that neuropatch thing. Who's to say they won't use it? Oh God. They might not want this out."

Chris threw his hands in the air. "And away we go with all the foil-hatter conspiracy theories. They who? Do I make my reservations for Buenos Aires now, or should I wait until next week?"

"Look, man. Hollywood tends to exaggerate a lot, but do you really think those writers are dreaming all that stuff up out of the blue? I don't want to be the 'I've seen a lot of things, man' cliché, because I'm not, but I've heard the stories, and our handlers used some of the wilder examples for training. They were there! Some of the crazy stuff really does happen, and from what I've been told, a lot of madness that we'll never hear about because it will forever remain classified. You have to trust me on this. I know I deceived you, but that's my job. Right now, I'm just as paranoid as you. From what I understand, it's not just my employer we have to worry about —there are others."

Chris calmed himself. "*Okay.* Suppose so. What do we do?"

With his back turned to the closest camera, Matt signaled Chris to look at him secretly pointing at it. "Don't look at the camera directly, but we have to assume they will know about this soon."

"All right." Chris' anxieties began to climb. His voice picked up volume. "What do we *do* about it?"

"I'm not sure now. I think we have a few days perhaps. Kattner hasn't gone to Washington yet, so we have some time. Maybe we should just finish working and leave normally at the end of the day. If we picked up and ran, well . . ."

Chris nodded, "Red flag, I agree."

He stepped over to his station and resumed testing for the two prototypes, keeping his head down until the last few minutes of their shift.

Later that afternoon, he motioned Matt over. "You're going to like this. Check it out."

Chris opened his first prototype, the laptop. After a brief booting sequence, he toggled its disc eject button. Instead of a plastic tray, an elaborate filtering mechanism sprung from its place.

Matt looked at it with a puzzled expression. "What is that?"

"Shrink just sent it back. I added a static filtering chamber. I'll have to test it elsewhere, but in theory, I should be able to eject the tray, run some material through it, and filter the results onto the soft drive."

"Sweet! It'll be like going out and catching a lot of tiny memory fragments."

"Exactly. And, if what I think is true, you really *can* be the fly on the wall."

"Problem." Matt winced. "Still kinda big. Can't be concealed."

"We'll see. Since it looks like any ordinary laptop, I think I can get it out of here without much scrutiny."

Matt looked over at the other prototype soft drive device and asked, "What about that one?"

"I'll be doing the same modification to the disc player version, but I'm not taking it with me. Too much of a curiosity. Why would I have a disc-player in the first place? Questions . . . and it will certainly raise eyebrows. I'll take the laptop, and since it has onboard processing, maybe more can be accomplished with the data than basic playback."

"Makes sense."

"You have my cell number, right?"

"Ends with 1101?"

"That's it."

"How predictably binary of you, Doctor Miller."

"Why, thank you. Wait . . . so, what is your rank? I'm assuming you *are* an officer."

"Commander, yes. Lieutenant Commander, actually."

"Lieutenant Commander Jacobson—got it."

Chris glanced at the large digital clock on the front wall. "You can get out of here if you want, Matt. I am going to finish up on the other unit then try to run home."

"Thanks. I should warn you—if you see anything out of the ordinary, let me know. Just ring if you see anything weird. Anything, but mind your words in case others are listening. Assume they are."

"Okay, thanks."

Matt closed down his station and waved towards Chris on his way out. Chris carefully nudged the newly modified filtering tray into the laptop and shut it down. He then turned his attention to modifying the disc player prototype. By the end of the day, Chris finished all modifications to the other unit, closed its lid, and carefully placed it in its secure locker. He slid the laptop cautiously into his attaché, then powered down his station and exited the lab with a brisk pace.

A red flashing beacon and a loud buzzer shrieked through-out Level 9, drawing the attention of a couple cleaning techs working in the biomechanics laboratory. Chris suddenly realized that he tried to actuate the rotating airlock door by pushing on it instead of mashing the large green button on the right side of the doorway. Confirming the error, he pressed the button, which deactivated the red warning beacons and activated the familiar yellow ones. To his relief, the door star-ted to revolve. Once inside the glass-walled inner air-cleaning chamber, he gestured towards the two techs by slapping his skull and shrugging his shoulders in a "What was I thinking" fashion. The techs laughed. One went so far as to slap the other on the arm and point as if to say, "To be so smart, he's a complete idiot!" *Fair enough*, Chris thought. *As long as it diverts their attention from the briefcase, I'm fine.*

Chris broke out in a full sweat by the time he entered the Green Room. Stripping off the body condom, the evaporating lotion and 20°C air conditioning treated him to the refreshing coolness of freedom. He opened his locker and got dressed—boxers, socks, trousers, shirt, belt, and then a conservatively-striped blue silk tie with a fast and simple four-in-hand knot. He eschewed his contact lenses for the chrome-rimmed eyeglasses he kept as a backup, then slipped on a pair of well-worn brown leather oxfords given to him by Suzanne a few years ago. Without delay, he blazed out the door. As soon as he hit the hallway, Chris noticed a security guard staring him down as if to question the contents of the case. Chris became nervous. The sweat returned.

"Doctor Miller, could you step over here for a minute, please?"

"Um, yes. Is there any problem?" Chris tried to focus on escaping the lab without any questions raised.

Discreetly, the guard started to smile while pointing down at Chris' lower half.

"Your left shoe is untied." He whispered.

Shocked, Chris did a double-take while looking down, thinking the guard would make a comment about the case instead.

"Oh, it *is*."

"Yes. I didn't mean to embarrass you."

Chris put the case down to tie the shoe.

"I can hold that for you if you like?"

"Oh, no. No. That's okay. I can manage." Fearing the guard might question the irregularity of the case's weight, Chris waved him off and quickly retied his shoe before heading to the elevators.

Chris' nerves were tightly strung. He refocused on escaping the lobby and headed for the relative safety of his car. Within two short minutes, he managed it without falling apart. Carefully, he placed the attaché case in the passenger seat, jumped in, and fastened his seatbelt. The Rabbit faithfully ignited with its familiar metallic gurgle. Chris backed up and exited the garage, checking his rearview mirror all the way, expecting to see someone chase him down at any moment. After the rise of the Amerimem's main exit gate, he was able to breathe a sigh of relief. Not looking to challenge Stevens Hill today, he took the much-despised second gear near the top while grinding possibilities and probabilities. Close to home, a wild notion struck him.

The Closet

Chris rattled through the gates of Sonno Dolce towards Smiley's to retrieve Emily. Parked at the foot of their driveway, he opened his door, swung around, and dropped both feet down. In that moment, a soaking wet Snickers bolted from the house and trumpeted Chris' arrival with barks and sniffs. Then came the shake that irrigated everything within a ten-foot radius. Chris removed his glasses and started to wipe them, water dripping from his face. The dog retreated as Patricia and Emily bounded outside in swimsuits.

"Hi Patty," said Chris. "How's the water?"

She giggled and bashfully nodded. Emily laughed and grabbed her father's arm so he could inspect her hand. "Daddy, look! It's wrinkled."

"You stayed in the water too long."

"Uh-huh. Missus Smiley said the same thing."

"It will return to normal in a few minutes. Collect your belongings so we can go home."

Patricia whispered something in Emily's ear, and then looked up at Chris with a beaming grin.

"Dad?"

"What?"

"Patty asked if I could spend the night. They want to take me bowling."

"Oh, I don't know about that, Em. We don't want to wear out your welcome. Missus Smiley needs a break."

Jennifer approached from the entryway. "It's fine with me, Chris; I don't mind. Those two have become inseparable and well, you know she's like our second daughter."

"You leave me no argument." Chris smiled. "I suppose there's no real reason to keep her away then, but not overnight; we have some chores to do in the morning."

Chris searched around in one of his front pockets, found a couple of twenties, and gave them to Emily. "Don't spend it all."

She frowned at the notion. Patricia dragged her inside, incessantly giggling at their evening's prospects.

"What do we say, Patty?" Jennifer demanded.

"Thank you."

"Thank you, what?"

"Thank you, Mister Miller."

Chris laughed while he restarted the Rabbit.

"You're welcome, girls."

He thanked Jennifer and sped home. He climbed to the top of the driveway and parked on the garage's right side, closest to the mud room's door. The diesel spiraled into a slow coughing death. Chris breezed into the house and made for the kitchen, plopped his attaché on the counter, nabbed a fresh glass from the dishwasher, and then reached into the refrigerator for a filtered pitcher of water. He poured a full glass and held it to his perspirative forehead for a few moments before quaffing it down.

He stepped upstairs to the master bedroom, placed the case on the bed, stripped off his clothes, and jumped in the shower. The day's events percolated as he gazed into oblivion, letting the hot water steam the air while beating down his tense back. Twenty or so minutes went by in a blink. *Enough*, he thought. Shutting off the water, its last trickles audibly ran down the drain as he opened the shower door. He grabbed a towel, dried off, wrapped himself, returned to the bedroom, and sat on the edge of the bed next to the attaché. He stared at a particular selection of Suzanne's clothes beyond in the closet, still hanging—untouched for two years. Pausing at each moment, he remembered the last time his wife wore each garment.

Wool jacket. Tahoe skiing. White blouse. Dinner with Jack at the club.

He arrived at a short black skirt, remembering a good time with friends at a local restaurant. He recalled the cab ride home because they were energetically buzzed, and that Emily was attending a slumber party that night. He remembered the vision of ravishing his wife and the hours of passion that followed. Chris lost himself in their best lovemaking. It had been a while, he thought. Probably long enough. He began to think he might be torturing himself unnecessarily. Still, the sensations of that night lingered. He knew they would forever.

Unconsciously maintaining the trance, Chris turned around and felt the attaché resting against his thigh. He wondered if he should dare experiment with his own life—a laconic mental exercise if there ever was one. He suddenly snapped out of his stare and flipped open the case's latches. He retrieved the laptop, flipped it open, and held the power button down, allowing the boot sequence to begin. Less than a minute later, the native Linux interface featuring the Amerimem logo splashed onto the screen. Chris navigated to his application and executed it. After the program opened, he toggled the filter tray's eject function. The fragile tray quietly slid open from the side of the laptop, exposing its collection membrane to the open air. Almost immediately, the program recognized dozens of the trapped fragments and began parsing their contents. Chris quickly slid the tray closed before too many were collected, thinking that the application would crash if he didn't. Seconds ticked; the algorithm concluded its assessment of the fragment contents—revealing two as containing intelligible media.

He clicked on the first fragment's file and ran it. A window appeared only to play a series of bright white flashes and a blip of audio that sounded like barking. *Barking?* He presumed the barking was likely Snickers since he was the only dog in recent contact that could have transferred any fibrous matter. Chris selected the second file's icon. The player initiated the characteristic bright white flashes until a new scene appeared from within the static. From Suzanne's point of view, she embraced Chris in a hug before backing off to admire her new jacket. It was the same wool jacket still hanging in their closet. "I love it, my Hudson," she declared with an embrace as the image dissolved into the series of white flashes.

The laptop's screen began to shake from Chris' trembling. He was in shock, mesmerized by an overload of emotion and possibility. He considered his new connection to Suzanne, and a strong thirst for her essence suddenly overtook him. His scientific side briefly interceded the new romantic fantasy, but only briefly. Chris' comprehension of his little discovery blossomed. *Petitio principii, indeed. Albert, you were a brilliant man!*

Chris excitedly hopped off the bed and snatched a comb from the bathroom. He took it into the master closet and waited several moments to let the air settle. Carefully, he clicked on the tray ejection icon, releasing the filter tray from the laptop's side. Smoothly, he raked a sleeve of Suzanne's jacket just above the filter tray. In seconds, new fragments began registering—first a few, then hundreds. Chris closed the tray and went back to the bed to sit down. 915 fragments registered, eventually acknowledging only five with any presentable content. Chris feverishly clicked on their icons to view the contents. The first started with the flashing, and then played another hazy scene from Suzanne's point of view. She walked towards her car, twisting her ankle on the last step in the garage, screaming in pain before the image faded. The second fragment showed her chatting with Jennifer Smiley about a Christmas play that both Emily and Patricia would be attending.

"Huh," Chris said under his breath. "I don't remember that conversation."

The third fragment brought tears as it displayed the heat of a senseless argument he had with Suzanne. Chris stopped and felt like he wasn't doing himself any favors by dredging up history—new or otherwise. Intoxicating curiosity may get the better of him. *Is this toxic?*

Fragment 4 displayed a much longer scene, this time from his viewpoint. Suzanne was frantically stripping her clothes off in the heat of another high-intensity moment. Chris never thought he would see her naked again, much less in this fashion. Yet, there she was. Her striking beauty paralyzed him; it was Reason #1 of many reasons he fell in love. Just as quickly as she appeared, she faded within the static haze and silent bright white flashes. Chris touched the screen. More tears welled in mournful acquiescence.

He decided not to open any more of the fragment files. It was too much to bear, and he was harming himself, answering his own question. He knew that much, and he knew it was time to let her go—to free himself. Now that he had seen her alive again, and with new experiences, he realized the addictive danger. *Where would it end?* Would he forever search for more fragments—any fragments—even those from her childhood home? His heart wept with renewed grief from her loss, and he couldn't bring himself to move from the edge of the bed. Several moments passed while Chris' mind thawed. The laptop, still waiting to execute Fragment 5, lapsed into hibernation mode. Chris would not reboot. Instead, he powered down, tucking the computer into his midsection and whimpering himself to sleep.

Just before consciousness escaped him, the doorbell rang. Chris forced himself up and threw on his robe before heading downstairs to the front door. Jennifer was dropping Emily off from their bowling trip.

"Jeez Chris. You look terrible. Everything okay?"

Rubbing his eyes and still sniffling, Chris answered, "Yeah, I'm fine. Come on inside, Em."

"Goodnight, Emily. We had fun tonight."

"G'night Missus Smiley."

"Jen, wait," Chris stopped himself from closing the door. "What did she score?"

Jennifer batted a lash. "185 and a 203. Rails up, of course."

"Ah, right. Not bad, though. Okay, thanks."

"See you guys Monday if not before. Have a fabulous night you two!"

"Thanks Jen."

Already bored in the throes of the evening's anticlimax, Emily went straight to her room and immediately jumped on the monkey phone with Patricia. Chris went back to his bedroom, dropped the robe, and climbed in between his golden Egyptian cotton sheets, falling directly into a deep, dreamless sleep.

Emily awakened the following day to the sounds of a local radio station jockeying one of her favorites (this particular week) by *Four Frisco*. Her father was also in the room, dressed in his robe, fiddling with Xeno while holding the computer laptop. Startled by the unannounced intrusion, she immediately sat up, furled both brows, and yanked the earbuds out of her ears.

"What are you doing?" She yelled.

"Oh, just a little experiment with your friend here. Did I wake you?"

"You scared me!"

"I'm sorry, honey. I'll be out of here in just a minute."

Chris toggled the filter tray and, as it slid open, he combed one of Xeno's arms, attempting to collect fibrous matter. After the fragment register passed 500, he closed the tray. While the laptop processed, he looked back at Emily, winked, and exited.

"Go back to sleep if you want, Em; it's still early."

He shut her door and returned to the master bedroom. With three pillows at his back, he reached for his cup of coffee while the laptop completed its filtration. Only two fragment files appeared, much to his disappointment. He clicked on the first one, producing the familiar bright white flashes. Within the static, an image of a carnival slowly materialized through Emily's perspective. She was holding Xeno just after Suzanne won him at the balloon race, and they were walking to the bumper cars. Voices were crystal clear on this fragment.

"Come this way sweetie, we'll bash your daddy at the electric cars."

"Yes!" Emily hissed.

The fragment fizzled.

Chris' eyes immediately flooded, crying *and* laughing. He decided to click on the other fragment, hoping for more of the same scene. Emily straggled into the room at the same time, scratching her eyes as she wondered at the computer's flashing screen.

"Daddy. I'm hungr—"

She abruptly froze. Urine ran down one leg, and she began shaking uncontrollably, eyes locked on the laptop's screen. Chris turned around to look at it. Xeno. His eyes were glowing yellow, and his oversized incisors protruded from an exaggerated red grin. He was coming at Emily from the doorway he just demolished, going for her legs, then his face filled the entire screen. As the fragment faded into the flashes, his voice started to fade—sounding like someone who had choked on fifty years of cigarettes and broken mirrors. It appeared as if he were looking at Emily at that exact moment.

"I told you. You can't hide from me," he gurgled.

She screamed and collapsed directly on the puddled floor, sobbing.

Chris shut the laptop and ran to her side. "What the hell was *that*? What *was* that, Emily?"

Emily had difficulty controlling her shock. Chris tried to calm her down by holding her tightly. "Xxxeno, Daddy."

"No, sweetheart. Xeno is a doll. Who was that?"

"I'm telling you. It's him! It's Xeno! I thought I was asleep when he came. You said it was just a bad dream!"

"It is, sweetie. It is a dream! And now it's over. Let's get you cleaned up and get some breakfast."

It took several moments for Emily to calm down. She nodded and sniffled as the tears soaked her face. Chris cradled his daughter into the bathroom and ran the shower.

"Go ahead, it's okay. Leave your clothes on the floor; I'll take care of them later."

Emily paused by the shower as Chris walked back into the bedroom.

"No, Daddy! Don't go!"

"It's okay, Em. I'll be right outside. Hurry up and we'll go to Benny's."

The apparition perplexed him. *That wasn't real, was it?* Chris reasoned that it must have coincided with Emily's nightmare from a couple of weeks ago. *Ahh, dreams too? Really?* He began to understand that the soft drive reads fragments generated from the actual thoughts of people—not solely what their senses recorded, but their cognitive interpretations as well. The thought occurred to him concerning manipulative applications. It was an ugly thought.

Emily dripped out of the shower and toweled off. She wrapped herself and exited the bathroom to where her father was finished cleaning the floor. Chris brought her back into his arms, damp towel and all.

"Emily, I need to ask you about what was on the screen."

In the relative safety of her father's arms, Emily managed to consider it for a second. With her eyes staring blankly towards the distance, she painfully recalled the episode.

"What you saw a minute ago? That was him? You sure?"

"Uh-huh."

Chris held her tight as she welled up with tears again, burying her face in his chest. "It's all right. He can't hurt you honey because he is simply a doll in a dream, nothing more."

Emily continued to cry. Chris knew this was one of those moments he wished Suzanne were still around. She was the emotional healer of the family, and she always selected the best words. Emily slowly wound down. Chris carried her back to her room and placed her on the bed.

"Get dressed, little trooper. We'll go eat now."

Emily's eyes widened as Chris turned his back to leave. He spun back around to see Emily pointing at Xeno sitting atop the chest of drawers next to her door. Chris laughed and took the doll with him to his bedroom. There, he placed Xeno on top of the back shelf in the large walk-in closet. He pondered all the history that could be floating around in that confined space, locked within the fragments. A minute later, the closet's lint got the better of him.

"ACHOO!"

Well, that kinda says everything, doesn't it! He thought.

Emily reappeared in the hallway several minutes later. No music player or skimpy top.

"Change of heart?"

"I'm not in the mood."

Chris laughed as they walked downstairs. The hum of the garage door slowly opened to the blazing Valley sunshine. They climbed inside the car and fastened their seatbelts. Chris fired the diesel and backed carefully down the driveway. As the garage door closed, he slid onto Collina Alta Court and gurgled away from Sonno Dolce.

Break Fast

They arrived at Benny's during its peak that Saturday. It was the busiest breakfast joint in Cupertino, possibly because it catered to those who wanted their regional favorites prepared using authentic, traditional methods. Diverse Californians distributed themselves several ways when choosing a submenu. New England selections included bagels and cream cheese, scones, corned-beef hash, and English muffins. Benny's Southern featured lard-cut buttermilk biscuits and milk sausage or sawmill gravy, grits, chicken-fried steak, and banana pudding for dessert. The independents opted for a little of everything, but the restaurant's notoriety arose from their traditional pancakes with eggs, bacon, and skillet potatoes.

Benny's sustained a 40-person line stretching through the front door at any given hour. Chris and Emily's wait was mercifully brief before a hostess escorted them to a tight booth towards the rear of the main dining room. A young brunette waitress immediately appeared and placed two glasses on the table, filling them with fresh iced water. She adjusted her oversized black frames and cued her tablet.

"What can I get you two to drink?" She flicked her ponytail from her right shoulder.

Chris glanced over the top of his menu at Emily. "Go ahead, honey."

"I'll have a Doctor Pepper."

Before the waitress recorded Emily's order, Chris interrupted. "It's too early for that, Em. How about some orange juice?"

"We have apple, orange, and grape," added the waitress.

"I want apple."

"And you, sir?"

"I'll have a double espresso with a shot of caramel."

Beguiled by Chris' unusual order, the waitress paused to moisten her lips almost seductively, then continued tapping the order on her tablet. "Interesting. I'll have that right out."

With a swift pace, she whisked away to take care of another table on the way back to the server's station.

"Do you know what you want, Em?"

"Yes."

"Then you mind telling me so I can place the order?"

She turned her menu around and pointed at a plate of pancakes.

"Is that all?"

Emily moved her finger over to a plate that included hash browns. "I want that and that." She also pointed to some sausage links.

"Sounds like your appetite is healthy."

She smiled. "I didn't know it could talk, Doctor Miller. Have you been hearing these voices often?"

"Figure of speech so can it, smarty. Here comes your juice."

The waitress placed a small plastic glass in front of Emily. "Your juice, young lady . . . and here's your double espresso with the shot of caramel, sir." She set the serving platter down and squatted in front of the table for a straight line of sight. "Are you ready to order, or do you need a few more minutes?"

Chris looked at Emily. "I believe we are ready to order."

"Fire away."

"She is going to have your Number Two with hash browns and sausage."

"How do you want the hash browns cooked, sweetie?"

Emily pointed towards a picture in the menu.

"Okay, hash browns crispy. And how do you want the sausage? Links or patties?"

"Links."

"Perfect, and for you, dad?"

Chris sheepishly blushed, "I'll have the Starving Redneck."

"One Starving Redneck." The waitress repeated loudly to Chris' embarrassment. "Okay, which gravy do you want for the biscuits? White sausage milk, or sawmill?"

Chris wanted the process to conclude before any more damage could be done. "Sausage."

"Do you want cheddar cheese in your grits?"

"Please. Oh, and make the hash browns the same as hers—bacon instead of sausage."

"Got it. And your eggs?"

"Scrambled . . . well."

"Okay, great. Your order's in. I'll be back in a few minutes."

"Thanks."

Emily guzzled her apple juice. Feeling the effects from an instant sucrose rush, she started bouncing around her bench.

"Can I go over to Patty's after this? We want to go swimming."

Chris looked at his watch and considered the day's schedule. "I don't see why not."

"Woohoo!"

"Not so loud, Em." Chris noticed an elderly couple's reaction. "I need to get some chores done around the house."

"Okie dokie." Emily's hyperactivity caused another turn-around from the adjacent booth.

"Em, be still!"

Benny's was renowned for speedy fulfillment and, predictably, the waitress appeared a few moments later with their meals. Emily immediately went to work getting the pancakes up to her standards by slathering voluminous clods of butter over each layer, and then drowning the lot with syrup—inevitably soaking the entire plate, including the hash browns and the sausage links. Chris' eyes bulged as he drew the last sip from his espresso, chasing it with a swig of water from a glass dripping with condensation. He grabbed some Mexican hot sauce from the carousel at the end of the table and slung a few drops on his eggs. They made short work of their plates without much conversation. By the end, Emily's pancake soiree had maple syrup trickling from several places underneath her chin. Chris dunked a fresh paper napkin in his water to clean her face. He reached across the table with the napkin and forgot the proximity of his jacket's unzipped front, which created another mess by sliding through his sausage gravy.

"*Great.*"

Emily giggled. Chris started to blot the dripping gravy when his cell phone rang. Fumbling around, attempting to avoid a bigger trainwreck, he retrieved the phone from the other side of the jacket and checked the display.

Who is this? He thought. "Hello?"

"Chris . . . Matt."

"Oh, hi Matt. I wasn't expecting—"

"Sorry Chris, I have to be curt. Look, I've just been tipped that there's a move on a priority intel target in Santa Clara."

"Us?" Chris's sudden high pitch echoed across the dining room. A few patrons turned around, which he noticed.

"Can't confirm it, but my gut says they wouldn't be calling me out of the blue. I think we should grab the other unit, just in case."

"Huh? Why?"

"Instinct. Your security is top-notch, but not good enough for the pros. I'm not talking about a few local weekend mercs, I'm talking about the hardcore international troublemakers. Wait, where are you? I hear people in the background."

"We're at a restaurant, why?" Chris started scanning around the room, paranoid.

Matt paused. "Look around and make sure nobody's paying attention. If none, we'll continue, but you have to keep your voice down."

Everyone in the restaurant was staring at Chris. He studied those in close proximity, turning around after a few moments. He turned back around to check the people behind him who were now wondering why the man on the other side of their booth had turned around. Their faces said, *What? What do you want from us?*

He sat back down and cowered as far as he could below the top of the booth. "Yeah . . . nobody." He breathed.

"You don't have to whisper, Chris. Just keep it down."

"Okay. For God's sake, please go ahead!" He loudly hissed.

"What I was saying, was that I think we should take the other soft drive so nobody can steal it."

"*We* are stealing it!" Chris said with a volume difficult to be considered a whisper. "Why not call the police?"

"That's a problem. I'll explain later. You need to come to the lab right now."

"Really? Now?"

"Yes, now. Right now. How far are you from the lab?"

"I still have to pay; it'll be at least twenty minutes."

"Can't you hold it?"

"Pay! As in the bill."

A woman two booths away turned around with a scowl.

"Okay, fine. I'll meet up with you at the usual spot at ten after eleven."

"Matt, Emily is with me."

"She can wait in the car, can't she? Hurry up!" Matt hung up, leaving Chris momentarily disoriented.

"Miss?" He attempted to flag his waitress and interrupted her taking another order three booths down. She glanced at him slightly annoyed and continued with the order.

"Miss!"

She gave him a contemptuous glare, pointing at her tablet. "I'll be right over, sir."

"Emily. Get your sweater, we're leaving."

He stood up in a nervous hurry and helped Emily climb out of her bench. "We have to stop by my office for a few minutes, sweetheart. When I get done, I'll take you to Patricia's."

"Ugh!" Emily pouted. "How long is *that* going to take?"

He held her hand as they approached their waitress, still taking the other order.

He tapped on the waitress' shoulder. "Miss, I'm very sorry to interrupt. I have to leave, like, right now due to an emergency. Do you have our check estimated?"

The waitress scrunched her eyebrows, and her pleasant smile quickly changed to one of deep concern as she feverishly swiped across her ordering tablet. "One moment; I have to close your ticket and cancel the order."

"I just need a ballpark guess. I'm very sorry, I just need to leave."

"All right," she sighed. "You guys had the pancakes with hash browns and links with a Redneck, a juice and a double espresso?"

"Yes, that's us."

"Probably around $45."

Chris reached into his pants' left pocket and retrieved a small roll of cash. He recalled as a boy, his father advised that when he became a responsible working adult, he should always carry at least $200 cash for emergencies—car trouble, helping a friend, etc. Chris typically carried double that amount. He thanked his father often because the idea mostly saved Chris time—his most treasured commodity.

He shoved a folded hundred into her hand "Keep it. Thanks, and sorry!" then made for the exit with Emily.

Amazed, the waitress became fluttered as she stared at them racing out the door. Her bounce and smile quickly reappeared as she returned to servicing the disrupted table. She flicked her ponytail from her left shoulder while squatting for the next person's order.

Chris checked his watch. "I hope he's wrong about this."

Sonno Dolce

Chris made Amerimem's main gate in short order, taking the prattling Rabbit into the security lane to swipe his pass. There were no friendly greetings on the intercom system. The light on top of the code box simply turned green. A moment later, the gate swung upward, and the unidirectional tire shredder lowered, allowing access to the garage. *That's odd.* Chris suddenly remembered it was the weekend, and weekend protocols were skeletal. He slipped into the garage entrance and over his normal parking spot. Matt was waiting a couple dozen spaces away. Chris turned off the car's ignition, unbuckled his seatbelt, and jumped out.

He turned back to Emily. "Wait here, sweetie. I'll be back in a few minutes."

Matt hopped over and shook his hand intensely. "Sorry, Chris. My source relayed an imminent timeframe, and mercs or whoever they are, don't take weekends off."

"Okay," replied Chris with a drop of skepticism.

"Emily, I take it?" Matt waved, but she didn't notice, having already indulged herself with the car's antique radio.

"Yep. All nine-point-four adolescent years of her."

"She's adorable. You ready?"

"I suppose." Chris gazed towards the garage's exit with a hint of dryness in his voice.

Both men trotted across the second-floor skywalk to the main administration building.

A low rumble resonated through their feet.

Chris turned to Matt. "Did you feel that?"

"No, what?"

"Not sure. It felt like a tremor. Too short, maybe."

"Don't you get those all the time out here?"

"Well, yeah—but never *that* short."

Chris thought nothing more of it and they continued towards the entrance. After swiping their cards at a terminal on the side of the main doors, they walked through Amerimem's ornate glass and steel vestibule into the lobby. The room was completely devoid of personnel.

"Okay, I know the front gate is automated on the weekends but there's definitely supposed to be *someone* in the lobby."

Matt's pace quickened over to the security desk. He didn't see anyone at first, so he shifted around to the rear of the kiosk and noticed part of a uniform on the floor.

"Chris! Get over here."

Chris rushed to the entry of the kiosk and discovered the corpse of a female security guard in a fresh pool of blood.

Matt rolled her over. "Damn it!"

"Oh, my God, that's Julie!" Chris became a trembling mess, nearly collapsing before Matt grabbed him by the arm.

"Get ahold of yourself! I need you on your feet and clear-headed, got it?"

Just as he said it, their eyes caught movement at the end of the hallway. A familiar short tone bonged, then a signal light over one of the main elevators turned green. Three men exited wearing thermal vision headsets, black jumpsuits, black Kevlar vests, and accessory belts fully stocked with a variety of armaments. Two were carrying foreign bullpup-style assault rifles, certainly not MP5s or M16s to Matt's observation. The third, a tall and toned man with a lengthy blonde ponytail, carried a rocket propelled grenade launcher strapped over his right shoulder. From 80 yards away and in split tick of mutual recognition, Chris noticed that one of these men—a serious-looking type with a headset video transmitter stretched over a plain black patrol cap—was clutching the disc player soft drive prototype.

"Matt, he's got the other drive!" Chris pointed.

The raider toggled his headset's microphone and spoke in a language Chris didn't immediately recognize. He then switched to English with a thick Germanic accent. "You see zem on your monitor? Yes? Good. These are ze two we are looking for?"

The man lifted his rifle, aimed it at Chris, and walked swiftly towards him along with the other two militants. "Doctor Miller, you come with us!"

Matt immediately yanked Chris's arm, "GET DOWN!"

One of the other men opened fire in Matt's direction as he and Chris dove behind the thick wooden walls of the kiosk. Wild shots shattered the large pane of glass in the corner behind them. Matt reached into his shirt pocket and emptied its contents onto the floor. He grabbed his car keys and threw them at Chris. "Run to my car and get it started; I will be right behind."

From nowhere, Matt produced an H&K Mark 23 tactical .45 pistol. He braced himself on the desk behind the upper counter and blasted two rounds towards the aggressors. The first shooter clutched his right shoulder as his right inner thigh flew apart. He collapsed onto the floor, immobilized. Chris frantically held his ears and froze in awe at Matt's assertiveness.

"I said GO, damnit . . . and keep low!" Matt yelled.

Chris determined that his best path to avoid stray gunfire was the gaping new exit created by the destroyed windows. Tiptoeing over the thousands of jagged shards, he made his way out of the building and across the road to the garage's stairway. The wounded militant fired three shots Chris' direction before the commander ordered him to stop. "We are zupposed to bring that one back alive."

"Tell that to my goddamn leg!" He grunted as he noticed the welling of his femoral artery. Unchecked, it would bleed out within a few minutes.

The RPG-toting merc stood up to aim his rocket. "You didn't say anything about anyone shooting at *us!*"

Matt didn't hesitate. He aimed and fired, blowing the prototype drive out of the leader's hand. From a few feet away, the man noticed circulant leaking from the bullet hole, and from that alone, he knew that the device was finished. He turned around towards Matt and released the safety on his rifle.

"Take ze bastard out, now!"

Both militants broke cover, stood up, and furiously shredded the kiosk. The desk was no match for the barrage, as small wooden splinters littered the air. Matt immediately ducked behind the far side of the desk and rushed for the same exit Chris used just moments before. The ponytailed man aimed his RPG at the kiosk and launched it. Matt dove through the shattered wall just as a tremendous explosion that fragmentized the entire glass façade of the main entry. The noise was deafening. Matt narrowly escaped the deadly blast radius and, in a daze from the concussion, suddenly realized that a credit card-sized shard was protruding from his left shoulder blade. He winced as he yanked it from his flesh, and picked up speed fleeing towards the garage, neglecting the warmth oozing down his back.

The smoke cleared, and the two remaining operators raced forward to inspect the debris. The only human remnants discovered were the bloody clumps of the security guard they dispatched earlier.

"Go get ze doctor and bring him back. I will assist Ernst out of here. GO!" The lead operative grunted.

The ponytailed gunner, frustrated in failure, hastily exited the front area, and bolted towards the garage.

Matt, nauseated from the concussion and bleeding, arrived a moment later at the Volkswagen. Chris had the passenger door open and was about to yank Emily out of it. She had been unaware of the commotion because the radio's volume was as high as it would go. Chris' exasperation surprised her.

"Emily! Get out of the car and run as fast as you can to that Mustang over there, right now!"

"Huh? Why?"

"Don't argue with me, honey; just do it!"

As soon as she climbed out of the passenger seat and closed her door, a deafening whoosh thundered overhead. A percussive detonation instantly disintegrated Matt's GT500. Emily screamed as Chris froze. Matt, who was closest to the explosion, got back on his feet and faltered to Chris and Emily. "This is getting old real fast!"

The ponytailed militant closed to just 50 yards, hastily reloading the RPG. Matt drew his .45 and blasted several rounds his way, forcing him to take cover behind a concrete column.

"Chris, get your car going, NOW!"

Matt fired another round, which pocked the column within inches of the ponytailed man's eyes. Chris grabbed Emily's arm and dragged her gently to the driver's side of the Rabbit. He released her while opening the rear door, and yelled for her to get in. He hesitated for a moment to assess Matt's situation.

Matt volleyed two more shots at the corner. "COME ON, GET OVER HERE!"

Chris panicked in starting the car, over-revving the engine and creating a huge mass of black smoke. He slammed the shifter into first, nailed the accelerator, and managed an elongated squeal from his front tires. He had never punished his friend this severely. Once he arrived at Matt's covering position, he reached over and flung open the passenger door as he hit the brakes. Matt sent yet another two rounds at the column as the gunner attempted to break cover, buying only a moment before another rocket surely gave chase.

Matt dove into the seat and slammed the door, "GO, GO, GO! Get us out of here!"

He rolled down his window as fast as he could, taking one last shot at the corner column, missing it completely. The merc knew it was clear to aim. Chris unexpectedly lurched the car, but recovered in short order. As they attempted to speed away, the more than slightly annoyed gunner swung around and locked his sights on the car as it gathered momentum. Matt looked back and recognized that the man was about to fire. He grabbed Chris' steering wheel and yanked it over to the right, causing the car to dive behind another support column just as the rocket flew past, striking at the end of the garage to the right of the exit. Shattered concrete and steel rebar rained on the front of Chris' Rabbit as it sped past, spidering the right side of his windshield just as it saw the daylight of the exit. The merc slammed his launcher onto the concrete floor in disgust, kicking it and shouting foreign expletives that reverberated throughout the entire garage.

His commander emerged from the rubble at the front entrance, lugging their injured comrade. "You let zem ezcape?"

"Nein!" The merc growled. "The sidearm kept me pinned; he had another car."

"You . . . pinned? This is a shame, Stefan." The commander noticed the damaged RPG launcher. "No bother; I know exactly where zey are going." He toggled his headset and spoke in German. "Brownstone is a negative. Secondary target initiated. One casualty. Acknowledge."

His headset crackled, "Affirmative. Return at once."

With the distant sound of approaching sirens, the plunderers walked down to the bottom of the garage where their van awaited.

"Don't slow down; run through it!" Matt yelled.

"But—" Chris remained skittish with the accelerator.

Matt grunted in pain, grasping his shoulder. "DO IT!—before we all get killed."

With that, Chris hit the floorboard, running through the collapsible swing-down gate at Amerimem's exit and tearing it off at the post. "Hey, that's going to leave a mark!"

Matt and Emily looked at Chris as if he had lost his mind.

"I'm just sayin'," said Chris.

Emily noticed the gash on Matt's shoulder. "YOU'RE BLEEDING!" She squirmed at the sight of his blood, dripping all over the left side of the front passenger's seat.

"Yeah, well. It comes with the job." Matt grinned as he looked back. "And, you're the famous Emily?"

"Uh-huh," she slid back in her seat.

Chris flew down his usual path to home, the engine wound tight.

"Well, it's finally nice to meet you, Emily. Your father said a lot of nice things about you. My name is Matt."

Emily didn't say anything. She stared at the trees racing by. She had never been driven this fast, and it scared her as much as it excited her.

"It's okay to speak with him, honey. He's a friend."

"Nice to meet you too, Mister Matt."

"Thank you, Emily. Can you do me a favor?"

She hesitated to respond.

Matt ripped a piece of cloth from the front of his shirt and folded it carefully into a multi-layered square. He then handed it to Emily. "Can you press this up against my cut real hard?"

Chris' head spun towards him, brow furled.

Trembling, Emily took the cloth and kept it tight against the back of Matt's shoulder, slowing the blood flow.

Chris glanced over his right shoulder at them. "You need a doctor. That's going to take stitches!"

"Maybe. I just need to find some clean cloth and some tape. They'll slow it down enough for me to thread it."

"What do you mean, 'thread it'? You need a doctor!"

"Can't!"

"Why?"

"They'll look for us there. This isn't over!"

"What's not over? What are you talking about?"

"Look Chris, they had the other prototype in their hand. Use that massive noggin of yours. If they knew about that one, they know about the other. Where is it?"

"Home."

"Then we need to go there right now."

"That's where I *was* going!"

A plain white van's tires squealed loudly in the background. Matt turned around and marked the van about a quarter mile back.

"Sucks being right sometimes," he muttered. "Chris, you're going to have to step on it."

"Um, Matt?"

"No time. Hit it!"

Matt reached into one of his pockets and produced a fresh clip for his pistol. Ejecting the spent clip, he jammed the new one into the grip and slowly cocked the weapon. His shoulder complained. Emily pulled away in anticipation.

"Cover your ears, Em. This is going to be loud," said Chris.

Matt turned around, aimed the pistol with his left hand through the door's window opening. He fired three times towards the van, striking the radiator and exploding one of the front tires. The van somehow continued its pursuit, now with a gunman dangling a rifle out of its passenger-side window. Emily screamed as she heard explosion from behind, knowing that they were shooting at *her*. Chris raged onto Stevens Hill as fast as he dared, tires squealing in the bend, managing a record 72 MPH in the straight before reaching the long incline. He never checked his speedometer until, slowly and steadily, the car started losing momentum. The van, having troubles of its own with the loss of radiator coolant and a blown tire, also struggled to climb the hill.

"Can't you go any faster?" Matt shouted.

"That's what I was trying to *tell* you! You don't think these things achieve 56 miles per gallon with a V8, do you?"

Succumbing to gravity, the car's lack of power forced Chris to compensate by shifting into third gear, but it was still too soon.

"Oh, you gotta be kidding me. This will go down as the slowest car chase ever!"

Angered, Matt turned back around and fired twice. This time, he struck the gunman through the windshield and took out the other front tire. The van slipped off the shoulder and crashed into the ditch.

"HA!" Chris yelled. "You got him!"

In the excitement, Emily slapped Matt on his wounded shoulder. "Way to go, Mister Matt!" Matt winced to the point of tears. "Oh, sorry, sorry!"

"Arggh." He barely whispered. "That's all right, little one. Can you put the cloth back on there with some pressure?"

"Uh-huh."

Chris' car continued its deceleration, but crowned Stevens Hill before the downshift. In triumph, his inner-geek returned, "Hey, I didn't have to—" He noticed Matt's suffering just after he turned his head. "We'll be there in five minutes. Hang on. By the way, have you figured out who they are yet?"

Panting from the excruciating pain, Matt placed the pistol in his lap so he could help Emily hold the patch. "I don't know who they are, exactly. All I can tell you is that they aren't from here."

"Yeah. The accents. I couldn't quite place the language."

"Well, I *do* know that they were using newer Swiss rifles."

"Swiss? I don't get it."

"Me either, but they aren't the only ones who use the weapons. There are others, including whatever euro-garbage outfit is using them to frame someone. It's pointless to speculate."

Chris brought them through the entrance of Sonno Dolce—towards the northwestern corner of the subdivision and finally onto Collina Alta Court.

Matt noticed a conspicuous silver sedan with dark tinted windows parked on the corner. "I don't know how much time we'll have. That car down the street—have you seen it before?"

Chris looked in his rearview mirror. "No, but I don't keep up with everyone in the neighborhood either. Suzanne did that."

"Emily?" Matt asked.

"No, sir."

"Okay, Chris. When you get to the house, do *not* pull into the garage."

"How do you know I have a garage?"

"Do you see any houses around here that *don't* have a garage, smartass?"

"Touché but watch the language around my daughter."

"I hear that word all the time," said Emily.

Both men turned around. She pretended to be surprised. Chris gave his evil eye and turned back around to pay attention to parking. "I don't doubt it."

Chris was the first out of the car, and he unlocked Emily's door a moment afterward. He ran around the car and helped Matt climb out.

Matt was panting heavily, but managed to stay on his feet and balanced as he assessed the Miller's house. "You and Emily wait here until I clear the house."

Chris held her tight and threw his keys to Matt. "You'll need these."

Matt's eyes scrutinized every corner and every shadow as he approached the front entry and peered through the windows on either side of the double doors. He detected no threats, so he inserted the key slowly. With caution, he opened the door wide, allowing bright sunlight to flood the interior. Room by room, he methodically snaked his way around, making sure all the nooks and crannies were clear of concealed peril. He made his way back to the front door and lowered his weapon, signaling for the others.

"Nice place. You could do better on *your* salary though."

"Suzanne wanted it. Less conspicuous and demanding, she said—where Emily would be around a lot of nice, unassuming families—no pretention or competition. This is where we settled. She was right, to a degree. No pressure, less overhead. We're comfortable."

"I see." Matt winced from his shoulder. "Hey man, I'm going to need some cotton, scissors, duct tape if you have it, and liquid toothache reliever."

"Toothache drops?"

"Yes."

"I'll see what I can do."

"We can't stay long, you know. They want the other unit, so take only what you both need for a few days. Snag that laptop of yours then we need to get on the road."

"Where are we going?"

"Anywhere but here."

Chris looked puzzled, and his breathing shortened. All he knew was that he was the defenseless target of unknown gunmen. His mind started to break.

"I don't understand why we just don't call the police. It's the correct thing to do, problem or not. We run and we're guilty. That's our optics. Oh God!"

"You can't." Matt checked his pistol by instinct, which unnerved Chris further.

"I'll just pick up the phone, dial 911, and they'll be over here to protect us. Come on, what's the problem?

"We just can't. It's risky—too risky."

"This isn't some low-budget '80s flick, *Matthew*. I can't tell you how many screens I yelled at. 'Call the cops!', I screamed. Do they? Never! Are you kidding me?"

"Okay, fine. How about a little reality check? Those guys don't care about your good 'ole boys in blue. For all I know, as soon as you pick up your phone, they'll be monitoring and know exactly where we are. I'm pretty sure they know it already and are regrouping. I'm stumped as to why they aren't here; it's strange. Please, just get your stuff together and let's get the heck out of here before they do show up."

Chris sighed. "All right. If that's what you think we should do, fine. Give me your plan. I need a plan. We need a safe place to go and figure this out."

"Where's the stuff I asked for?"

"You'll find the first aid kit in a cabinet under the center island in the kitchen. I think there's some duct tape on the wall behind the workbench in the garage. I'll be back in a minute to help you with that."

Emily shook from the commotion. "Daddy, I don't want to go. Why do we have to go? Can I stay at Patty's?"

Chris picked her up and hugged her tightly. "I'll see, sweetheart." *That might actually be a good idea, he thought.* "Go upstairs and get your overnight bag together, I'll be up there to help you in a minute."

He set her down and she ran upstairs. Chris headed for the garage.

"That's not necessary, Chris. Your kit had everything. Tape, gauze, antiseptic, alcohol, and the toothache drops, too. The cut's not as deep as it looked. I can get away with a just a few stitches if you've got some thread and a small needle."

"Suzy had a small kit she kept near the living room. Hang on."

Chris ran to the living room to retrieve the sewing kit while Matt cleaned the wound with alcohol. He drenched it with the toothache liquid, which provided a weak topical anesthetic.

"I'll need a mirror unless *you* want to do this. Tough reach."

Chris became queasy while staring at the gash. "No thanks."

He ran to the bathroom near the garage and returned with a small hand mirror. Matt managed to prep a sewing needle with some black thread. He instructed Chris where to hold the mirror while he worked. Wincing at each insertion, he repeatedly penetrated the upper layers of flesh, causing additional bleeding with each loop.

"Sponge that once, would ya?"

Chris wiped the wound, and then Matt slowly looped the last stitch. With the cut mostly closed, the bleeding slowed to just a small droplet every few seconds.

"Okay, I'm going to sanitize this over the sink one more time with some alcohol and antiseptic, and then I'll gauze it over. I can take it from here, thanks."

"No problem." Chris watched him tape the gauze down tightly over the stitches.

"I don't suppose you have an extra shirt. I think we'd look a little conspic—"

Chris interrupted, "Of course. Let me see what I've got. Better get a few shirts, and maybe a jacket."

"Don't forget the laptop."

The men walked around the corner and headed upstairs to the master bedroom. Passing Emily's door, Chris checked in on her packing activities. Of course, the first thing she did was place her music player on charge. After that, she tossed a selection of clothes on her bed, just as her mother taught her before vacationing in Tahoe.

"No, Emily. You can't take all of those. Just a couple night's worth. I don't know where we are going or if the Smiley's can take you, so get your jacket . . . and some jeans."

"Which jacket?" Emily owned several.

Chris looked in her closet and pulled out a light blue fleece hoodie. "Here. You can wear this anywhere and it's warm."

Matt continued to the master bedroom and began looking around for the laptop. Not finding it at first, he turned to Chris. "Hey. Where is it?"

"Christ sakes, it's in the first drawer under the TV!"

Matt accidently opened the second drawer by mistake. About the time Chris walked through the door, Matt held up a copy of *Stiffed at the Counter.* "Ah-ha!"

"Gimme that! Emily doesn't know about those." Chris quietly ran to take the video out of Matt's hand.

"Well hey, I understand. Been a while. Easy way to go if you don't want to get back in the game yet. No Reno embarrassment . . . I get it."

"No, that's not the deal. Suzy and I . . ."

"Don't! I don't need the visual."

"I need to get my stuff."

Matt shoved the video back in the drawer. Chris opened a couple other drawers and pulled out some boxers and black socks to match his sneakers. He opened yet another drawer and grabbed two pairs of blue jeans. "Shirts and another jacket, that'll be in the closet," he mumbled.

Matt, sitting on the bed in front of the TV, heard a single metallic click from the closet, causing him to throw his hand in front of Chris, blocking his path. He raised his other hand's index finger up to his lips. Pulling the pistol from his beltline, he covered the rear slide area to muffle the sound of him releasing the safety. Slowly, Matt approached the door from the side and reached for the knob. A thunderous spray of automatic gunfire erupted, instantly shredding the middle of the door with splintered holes. As soon as the burst stopped, Matt swung the door open and fired a single shot towards the back of the smoke-filled closet. Unintentionally, the shot exploded a flare attached to the intruder's vest, igniting the surrounding clothes.

"Get your stuff and get out of here . . . NOW!" Matt yelled.

The gunman, burning from the flare and the cauldron of flaming clothes around him, screamed "I'M HIT!" in his headset before the flames consumed him. Howling as his flesh charred, the gunman was mercifully put out of his misery by a second round from Matt's .45.

As the smoke cleared Matt's barrel, the sound of shattering glass exploded from downstairs. Presuming it was a second gunman, Matt ran down the hall and tumbled down the stairs catching the intruder off-guard in the opening between the kitchen and the front entry. Matt dove across the entry, sending two taps from his Mark 23 while airborne. The first round was involuntarily inhaled through the man's left nostril, exploding the back of his skull. The other, to his right inner thigh, contributing to his immediate and permanent collapse. Matt stood up and checked the rear of the house for more potential corpses. *Well,* he thought. *They know we're here.*

Chris rescued a couple of shirts out of the front of the closet before its total destruction. The fire was raging out of control, and Chris knew there was no chance to stop it. Gagging from the toxic smoke, he managed to retrieve only one long-sleeved T-shirt before being overwhelmed. Coughing and wheezing, he stared into the back of the closet to witness Xeno's smile consumed in flames along with Suzanne's clothes. In that pixilated snapshot, he realized his life was taking another major turn.

Snatching the attaché case from the other side of the bed, Chris dumped the contents and stuffed the case with his clothes and other necessities, placing the laptop safely in the middle. In his panicked rush, he forgot that Emily was just down the hall. When he opened her door, she was obliviously dancing around the room, earbuds in at full volume. She was ready to go but distracted all the same. Chris came up from behind and twisted her around, jerking her earbuds out by tugging on each of their cords. Seeing and smelling the smoke billow in from the hallway, Emily stood paralyzed.

"Come on, we have to get out of here."

"What about my new phone?"

"You won't be needing that."

"What about Xeno?"

"You don't have to worry about him anymore." Chris looked back towards his bedroom. "Come on, let's go!"

They ran down the stairs and found Matt still surveying the cadaver he created. Emily shrieked.

Taking the assassin's weapons, Matt made a puzzling observation. "You see this?"

"Yes, it's an assault rifle. Can we go?"

"It's definitely a rifle like the one those guys had back at the lab, but these are marked."

"Yeah, and?" Chris motioned with his hand to speed up.

"I only know of a couple of regiments using these, and they're both Swiss."

"Okay, so for some reason the Swiss are after us. Didn't you say that before? LET'S GO!"

Matt, still perplexed, grabbed the rifle, and slung it around his right shoulder. He then unfastened the accessory belt from the gunman's waist. It contained two extra ammunition clips and four concussion grenades. He picked up the belt and carried it with him out the front door, much to the dismay of a few neighbors gathered down the street to see what the loud noises and smoke were all about. Naturally, they gasped and reached for their phones, fumbling to snap photos and call the police.

"No, No! He's with me!" Chris tried to explain at a distance, but the doors were already slamming. Again, distant sirens signaled the need for an expedient retreat.

Matt climbed into the Rabbit's front passenger seat. Emily opened the driver's side rear door and hopped inside. Chris turned around to look at his home—smoke and flames now consuming the right side with its windows shattering one by one. The destruction reflected in the welling of his eyes. He couldn't calculate what was happening to him. He stood motionless as the timbers began to creak.

"Chris, COME ON!"

He climbed into the driver's seat, started the car, and raced towards the Smiley's.

At the driveway, he and Emily opened their doors, but Chris sensed something out of place as soon as he stood up. *Snickers wasn't barking.* He turned around to see the black plumes and orange glow of his house from over the treetops.

"That's odd. Where's the dog?"

They walked up the driveway and around to the front entry. Still no Snickers. Ringing the doorbell and knocking brought no action and still no dog. Chris reached for the handle and found the door unlocked. He opened it and poked his head inside but saw nothing.

"Hello! Anyone home? Patty?"

Nothing.

"Now that's *really* odd," Chris mumbled.

He swung the front door open further and stepped inside to have a look, spooked. Emily decided to follow him without his knowledge. Chris walked past the front entry area and entered a wide hallway that separates the kitchen's bar from the adjacent family room. He turned his head to the right and made a discovery that shook him to his core. Jim Smiley was face down on the kitchen floor in a large pool of blood.

Emily screamed at the top of her lungs, "DADDY!" Her shriek jolted him in surprise. She was trembling and crying, but Chris didn't know why. She was not in position to see Jim on the floor behind the counter, he thought. Looking across to the family room, Jennifer Smiley was seated against a wall with her hands tied from behind. Someone placed a clear plastic bag over her head and closed it off with duct tape strapped around her neck. During her final struggle, she vomited inside it—the residue left to gather in the lower front of the bag below her chin. Chris ran to block Emily's sight of her. Matt dashed inside the house with the rifle and chambered a round.

Patricia, Chris thought. "Patty. Where's Patricia?"

He turned Emily around and hugged her to the point of squeezing. Matt instinctively knew what had happened to the Smileys. He studied those tactics in the torture defense modules at The Point. *Savages!*

Chris pointed up the stairs. Matt nodded and methodically made his way up to the little girl's room, finding the door tightly shut with some faint whining emanating from the other side. Without a second consideration, Matt kicked the door open and jumped inside. Sitting next to a pair of motionless young legs was Snickers—mostly silent but whimpering slightly. His head was draped across the small of poor Patricia's back and his nose was plugged with mucus.

Matt stepped back downstairs with a cold stare, shaking his head. Chris closed his eyes in rage and Emily felt it, clinging to him tightly.

"Where's Patty?" She sniffled.

Chris had a loss for words.

Matt cleared his throat. "She is with her family."

Emily burst into louder uncontrollable sobbing, so Chris picked her up and placed her head on his shoulder.

"We need to leave before any of the others return. There will be more." Matt said.

"That does it!" Chris yelled. "I'm through. We need to call the police, the FBI, CIA, somebody. EVERYBODY! This has gone far enough!"

"We can't."

"You mean to tell me I can't trust my own government to take care of this. To protect us? Isn't that their first mission? Why the hell am I paying taxes?"

"Don't be naïve, Chris. I told you. As soon as you dial, they will know. Believe it! We need to disappear. You can send a nastygram to the IRS later."

"And go where, Matt. What's your grand plan? Something I don't need to know? I NEED TO KNOW!" Chris was cracking, and Matt fought to stay calm. "You say they'll know if I call, well gee, doesn't it make sense that if they have the police tapped, they probably have the phone company too?"

"You need to work with me here, Chris. I don't have an exact plan, but there are people I trust back east. I have a friend in Washington that may be able to help. Getting to him is the problem. And yes, the phones may be compromised."

"Wait . . . Washington? As in DC? All the way across the country? Great. It couldn't have been a field office or base just around the corner. Not even in the same state. No—has to be across the entire country. Okay, Matt, why is getting to Washington, DC a problem?"

"Daddy, stop yelling!" Emily held her ears and started crying again.

"They will be looking for us. We can't just waltz into a public transportation hub, you know. We'll show up on surveillance. Think about this: if they knew enough about you to come here, then we must assume they know everything about you. Worse, I just exposed myself."

"None of this makes sense to me, Matt. If that *is* your real name. You say you're an operative for the government who is spying on private companies and acquisitioning technology it feels fit to take without public knowledge. Now you're telling me you're renouncing your oath, going AWOL, or whatever it is that you call it, and they will brand you a rogue, or worse, an insubordinate traitor—for what reason I'm not quite sure. And if that wasn't enough lunacy, you're also telling me it wasn't your employer that raided my laboratory, but mercenaries for God knows who, and God knows why. Now, you want me to just drive to DC, no questions asked, no calls to the authorities? Tell me, Matt—why would any sane person on this planet give you more than a millionth of one second?"

"Because you and this sweet little girl right here would be just like those people behind you if not for me."

Chris' expression changed abruptly. The logic always won.

Matt reached for Chris' hand. "Please, it's the only way I see right now. We can discuss this in the car if you like. *After* we get moving, that is."

Chris slowly took Matt's hand and shook it reluctantly. The debate was over, but the skepticism remained. Chris followed Matt out the door, carrying Emily. As they climbed back inside the car, the sirens had grown much louder. Emergency vehicles were at Sonno Dolce's entrance—dozens of them. Chris began to ease away from the Smiley's driveway. A ladder and two pump trucks shot by the crossing street at the end of the block two hundred yards away.

"Hang on a minute. Let them pass," said Matt. "All of them."

An ambulance, a sheriff's cruiser, and one unmarked sedan with flashing lights followed a moment later. The Rabbit gurgled patiently while they waited. Something caught Chris' right periphery. Snickers trotted out of the Smiley's front door and over to the Volkswagen, whimpering.

"Here Snickers. Come on." Emily cried. "Here, boy!"

"No. No, we can't." Matt said.

Chris looked at Emily, welling a tear. He jacked the emergency brake, placed the shifter in neutral, and jumped back out of the car. He took Snickers by the collar and opened Emily's door.

"Slide over."

Emily unbuckled her seatbelt and moved to the other side.

Matt scanned the street ahead for undesirables. "Great, another passenger."

Chris wasn't having any of it. "He has no family. They would stick him in a pound for euthanasia. Nobody would take him at two years old, let alone four. His odds are better with us."

He held the rear door open to let Snickers inside. Without further prompting, the dog jumped in and laid down next to Emily, placing his head in her lap for scratching. Chris climbed back inside, released the brake, and pointed towards Sonno Dolce's exit. "I need to know where we're going."

"North. The best way to get lost is in a crowd."

Emily, still shaken by all she had undergone, found Snickers' friendship calming. She rested her sniffling head on his while she scratched it. Chris knew the dog's strategy was impeccable. He wasn't so sure about Matt's.

How Soon They Forget

"*Biasimevole*, Narciso! Our operations mandate extreme caution to be executed in a discreet, escapable manner, yet *you* unilaterally decided to risk global attention? There will be inquires to be sure, and these authorities will not simply go away. Everything cannot be sanitized! How do you explain it, Narciso?"

Esposito's eyes suddenly wrenched to steely-gray and squinted. "Might I remind His Eminence, there was no way to anticipate Doctor Miller's improbable confederation with an embedded Brownstone operative."

"Improbable? Spada Sacra do not believe in the folly of chance. Obviously, this operator is a spy."

"Fortuity aside, Your Eminence, we could not predict such an alliance."

"This is not important, my son. What *is* important is that others are not aware of us! You had those imbeciles masquerading around with identifiable weaponry?"

"This was a prerogative mandated by the *Fachoffizier*, Eminence."

"A harlequin! We decide, not him. There will be questions, and it will only be a function of time before hibernating bears awaken. Where are they now?"

Esposito grinded teeth. His ascension to Spada Sacra's second in command was one of the fastest in the organization's recorded history, yet his ego was constantly checked by his master in a show of titled superiority—and he savored the succession that would come soon enough. Sooner if necessary.

"According to our sources, heading to the city of San Francisco."

"That is not what I asked, Narciso."

"We do not have a current location, although—"

"Find them. Bring the scientist to me, and do not lose the device this time."

"Yes, Your Eminence."

"Daddy, I'm hungry."

Matt turned around and looked at Emily with complete astonishment. *How could she possibly want anything to eat after all that?* Chris checked the rearview mirror and saw Emily pointing towards her mouth. Snickers was sitting up, panting heavily from the hot vinyl seats. His hair was slightly longer than a purebred Labrador's, evidence of a Golden mix, and wind blasting through the open windows created a swirling hair storm.

Chris checked the fuel gauge. "There's a gas station ahead at the Sand Hill exit. We should probably stop."

His Rabbit bickered with every incline, only to befriend the valleys some moments later. It soon rambled across an overpass traversing the two-mile-long Stanford Linear Accelerator. San Francisco's suburbs lay just beyond.

U.S. Interstate 280, better known as the Junipero Serra Freeway, was named to honor a Spanish Franciscan friar that founded many of the area's missions predating the American Revolution. The friar achieved notoriety not only from his mission work, but chiefly because he endured his later travels in debilitating pain due to a leg injury incurred after falling off a mule. Choked with fast moving traffic and constant undulations, the Junipero showed no mercy for the tired Rabbit. Its temperature gauge started to climb. Frustrated drivers were forced to overtake the decelerating heap, shaking their heads as they passed. Friar Serra wouldn't be the last pilgrim to limp on this trail. It became obvious to Chris that his car needed a break before it overheated. He exited the interstate and proceeded east for a mile before locating the first service station. As soon as they stopped at a diesel pump, both men jumped out of the car. Chris immediately reached for his wallet and pulled out a debit card, inserting it into the pump's validator. Matt, still sluggish from his injury, looked up and saw Chris pulling the card out of the machine.

"NO!" He yelled across the car's roof.

"What?" Stunned, Chris took his hand off the pump handle.

"Ugh. My fault. I should have warned you. Now they know exactly where we are, *and* our direction. Sorry, I didn't think about this. Just remembered."

"Huh? How?"

Matt pointed to the card. "Doubtful they have someone right around the corner, but they probably have the capability to have someone intercept us within ten to fifteen minutes, or less. We'll need to leave, and I mean very soon."

"Oh God! I didn't think about that. You're right; I should have used cash."

Chris reached into his front pants pocket and found over $100 in mixed bills. The amount was far less than needed for the journey to DC, Matt concluded.

"Chris, look. That's my fault. I must assume they know we're here already, so it won't matter if we swipe our cards. They can't know where we are ultimately going. Oh, geez." Matt had another revelation. "How could I be so stupid? Our phones!"

"What about them?

Matt suddenly remembered his was likely destroyed along with his Mustang. "Turn yours off. They'll triangulate your signal if it's turned on."

"Oh, for the love of—" Chris fumbled for his phone and shut it off in a panic. He quickly regained his composure and returned to their immediate problem. "We'll need cash, Matt. As much as we can get."

"Exactly."

Matt reached back for his wallet and handed Chris his bank card. "Here—take this. There's a $500 limit, so max it out. The PIN is 0824, got it? Do the same with your card. I will finish the refueling while you take care of that and your daughter. Do it quickly—we don't have all day."

"Got it. Come on, Em."

Chris knocked on Emily's window and motioned her to come along. She opened the door and Snickers immediately jumped over her and onto the pavement, running towards a hedgerow between the parking lot and the main road. Before he made it, the dog ran directly into the path of a circling car. The driver slammed on the brakes and laid on their horn. Emily chased Snickers and attracted a stern caution by a panicky old lady who could barely see over her steering wheel, yet was able to leer through her window and thrust a bony finger. "Keep that dog on a leash, young lady!"

Ignoring her, Emily continued across to capture Snickers, who as it turned out, only meant to relieve himself. Emily called Snickers back to the curb afterward. The Lab shimmied to her side where he sprawled on the pavement, his mouth wide open, panting heavily, and his tongue unfurled in a waterfall of bouncing flesh. The beldam driver raised her nose and huffed away, revealing Chris racing inbound.

"Come on. Let's take Snickers back to the car so we can get something to eat, okay?"

Emily grabbed the collar and struggled to coax Snickers back in the car. He weighed considerably more than her and leveraged it to his advantage. After a few failed attempts, she eventually convinced him that the Rabbit's vinyl seats were better than scorching asphalt. Snickers sniffed the rear seat and climbed aboard, draping himself across the shady side of the bench. Emily closed the door and joined her father as they entered the store. There was an ATM located on the back wall by the restrooms.

He relocated his debit card, swiped it past the reader, and entered his PIN. After a prompt, he selected the maximum $500 allowed and waited. *That's one thing going right today at least.* He stuffed the cash and his wallet in a pants pocket, and then reached into his other pocket, producing Matt's card. He swiped it and the machine prompted for the PIN. Chris paused for a second to recall the number.

"0824," Emily blurted without hesitation.

Chris turned around astonished, but she rolled her eyes, mouthing the words to a song in a smug display. Chris continued with the transaction and waited for the cash. Another $500 appeared from the dispenser below the screen. Surely, $1000 would get them to DC, he thought. Gas, food, lodging. It's only three days away, maybe just two or even less if they didn't stop. A bit more reality was settling in than Chris desired.

Walking over to the fresh food section, he and Emily stared incredulously at some hot dogs that had slowly atrophied to wrinkled twigs.

"Sandwich?" Chris rummaged a nearby cooler. Emily nodded and looked at them. She selected a thick bologna and cheese on white bread sandwich. Chris grabbed two turkey and Swiss on wheat sandwiches, and then snagged some chips and a few candy bars on the way to the dog food.

"I don't believe it."

"What?" Emily asked.

"Look! They have leashes."

Next to the dog food was a small selection of pet needs, including a few short nylon dog leashes. Chris added a six-foot blue leash, a can opener, and four large cans of dog food to his overestimated cradle. His arms took notice. Returning to the cooler, he and Emily nabbed some soft drinks and two liters of cheap bottled water. *The dog.* With the ability to carry no more, Chris and Emily brought their comestibles to the counter. When it came time to pay, Chris reached for his wallet to retrieve his debit card. He paused, then handed debit card to the cashier. *We're still in the same place, why use cash now?* The clerk bagged everything and completed the transaction. Chris handed Emily her soda and they returned to the car. Matt had completed refueling and sat in the back, playing with Snickers. Emily opened her door and climbed inside. Snickers assailed her, investigating all the new smells her clothes picked up from the store. Chris handed the grocery bag to Matt, who began inspecting its contents. "What did you bring me?"

Chris jumped in the driver's seat and started the engine. "A turkey sandwich and chips. You can have a water or one of the sodas. I'm saving one bottle of water for the dog."

Chris handed him his debit card and $500.

"Thanks. We'll make it, don't worry."

Matt removed one of the dog food cans and turned around to Emily, grunting a little from the wounded shoulder. "See what your daddy bought you?"

"No!" She replied as she pushed his shoulder away. "Where's my sandwich?"

Matt winced. "Let me guess." He pulled out the sandwich with white bread and held in front of Emily. "You got the bologna, didn't you?"

"Gimme!" Emily dove for the sandwich. At the same time, Chris sprung the clutch. The car jerked forward, causing Emily more difficulty.

"Very funny."

Chris steered back onto the freeway while the others dined. As soon as he settled into slow lane's pace, Matt handed him a sandwich and a cola. Matt finished eating and cranked open a can of dog food. Making sure he didn't leave a sharp edge, he passed the can back to Emily. Snickers whined with anticipation. Continuing to devour her sandwich using her right hand, Emily held the can with her left, allowing Snickers to lap up the beef product feverishly with his gargantuan tongue.

Despite the lacking horsepower, Chris managed to keep them above minimum speed limits. Matt scrutinized each passing vehicle, maintaining a high state of alert. Thirty minutes up the road, Snickers began to whimper.

"Daddy, I think we need to pull over."

Chris looked in his rearview mirror at the situation and dismissed the situation. Even in heavy traffic, the run from Santa Clara to Fisherman's Wharf was under ninety minutes.

"He'll be okay, Em; we're stopping soon."

Emily shook her head. Chris maintained focus on the road. He daydreamed about one of his first dates with Suzanne over a dozen years ago—catching a bus to Pier 39 for day sailing, then returning for drinks at the aquarium. He recalled being quite ill on that date. His land legs were three hours disposed before making a mess of a restroom stall. It was a supreme test in patience for Suzanne, and she passed with flying colors—patience not being one of Chris' virtues, or Matt's. The dream broke when Snickers' whimpering became to out-and-out crying.

Emily tapped her father on the shoulder. "I really think he needs to go."

Before Chris could reassess the situation, Snickers started convulsing. Emily panicked because she didn't know what to do, and this big dog was right next to her, uncontrollably retching. Snickers held his head just above Emily's lap, and with one last major convulsion, expelled a hot combination of bile and the entire can of food he just ate.

Emily screamed, feeling the warmth of the emesis across her legs. "UGH! Daddy!" She started to cry.

"Oh, dude, that's disgusting!" Matt held his nose and felt like heaving.

Chris slammed the brakes and pulled the car onto the emergency shoulder. Once stopped, he jumped out and grabbed a towel from the back. He ran around to the right side of the car and opened Emily's door, allowing her to flee.

"Matt, get the leash and take the dog over to the grass over there, would ya?"

"Uh . . . sure." Matt held his nose and felt queasy. "No problem."

Emily squirmed as Chris wiped her down. Her pants would require more attention. He returned to the car and grabbed another bottle of water. Matt escorted Snickers far from the road and into the grass. The dog convulsed once again, launching another salvo. Matt led him away before an inspection occurred.

"Uh, I think he's finished."

Snickers shook his head, licked his mouth a few times, and looked up at Matt, tail wagging. Chris shifted his attention to the car's rear seat and toiled to scrub it. Using the rest of the bottled water, he managed to remove most of the foul mess, odor excepted. A California Highway Patrol interceptor eased in behind them with his emergency lights flashing. Its driver was visible behind the windshield's glare, speaking into a microphone. Chris looked up at the officer, forgetting about the soiled towel in his hand.

"Damnit!" Matt yelled in a muffled tone.

"What?" Chris remained fixated on the patrolman.

"He's reporting our location!"

"To whom?"

"To anybody with a scanner and the ability to trace your tag. Assume those guys from the lab are listening."

Chris put the towel down and started to approach the officer. Abruptly, the patrol car's public address speaker blared, "Please remain where you are, sir."

The patrolman pulled his cruiser onto the grass between Matt and Chris' Rabbit and climbed out. He spent several moments assessing the situation, and while doing so, caught a whiff of the dog vomit. He covered his nose and turned to Chris.

"Sir, are you the driver?"

"Yes," Chris replied.

"I'll need your driver's license, proof of insurance and registration, please."

Chris reached back for his wallet and handed the credentials to him. The patrolman returned to his car, spent a few unnerving minutes examining them, found everything in order, and returned.

"Do you need any assistance, Mr. Miller?"

Mr. Miller? It had been several years since anyone called him that, but Chris walleted his cards and fumbled for some words. "Uh, no. No thanks. I think we're good."

Curious, Emily came to her father's side to have a peek inside the patrol car. The officer looked at her and smiled.

She looked back at Snickers. "He's sick," she said.

The patrolman looked towards Snickers' direction and nodded, catching another dose of putrid odor.

"That much is apparent, young lady." He turned back to Chris. "Mr. Miller, try to get underway as soon as you can." With a smile, he motored away.

Chris waved and looked towards Matt. "Thanks, we will."

Matt looked concerned, attempting to guide Snickers towards the back seat of the Volkswagen. "We need to get out of here and off this interstate right now."

"There's a big park about ten minutes up."

"Hmmm." Matt paused. "That will have to do. We should stay off the road for a little while. They'll have the city full of eyes. Our chances will significantly improve after dark."

He let Snickers climb in, and then took the front seat. Emily, still wet on her legs, reluctantly sat in her usual place. She kept pushing on Snickers' head to keep it at a distance. He thought she wanted to play.

"Ugh—Daddy!" Emily held her nose. The stench was overbearing.

"Oh, man . . . no!" Matt furiously rolled his window down.

Chris motioned to Emily. "Roll yours down too, Em. As soon as we get moving, this will all go away."

He was wrong. Emily struggled with the window crank and managed to get the glass most the way down. Chris slowly brought the car up to speed and merged back onto the interstate. With the wind whirling hair and stench throughout the car's cabin, he winced repeatedly.

"Geez. Sorry guys. We'll be off the road in a few minutes."

As the hilly landscapes passed by, Chris found the exit sign he wanted.

HWY 1 – 19TH AVE 1/4 MILE

He maneuvered toward the left exit lanes and then continued north on 19th. A few blocks down the road, Matt spotted a service station.

"Pull in here."

"Why?"

"Just pull in; I'll only be a minute."

Chris directed the car into the parking lot. Matt jumped out and walked swiftly inside. Roughly two minutes passed. He emerged with a small bag. Opening his door and climbing back in, Matt reached into the bag and removed a can of cherry-scented car deodorizer. He opened the can and handed it to Emily.

"Here. Place that in front of you, under my seat. It'll knock the smell down."

Emily whiffed the can. "This smells like the school's bathroom."

Matt reached back into the bag, pulled out one of those generic cardboard pine-scented air fresheners, and hung it from the rearview mirror.

"There! All better now?"

Chris rolled his eyes and maneuvered the car out of the parking lot and back onto 19th Avenue, continuing north.

Rumbling past State University, the mall, and a few blocks of elder Queen Anne and Revival-styled homes, the road disappeared into the densely forested bisection of Golden Gate Park.

"Taking this one," Chris said.

He drove the car around to Stow Lake Drive and found a parking space near a walkway leading to the top of Strawberry Hill.

"Come on, Em; I'll show you where Mommy and I used to date."

Matt took the leash and attached it to Snickers' collar. He and his new pal followed Chris and Emily across a footbridge and up a steep hill. At the top, they found a magnificent view of the surrounding San Francisco area, including Chinatown, the harbor docks, and the tops of the Golden Gate Bridge towers.

"We should stay here for a couple hours," Matt said.

Finding a bench, the three sat facing towards the west to catch some sun. The wind was a gentle, occasional wisp— letting the warmth of the city radiate over them. Emily stuffed music into her ears, and Snickers decided to take position underneath their bench.

"We used to catch sunsets here."

"You're never going to get over her if you keep digging her up, man."

"I don't want to forget her or all the good times we had. I can't."

"Long road . . . I—"

"Besides, the older Emily gets, the more I see Suzanne in her. That will always be a constant reminder. No way around it."

"Fine, but you could have picked any place in this park. Why here?"

"Come on, look at it. Emotional times like this. You see that clearing behind us? There's something about this place— calming and removed. Yet, it's in the middle of everything. You still feel connected, but at a distance. It's peaceful and it helped us—I mean it helped me forget any troubles I may've had."

"Hippie!"

"No, I'm serious. There are only a few places like this that offer the same comfort."

"If you say so. I *do* like the view."

Several moments ticked by as the sun raced towards the horizon.

"We've been lucky, haven't we?" Chris asked.

"Very."

"So, where do we go from here? What's our route to DC?"

"We'll take the northern run. Head to Reno, then east. I figure it will take at most three days, maybe less if we take shifts."

"You able to drive?"

Matt lifted his left arm slightly, still flinching. "We'll find out!"

Emily dropped her head into her father's lap—turning her body around to lay down using the rest of the bench.

"That's fine, but if you get drowsy, you'll let me know, right?"

"Absolutely." Matt nodded.

Chris gazed at the horizon as the copper giant gently dipped beneath the grey haze, ushering a crisp breeze across the hill.

Leg of Lam

"I'm cold."

The temperature plunged further than Emily could tolerate. Even with Snickers' warm fur draped over her feet, the brisk pacific winds were biting in the waning after-glow.

"Okay. We're leaving now." Chris tapped Matt's uninjured shoulder. "We should be on our way."

Matt arose from his state of semi-consciousness, having dozed off to one of the most beautiful sunsets he had ever witnessed.

"Yeah." He raked his hair back and rubbed his eye sockets. "Come on, Snickers."

The wagger led them down the hill and across the footbridge. Matt froze just as he reached the side of the car.

"Check the van over there to the left, about a hundred yards out."

"Another one of those?" Chris whispered loudly. "Jesus!"

"Get that car started, now."

Emily's eyes began to well, and she produced a reticent sniffle. The group scrambled to get inside.

Matt glanced back at the van and saw a gun barrel protruding from the passenger-side window.

"GET THIS THING STARTED!" he screamed.

Chris turned the ignition key; the warm-up light flashed.

"WHAT? I didn't think it was that cold!"

"It won't start?" Matt turned back towards the van, now fully accelerating towards them.

"It's going to take a second." Chris snapped. "Oh God, please don't take more than a second, baby!"

No sooner than he finished saying it, the light blinked off with a click, and Chris rumbled the car to life. He scorched the transmission in reverse, backed out, and slammed the shifter into first, speeding away towards the northern exit. The white van's tires chirped in pursuit. A man in a black balaclava emerged from its passenger window and took aim with his rifle. He blasted two rounds at the Volkswagen, striking the embankment just beyond the car's front bumper.

"Emily, get down!" Chris yelled.

Zigzagging his way through the series of park exits, Chris rammed the car back onto Highway 1, heading north towards the Presidio. A disorganized mass of traffic blocked his lane at the Fulton Street intersection—the park's northern border.

"Don't stop; go through it!" Matt looked back for the van. It was less than 30 yards away.

Chris made several glances in every direction, then stomped the accelerator, bolting around stopped traffic and straight across the intersection. A bus slammed on its brakes just ahead of them and laid on its horn. Chris never saw it and didn't bother looking back until Emily said something.

"Dad, what does a stoplight camera do?"

"DAMNIT!" Chris checked the rearview and saw the bus stopped in the intersection. "Now I'm going to get a ticket."

A loud explosion from behind broke his engine's cadence.

Matt checked rearward again. "Don't worry about the damn tickets, just get us out of here!"

Accelerating as fast as the car permitted through the next two blocks, Chris suddenly threw the steering wheel to the right, squealing the tires as he drifted onto Geary Boulevard, heading east. Struggling to make the same turn, the top-heavy van managed to stay within fifty yards, taking shots at any opportunity. Their aim was carelessly poor, creating collateral chaos from each barrage. Multiple cars parked to either side received the brunt. Shattered windows, holes in the bodywork. Storefronts destroyed. Pedestrians trampling other pedestrians. Dozens of phones dropped onto the pavement and flying apart in panicked 911 dialing. Chris tried desperately to lose the van, nailing the pedal to the floor and ferociously weaving through dense traffic on the three-laned street.

"Daddy, you passed another one of those camera signs."

The van struggled to keep up with the handling of the Volkswagen until the first hill with a significant grade appeared in front of them. The car choked and convulsed, forcing Chris into a lower gear. The van closed on them, and its passenger unleashed another furious volley, one impacting the car's rear bumper. Chris and Matt winced from the sound of more shattered glass just off their sides. Matt noticed the gunman's inaccuracies and an ever-so-slight smirk appeared on his face. That was, until he heard a bullet sizzle past, less than a foot over his head.

"If we stay here, we're going to run out of road." Matt yelled.

"Another one." Emily pointed back at a camera.

Chris became overwhelmed by the chase and specter of additional traffic tickets.

"Okay," he said with a sarcastic tone. He slung the wheel left at the next intersection and then made another squalling right turn two blocks down onto Bush Street. Another menacing hill loomed in front of them several blocks away.

Chris desperately examined each alleyway for an escape—anything that the van couldn't manage. His car possessed handling supremacy and he meant to take advantage of it. As he checked his periphery, another van appeared in front of them, blocking the road. He saw a flash of gunfire from the passenger side of that van and felt the bullet's impact as it smashed a headlamp. Chris flung his steering wheel to the left in a controlled skid and made a fast turn under the Dragon

Gate—the one-laned entry to Chinatown's famed Grant Avenue.

"ARE YOU NUTS?" Matt screamed. "It's uphill *and* it's narrow!"

Laying on his horn and dodging pedestrians, Chris churned up the lantern-lit street in second gear. The second van had little difficulty in keeping pace but couldn't open fire with so many people around. Instead, the gunmen rammed them from behind. Chris almost lost control, sideswiping a fresh protein kiosk and releasing some of its live contents. The gunmen kept pursuit, indiscriminately squashing chickens, snakes, and frogs in its path while paying no attention to the Cantonese-laced screams of the shopkeepers whose lives they just upheaved. The van hammered the Volkswagen's bumper again. Chris momentarily lost control, fishtailing and slamming the right side of his Rabbit on the rear clip of a parked sedan. Emily screamed. Snickers dove for the floorboard, what little of it there was.

Chris righted the car quickly, shifting back into third gear to hopefully accelerate away while the grade was level.

"We need to get off this street—it's too narrow to maneuver!" Matt shouted.

Chris looked for any path of escape and took the next street to the left. Sighing with the discontent of a bad decision, he demanded everything the car had by downshifting from third back to second gear, building momentum.

"NO Chris! We need to go *downhill*—downhill, if we want to get away!"

"I know that already." Chris angrily threw the gearstick into third. "I can't see around corners!"

The van made the same turn and quickly caught up. A shot ricocheted off the left.

"DOWNHILL, CHRIS!"

Chris spun the wheel to the right, skidding and barking the tires as they hopped from overexertion. He had a crazed look on his face.

"Oh, you want downhill, huh? I'll give you downhill!"

No sooner did he complete a right turn onto Hyde Street, he whipped the car sideways in a speed-controlled drift into the entrance of Lombard Street's steep downhill chicanes. In doing so, he came within a foot of nicking a traffic cop who was directing the never-ending conga line of tourists taking the famed eight turns.

The stunned officer jumped out of the way.

"HEY, YOU CAN'T . . ." blasting his whistle repeatedly afterward.

The pursuing van screeched around the corner and struck the policeman's elbow, displacing the whistle. He spun around and grabbed it in pain, then reached for his radio and relayed an alarm to a second officer located at the bottom of the hill, as well as an emergency plea for help to his dispatcher.

Honking his horn, Chris desperately tried to hurry the long line of tourists, but they were in no rush. Frustrated, he swung the Rabbit around and started passing other cars on the narrow road, easily violating the 5 MPH speed limit. Standing on porches and the railed staircases lining each side of the street, homeowners and curious onlookers gawked at the suicidal invaders. Many of them lit the switchboard monitors of San Francisco's emergency services. By flashing his lights and maintaining his hand on the horn, Chris managed to plague most drivers over to one side or into one the many private driveways along the way.

"YOU *ARE* NUTS!"

Matt grabbed the handle over his doorframe with both hands in order to stay upright. Snickers kept his composure in the left-rear floorboard and Emily hung on for dear life. Chris swung to the far right side on one of the sharp left turns, scraping a short concrete wall that protected one of the many meticulously-landscaped terraces. In doing so, Emily's door sheared away, leaving a gaping hole just to her right with only the seatbelt to keep her from falling through it. She screamed, cowering towards the middle of the car. Sparks flew past her doorway after Chris scraped the wall a second time. He passed two more shocked carloads before the next curve and attempted to pass another two on a hairpin right turn just ahead. The car in front of him panicked and opted for a driveway, but the other continued in ignorance. Chris tried to get around it in the turn, but instead received a blow to his right-rear corner from the pursuing van. The VW spun wildly left. Chris countersteered and used an adjacent driveway's width to pass the car in front. The van's passenger, now two vehicles back, pulled out a large-caliber handgun and blasted at the Rabbit, penetrating the roof, and exploding the rear driver's-side window. Emily squealed and covered her ears. The enormous concussion from the gunfire between the buildings sent spectators fleeing up and down the stair-cased sidewalks. Pedestrians within two blocks ran away from Lombard, phones in hand.

Chris glanced back to make sure his daughter was okay. She was anything but. "Hang on, Em. We're almost out."

In doing so, he lost focus, not noticing that the white van had regained position just behind him and wasted no time letting him know it. Again, it violently rammed the small car as it traversed Lombard's second-to-last curve. Chris couldn't make the correction in time and slammed head-on into a previously damaged portion of the protective concrete wall. The wall gave way to the car, sending them sailing over a flowered terrace, across a driveway, and over the next terrace guarding the final curve. Heavily damaged, but still operable, Chris nailed the accelerator and continued downhill on Lombard, now a straight run to the intersection with Leavenworth Street. A policeman at the bottom, who took position around the corner of the last apartment at the first sound of gunfire, emerged to give everyone a stern whistling. By that time, the Rabbit was halfway down the next block. The van made it to the bottom of Lombard's curves and continued the pursuit, ignoring the officer's angry tweets.

"Don't stop for anything." Matt demanded.

"That's what I'm doing!"

Emily was leaning as far as she could to the middle of the car, the howling wind from her open doorway increasing its velocity. Shaken, Snickers kept his head down on the floorboard. Chris laid on the accelerator as they sped past 60 MPH. Passing other cars left and right, their distance increased from the van, now a full block away. Chris suddenly slammed his brakes to avoid a semi rig crossing the next intersection. The brake pedal went to the floor and stayed there. Chris' eyes went wide in disbelief, then in a split-second, nailed the accelerator, deciding to outrun the potential collision. In doing so, he spun the steering wheel right then left, purposely flicking the car on an elliptical path around the danger. His evolving adeptness at handling his old car shined through, reaching the other side of the intersection unscathed. The van was forced to wait, stymied by the same truck who, in reaction, jackknifed to a stop in the intersection.

"We've got a problem." Chris said coldly as he tapped on the brakes.

"What do you mean?" Matt turned his head around and noticed the tapping.

Chris glanced at him. "I think the . . . yes, Damnit! The brakes are done."

"What?"

"The brakes are DONE, as in OUT!" Chris demonstratively stabbed the brake pedal several times in wild fashion.

They had advanced several blocks towards the bay at this point. Just ahead, what appeared to be a clear road from the top of Lombard now disappeared into blackness beyond the streetlights. The two suddenly realized they were about to run out of road.

"I don't like the look of this," Matt said.

Chris deliberated ways to decelerate the car, eyes darting about its interior. He attempted to downshift from fourth gear to second. With a high-pitched grind, the transmission's synchronizers disapprovingly rejected the notion. Chris desperately tried again and managed to pound the stick into third, slowing the car somewhat. There was a slight grade helping, but it wouldn't be enough.

"We're running out of road, CHRIS!"

Chris desperately tried to downshift again, but the transmission wouldn't have it.

"Don't you have an emergency brake?" Matt panicked.

A concrete retaining wall blocked the end of the street just ahead of them. Chris looked at it and then down at the emergency brake handle, shaking his head because he hadn't remembered the most obvious solution. Yanking on it as hard as he could, the car's rear tires locked, making a horrific noise, but not slowing the car as quickly as he hoped. As they neared the end, Chris skidded off the pavement, steering towards a narrow gap in the wall next to a condominium building.

"NO!" Matt screamed as the car came to a rest.

Terror gripped Emily in silent shivering as the car teetered over the edge of a 120-foot-high cliff overlooking Pier 27's docks. Chris gulped, catching a glimpse of the Bay Bridge ahead to his right.

"Oh God, what have I done!"

Emily screamed at the top of her lungs, alarming Snickers. Matt braced himself against the back of his seat, looking down as the car's nose slowly dipped downward. Over they went, down an eighty-degree slope with no control. Chris kept his arms locked on the steering wheel and closed his eyes. Matt pushed against the glove compartment in dreadful horror. Emily bounced wildly against her seat restraints. The gentle rush of air coming through her door became a loud roar as the car built velocity down the cliff. No sooner than they began falling, the car suddenly reached the bottom and crashed into a thicket of junipers, providing a supple cushion. It diffused the amassed kinetic energy—but not all of it. The car spilled out from the thick brush and onto the street below. Before anyone could catch their breath, gunfire blasted from the top of the cliff. Bullets and their shrapnel ricocheted on the pavement next to their rolling jalopy. To Chris' amazement, the car was still running. He intuitively slammed it into second gear and made for the boat docks directly in front of them.

"Oh my God, that was INSANE!" Chris looked back. "I can't believe we just—"

Matt pointed to a pier straight ahead. "Let's ditch it in there."

"Ditch what?"

"This car!"

"I'm not—" Chris started to dismiss any abandonment until several more gunshots ricocheted to his left. The wrecked and wobbly heap tumbled across The Embarcadero and into the pier's dockage areas.

"Take it to the end—all the way," Matt said. "We'll need as much time as we can get."

Chris goaded the now-coughing diesel towards the end of the docks where several other vehicles had parked alongside a warehouse. Not seeing any other available spaces, Chris parked it under a large motor yacht, freshly removed from the water and slung on a massive mobile gantry crane.

Matt hopped out. "Get your stuff fast. We need to take cover and find a boat. That's the only way out of here."

Chris ran around to open the car's damaged hatch. With difficulty, he pried it open and grabbed Emily's backpack along with his attaché case. Matt waited for her to exit the car, and then he reached for Snickers' leash. The dog growled somewhat, upset by the trauma and reluctant to leave the sudden calm of the rear floorboard.

Matt gave a stronger tug on the leash. "Come on, boy!"

Snickers tucked his tale and bounded out of the doorway.

The echoes of screeching tires interrupted the quietness of the harbor.

"Over here!" Matt pointed while looking back at the cache of weapons he had no time to retrieve.

The group ran to an empty portable office at the end of the parking lot. Matt kicked open the door and scrambled inside with Snickers, motioning Chris and Emily to hurry. Just as they closed the office door behind them, a white cargo van came to a grinding halt fifty yards away from the rear of the hissing, dripping, heap of a Volkswagen Rabbit. Two heavily armored men cautiously approached the car with their rifles pointed at the windows.

"Damnit!" Matt whispered. "Shoulda brought a rifle instead of this dog."

"Shh!" Chris took the leash from him.

One of the operators stopped several yards away from Chris' car and clicked the transmit key on his headset system. "It appears to be empty," he said.

A response tinkled in his earpiece, and the operator nodded to his comrade. "He said he didn't care what it looks like, and to go and see for ourselves."

"So we go," the other replied.

They slowly approached the car, maintaining aim on the windows, leaving little opportunity for a surprise ambush. The first operator arrived at the driver's door. Shading his eyes, he peered inside and found nothing. He turned around to share the news with his comrade and noticed Matt inside the trailer holding a large controller module. Silent expletives escaped from the soldiers' lips as Matt hit the release button on the gantry's remote. The huge yacht instantly dropped on top of them, and onto Chris' first love. All disappeared beneath it.

"AH!" Chris stood up breathless, stunned, not believing what just happened. The shockwave rocked the ground like an earthquake. "MY CAR!"

Matt put down the remote. "Ended up being useful after all."

"I don't think I'll be eating pancakes for a while," quipped Emily. She hated that car.

Snickers looked up at her and barked once.

"But—" Chris whined.

Matt interrupted, "Never mind that, we've got to find a way out of here."

"Well, she might not have meant much to *you*!"

"She?" Come on, let's go. I have an idea."

"Why don't we take their van?" Chris bawled.

"Probably tracked," Matt said as he walked towards the door. As they stepped out of the trailer, the unnerving sounds of more screeching tires echoed throughout the docks.

"RUN!" Matt yelled.

The group bolted inside a massive dry dockage warehouse through one of its colossal entry doors. Inside, some workers dropped what they were doing to gape at the strangers.

One of them shouted, "Hey, you can't come in here!"

"Come on!" Matt hurried.

Chris kept pace across the vast concrete floor, but Emily struggled with her overstuffed backpack.

"Come on, Emily! We have to go."

Tears emerged from the corners of her eyes, but she continued scrambling across the floor with her father as fast as she could. Matt scurried ahead and made it through the doorway on the eastern side of the massive boathouse. Once outside, light that spilled from the warehouse's doorway quickly faded. Ahead were some dimly-lit and rickety boat slips, many of which were empty. Chris heard more tires squalling on the other side of the building. Looking back, he faintly discerned one of the dockworkers pointing towards the yacht resting on his car. Two gunmen paced towards the scene. Once there, they examined the hulking *Say Ya Nora,* a 75ft express motor yacht. From under its crushed bottom ran a river of blood and fuel towards the seawall. One of the operators looked back and saw a similar van to theirs, still idling with both doors open and its interior light illuminated. After inspecting it, one of the men unsnapped the holster to his side arm and walked towards the long boathouse where a handful of curious workers stood by the door. A husky stevedore—wearing black rubber galoshes, blue jeans, a windbreaker, and a hardhat—stepped backwards as the barrel of a pistol had him perfectly framed. Slowly he raised his hands.

The operator coldly flipped the weapon's safety. "If you saw something, I want to know about it right now. I will not ask a second time."

Without hesitation, the dockworker pointed towards the gaping doorway on the other side of the building. His inquisitor looked him straight in the eye before pointing towards the other door and motioning his comrade, "Let's go."

Matt, Chris, and Emily disappeared into the darkness of the eastern slips, where their available options all but disappeared.

"What's the plan, Matt?"

"Shssh! I know where we're going, just relax."

A few slips down, Matt found precisely what he wanted.

"There," he said.

Chris saw nothing. "There what?"

"Down there; it's perfect."

Chris looked further down to see what Matt was pointing towards—an older, inflatable dinghy. 18-footer, dark gray. No motor, but it had two worn, plastic oars and importantly, its deck appeared dry, *mostly.*

"What?"

"Get down here," Matt insisted.

Chris slowly made his way down to the boat and nearly slipped when he stepped on its slick, rubbery deck.

"Chris, we can't go back. Those men have the docks covered, and you hear the sirens, right? For all we know, they'll think we died in the car. That might buy us some time. The thing is, we need to get out of here quietly. I don't have time to untie and hotwire some other boat, even if there was one available. Not to mention the noise would make. This is perfect."

Chris considered it and agreed.

He turned to Emily. "Come on, honey."

"I don't wanna."

"We don't have a choice, now hand me your backpack."

Chris took the backpack and laid it down on the damp deck. Reaching up, he lifted Emily and sat her on the boat's inflated center transom. Snickers whimpered with his leash dragging, realizing he was not quite onboard with his new family yet. Chris attempted to resolve the situation by persuading Snickers to jump into his arms. "Come on, boy."

"Shssh!" Matt looked around to see if anyone heard them.

Snickers, hesitant at first, leapt when Chris encouraged him the second time. He landed broadside against Chris' chest and became cradled in his arms. The inertia, however, was too much for Chris. As soon as he caught the dog, they fell backwards. Chris landed with his rump on the deck, but he held on.

"Good boy."

Chris felt the cold condensation seep through his underpants as he let go of the dog. Matt untied the last line, took position at the port bow side, and began paddling out of the slip.

"Grab the other oar and take the rear. When I get the boat straightened down the channel, paddle with me."

"Where are we headed?" Chris asked.

"Okay, now!" Matt said.

Chris didn't budge. "Where are we *going*, Matt?"

The boat drifted just past the end of the pier.

Matt, looking forward and to the left, said, "You see those lights through the mist? Over there."

Peering through the light fog, Chris instantly recognized the small clump of lights less than two miles away and started paddling in unison with Matt.

Searching up and down the docks, the two gunmen grew frustrated. Realizing the enormity of the docks themselves, and that their search time had expired due to the sirens in the background, they headed back through the boathouse's main doorway. This time, there were no curious onlookers.

The leading operator holstered his pistol as he climbed into the driver's seat of the first van.

"Take the other van. We must go."

With spinning tires, both vehicles escaped the pier undetected. The dockworkers scampered out of the doorway as the sirens approached. No less than fifteen patrol cars thundered onto the pier, tires barking as they drew up in front of the small assemblage of the curious and concerned. Heavily-armed policemen jumped out and crouched behind their car doors. Shaking his head, the same dock worker that had the gun pointed at him earlier raised his hands.

"Hellooo overtime."

Rocked

"ALCATRAZ?" Chris yelped.

"It's not a problem. Keep it down!" Matt flipped around to check if any emergency crew or dockworkers were searching for them, but the bay's mist had already cloaked their exit.

"I see a problem. You could've put us ashore anywhere in the immediate arbor, but *nooo*—you think an old, completely-isolated prison is better suited?"

"Look, we go anywhere else in the bay and someone sees us—and they *will* see us—they'll call it in and we're done. We go over *there* and beach on the backside's rocks, no one will ever know."

"And just how do you plan to get us back from there undetected?"

"Easy, we wait until just before daybreak and paddle across to the other side. What is that—Sausalito?"

Chris clinched his teeth and mumbled, "Simply, he says."

Emily shivered quietly from the murky bay's damp chill. Its infamous fog was faintly thinner that evening, but Alcatraz was invisible at sea level, save for its powerful strobing bea-con. The waters were soupy and calm, and just over a half mile away from Pier 27, the city's noise faded into reticence—only broken by the rhythmic penetrations of the oars and the occasional distant soundings from Alcatraz and the Golden Gate Bridge. The enormity of Chris' situation suddenly hit him—the attempts on his life and Emily's, the destruction of Andromeda, the total loss of his home and everything in it, and finally, the bloated, ashen faces of his precious friends—

murdered. *Why them?* Anger gripped every muscle in his face—eyes squinting, teeth clinched.

Matt suddenly stopped rowing and motioned Chris to do the same. His trained ears could not discern much within the white noise. A lesson he learned years ago—that the natural noise of water or air masked most of the human's audio spectrum. Waterfalls, crashing waves, a brisk wind flowing through a sea of trees. San Francisco Bay was an audio haystack. Having spent his youth (or *misspent,* his mother would say) in the arcades, pool halls, and bowling alleys many years ago, Matt learned to filter and pinpoint desired sounds from the discord with laser-like focus. He could be engrossed in a multi-player Formula One race, yet still know when Kano ripped a heart out, even from the other side of a large room. *Flawless . . .*

Snickers started whimpering.

"Shssh!" Matt woke Chris from his subconscious staring.

"What?"

Matt motioned again to keep it down. Pointing at his ears and looking to the left, he slowly recognized the slight and steady increase in the sound of churning water. A colossal, dark mass penetrated the fog and obliterated everyone's ears with its foghorn. Lasting an eternal four seconds, Matt and Chris realized they were about to cross directly in the path of an oncoming container ship.

Without prompting, Chris frantically whipped his oar into the sea and backpaddled as fast as he panicked to move it. Matt's attempts to get his attention went ignored.

"DAD!" Emily screamed, finally breaking Chris' concentration.

"Chris, stop!" Matt yelled. "You're rowing us in a circle."

Chris could not see Alcatraz's flashing beacon any longer. The bow of the immense cargo ship stormed by some 60 yards ahead.

"We need to reposition ourselves for what's coming." Matt hollered. "When I tell you, start rowing forward and fast!"

"What's coming?"

"The wake."

"The what?"

"The ship's *wake!* It'll be about five feet high. Now, get ready!"

Chris started to debate, but as soon as he lifted his finger, another deafening blast from the ship's foghorn paralyzed them. The oars were dropped as everyone smashed their hands over their ears. Snickers screeched, then resumed barking.

Matt let go of the sides of his skull and regripped his oar. "Here it comes!" He shouted above ringing ears.

Together, the men increased their momentum, paddling as fast as they could. The bow flung Matt upwards to meet the wave's crest, and he rode it admirably—his Class 4 kayaking experience paid in full. Emily didn't fare quite so well. The wake threw her from the center transom, and she tumbled towards the stern near her father. Soaked from the spray and the damp bottom of the flimsy craft, she started yelling. Chris used his left arm and helped her up to sit beside him. When the hulk's huge transom flew past, she settled down. Within the relative calm of the freighter's propwash, Matt struggled to ascertain the ship's name as it disappeared into the darkness. "Alabama," he mumbled.

"That sounds familiar," said Chris.

"Glad to be stateside, I'd guess."

Alcatraz's flashing beacon and dim lights slowly reappeared as the men resumed their cadence.

"Chris, don't row towards the middle of the island. Point towards the right because of the ebb tide current."

"If you say so."

Chris' directional management frustrated Matt initially, but they found their rhythm in short order. For twenty minutes they rowed against the current, slowly making way towards the eastern shore. Alcatraz—at first a distant, vague, bundle of orange sodium-vapor lights—gradually materialized. Chris paddled on, surveying the main building and a lighthouse that was awash in light. He could see a sheer cliff overhanging their rocky destination, and the switchbacked walkway leading up its face.

Her head drooped, Emily became entranced by the constantly rippling floor of the boat. Each swell created from Matt's oar traversed the bottom from bow to stern. Every wave warped the rubbery fabric, and she felt it on her feet as if she was directly connected to its surface. She noticed a singular point rising from the flexible bottom. Another ripple came past, front to back, and another. And then one came from behind and disappeared just before Matt's feet. *Just a weird wave,* she thought. Although somewhat curious, she was too sleepy to give it much attention. That was, until it happened again. Her feet rose as the elastic floor stretched around a single point as it made its way to the bow. Snickers growled. Emily turned around to ask her father what it might be, and Chris paused briefly to watch the deck. When the last ripple of water subsided at his motionless oar, the front of the boat exploded out the water. Matt flew several feet into the air and over the side, creating a loud splash that ended the relative silence of the past few minutes. A large, dark fin disappeared below the surface from just past the bow of their defenseless tender. In a panic, Chris sloppily made his way to the starboard side to rescue Matt. *An errant killer whale playing with dinner?* Chris heard of the bay's dangers—sharks, hypothermia, currents that sweep you into the ocean. He knew those were primary considerations in the decision to make Alcatraz a prison. While not inescapable, it had inescapable deterrents, and quite possibly one of those deterrents just tossed Matt into the bay.

Matt desperately flailed towards the boat as Chris extended his oar to him.

"Take it!"

Matt reached for the oar and missed on the first try. Stretching and straining further, Chris held out the oar as far as he possibly could. Matt's fingertips hooked an edge and Chris braced himself while carefully hauling him portside. Matt choked on salt water and clung to the rubber gunwale, coughing and spitting.

Chris extended his hands. Matt continued panting. "Hang on a minute."

"You need to get in here right now; there's something you don't know!"

Before Matt could respond, he felt something slick bounce against the front of his legs. The force attempted to push him away from the side of the boat. Emily looked at the middle of the floor to see the point sticking up several inches and running from back to front again. This time, the rise in the floor froze, and then grew larger.

"Matt?" Chris' voice stuttered.

As Matt clung to the boat, he felt a large mass slide across his legs and under his feet.

"Oh God," he whispered.

The creature abruptly thrust upward, launching Matt airborne once again. This time, he landed on the flat of his back *inside* the boat, shuddering the entire craft from the impact. A moment later, just to starboard, a plume of water sprayed upward in a geyser of escaping air.

A blowhole! Chris thought. "That's *not* a shark!"

"Daddy!" Emily threw both arms around his legs and squeezed.

Matt gaped over the side as a massive tailfin rolled over in the water, disappearing into the deep. Snickers jumped to the side of the boat and began barking wildly. A tail that was as large as their boat emerged from the deep and towered in front of them for several seconds before crashing into the water, drenching all aboard from the spray.

Chris wiped his glasses. "It's a humpback, I think!"

Snickers, now soaking wet, gave a small whimper and grunted while shaking off the saltwater, attempting to settle back in the sloshing floor of the boat.

"What the devil is it doing here?" Matt shivered from the dowsing.

"It's not entirely uncommon, albeit rare. A couple of them swam up the Sacramento River some years ago, and another was famous for it in the eighties. It was all over the news."

Now further away, the head of the giant whale flew out of the water, and the percussive sound of air explosively escaping its blowhole commanded attention.

"Tremendous." Chris turned to relocate Alcatraz's eastern rocks.

Matt sighed. "Umm, I seem to have misplaced my oar, and it's a fair assumption you don't have it."

"Oar?" The water was a swirling black mass to Chris. Only the crystalline peaks from reflecting city lights randomly dotted the water. "No."

"Damnit!"

"Hey!" Chris gestured as Snickers barked once.

"Sorry, Emily; I didn't mean it. Chris, you'll need to take us in. It's only a few minutes away."

Tired but dry, Chris scratched his head, cleared his mind, and didn't offer a word in rebuttal. He simply swapped positions with Matt and started paddling.

"You'll need to alternate each—"

"I know."

Chris developed a cadence and brought the craft upon the boulders protecting Alcatraz's southeast shore. The waves calmly lapped at it, allowing them to exit the inflatable boat without much difficulty. Matt jumped out and helped Chris drag it the rest of the way onto the rocks where Emily could debark without getting wet. A jagged cliff rose dozens of feet in front of her, and it protected the island from many assaults, but not the kind that took place this night.

"Get your stuff." Matt said. "There's an abandoned guard shack or something up on the first tier. We'll bivouac there until daybreak."

"Then what?"

"I don't know."

"WHAT? I thought you had a *plan*?"

"Yeah, I had a plan to escape the *docks*. I didn't think too much about getting out of *here*, other than rowing out in the morning." Matt turned to face him. "With one oar?"

"So we're trapped. Fantastic."

"No! No, we're not. We still have a good boat and what's left of our health. The solution will come but I need to dry out."

Trudging up the zigzagged walkway, they made their way around an old rusty fence to a small concrete building overlooking the bay and the bright lights they left behind. Opening its creaky old door, Matt found the room empty. He stripped off his shirt and hung it on a nearby tree branch to dry.

"I don't suppose—"

"Yeah, hang on a minute." Chris interrupted.

Emily sat on the floor and propped her head up on her backpack as a makeshift pillow. Chris opened his attaché case and handed a shirt to Matt.

"Thanks. Look, I know we'll get out of here and out of this mess."

"Time will tell. I'm just tired."

"Daddy, I'm—"

Matt's brow furled. "You've got to be kidding me."

Chris fumbled around with the case and realized they abandoned their food during the escape. He dug into his inner jacket pockets and felt the two candy bars he purchased back at the convenience store. He gave one to Emily and held the other in front of Matt's face.

"Better than nothing."

Chris split half of his bar and handed it to Matt. Placing the small hunk of chocolate in his mouth, he slipped on the fresh shirt and found a corner to lean against. Chris cuddled next to Emily as she finished her snack. After the last bite, she yawned and found a comfortable spot somewhere between her backpack and her father's chest. Snickers paced to Matt's right side, made three tight circles, and plopped down against his legs, dropping his head onto Matt's lap.

"You see this?" Matt pointed to Chris as he finished his dinner.

The aging cinderblock shack did little for warmth but everything for wind protection. It also squelched the intermittent foghorn blasts from passing freighters and those from Alcatraz, emanating from somewhere further up the hill. They remained close enough to the bay to hear wake water crash along the rocky shore down below, and, after a while, nothing mattered—only the blackness of a deep sleep.

"What of it then?"

"Nothing, Your Eminence. It merely means we are not alone."

"And, you dare call it *nothing*? I understand the importance of this, but our risks—our costs—are broaching intolerability. Who?"

"We do not know." Bishop Esposito pointed at the translucent monitor. "Our team was surveilling, not engaging. The imposters went out of their way to imitate us during the chase. See for yourself."

Realizing the repercussions of lost control, His Eminence, Cardinal Vasco Tagliabue, recessed into the deep confines of his well-appointed chair. Gazing downward in deep thought, he stroked the finely entwined golden rope of his pectorale. His thoughts were not easily discernable by Esposito, but his constantly changing facial expressions said enough. The cardinal continued in this manner until his anger gradually transitioned to cognizance. His ancient eyes darted around behind the thick glass of his bifocals. He removed them moments later to pinch the bridge of his nose, soothing a fresh headache. There were so many.

"It may have been premature of me to sanction this operation. I see no immediate risk unless this Doctor Miller seeks the attention of the press, of which I have seen no proclivity or evidence. Yes, naturally we remain hopeful to acquire the device and its sires, but not at further risk of exposure. These operatives you have shown me, I consider them non pectore, yet symbiont, Narciso. We shall consider them as proxy until the appropriate time."

The cardinal's chair slowly turned away from the screen and towards his rather perplexed protégé.

"I want you to manage this, Narciso."

"But, Your Eminence—"

"You must discover the nature of these people who wish to lay blame at our feet. They obviously know about us. We must know more about them. They will do Our Lord's work at no significant expense to us."

Esposito bowed, gave his *Signum Crusis,* and turned around to exit.

"And take the *Monsignor* with you. He might be useful."

Esposito slowly turned back around and bowed again, but with a slight pause, reasoning the cardinal's appointments. The bishop's grimace swiftly changed to a grin of malevolence. As he departed, the sentries on either side of the great archway reaffirmed their allegiance. Esposito glided into a cavernous hallway below its towering, vaulted groins, decorated with millions of tiny tiles depicting the scene of Jacob blessing Joseph's sons from his deathbed. He made a left turn and stepped down another vast hallway, his shoes echoing his imminent arrival against the walls. Along the way were several guarded archways, and his was the last on the left near the end of the hall. Paying his personal guard no attention, the bishop sat behind his desk to the immediate right of the entry. He punched a couple buttons on his phone's intercom and waited for a response.

Monsignor Trovarto stared at the light blinking in front of him. The phone rang three times—twenty-one seconds to be exact—as he pondered the call. In that brief moment, the priest presumed the caller's identity, the likely reason for the contact, and what he would probably be asked to do. He continually suffered from a combative relationship with Esposito over his aggressive nature, and Trovarto wasn't alone in his suffering. It was widely known that Esposito minimalized his menial duties as a bishop of the Catholic Church. It's what earned him the position of primary enforcer for the Spada Sacra—much to the loathing of his contemporaries, yet much to Tagliabue's satisfaction. In twenty-one seconds, Monsignor Trovarto deduced that particular call would beget the most important undertaking in his life. It overwhelmed him briefly, but that was nothing new.

"Yes," he responded.

"Prepare for Washington, departure in two hours."

The line extinguished before Trovarto could field any questions. Protocols were no inquiries; he was simply to be at the motor pool in two hours. Trovarto pressed the speakerphone button and replaced the handset, recessing into his thoughts. The monsignor quickly detailed a short travel manifest and summoned one of his sentries.

"Take this to provisioning; I debark in two hours. Please be swift."

The courier took the communication in hand, gestured, and walked straight down the hallway at a brisk pace. Trovarto summoned his remaining sentry.

"Go with him. It will take both of you."

"But—" The guard started to question the order, as it was a breach of protocol for him to vacate the doorway when the office was occupied.

"It is not a problem. I am leaving in a moment. Go on."

The guard gestured before turning around. After he disappeared down the hallway, Trovarto closed the arched doorway to his office. Reaching inside his cassock, he produced a plain black metallic and rectangular bar that measured about nine centimeters long, four centimeters wide, and just one centimeter thick. Holding the device in his left hand, he pressed his right index fingertip onto the middle of the rectangle for three seconds. A dim green point of light emanated from under the surface of the device, just in front of his finger. He held the device close to his face and listened for the cue.

Leave your message now.

In a muffled voice as not to gain the attention from other sentries down the hall, he stated, "Destination Washington, DC, without delay. Advise, *s'il vous plaît.*"

Trovarto released the tiny device. The light disappeared, and he tucked it deep within his cassock. He placed his left hand over his mouth with the index finger across his upper lip and thumb under his chin. *Washington. They warned me about this.*

Clasping his modest olive wood rosary and kissing its crucifix, he softly whispered, "*Aiutili, Dio.*"

Pelican Island

Matt cracked his eyelids just before daybreak to the irritable sensations of incessant whimpering and the prodding of a wet nose. Snickers kept a tight schedule, and that usually meant rising with Master Jim Smiley before the day's heat made for unbearable homebuilding. Groggy from blood loss, Matt checked his watch. 6:02, but his body, particularly his left shoulder, signaled it had only been a couple hours since he propped himself against the wall. Rubbing his eyes and yawning, he struggled to stretch with pain's paralysis. He felt his stitches flex, and a razor-like sharpness shot through them. He winced in a stifled breath and reached for the shack's door with his right hand. Frigid air blasted the room, startling Chris and Emily. Snickers wasted no time and dashed for the nearest patch of grass. Matt struggled for warmth as he waited; the crisp breeze ignored his T-shirt completely. It wouldn't be long before the uncontrollable shivering started, so he occupied himself with the landscape.

The southern shores of Alcatraz offered little amusement for him besides the blinding flash every five seconds from the old lighthouse and the intermittent blast of the island's foghorn every few minutes—something they somehow tuned out during the night. The surf rhythmically splashed the rocks below, and the city's illuminated shores glistened just beyond the morning mist. Torturous temptation for former residents.

Matt stepped to the cliff's edge to relieve himself and made a startling discovery—their transportation was missing. The stolen boat slipped off the rocks during the night and drifted out to sea with the tide. Matt suddenly forgot his physical condition as he scanned the shoreline. Nothing. *How do we get out of here now?*

Tourist embarking and debarking was located across the old parade grounds on the northeastern shore. Matt momentarily looked towards that direction, and a jolt of lightning—a plan—electrified his mind. He felt a light tap on his shoulder and turned around to see Chris offering a light windbreaker.

"Thought you might want this," said Chris.

Not without tremendous pain, Matt gratefully donned the dark blue jacket as they caught a hazy sunrise over the Oakland skyline.

He paused for another moment and looked back across the parade grounds behind them. "Before it gets too bright out here, I need to check something out."

"Yeah, why?" Chris asked.

"I hate to tell you this, but the boat's gone."

"What?" Chris walked over to the cliff's edge and looked down. "How?"

"Tidal currents? It doesn't matter; we'll have to leave by another method now."

"For the love of Christ, I can't take any more of this!"

"Settle down. We should be able to take one of the tour boats, but I had to think it through. We can't just appear first thing in the morning and hop on the first shuttle out."

"They're going to remember us, Matt. And don't forget we have a dog. Something told me it might have been a bad idea at the time, but I'm a sucker, you know. Damnit!"

"Exactly, and I may have a way around that, but first things first. It's only just after six and I don't think the first boat comes until nine or so. That's what I need to nail down. The park rangers probably arrive before anyone else. Maybe they have someone posted all night, so we need to disappear until some tourists show up. We can walk around legitimately then

. . . maybe. I'm guessing they don't check visitor passes once they're already *on* the island."

"I've been here twice with Suzanne. No, they don't. I don't recall any dogs on the island either."

"Leave that to me. Back in a few . . ."

"What?" Chris asked too late; Matt had already gone. He adjusted his glasses, mumbling, "Leave it to him, sure."

Matt paced along Alcatraz's old residential ruins heading towards the former recreation building's outer wall. Making his way around to the northern part of the island, he reached the end of its upper terrace, crouched down and looked westward. At the end of the wide walkway between the old medical officer's quarters and Building 64, were two rangers in a steep cadence climbing towards the main cellblocks above. Matt froze, slowly backed away from the corner, and took a deep breath. Deciding that walkway was too risky, he dashed across to the southeastern foundations of Building 64 and wildly exhaled. He moved to climb down the short, wooded embankment to reach the bottom. Once there, he took a staircase leading down the side of the Building 64's basement towards the docks. He noticed an empty National Parks Service tender moored to the western side, and he reasoned it belonged to the rangers he observed moments earlier. Scrambling down to the debarkation point, Matt found what he wanted—a schedule detailing shuttle departure times.

He looked back across the courtyard at the cracked yellow paint on Building 64's façade over its bookstore. Above an old United States Penitentiary sign was "Indians Welcome" handwritten in faded red paint. Matt stared at it for several moments before heading back. He quickly ascended the staircase leading up the side of Building 64 and jumped over its rail to a wooded embankment. While climbing it, Matt took a quick look down a separating walkway towards Alcatraz's western end, then he snuck across to the parade grounds. He started to dash across it and was immediately paralyzed by something he had forgotten when he strode across the parade grounds a few minutes earlier. Stunned and covering his ears, he instantly realized he had stumbled directly in front of the island's massive foghorn. He stumbled briefly and cowered while racing towards the horn's flank to lessen the blow, ears writhing and ringing. By the time he arrived at the decaying guard shack, his headache subsided somewhat. The ringing remained. He opened the door and found Snickers curled up alongside Emily, still snoring. Chris peered through the shack's salt-stained windows, framing a gorgeous sunrise. He spun around to find Matt taking deep breaths, slightly off-balance and still nursing his right ear.

Pointing to it with his other hand, Matt said, "I forgot about something."

Chris chuckled. "The foghorn, no doubt."

Matt nodded.

"Yeah, I don't know how we slept through it. What did you learn?"

"The first departure isn't 'til 10, then every thirty minutes. I guess we should try to leave on the second."

"Why the second?"

"Okay, check this . . . According to the schedule, the regular tour operator has two boats. Think about it. We're trying to sneak out, so we don't want to get recognized, right?"

"I suppose we *are* famous."

Matt cringed. "I presume they want a boat at each dock so they're not interfering with each other. The first tender drops off their first load at nine, then goes back. Why? Because he just dropped his first passengers. Those people obviously don't want to leave yet, and there's no reason for the first boat to stay, so he departs for his second load. Before he returns, the second boat arrives here at nine-thirty. That boat doesn't stick around either, still too early. The first boat returns at 10. This time, he takes passengers. I'm thinking that it takes more than an hour to see the entire island, and if any people actually jump on his boat to go home, it's maybe just a few, and the crew would likely remember their faces. The second departure will have more passengers, and the crew would presume most came from the first boat, so . . .."

"That makes sense. What about the dog?"

"Work in progress."

Chris detected something in the distance and turned around.

"Shssh." Chris held his finger up to his lips. "You hear that?"

"You kidding?" Matt pointed to his right ear.

"Get down," Chris whispered loudly.

A beam of light pierced the shack's western windows, tracing across the wall. It disappeared a moment later, then a loud metallic pop preceded the grind of small wheels rolling across fine gravel. Matt eased over and slowly cracked open the shack's door to have a better look. A ranger was making her rounds in an electric golf cart, traipsing around the old parade grounds towards the front walkway overlooking the docks.

"Well?" Chris asked.

"Ranger," Matt whispered. "We probably won't see her again."

"What time is it?"

Matt checked his watch. "Close to seven."

"I suppose we'll have to sit tight for a while."

"Until the first tour arrives, then we can move around. I saw a gift shop on the other side. It'll have food, yes?"

"Light snacks if memory serves. Emily will be okay until she wakes up."

Matt looked down at her blissful face. "Well, she has the right idea. I could use another couple of hours."

Matt sat against one of the concrete walls of the shack. Slowly, his head drooped to one side, and he drifted away.

Chris' anxieties were getting the better of him. He gnashed his teeth on the details of their escape and plans after they made it back to shore. It took an extra twenty minutes for him to revisit the Land of Nod.

There was a pounding at the shack's door. A man wearing tall black boots and a white jumpsuit with a clear plastic protective facial shield, violently kicked it open. Brandishing a large caliber handgun, he pointed it at Chris and demanded in a plain voice, "Let's go, Miller."

Chris looked back for Matt and Emily, but they were missing. Snickers too. The man grabbed Chris by his left wrist and flung him outside to the waiting arms of several more men who were similarly dressed. At first, Chris was stricken with a sense of displacement and loss—wondering what happened to his daughter. In anger, he turned back to the men, who were now laughing hysterically. Chris remembered the tone of those laughs, and it confused him further. The men gathered around him in a tight circle. Chris tried to see their faces, but the plastic shields were tinted too dark. He spun around and faced yet another man. His shield was translucent, and his face was barely recognizable—that of a young teenager's, which seemed further irksome. *Bobby?* Chris thought. The boy laughed hysterically, and soon the rest of the strange jumpsuited men joined him.

The boy poked him in the chest. "You're going in the water, *Piss.*"

Bobby! He's the only prick that called me that.

"Bobby, wait!" Chris yelled as the men firmly grabbed each of his four limbs. They lifted him off his feet and swung him back and forth towards the water.

"ONE, TWO, THREEE!" They yelled.

As they let go, Chris knocked his head against the concrete wall of the shack, shocking him awake. His pulmonary reflex also startled Matt.

"What? What is it?" Matt yelled.

"Ow!" Chris checked for blood. "Nothing. Just a stupid little nightmare."

"My father once told me strange places tend to stir the imagination."

Emily twitched, first outstretching her arms, then her mouth opened widely in a ferocious yawn. Snickers did much the same, licking his nose a few times, and flapping his ears.

Matt pulled the jacket sleeve back over his watch. "8:56. Good timing! Okay, the first boat should be here any moment. Sit tight until I return."

Jogging up to the old parade grounds and concealing himself against the northern wall, Matt slithered his way back to within view of the docks. Just after 9 a.m., a double-decker ferry docked and unloaded well over 500 passengers. Matt observed how they dispersed before heading back. Two park rangers took position in front of the inbound queue, checking passes and providing instructions. About twenty people formed a group to the rangers' rear, delaying their tour until the boat fully emptied. The others investigated the dockage area briefly, either drifting towards Building 64 or beyond the old guard tower on the western end. Matt returned to the shack and found Chris sitting quietly with Emily, now fully awake.

"Dad . . ."

Chris interrupted, "You see, Matt? It never ends."

Matt bent down to shake Emily's hand. "Good morning, Miss Hungry. I am pleased to meet you! My name is Mister Matt."

"The Funny Man has come to breakfast," Chris laughed.

"You mind if I take her with me to the gift shop? Someone has to stay here with the dog until I return."

Apprehensive, Chris acquiesced and looked down at his daughter. "If that's okay with Em."

Emily nodded and took Matt's hand. Chris secured the door behind them while Snickers whimpered. Making their way across the parade grounds, Matt and Emily entered the walkway between Building 64 and the main prison. At the end was the well-stocked gift shop.

"Not too much, sweetie. We'll have a big meal later."

Emily reluctantly nodded, snatching a green-colored soda out of the cooler and a marshmallow cookie treat. Matt grabbed two bottles of water and two bags of potato chips. While doing so, a small display next to the front counter caught his eye.

Perfect.

Emily placed her items on the counter, as did Matt. After doing so, he stepped in front of the counter's display, took one more item, and placed it on the counter.

"That will make it $17.45," said the cashier.

Matt reached into his back pocket and retrieved a damp wallet. His money was still soaked, and he noticed that the cashier was somewhat intrigued by the wet $20 bill in her hand.

"We had a small accident before departing the docks."

"You fell in the bay?"

"No," Matt improvised. "Restroom."

Her eyes went wide, and she dropped the bill on the counter.

"No, no . . ." Matt laughed. "The sink. It's just water."

She pursed her lips and delicately pinched the twenty, placed it under cash drawer, and withdrew Matt's change. "$2.55. Thanks."

Matt and Emily climbed back towards the parade grounds. Avoiding the foghorn, they detoured through the residential ruins and then down to the shack. Matt opened the door and handed a bottle of water and a bag of chips to Chris. He tossed them down his throat while Emily made short work of her cookie and soda. Snickers begged and Matt obliged with an occasional chip, as did Chris.

"Speaking of which, what are we going to do about him?" Chris asked.

Matt finished his bag, handing the last of it to Snickers. Holding up his index finger as if to say, *wait a minute*, he reached into his front pants pocket and withdrew the nylon leash they bought in the convenience store the day before. Carefully, he fastened one end to the Snickers' collar, and then tied the opposite end to the other side of the collar in an anchor hitch knot, making a loop across the dog's shoulders. Matt stood up and retrieved the item purchased from the gift shop from of his front shirt pocket—dark sunglasses. He confidently slid them on his face and took Snickers by the leash's loop. "Voila!"

"Genius," said Chris.

"Like it?"

Emily furled her brow. "I don't understand."

"Mister Matt is now our sightless friend, and the blind, as you know, sometimes use a seeing-eye dog."

Matt practiced with Snickers outside the shack to make sure he would play the part. "He must have been a service dog in a former life. He's perfect! Let's go."

Chris finished his chips and gulped a mouthful of water. Before finishing the bottle, he looked down at Snickers. With a brief sigh, he knelt, cupping his hand to receive the water he started pouring. Snickers shook his head as if to thank him and eagerly lapped up the water as fast as Chris poured it.

Matt looked down the empty path heading towards the prison's southwestern end.

"We should blend in from the back. If for some reason the cashier is in front of the store or notices me pass, they'll know something's up. Okay?"

"What time is it?"

"About 9:30. We have a good hour to kill before our boat arrives."

As they ambled along the southwestern pathway, Matt struggled to maintain his charade, and Chris often caught him looking.

"Stop moving your head."

"What?"

"Stop turning your head, Matt.; you're supposed to be blind, remember?"

"Oh. Right. Easy to forget."

They continued down the path along the edge of a jagged cliff. Down below, a deafening hoard of cormorants roosted along the boulders. Matt preferred the foghorn up the hill, he thought. The trail terminated after Baker Beach at the end of the laundry building. To the right was an old staircase leading up to the recreation yard.

"We should probably climb up there and be seen with other visitors," said Chris. "This way . . ."

"I can see it for myself."

"No you *can't*, Matt! Play the part, okay?"

The four ascended the steep staircase leading to a doorway in the southwestern side of the old recreation yard. A few tourists sat at the far end, narrowly avoiding the few concrete tiers that were scattered, covered, and splattered with decades -old cormorant guano. A staircase to the right of the tiered seating led to yet another hallway, then up a stairway to the main prison level. Matt guided Snickers just to the left of the doorway at the top of the staircase and sat on the top tier next to the exit.

"We should wait for a few minutes. I don't want anyone taking a close look at this makeshift harness. When the time comes, we'll walk directly across and down to the docks."

"Ewww!" Emily shouted.

"What?"

"Snickers is sticking his nose in the bird poop."

Matt looked down and yanked on the harness. "No!"

"Matt, stop looking."

"What is this place?" Emily finally asked.

Chris never thought to tell her. "It's an old prison for extremely bad people."

"How bad?"

"The worst. Murderers, thieves, and other lawbreakers. Particularly, escape artists. This was a maximum-security prison. The worst people from the worst prisons were sent here."

"What did they do *here*?" Emily pointed at the empty yard below.

"They were allowed to come here and see the sun, maybe play some games, or just sit here like us and talk with other prisoners. It was considered a privilege."

Emily struggled to repeat the word. "Privel-ige. What is that?"

"A privilege is something you get to do, but only if you're good and earned the permission to do it; for example, talking on your phone."

Emily turned around with wide-open eyes, and sulked as she remembered she no longer had a phone, nor anyone to call. Chris suddenly realized he accidentally threw salt in her wounds and tried to make amends.

"You will have another. Maybe a cell phone this time."

Chris was happy that he could still coax a smile from her, even if it was half-hearted. She understood that emotion more than any other, it seemed. He figured a phone's benefits outweighed the potential health hazards, so long as Emily used it in moderation. He recalled a story involving a neighbor who ran into trouble with their homeowner's association because his daughter racked up $4,700 in data charges. "But no internet or texting."

"Aw, man!" Emily's grimaced.

"So get her an unlimited plan," said Matt, growing fidgety. "I don't know how much more of those screaming birds I can take. They weren't doing it this morning."

"Then let's go. We'll take our time."

Matt resumed his act, grabbing Snickers' harness, and awkwardly standing up. After climbing another stairway, they entered Alcatraz's dining hall. The floor was old and spent. All surfaces, were hard and cold, reflective of the prison's persona. When the room was fully occupied, there were many bodies to soak up the sound. Voices of passing visitors created a ghostly wash of reverb. With no intimate knowledge of one of the toughest former penal facilities in the nation, the deserted spaces echoed every visitor's curiosity. Continuing, they made their way into the shower room. Intrigued, Emily spoke up.

"What is *this* place?"

"This is where they bathed," said Chris.

Puzzled, Emily continued looking around the room for shower stalls. Chris noticed her reaction, anticipating the result. "They took showers out in the open. Many at the same time. No place to hide from the guards, understand?"

"They could *see* each other?" Emily gasped.

"Naturally."

"Uh uh, not me!"

Matt chimed in. "Don't do bad things and you won't end up in a place like this."

"Exactly." Chris nodded.

They turned around a corner and the main cellblocks revealed themselves. Chris ushered them to a specific area to make another point with Emily.

"D-Block," he said.

Gazing upwards and outwards, they saw three levels—dozens of cells. The chambers on the bottom were dark, fronted by thick steel doors with grated steel mesh protecting small windows. Just behind those doors were more doors and they were solid, allowing no light when closed. Emily wondered at these tiny rooms.

"They could take showers in *there,*" she said. "Nobody would see them."

"These rooms are for absolute the worst people, Em. They were not allowed to come out for days at a time. Sometimes weeks or even months—not even to eat, and certainly not to go outside. Solitary confinement. If they were really bad, they weren't allowed to see the light of day. They would close that rear door and turn off the lights—total blackness. It's similar to when I send you to your room, except there's nothing to do, you can't see anything, and you don't get to come back out."

Emily shivered. "Umm, let's keep moving."

Matt noticed a tour group entering from the other end and, preferring no scrutinization, obtained Chris' attention without leery appearances.

"The next cellblock sounds bigger. Let's go."

Chris looked down the block and spotted a female ranger, probably the same one from this morning he thought, leading a group of about twenty people through the entrance at the opposite end. He overheard her explaining the Oriental Cell and its brutal history, breaking the toughest convicts by stripping them down and locking them away in its cold, barren darkness.

They walked over to the main cellblock to comingle with the fifty or so loose visitors exploring the four-story open interior. The cells still housed their original porcelain sinks, toilets, and fold-up shelves for sitting, writing, and storage. The cots, however, were removed. One cell had been meticulously restored to the prison's heydays of the 1930s when Al Capone was incarcerated for tax evasion. Emily's eyes grew wide when she realized how little space these people had.

"Matt, what time is it?" Chris asked.

"You want me to look at my watch *here*? With all these people staring at Snickers as it is? I shouldn't even be *wearing* a watch."

Chris stepped over and discreetly removed the watch from Matt's wrist. "10:07. We should probably make for the docks, right?"

"Right. If we miss our boat, it will be another hour before the same one returns."

Passing dozens of visitors on their way out of the Cellhouse, only a few paid any attention to Snickers. If anything, they smiled in approval. Winding past the last cells, around the visitation room and the warden's office, they finally found the exit to the stairway that led to the docks. A ranger stationed on its decking glared at them and walked over.

"That's a nice animal you have there, sir."

Matt turned towards the ranger's direction and made sure to not lead with his eyes.

"Thank you. His name is Snickers."

"Ah, nice."

As the ranger bent down to pet the dog, he detected something slightly out of place.

"His rabies tag is expired, you know."

Matt was relieved that it wasn't about the harness, but he was confused as to what to say.

"What? We visited our vet just last week and they told me he was up to date. Had no reason to distrust them. Damnit! That's the last time this happens." He turned to Chris. "Can you believe this?"

"Not the first time," said Chris. "Remember that convenience store clerk who tried to hand you a one-dollar bill instead of a ten?"

"Yeah. Complete jackass. Look, I'm very sorry Mister . . ."

"Ranger Evans, sir." He continued scratching Snickers behind the ears.

"Ranger! Goodness. My sincerest apologies. I can assure you he's had the shots. They made me restrain him while they did it. I felt him wince."

"Oh—I believe you, sir." The ranger stood back up. "By the way, there's a ramp a few paces behind you if the stairs are too much trouble."

"Thank you. Snickers tends to rush a bit on stairs."

"Don't forget to hit the bookstore on your way out; the proceeds help maintain the park."

"Will do."

"Thank you," Chris added. "Emily, say thank you to the nice ranger."

"Thank you."

The ranger smiled and disappeared inside the prison.

Matt exhaled deeply. "Jesus, let's just get out of here."

The walkway hairpinned its way down the sheer embankment separating the main prison from Building 64.

Matt peeked under his rims. "Don't see any ferries yet. If you need to use the restroom, now's the time. When you get back, I'll go. Just hold Snickers."

Chris brought Emily to the ladies' restroom door. "I will meet you back here. Don't take too long; we don't want to miss our boat."

She nodded and went inside. Moments later, Chris traded with Matt and took over Snicker's leash. The same female ranger from the earlier tour descended the stairwell near the restroom entrances and couldn't resist petting the dog.

"He's adorable!" She said, bending down to scratch behind Snicker's ears. "Probably not a good idea to take him in the restrooms, huh?"

Chris attempted to make his excuse seem logical. "Not really. Canes and astute hearing work better in there."

"I bet. What's the case for?"

Chris tensed up for a moment, realizing that his attaché case probably seemed out of place. Plenty of tourists were wearing backpacks, but none carried briefcases. "I'm doing research for a lecture and my computer is in there."

"Lecture? You a professor?"

"Sort of. Technical advisor in silicon."

"No shortage of *those* around here. Do you mind if I have a look? We can't be too sure these days."

"Not at all, but if you turn on the laptop, I'll need an NDA."

The ranger glared up at Chris with a dry expression as she knelt to open the case. A pair of patterned boxers covering the thin laptop.

"Oh, that's cute!" The ranger looked at Chris and batted her eyelids a few times too often. "And the computer fine." Laughing, she closed the case.

Chris pretended to giggle along. "Wait," he said, "What's so funny?"

"Well, take care big fella." The young ranger patted Snickers on the head and went into the gift shop.

Chris breathed another sigh of relief. Emily returned ready to go. Matt soon followed.

"Where are your sunglasses?" Chris asked.

"Oops! Right." Matt reached back into his front shirt pocket for the sunglasses and took Snickers' harness back in hand. "Come on. Let's get to those docks."

From the front side of Building 64, they traveled down the stairway to find only a handful of tourists waiting to leave.

"That's too bad," said Matt.

"Why?"

"I could have seen more, first trip here and everything. The place kinda fascinates me."

"Really? Which part?"

"The stories on the wall placards. Capone, the Birdman . . ."

"Sure it wasn't the shower room?"

"Oh, *funny*. Look! Here comes our ride."

Gradually, the triple-decker ferry, *Alcatraz Esteem*, slipped into the front dock on its starboard side. The crew jumped out, roped the dock cleats, and handily attached the small gangplank, allowing hundreds of fresh visitors to debark. Minutes later, the operator walked over to the front railing that was pinning the small queue of twenty or so departing visitors.

One of the ferry's mates took a long look at Snickers. "You guys must have been on the first boat because I would have remembered this cutie-pie."

Snickers was reluctant to hop on the metal gangplank, spooked by the previous night's boat ride. He whimpered and whined, so Matt disciplined him and then asked for help across the slowly pitching ramp.

The mate quickly nudged Snickers in the correct direction, allowing Matt to continue onto the boat. "This happens almost every time," he said.

Chris and Emily landed on the ferry's main deck. "I don't doubt it," said Chris.

Staying on the inside, Matt sat on a bench towards the back of the boat, well away from the bulk of the other guests who typically went for the top deck to get a better view. Chris and Emily took their seats.

"ETA is ten minutes," Chris said. "After last night, it will seem like nothing."

Emily leaned against him the same way she did that morning—exhausted and hungry. She yawned as the ferry chopped its way to Pier 33, just two docks over from the calamity of the previous night.

"We're going to need a car," said Matt.

"What about a rental?"

"Come on, man! You have to use identification for that, not to mention a credit card."

"You mean we need to *steal* a car."

"Right."

"And how do you propose we do that?"

"Eating bugs and kicking ass . . . tail" —Matt reminded himself that Emily was within earshot— "aren't the only combat survival skills taught to special ops. Problem is, we have to find a car that's already open. I prefer not to break windows. Draws attention. When we get to the main parking lot, we'll just test some doors."

"And then what?"

"I'll show you a trick."

Esteem docked and the operator soon extended its gangplank. Chris stood up and Matt grabbed him by the arm.

"Hang on a minute. Let them go ahead so we don't accidentally select one of their cars and get caught in the act."

"Good point."

By four minutes, the majority had departed the ferry. Matt motioned and they stood up, walking towards the ramp. Sensing solid ground, Snickers was eager to get off the boat.

"Settle down, Snick." Matt yanked on the harness.

Nobody in the exiting throng paid attention to him as they departed the docks, walking towards The Embarcadero.

"Matt, there's hardly any parking here, I forgot. We'll have to go down the street. I know of a larger lot and it's less exposed."

"What about that garage over there?"

"Wouldn't it be manned?"

"Only at the gate. Most people will have the ticket on the dash too."

"Fair enough. Let's go!"

As soon as they rounded the corner past the parking in the ferry terminal area, Matt stalled to straighten Snicker's leash and remove his sunglasses.

"Much better. Look! The Lord blesseth me, for I can see again!"

"Halleluiah!" Chris shouted as Emily giggled.

"Ooh—that actually hurt a bit." Matt put the glasses back on.

Entering the parking garage, the first floor was in full view of the ticketing kiosk. Matt made a quick assessment, noticing the attendant's viewpoints and the camera positions on the floors above that appeared on his security monitor. By the luminescent glow, the attendant was too busy texting and barely lifted his head as the group walked past.

Matt pointed upwards. "Let's take the stairs. The second floor's camera only displays the first dozen or so spaces."

They reached the last step and walked past the first ten parking spaces. Matt turned around. "Okay . . . my trick will work on just about any modern car, but we need to find is one that's open. It may be difficult since most people make sure their car is locked, but we can try. Miss Emily?"

"Yes."

"Lift up or pull on the door handles of each car—all of them. Just run down this line of cars here and test the handles. If one opens, quietly come get me or your father. Understand?"

Emily excitedly nodded and ran off. Chris selected his row and so did Matt, who had to work a little slower due to Snickers' leash and a dull throbbing behind his left shoulder. Seconds passed and nothing. At the other end of the row, they regrouped.

"Okay, we have two more floors, so let's get up there," Matt said.

At the top of the next stairwell, they traced around the camera's view. The security guard was still preoccupied with his phone and never took notice.

Chris tapped Emily's shoulder. "Same job, be fast."

Matt walked over to the third row and started pulling handles. Chris plowed through every prospect on the second row, reached the end, and started working Matt's row from the other direction. He was at the third car before noticing someone climbing out of a sedan between him and Matt. Chris stopped cold, but she gave him little attention. As the older woman made two attempts to roll out of her driver's seat, Emily's voice echoed from the opposite side of the garage.

"Found it!"

Chris looked over at the woman and shrugged his shoulders. "Forgot where I parked."

Walking rapidly towards Emily's direction, Matt arrived the same time as Chris.

"You're becoming quite the excuse-maker."

"Yeah. Sickening, isn't it?" Chris replied.

"Oh no."

"What's the matter, Matt? She found one. Get busy!"

"I can't believe it. You guys must have a thing for ugly."

"What?"

"I *hate* those! They're even uglier than a VW Thing, or those Scion boxes from a few years ago!"

"It's not that bad, Matt. Besides we don't have much choice."

"Ugh! It's what you'd expect to find in a design studio equipped only with a ruler and a box of Crayolas. And people buy this crap!"

Matt drooped his head in shame, noticing his reflection in the bright orange paint of a Pontiac Aztek.

You've got to be kidding me.

Chris and Emily dumped their bags in the rear, then hopped into their seats. Matt reluctantly crawled into the driver's seat and looked around in disgust.

"All right, Mister Matt. We're all dying to see your fantastic magic trick."

"Give me a second for the nausea to recede."

Matt analyzed the controls briefly before initiating his sequence. First, he switched the wipers to their fastest intermittent setting. He pressed the driver's door lock button four times, the right-rear window up button twice, pressed and released the brake pedal once, and then he bumped the turn signal indicator down twice, then up once. The lights on the instrument cluster illuminated, indicating a pre-starting condition. Matt turned to Emily in the back seat and winked one eye before pressing the washer button at the end of the turn signal stalk. The engine started without hesitation.

Chris' jaw dropped halfway down his chest in disbelief and Emily blurted out a quick "Yay! Can we go eat now? I'm starving!"

Chris turned around, "You're always hungry, but we can't eat just yet." Turning to Matt, he continued, "Obviously, I see *how* you did that, but I'm curious on the background. Does it work for *all* makes?"

"Yep, pretty much. From the time they first installed ignition computers, manufacturers secretly programmed back-door coding in case of a national emergency. If the military found themselves in need of transportation, they don't have time to ask permission or hunt down keys. Of course, you can imagine they don't just go around telling everyone. We don't use it unless we absolutely have to, and only the top clearances are briefed."

Chris reclined. "Incredible. It makes perfect sense, but if it ever got out . . ."

"High profile grand theft galore." Matt adjusted the rearview. "I've been told of a few that quit just for that reason. You lift a couple high-end models and that GS-12 pay looks like chump change."

"Ever done this before?"

"No . . . well, only simulated."

Matt removed the parking slip from the dash and examined it. "This is four days old. Well, that's good news. I bet the owners are off on a cruise. They won't be missing this crate for at least a few more days."

Matt sped down to the first level and stopped at the attendant's booth. While donning his new sunglasses, he handed the parking slip to the attendant before he got a good look at his face. The attendant never made eye contact. In fact, he never bothered.

"It's sixteen dollars."

Matt looked over to Chris and held out his hand. Chris hurriedly dug in his pocket and pulled out a twenty. Matt gave the attendant Chris' twenty, received the change, and handed it to Chris.

"You have money, why me?" Chris asked as they pulled away.

"I remembered mine is still soaking wet from last night. I don't want to give him anything *else* to remember."

"What do you mean by that?"

Matt sarcastically laughed as he made a left turn out of the garage, heading northwest. "Wait . . . you're not kidding."

Salen

Bouncing along the Golden Gate, Matt broke his fixated gaze across the bay—Alcatraz hazy and looming in the distance as if a mirage.

"We're not safe here. Reno would be better," he said.

Chris blankly stared at the traffic ahead while Emily rediscovered her music pacifier. Once plugged in, she ignored everything outside her bubble, including her insatiable appetite.

"Wouldn't the secondary roads be more desirable?" Chris asked.

"This is hiding in plain sight." Matt nodded towards the midmorning traffic. "We should stay on the interstates so we're not sticking out so much with this clown car. I mean, *really.*"

"Okay, okay, it's not the perfect car, I get it. Beggars can't be . . . And how are we going to accomplish this?"

"What?" Matt asked.

"Driving across the country. Are we taking turns or driving straight through? Are we stopping each night? How?"

"If we stay on the highways and take turns, it'll take two days. If we stop each night, it will take at least three."

"Why don't we stop tonight, get a good rest, and then drive straight through. I don't know about you, but Alcatraz left me with an aching neck."

Matt paused and briefly recalled the night before, trying to decide which was worse—the shoulder pain or that damned foghorn. "Okay, but not in a small town. Not with this pumpkin."

"Yeah, yeah. I get it already! We need to stop soon for lunch. Someone will be hitting the alarm soon."

"Ah, yes, Miss Hungry. Well, Vallejo might fit the bill. Multiple restaurants surround the amusement park there."

"Not literally *stop*, I meant a drive-thru. The further we get away from San Francisco, the better."

"Reno then?"

"Sounds good."

● ● ●

"Only two, sir."

"Which two?"

"Our two, sir."

Teeth grating, a higher-ranking officer reviewed video footage of a crane slowly hoisting *Sa Ya Nora* off Chris' crushed Volkswagen and two flattened piles of red and black pulp to either side of it.

"So, they're alive and in possession of the device."

A senior analyst turned from his monitor. "That is the assumption, sir."

"Splendid. Have surveillance resume their sweep."

"What about Jacobson's key, sir?"

"Not yet. He'll materialize soon enough, but we need to expedite it."

"And what about our men, sir?"

"Standard protocol. They ceased being ours the moment they failed. Issue a Directive 3 for Jacobson."

The lieutenant removed his cobalt blue beret. "Yes sir."

Continuing to massage the receding hairline just above his right temple, Colonel Carl Osterhoudt acknowledged the full impacts of their escalating concern. Classified operations in covert wars were nothing new to him. Having secretly survived the Mogadishu '93 debacle and used for barter by Mohammed Aidid, his soul remained an ethical dichotomy. The difference this time was the possible ramifications if this operation failed.

Osterhoudt remembered what it was like to be a field operative, and he craved thoughts of a return, but that was almost a decade ago. Now, he had a manufactured family and a large estate surrounded by so-called colleagues in their DC suburb enclave off Persimmon Tree Road—The Congressional Country Club a stone's throw away. If he were to jeopardize this one somehow, he knew the consequences. Begrudgingly, he obeyed his implicit orders: Locate and recover Doctor Christopher Miller and his device—spare no resources. Under no circumstances was discovery acceptable. Jacobson is disposable.

Why was this so damned important?

"Sir?"

"What is it?"

"You're ordered to depart for Travis immediately, sir."

Osterhoudt stood up straight and took a deep breath. "Finally."

● ● ●

"Dad, look!" Emily shouted from the rear cargo area. Her music player's charger was plugged in to an AC power receptacle on the rear side panel. "I can recharge!"

Chris turned around and noticed Snickers displaced and shivering in the rear floorboard. "That's great, hon. Don't you think Snickers should have his seat back? And get your seatbelt back on!"

She had forgotten all about him, and when she wiggled her way back and buckled her seatbelt, Snickers met eyes with her. He appeared sad and shook nervously, wondering why Emily wouldn't allow his head on her lap.

Chris tapped her knee. "When you complete charging, I want you to take the laptop out of my case and put it to charge. Can you do that for me?"

"Yep." Emily nodded and continued bobbing to her tunes.

Matt navigated the Pontiac around the capacious San Pablo Bay to the city of Ignacio, then onto Highway 37, eastward. With little entertainment, the lifeless landscapes sent Chris directly to slumberland. Several minutes passed and Emily noticed her father resting comfortably with his head drooping to the right. Her music player chimed in her earbuds, indicating a full charge. Following her father's instructions, she opened his attaché case, removed the computer and its charger, and placed both on her lap. Connecting the power adapter to the rear of the computer, she turned around again, almost standing as she reached to insert the plug into the power receptacle. She turned back around and discovered a tiny red light blinking on a top corner of the laptop. She wondered if she dare tempt the rage of her father, or worse, the wrath of the monster that possibly lurked inside. Emily frightened easily like most young girls. Unlike most young girls, her curiosity impulses often surpassed theirs. It was a cat-like nature to which Emily was predisposed, and probably the reason she loved horror movies. Chris occasionally wondered if he was nurturing something nefarious, but her happiness meant so much more.

After unplugging the earbuds from her music player and plugging them into the laptop, Emily held its power button down for three seconds. The screen lit and the boot sequence began. Fearing discovery, she looked at her father to make sure he was still asleep. The dynamics of road construction interrupted his occasional snoring, but not enough to wake him. Emily watched the boot sequence, then the transition to the opening prompt of her Father's program. "Awaiting input…" flashed. Taking it a step further, Emily looked around the case to try and understand what the prompt meant. Clicking her cursor around the screen had no effect until she managed to select the filter tray's actuator. It popped out the left side of the machine. Emily immediately covered her mouth in a muted squeal, cramming the filter door back into the laptop. Everything looked normal to her. She sighed. The program suddenly changed screens.

The signature bright white flashes flickered and gave way to a staticky scene of an old woman fussing with an elderly man as they drove down hectic urban street. As soon as the vision appeared, it disappeared into the static, and again to the white flashes. Emily glanced up at her father, making sure he was still asleep. A car passed on the other side of the interstate with its horn apparently stuck. Emily didn't notice that the bright white flashes continued with occasional static dancing across the screen. Matt, distracted by the horn, didn't notice the Aztek's battery gauge's slow ascent past 14 volts, then 16, then 18. Emily's full attention returned to the laptop when she began to feel the painful burn in her ears she experienced only once before. It instantly became unbearable. She grabbed the wires, but they were already so hot, the insulating plastic melted in her hands and burned a solid red line down both of her palms. Emily screamed at the top of her lungs.

"What?" Chris yelped, awake and dazed.

Matt swerved abruptly, almost losing control. The Aztek's horn spontaneously blasted, and Matt couldn't make it stop. Chris swung around to Emily, saw what was going on, and yanked the earbuds from the computer. He grabbed the laptop from Emily's hands and attempted to shut it down. Snickers barked wildly at it.

"EMILY!" Chris yelled. "Emily, wake up!" He shook her arms.

The horn suddenly stopped as Emily came to. She flung the wires out of her ears in disgust. The laptop's display finally doused itself in black and Chris turned to Emily, predictably angered.

"Did I say to play with this? This is *not* a toy, understand?"

"Yes sir."

Matt looked at the car's instrument cluster. "That's funny."

Chris turned his head back around. "Now what?"

"The voltage gauge! —was nearly pinned at the top. Coming down now."

"What does that mean?"

"Spike of some kind. Maybe had to do with charging or something. Who knows. These cars have a lot of tricks, but I've heard a lot of flaky stories too. Hardware bugs, electrical . . . you know."

"Well, it seems kind of odd with the timing. Maybe something to do with the internal inverter?"

"That would be my guess, too. For now, just keep the laptop off of it."

Chris looked back towards his daughter. "Not a problem."

Emily was stunned and exhausted. Another nightmare. She kept the earbuds off and stared into the comatose world outside. Flat marshes and high-tension power transmission towers stretched into oblivion.

Matt eventually crossed over the Napa River and back into civilization at Vallejo.

"Chris, wake up."

He yawned, rubbed his eyes, and examined the landscape. "Are we close to the park?"

"Not sure."

"It's rather large. You couldn't miss it. We typically arrive from the other side of the bay, so this doesn't look familiar. Wait, there's 39. Yeah, stay on 39. It's around the next bend."

"Okay."

"There. Get off at Exit 20."

"Roger that."

Chris looked back to Emily, who was coldly staring out of her window. "Hungry, sweetheart?"

She looked at her father with wide-open pupils, disheveled, but gesturing. Snickers, sensing a change due to the conversation and the car's deceleration, jumped up, flapped his ears, and started sniffing around. Hair storm. Matt casually made a right at the end of the offramp.

"Take the next left between the hotel and that gas station. I believe some restaurants are back there," said Chris.

They drove past the amusement park's roller coasters, and then made the left Chris suggested. Matt stopped in front of a sandwich shop next to the gas station.

"We can't leave Snickers in the car while we eat, so just get something to go. I want to keep moving anyway."

"What do you want?"

"A turkey club if they have it, or a chicken something or another. Chips and a soda. One with a *lot* of caffeine. Maybe an energy drink for later."

"Are you sure? I thought about taking a turn after this."

"Daddy, come on!"

"Can't siesta yet. I need to stay fully alert until we get out of this state."

"No problem."

Chris and Emily disappeared inside the sandwich shop as Matt enticed Snickers out for a walk by displaying his leash. As soon as Snickers saw it, he jumped outside, sat, and wagged his tail in anticipation of a stroll. Matt snapped the leash onto his collar, and they walked to a grassy area just behind the gas station. Snickers finished, and Matt ushered him to the back seat then eased the Pontiac over to the gas station. In a flash of intense anxiety, Chris exited the sandwich shop and lost sight of the car. It didn't take much longer than a split second to relocate their blazon chariot by the gas pumps. Matt finished refueling and restarted the engine with his classified defense maneuver. Chris and Emily climbed inside and launched into their long-awaited meals.

Chris opened his sack of groceries and turned to Emily. "The store actually sells dry dog food, so Snickers can have a small snack after you finish. Can you handle that?"

She almost threw up in her mouth remembering the last time she fed the dog.

"No!"

"Oh, come on, Em."

"He's going to barf on me!"

"Not this time. The food is different, and you're only going to give him a little bit until we get to a hotel."

Emily grunted as she nibbled on her sandwich. Snickers panted heavily looking at Emily while she ate.

"No!" She pushed him away.

Snickers cowered and shrank into the floorboard behind Chris' seat, never taking his eyes off her sandwich.

Matt entered the I-80 ramp, heading east towards Sacramento. Chris polished off his sandwich and dug into his chips. Emily's face was dripping with a meatball sub's tomato sauce she couldn't wipe while playing keepaway from the dog. Matt settled onto a long interstate straightaway and dove into his turkey club.

"Daddy, I need you to open this." Emily held up a small bag of dog food.

Chris stripped away its seal and handed it back to Emily with the top opened. She scooped a small handful and held it near Snicker's mouth. Without further prompting, the dog voraciously gormandized it. Emily recoiled in fear of losing her hand.

"Hey! Slow down, dog!"

Snickers glanced up at her, wagging his tail and expecting more food. She grabbed another handful, but this time she tossed the kibbles beside him on the seat. The pellets scattered, but the dog managed to locate each one no matter how deep it went into the seat's recesses.

"Emily, don't do that. You're going to get the back seat filthy and sticky from his saliva."

"He almost ate my hand!"

"Do you see that little handle on the seat next to you? Yank on it real hard; it'll pull down."

Emily examined it for a moment, pushed Snickers backwards a tad, and yanked down on the strap. An armrest fell down revealing two separate cup holders.

Chris turned to have a look. "Perfect, they're both waterproof. Okay Em, place some of the food in one of the holes. He can eat from that without making too much of a mess. When he finishes, pour some water in the other hole."

Snickers swiftly dispatched the small amount of food from the cup holder. Chris handed her an open bottle of water and she poured some into the other holder. Snickers quietly lapped it up, but since he was facing Emily's direction, she was becoming soaked. Turning her head away and holding up her paper napkin as a shield, she winced each time a cold droplet struck her legs.

"UGH!"

The dog continued until all the water was gone, and then he sat up to look out the window. Matt hit a switch on his door panel, opening Snicker's window just enough so that the dog could poke his head out and inhale the world. Hair storm. Emily closed the armrest, turned sideways, and propped her legs on the seat. She stared at Snickers enjoying the rush of wind and wondered what he smelled. Chris finished his chips, laughing at Matt struggling with his one-handed sandwich.

Skirting around the north side of Sacramento, they headed into the mountains of the northern Sierra Nevada range inside Tahoe National Forest. The drone of the engine would normally put everyone to sleep if it wasn't for the constant changes in elevation and direction. In little more than an hour, the sun faded, and the dim hues of Reno came into view.

Chris raked through his scalp and sat up. "What's the game plan?"

Matt set his turn signal to pass a noisy Lincoln. "Never been to Reno before, so not much of a plan. Maybe some cheap hotel that's not too far off the road. That's all we need. You said you've been here. Any help?"

Chris stuttered, "I'm, uh, afraid I can't remember the details."

Downtown Reno arrived quickly, and the Maple Street exit materialized soon after. Chris noticed the brightest lights just off his right side.

"Take this exit and let's see what the town is like. It should only take a minute," Chris said.

Matt hit the offramp onto Maple and then made a right heading down Virginia Street. In moments, they entered the casino strip—The Row, Circus Circus, Silverado, Eldorado . . .

"Look at this, Emily." Chris pointed to a large archway that said *Reno – The Biggest Little City in the World.*

"Why does it say that?"

"It's called an oxymoron, Em."

"A what?"

"Something that contradicts itself. Small town, but big city amenities—like San Francisco, or in this particular case, Las Vegas."

"I don't think this is a great location," Matt said. "Too far away from the road and too crowded."

Chris rolled down his window. "Everything in Reno is basically on this strip—I remember that much."

Matt stopped at the next red light, and Chris snagged the attention of a young couple about to cross in front. "Excuse me, are you from here?"

The couple gestured they were not. A tattered vagrant who was leaning against a corner behind them spoke up.

"I am."

"Are there additional hotels outside of town?"

"Which side?"

"Umm. The east side—off the interstate."

"'Fraid not. Not much there 'cept warehouses and the train depot. This is the main drag for hotels, young man."

He stepped forward and held his hand out.

Chris rummaged for a small, folded bill and slipped it to him.

"Much obliged," replied the old-timer.

The light changed and Matt sought a place to turn around.

Chris rolled up his window. "I guess this isn't *that* far from the interstate."

"Yeah, I know. I'm just wondering about logistics and the dog. I imagine most of the tourists around here travel without their pets."

"High probability, yes."

Matt found a modestly sized hotel and parked the car in front of the lobby. Chris hopped out and went inside. Only a few seconds passed before he opened the door, shaking his head negatively.

"They said that the only place that allows pets is that huge resort down the street. Said they have their own kennel."

"Perfect."

Matt drove them down the street and into the resort's valet area. A parking attendant scrambled to his window.

"Parking, sir?"

"No thanks. We may not be staying."

"Oh." The valet gestured towards a few spaces on the other side of entry. "Would you mind pulling over there, sir?"

"No problem."

Chris jogged inside to the lobby's check-in queue and waited for an available reservationist. The wait was short.

"May I help you?"

"Yes. We need a room. Two adults, one child, one dog. What's the rate?"

"We have a special with two double beds for $49 plus taxes and the Resort Fee."

"How much is that?"

"$49."

"So $98 plus taxes."

"Yes. By policy, your pet must overnight in our kennel resort. This is free with your room so long as he has an updated license. You are responsible for walking it until 11 p.m., at which time the kennel closes until 5:30 a.m. There is a designated pet area to the side of the parking garage."

"We are from California. Is that going to be a problem?"

"We'd be out of business if it was," she grinned.

"Nice."

"Your name?"

"Chris Miller."

"Okay, Mister Miller. I will need your credit card and driver's license."

Icy tingles went down Chris' spine, remembering what Matt told him about tracking. Pursing his lips, he grinded on how to proceed.

"Sir?"

Chris copped a slightly condescending tone. "You take cash, don't you?"

"Yes, for payment. The room must be reserved with a credit card for incidentals."

"I see. You won't take cash for that too?"

Confused, since she had never encountered a card refusal, the clerk summoned her manager. "Roger, please come to the desk."

A moment later, the reservations manager appeared from a rear doorway.

The clerk gestured in Chris' direction. "This customer wishes to secure his room with *cash*. He doesn't have a credit card."

The manager whispered into her ear, to which she responded with astonishment. He raised half his monobrow and turned to Chris.

"Sir, to confirm, you don't have a credit card and wish to secure the room with cash?"

"Yes. We had an emergency and just need a place to stay for the night. I promise we will spend some in your casino to make up for it. Please?"

After a short debate, the manager left instructions with the reservationist.

"Sir, he said we can accommodate you with a $300 cash deposit refundable minus any incidentals, and contingent upon an inspection at checkout. Is this acceptable?"

Chris breathed a sigh of relief. "Absolutely, thanks."

Chris signed off on the agreement and tendered the required funds while receiving room instructions and directions to the kennel. He strutted back out to the parking lot and slapped two door cards onto Matt's window.

"Wait. You didn't give them your debit card, did you?"

"Of course not. They accepted a $300 cash deposit."

"That's all?"

"Well, I did promise to spend some in the casino."

"We don't have money for that!"

"I know, but I think twenty dollars can be parlayed at the slots, or perhaps a low-ante blackjack table. I don't count cards, but Suzanne and I memorized the table a few years ago."

"What does that mean?"

"It means I *should* be able to hang even with the house over a period of time. Maybe better with fortuitous wagers. No guarantees though."

"I can live with that."

Chris grabbed Snicker's leash, snapped it onto his collar, and handed Matt one of the door keys.

"It's room 316. I'll be up there just as soon as I square away the dog. Emily, hand me his food please."

Emily tossed the small bag to him, and Matt sped off to the parking garage. Snickers tugged his leash all the way to the basement kennel. Once inside its lobby, he relentlessly snorted every particle in every crevice. The facility was spotless with modern suites for cats and dogs of different sizes. An attendant copied Chris' information, checked Snicker's tag, wrote down the registration number, and walked the dog back to his kennel.

So, they don't actually verify registrations, Chris observed.

"I will return in a couple hours for his walk. Thanks."

Chris headed back to the lobby and caught an elevator. Matt and Emily met him at their room's door. Matt swiped the key card through the lock mechanism and a small light on it turned green. Matt twisted the door handle.

"Emily, you and your father can take the bed closest to the window. The TV remote is over there, but don't buy anything."

"Buy?" Emily asked.

"Some channels won't be free, so be careful sweetie," said he father. "If the TV asks for money, just change channels until you find something you like."

"Okay." Emily bounced on the bed while pressing the ON button of the TV's remote.

Matt locked himself in the bathroom and stripped down. The mirror reflected his fully-cauterized shoulder. He removed the bandages and ran water in the sink to begin cleaning the freshly sewn wound. With a damp washcloth, he carefully scrubbed the dried blood away and lightly washed around the stitches. He turned the sink off and ran mildly hot water in the bath.

"Em, I'm going to go back downstairs. When Mister Matt finishes, I want you to take a shower and get ready for bed. Tell him I went down to the casino for a few minutes, and I'll be right back."

"What's a casino?"

Chris struggled to find the right definition without making his young daughter jealous, careful not to use the word, *games*.

"It's a big room full of machines that grownups use to throw away their money."

"Why? That doesn't sound very smart."

"You're right, it doesn't. I'll see you in a few minutes."

"Okay."

He closed the door behind him and slipped downstairs. Making a point to be noticed going into the casino, Chris exited the elevator and sauntered past the lobby, waving to the same reservationist from before. Once in the casino, he found an unoccupied penny poker machine, inserted a twenty, and started pressing buttons. Right away, Chris won a hand worth 20¢. Not surprisingly, he bet it all on the next hand and lost. Undeterred and with an even score, he tapped a 25¢ bet and played another hand.

Matt was satisfied with his fifteen-minute soaking and climbed out of the tub, steaming. Realizing that he could use some fresh clothing, he got dressed and considered the gift shop.

"Mister Matt, my dad wanted me to tell you he was going to be downstairs in the . . . place to lose money."

Matt chuckled and continued to put on his shoes. "He's been down there the whole time?"

Emily nodded as she lifted up her backpack to take out some clothes. "I am going to take a bath."

"That's fine. I'll go downstairs and get him. We'll be back before you finish. Remember this—do not open the door for anybody. Not a soul unless it is me or your father, understand?"

"Okie dokie." Emily shut the door behind him.

Matt left the room and went downstairs. Visiting the gift shop, he bought a couple inexpensive hotel-logoed T-shirts, one adorned with "She knows about Reno" on the front.

Uh—how redneck! There's a reason they are selling these for five bucks. With his purchase in a bag, Matt set off for the casino, quickly finding Chris betting his last 50 credits at the same machine.

"How much did we lose?"

"That's the last of a twenty, so that's okay." Chris hit the deal button. Two fives, an eight, the jack of diamonds, and the king of hearts.

"Suicide king. Hmm. Keep him and throw away everything but the two fives."

Chris turned around. "Why the king?"

"Got a feeling."

Chris removed the jack and the eight, then hit the deal button. In succession, the other fives appeared, giving him a four-of-a-kind hand and a payout of **10,000** credits.

"YES!" Chris pumped his fists.

Matt smiled. "It's only $100."

"Maybe to *you*. I never won that much in my life!"

"Well you can't say that anymore, now can you?"

"Don't rain on me!"

"Look, I bought these two shirts to get me to Washington. You can have this shirt back."

Chris smirked. "*She knows about Reno?*"

"Yeah, what about it? I bought them 'cause they were cheap."

"This town used to be the national divorce capitol. You didn't know that?"

"Let's get a drink to go. I'm ready to collapse."

"Right behind you."

Chris printed a payout slip and cashed it at an ATM, then strode over to the bar.

"Gentlemen?" The bartender looked at both men for their drink orders.

"We just want a couple beers to go." Matt said.

"We have a large selection. Anything in particular?"

Chis looked it over. "A Sierra is fine with me if you have it."

"Hmmm. I guess just a Lite," said Matt.

"Okay, a Sierra and a Lite—$7."

"Thanks."

Matt picked up his beer, handed the bartender a ten, and walked off.

"Thanks! You two have a good night."

The way the bartender inferred something in her salutation passed right over Chris' head, which wasn't at all difficult at that moment since he was still fondling the crisp $100 bill.

"Well, that helps for once," Chris said. "Do you mind taking Snickers out for his last walk? I'll stick the beer in the fridge."

Matt paused, not used to the responsibility of a dog. "No, no trouble." After handing Chris his items, he headed for the kennel.

Chris turned around and started to leave. He looked up just as a towering man, wearing an untucked white polo, jeans, high tops, and a side-cocked ball cap, got up and created a vacancy at a bustling $5 blackjack table. The dealer caught Chris' eye.

"Open seat, sir."

A half-lit, heavyset cowboy sat to the left, wearing a bone Stetson Gus, a scotch in his left hand, and a bouncy blonde around his neck.

He turned around. "You comin'?"

Pocket burning, Chris couldn't resist the green baize table and handed the dealer his Franklin. As Chris took his seat, the dealer forked over twenty $5 chips, neatly stacked. Chris looked around the table at the other player's banks. His was the smallest. The cowboy loomed over $5,200 worth in his pile by Chris' estimate. *Either lucky or a card counter . . . or just hit oil. Fracker.*

Everyone anted, and most played over the minimum. The cowboy shoved $200 worth in front him. Chris slid a single $5 chip to his ring and the dealer started working. Chris' first card? A five. The cowboy received an ace and sat back, smiling as he sipped his scotch. The dealer showed a queen and checked his other card with an electronic reader. No ace.

Second card. The player to the right sat with a 19. Next came a **10**. *Damn! Fifteen. I hate hitting on 15!* Chris started shaking his head. He was about to throw away cash and he knew it. The cowboy lamented the **10** for his own, and relaxed when the dealer flipped a king in front of him.

"That's my man!" He raised his glass to the dealer and smiled as his bimbo cheered wildly, as if she had just been plucked off a Sunday sideline.

The players to Chris' left carried marginal hands at best; a **16** and a **12**, respectively. The dealer raked $440 worth to the cowboy and returned to the man on Chris' right. Predictably, he held with the **19**. Chris paused and rolled his eyes as he tapped the felt. It was a seven, busting him.

"Comes and goes, partner." The cowboy nudged him on the shoulder. "I wouldn't be sitting here if I didn't hit the keno for $2,600 a little while ago."

The other players both hit face cards and busted. The dealer flipped his card, finally. A four. Chris sank, but the dealer wasn't finished. He dragged another card out of the shoe and turned it over. Six, and he now had twenty, beating all but the blackjack. Chris suddenly didn't feel so bad.

"How 'bout I spread some around and show you how this works." The cowboy nudged Chris' left arm again. He picked up a stack of $1 chips and placed one each on the side bet circles of each player. A matched hand to the dealer paid 30-1 odds.

"Sir, that's the last time I'll allow that," the dealer cautioned.

"Oh, it's not for me; they can keep it if they win. And, this is for you, my friend." The cowboy slid a $25 chip in gratuity to the dealer.

"I appreciate it, sir—I do." He pointed up to a camera over the table. "They don't like it."

"Gotcha." The cowboy siphoned his scotch-flavored ice.

The dealer raked in the loser's chips and reset the table for the next hand. Everyone anted the same amounts as before, except the player to Chris' right plunked down the table minimum. One by one, the cards zipped out of the shoe under the dealer's fingertips, flipped over at the last moment in front of each prospect. The player on Chris' right received a three. Chris was dealt another 10. The Cowboy received a jack, the next player an ace, a four to the stone-faced elderly woman on the far left, and the dealer scored a 10.

Second card for the player on Chris' right brought a five for a total of eight. Chris received a queen, and he breathed in relief, although the second-hand smoke started burning his eyes. The cowboy watched as another ace flipped in front of his stacks, scoring a second blackjack and another $440. Again, his blonde jumped up and down. He smiled and hollered for the nearest cocktail waitress. Before she arrived, he nudged Chris' arm once more. "You see! Fortune follows the bold."

By that time, the dealer had already flipped the two cards for the other players. A younger man to the cowboy's immediate left sat with his ace and an eight. The elderly woman now had 14. The dealer checked his hole card for blackjack using the electronic sensor. He kept the card down and shook his head, pointing to the player on Chris' right. He hit and received a queen, standing on 18. Chris passed, as did the young man. With the dealer showing a 10, the woman tapped the felt. The dealer sent her a royal massage, busting her with the king of clubs. The dealer cleared her betting square and then went to reveal his hole card—a queen.

The cowboy slapped Chris' shoulder. "Aha! I told you! 30-1!"

Chris laughed. "Makes up for the push, thanks!" Then the notion hit him. "You're right." He slid one of his $1 chips onto the cowboy's side-betting ring. "Let's test that theory one more time."

"Sir?" The dealer grimaced.

"Just returning the favor this once," Chris said.

The dealer rolled his eyes up to the camera and pursed his lips, readying another hand.

This time the betting went differently. Chris upped his ante to $25, while the cowboy reduced his to $100. The others also reduced their bets to the table's minimum, which was all the player on Chris' right could afford.

The dealer cracked his knuckles and dragged the first card out of the shoe. A five flipped over, causing the man to right to throw his arms up in disgust. Chris received an eight. The cowboy earned a deuce, the young man a jack, and the lady at the end, an ace.

"'Bout time for you, ain't it?" The cowboy laughed as he paid for his whiskey.

The lady at the end just smiled and nodded, but her eyes let everyone know she *was* excited.

The dealer turned over his first card. It was a six and he collected the cowboy's side bet. "Well, I see it ain't going to pay for me this go-round."

Second cards: The player to the right received an ace, bringing his total to six or sixteen. He just sat there and shook his head. The dealer reached for Chris' card and slid it across the table, flipping over another eight. *Eights. Aces and Eights. Dead man's cards to split, always.*

"Splitting?" The dealer pointed at Chris' hand.

"Yes." Chris picked up another stack of chips and slid it behind the second hand.

The dealer drew two more cards from the shoe. The first was a three, much to the enjoyment of the table. The dealer turned the second card over, and it was an ace, giving Chris a 19.

"Looks like easy pickins to me, fella." The cowboy earned a jack for a total of 12.

The dealer reached back for the shoe and pulled out a seven for the young man, and a lady for the lady, scoring her a blackjack. The table cheered for her as she collected $11 from the dealer, who cleared her square. The dealer pointed in front of the man to Chris' left. With the dealer showing a six, he wisely held with a 15. Chris' turn. The dealer pointed to his first hand.

"I'd like to double down." Chris picked up another $25 stack of chips and slid it next to the hand. The dealer drew a card from the shoe. It was a 10! The table clapped in victory. Any individual win was a triumph against the evil house, and they loved that. If anything, Chris would be ahead even if he lost the second hand, so when the dealer started to skip over it for the cowboy's decision, Chris interrupted, picking up another $25 in chips.

"And I'd like to double down on this hand too."

The table gasped.

"You sure, brother? Should stand on that other nineteen," said the cowboy, adjusting his hat.

Chris never flinched as he slid the chips behind his second hand. "Double please."

The dealer sighed and dragged a card from the shoe. A seven. Chris had a new total of 16 for his second hand, which looked good from his perspective.

With a 12, the cowboy asked for a card and was dealt an ace. He hit again for a five and stood on 18. The young man to his left was handed an eight, also giving him 18 to rest upon. With much anticipation, the dealer removed the hole card from his hand and flipped it over, revealing a jack for a total of 16. He was required to hit, so he reached back for a card, dragged it out of the shoe, and flipped it over. The table instantly erupted at the sight of his busting queen of hearts.

"Lovely ladies!" Shouted the cowboy, struggling to keep his hat atop his head with his bouncing blonde knocking him around in celebration. Amongst the clapping, Chris just sat and stared at the table with a fixated grin. The dealer reached for his tray and started the payouts, beginning with the young man. When he arrived at Chris' square, he counted out $100 in four stacks to match Chris' bet. Savoring his victory for a moment while the dealer finished payouts, Chris took a deep breath, stood up, and collected his winnings.

The dealer smirked. "So soon?"

Without hesitation, the cowboy reached for Chris' hand. "Smart as they come right there. Double and dash."

Chris took his hand confidently, "Well thanks, Tex. Time I mosey outta here while the gettin's good." He handed the cowboy's girlfriend the $10 profit from his side bet and flipped another $5 chip into the dealer's end on the way to the cashier.

The cowboy turned around to hug his gal. "You see that, Daphne?"

"See what? It's just a hundred dahlahs. Won't even do my nails!"

"That's not my point. I meant that's how it's done. Discipline, dadgummit!"

"Whatever you say, baby." She writhed against him with expectant eyes.

"I reckon there's a hot tub with our name on it." He spun his stool back around to the dealer. "We're outta here too, uh . . . Mike. Don't wanna miss tomorrow's breakfast, you know what I mean? Now assist me with those stacks."

Mike counted the cowboy's chips and converted them to larger denominations.

Chris collected his money from the cashier and, with an extra eighty-five springs in his step, headed upstairs. In the elevator, he suddenly noticed that the beer he was shuttling had become warmish and sweaty. He reached the hotel room, swiped his key card, and entered to find Emily on the far bed in front of the television, brushing her hair while watching a program on the Mouse Network. Turning around quickly in surprise, she appeared agitated.

"What took you so long?"

Chris glanced towards the bathroom. "Where's Mr. Matt?"

"He's not here, either."

Chris put the beer in the mini fridge's freezer, and the bag of T-shirts on Matt's bed. "I'm sorry, Em. It took a little longer than I thought. Earned us some extra money and tomorrow morning we'll have a nice big breakfast, okay?"

"I guess so. But don't do it again!"

"I promise."

Chris prepared to take a shower in the already steamed bathroom. "Mister Matt will be back here any minute. He's walking Snickers."

Emily paid her father no attention, completely fixated on her television show and her hair. Chris closed the bathroom door, dropped his clothes, and climbed into a hot shower. The water brought instant relief to his sore neck. Mesmerized, he let the water soothe him for a few extra moments before getting down to business. During this time, the bigger questions arose from the action over the past two days. Their escape was in the bag, but where were they going? Where was *he* going? For now, it didn't matter. Fatigue beclouded his mind again, making for moot logic.

Matt walked in just after Chris entered the shower, surprising Emily with a can of grape soda. "Did you brush your teeth already?"

She shook her head, "No."

"Then here." Matt handed her the soda, sat on the edge of his bed, and took off his shoes.

Chris emerged from the bathroom wrapped in a towel, rubbing the fog from his lenses. Matt held up a couple of items for Chris to see.

"Believe it or not, I found a paper road map in the lobby. Best guess is Salt Lake in six or seven hours after we leave. We'll grab a good meal, stretch the legs, then head for Cheyenne. I'll take over from there; we'll be in Chicago by the next morning."

"I like it." Chris winced as Matt reached into the refrigerator and retrieved both cans of beer.

Matt opened both and handed Chris' over. "Cheers then." Matt lifted his frail metal can and gagged instantaneously. "What the— Why is this so warm?"

Chris looked around for the ice bucket. "Took a short detour on the way here . . ."

Salen II

"Colonel, G-Com reports a facial recognition match. Tripped a link in Reno, sir."

"On screen." Osterhoudt studied the monitor capture. "That's him. Where was this taken?"

"Nevada Black Book feed, sir."

"How long ago?"

"Last night, 2321 Local, sir."

Osterhoudt checked his watch—0615. "Have they departed yet?"

"Checked out an hour ago, sir."

"Do we know what they are driving?"

"The hotel recorded their license plate, sir. Running it now. It's a late model Pontiac—" The officer sighed at the model description.

"Pontiac what, lieutenant?"

"Aztek, sir. Orange Aztek. Blaze Orange, sir."

Osterhoudt cringed. "That figures."

"The vehicle's registration appears negative, sir."

"Doesn't matter if it's stolen."

Studying the photograph, Osterhoudt opened his left-front breast flap, removed a pack of cigarettes, flipped one between his lips, and lit it.

"Sir, there's no smok—"

The colonel continued his first deep draw. "You can cry to your CO after requisitioning my transit to Wendover."

The analyst coughed. "Wendover, sir? There's nothing out there."

"That's where I need to go, so get it done."

Osterhoudt continued fogging the room, peering deep into the photo flickering on the monitor. He rubbed his temples in fathomless thoughts from the past.

● ● ●

The hotel room shuttered as Matt slammed the door, turning on the light nearest the Miller's bed. The smell of maple syrup, bacon, and coffee instantly cracked both Chris and Emily's eyes wide.

"Hey—you didn't have to do that." Chris reached for his glasses.

"I know; I wanted you to sleep longer since you're first to drive. I'll doze later. It's six and we need to get moving. I've already walked Snickers; he's standing by at the kennel."

"Wow. You did all that?"

"I got up an hour ago."

After finishing their breakfast, Chris helped Emily gather her belongings. Matt donned a fresh T-shirt after a quick shave and rinse. Chris did the same, and they made a last-minute dummy-check before leaving. Matt slipped down the stairs to fetch Snickers while Chris completed their checkout. A few moments later, Matt reappeared with the dog and escorted Emily to their vehicle.

A clerk retrieved Chris' booking. "Ah, yes, Mister Miller. I see you deposited *cash* contingent on inspection. Please allow us a few moments while we complete it. There is a bench along the wall over there if you need place to sit. This won't take a minute, sir."

The clerk summoned a porter on that floor to execute a quick inventory. Chris waited a few moments until a comment crackled over the clerk's walkie-talkie.

"Sir, it appears there is a pillow missing from your room."

"A pillow? What pillow? I didn't take any pillows!"

Chris became agitated and looked at the driveway just past the lobby's doors as Matt, Emily, and Snickers pulled up to the valet. Chris dashed out through the door and poked his head in the passenger-side window.

The clerk stood up. "Sir!"

"They said there is a pillow missing." At the same time he said it, Chris saw the pillow under Emily's head, resting against the door. "Em, you can't take that with you; that's stealing!"

"I told her it's okay," said Matt. "Blame me now, but you'll thank me later."

She looked up at her father in tears. The clerk ran outside and saw Emily crying. "Sir, we only charge $35 for pillows."

Chris paused to consider the money versus his peace-and-quiet factor. It didn't take long to absorb his daughter's tears.

Matt climbed into the front passenger's seat. "Is there a discount for two?"

Chris cut the clerk off before she had a chance to answer. "Just the one pillow, thank you."

They walked back inside and settled the bill. Matt fidgeted with the Pontiac's ergonomics until Chris trotted outside with his receipt and the $265 he recovered from the deposit. Jumping into the driver's seat, he turned around and began to lecture Emily about taking something without his knowledge, but she had already fallen asleep.

"Can't win." Chris muttered.

Matt fastened his seatbelt. "Nope."

Chris checked his mirrors while driving them out of the hotel parking lot and onto the streets of downtown Reno. Heading north to reacquire Interstate 80 eastbound, he pitted at a ramp-side convenience store for fuel and supplies. When they acquired all the provisions they felt necessary, Chris motored back onto the interstate and pointed towards Salt Lake City.

A few dozen miles ticked off the odometer before Matt broke the silence. "You know. I've probably been too harsh on this car."

"How do you mean?"

"Okay, I hate the way it looks on the outside. Hands down, it's nothing short of vomit—the chunky kind."

"Yeah, we're *all* aware of that."

"But the interior? That's another story. Rather decent actually, and it rides well for a floating cardboard box."

"Skin deep, then."

"Sort of. I just wish they made a few changes and got it right."

"That bugs you?"

"Not really. Not in the grand scheme of things, if that's what you mean."

"No."

"So why did they have to make it so, I don't know—controversial?" Matt asked.

"The style or the colors?"

"Both! It's like they went out of their way."

"Probably the point, don't ya think? Part of the brand language, perhaps? Ostentation breeds controversy, which breeds interest, and interest equals sales. All calculated, and some more so than others. We obviously selected the wrong one for aesthetics, but you're correct. Once you get past the sheet metal, it *is* a decent ride. You'd never lose it in a parking lot."

The miles marched and the monotony of northern Nevada's moonscape placed Chris in complete mesmerization. Matt and Emily indulged the road noise to entertain their unconscious minds. Crossing the Utah state line brought even less serenity. Chris began to think that God drew a complete blank here. Focused forward, allowing the cruise control to maintain a fraction over the speed limit, he never noticed the massive, white Peterbilt 388 grain hauler gaining on his rear at high velocity. The semi tractor filled his three rearview mirrors. He had no time to warn Emily or Matt. There was no option but to brace for impact and succumb to his automatic pulmonary reflex.

The truck slammed into their rear, exploding its rear window and compacting most of the space in the cargo area. Snickers yelped and dove for the floorboard. The impact propelled them to 90 MPH indicated. Emily shrieked and clutched her right elbow. Matt jolted awake holding his left collarbone from where the seatbelt made its impression.

"WHAT THE HELL?" Chris screamed, clutching the steering wheel with both hands, panicking to maintain control.

Matt spun around and saw the open cavity and the undamaged truck just behind—undamaged except for the now-rumpled collection of antique license plates aligning the front bumper. The truck was too close to see its driver. Matt knew the element of surprise no longer existed; the advantage of distance vaporized.

"He's gaining!" Matt yelled. "Don't let him get beside you."

"WHAT DO YOU THINK I'M DOING?" Chris panicked. "I should have known better than to pick a pumpkin ripe for carving! Em, what's wrong?"

"My elbow," she whimpered.

"Is it bleeding?"

"No."

"HANG ON!" Chris shouted, combating the wind noise. "I'll look at it as soon as I'm able."

The truck tapped the left rear of the Aztek's bumper, causing a sudden fishtail. Chris fought to correct it.

"I can't outrun him; we're over ninety and there's nothing left in the pedal."

"Well, you're going to have to do *something* because this isn't working!" Matt braced for another impact.

Chris steered the car back and forth across the seemingly empty interstate, avoiding contact with the menacing semi. He glanced towards the left across the median.

"I'm going to make an emergency stop. HANG ON!"

"Chris, what are you doi—"

Chris smashed the brake pedal to the floorboard. The truck had no other option but to blow past them on the right side. The truck's driver locked the rear tires of the trailer, sending them skipping across the pavement in a thunderous roar of smoking rubber. Chris immediately threw the steering wheel left, dove into the grassy median, and timed the westbound crossing of I-80 just in front of another car. Instead of retreating westward, Chris bounced over the shoulder and continued straight into a vast salt flat, keeping the accelerator floored.

Matt looked over to him, taking notice of the sheer determination in his eyes. "If you were worried about speed, this is *not* the place."

Chris didn't bother with an answer; he remained focused on the rearview mirrors.

The semi rig bowled over the same lanes and initiated its pursuit. Wind noise rapidly grew to intolerable levels, and Snickers buried himself under clothes in the rear floorboard. Emily was frightened by the deafening wind, and also by the lone shark swimming in her sea, vacuuming the injured prey's wafting blood trail. She could see it all too clearly through the gaping hole behind her. The truck was gaining on them.

"Chris, what are you doing? You can't outrun it. This garbage pail's probably got a governor set to 105. Besides, look at it! It's not made for speed."

"I'm not concerned about the speed."

The white horizon disappeared into a mirage-like reflective mirror. At this time of year, and at this time of day, the flat's percolated brine slowly evaporated in pockets, revealing shallow crusts of halite and gypsum. Chris maintained his speed, dodging and skiing across the ponds. As the truck's distance closed, a malevolent grin appeared on Chris' face. The largest pond was just ahead.

Matt checked their rear and turned towards Chris. "Whatever it is you're doing, IT ISN'T GOING TO WORK!"

A moment later, they hit the fringe. The water slowed them modestly at first, losing 10 MPH from the initial impact, and then a slow grind downward. Seconds afterward, the truck hit the pond's surface and rapidly lost all momentum, grinding to a near halt just before the other side. The soft crust at the edge proved too fragile for the heavy truck; its tires and axles disappeared beneath.

Chris turned around and saw it happen. "HA HA!"

Matt shook his head. "Okay, I was wrong. Maybe you *do* know a thing or two about science."

Chris executed a long turn and brought the Aztek around to stop at a distance over two hundred yards away, avoiding the small ponds that still contained danger. The Peterbilt's door obscured any chance for identification. Matt's eye caught a flash from the truck window just before one of the Aztek's side mirrors exploded next to him.

"GO, GO, GO!"

Chris stomped on the accelerator, spinning the tires in the salt as they regained momentum heading towards the interstate. They were five hundred yards downrange, and Matt heard the sharp crack of supersonic compression a foot over his head.

"JESUS, MOVE IT!"

"Did you see them?" Chris asked.

"No, but that's the unmistakable sound of a .50 cal."

"Any idea whose it is?"

"No, but if it was my detachment, they'd have more assets on me than some guy in a truck, unless . . ."

"I don't think it matters. We're out of here." Chris kicked the accelerator down.

"Not yet we aren't! That rifle's got a two-mile range."

Chris dodged small rocks and weed patches at the interstate's shoulder, illegally crossing to the westbound lanes as they sped away from Bonneville.

"Emily?"

"What?" The wind's noise increased, making conversation difficult.

"How is your elbow?" Chris yelled.

She held onto it tightly. "It's fine!" But her face showed anger.

"I think you hit your funny bone, sweetheart," he shouted. It'll go away in a minute."

"It's not funny to me!"

"I know. Whoever came up with that name had a weird sense of humor."

"Humerus." Matt pointed towards her arm. "Latin name for that bone." He turned away from Emily. "Chris, we can't stay on *this* road. Someone knows we're here, and they know we are headed east."

"We'll be in Salt Lake in less than an hour; what do we do?"

"North. We should head north."

"North? Why north?"

"I figure they, whoever *they* are, will be looking for us on this road. Even if they guess our course change, which would be the most logical direction?"

"I think probably south—try to get over to Denver instead of Cheyenne. There are more routes east or south from there."

"Right." Matt unfolded a roadmap. "So, I say we take the opposite direction. Head north into the Rockies, then east across the top. According to this, we can run up I-15 into Montana."

"Montana?"

"Lost your hearing? Yes, Montana! When we get to Butte, we can grab I-90 and head east again. They won't be looking for us there."

"What about this car?"

"We'll acquire another one ASAP. Bad enough it stands out like poo in a pool, but damaged?" Matt gagged.

Salt Lake City's skyline oscillated in the haze. Chris took I-215 North around the airport and towards Ogden. With the fuel gauge bouncing off empty, he took the first exit after joining I-15 on the north side of the city.

"Leave it running." Matt jumped out and inspected the damage. "Oh dear."

Chris walked around, mouth agape. "It's destroyed! We're going to get pulled over for this. Look at the taillights!"

"Do they work?" Matt lifted some pieces of dangling plastic. "The bulbs are still here."

Chris climbed back into the wreck and tested the brakes.

"Okay, they still work." Matt reported.

"Daddy, I'm cold."

Chris turned around and saw her shivering.

Matt looked across the street at a large department store. "Hey—pick me up over there in a few minutes."

"Huh?" Chris turned back around to the open driver's window.

Matt trotted across the street and vanished between a myriad of parked cars.

Chris stepped back out and continued filling the tank.

"Daddy?" Emily cried.

"I think Mr. Matt heard you, Em. We'll have to deal with the wind until we can find another car."

He finished refueling and drove up to the station to let Emily use the restroom. Upon her return, Chris brought the car across the street and up to the department store's loading lane. Matt appeared after a few moments pushing a full cart. Hopping out to give him a hand, Chris assisted in loading two blankets, some hand warmers, a small bag of dry dog food, a metal bowl, a 12-pack of bottled water, a roll of clear red tape, three deli sandwiches, and some chips.

Chris grimaced. "We'll be sick of sandwiches before this is over."

"Take me back to the gas station. I need to hit the head."

"Yeah, same here. I couldn't leave Em with the back window in its present condition."

Matt looked at it for a few moments while placing the supplies into what remained of the rear cargo space.

"We'll make Butte in five or six hours if we're lucky. I'll take over for you there. Hey, grab some drinks for us while you're in there."

Chris glared up at him over the rims of his glasses. "I thought you bought drinks."

"Those are for the dog."

Matt unpackaged the red tape and carefully masked the broken taillights. Chris returned with some sodas, gum, and a few candy bars. Matt threw the remaining tape in the back and ran for the restroom. When he returned, the group embarked northward to the wide-open territories of Montana.

Butte was once a thriving mining metropolis on the Continental Divide. Lately, it had become a relatively sedate enclave catering to tourists, ranchers, and retirees. Chris remembered little of it as he joined I-90 in the middle of the afternoon, headed east. Matt scanned for replacements at the next refueling stop and located one, but Emily found it locked tight. Chris and Matt swapped seats and they continued east with Matt at the wheel. Leaving Butte, bounding towards chilly tangerine twilight.

"I'm cold!" Emily shivered.

"Change places with me and sit up front with the heater. Mister Matt will keep it warm for you."

Next stop occurred in two hours. Snickers inhaled his dinner and was taken for a short walk. They resumed eastbound. The icy wind fluttered from the rear, yet Chris managed to find peace and warmth under a blanket with Snickers at his feet.

"Now I understand what Jen was talking about," he said.

"Who?" Matt shouted.

"Jennifer Smiley. She and her husband are—*were*— Snicker's owners. They used to brag about having a live foot warmer in the winter."

Chris slowly drifted off into the wash of air.

● ● ●

"I say spare no expense and you steal a truck?"

"Excuse me, sir. This is the *Information Age.*"

"Don't condescend me, Colonel. I should have known better than to listen to you. What's your great excuse this time? You lost the most peacocky vehicle ever produced in these United States, and in the middle of Bonneville? If my ass wasn't on the line here, I would be laughing hysterically— but I'm not laughing now, am I."

"Are you done?"

"Do not provoke me, *Colonel.* Go ahead with what will surely be an entertaining excuse."

"Thank you. In the *Information Age*, anyone can post anything and everything online live—as it happens. There are no longer opportunities for damage control, no phone calls to resolve the situation, and no Piggly Wiggly trucks to use in a cover-up. You have to be smarter. Now think about this for a minute, if you will, *General, sir*. Sure, I had a helicopter at my disposal. I could have used a drone, too, but what happens when other drivers start snapping photos of a helicopter shooting at a helpless car, hmm? It's better to appear like it's just road rage or some other commonality."

"You took shots. What about that?"

"We were out of the public's eyes, and Jacobson's D6."

"No, I said bring me the doctor alive with the machine preferably intact. If anything, just bring the doctor. I am not concerned with the life of Jacobson or the doctor's daughter."

"I won't harm the little girl, Tutlow. That is against my principles and the Code."

"Do I need to get someone else, Colonel? Your code does not apply in this situation. It is top priority, understand? Top!"

"'Course it is, but I will not hurt the girl."

"Fine, don't bother with her. But, if it comes down to you losing the doctor over that little girl, I'm going to bother *you*."

Osterhoudt carefully plucked the cigarette from his lips and ground its cherry into the swollen calluses of his left palm. Exhaling the smoke from his last drag, he watched the surrounding shallow ponds evaporate in the morning's broil.

"Have they been reacquired yet?" Osterhoudt asked.

"No sir, they must come into another contact area before that happens."

"You have my location, don't you? Call my chopper from Wendover. I will return this afternoon."

The Eaten Crow

Dashing between mountain peaks off his right, a vivid sunlight strobed Matt's pupils repeatedly as he stared deep into the interstate's vanishing point ahead. They refueled in Billings later that evening, downing their meals on the run. Around midnight, just beyond the town of Hardin, across the Bighorn River, their path dipped southward into the gently rolling hillsides. Without warning or any flashing indicator, the engine suddenly ceased, the headlights extinguished, the heater's fan shut off, the steering went numb, and the slow dissipation of wind noise brought upon them a renewed trepidation.

Chris sprung from a daze in the back seat. "What's wrong?"

"I don't know!"

Matt struggled to maintain directional control. The vehicle found equilibrium between wind resistance and gravity, maintaining 50 MPH as it slipped down a long grade some ten miles south of Hardin. Matt fumbled in desperation to reinitiate the secret starting sequence, but the starter never engaged as he mashed the windshield washer button.

"What are we going to do?" Chris' voice pitched upward. "It looks like we're in the middle of nowhere!"

"Calm down. It's not as bad as it looks. We passed a small town about five miles back. I could hike it in an hour, and that's if I don't catch a ride."

The beaten Aztek came to rest just beyond a shallow valley. Matt hoped their momentum would carry the next hill, but it couldn't—too much wind. Maybe there was a closer town that direction, he thought. Maybe one with a store or some other opportunity to pinch another car. His printed map was not so detailed. *Damnit, no GPS! Damn you, Murphy!* He scanned the horizon for lights, any lights. Instead, it was just another long, flat rise into oblivion. *Risky.*

"Any clue? We can't just sit here all night without a heater." Chris pointed to Emily, who was rubbing her eyes.

"Could be another town just ahead. I can't see anything beyond the next hill. I could find out in ten minutes, though."

"You don't think it's caused by the onboard information circuitry, do you?"

"Not likely. It's completely dead, as if the battery also died, but I know that's not the problem. Terminal test with the tire iron sparked it. My guess is that it has something to do with those briny pools you skirted this morning. It wouldn't take much of that spray into the electronics to fault a connection. I've seen it before, just not so fast."

"Great. So, what you're telling me is that we're kaput."

"That seems to be the short of it, yeah."

Matt grabbed his other T-shirt and donned it underneath Chris' spare windbreaker. He climbed out, shut the door, and jogged up the hill to look for any signs of life—preferably human. He only made it a few dozen yards before a lone pickup truck eased in behind their car. Matt ran back to confront the dark figure that stepped out of it. Chris snapped around too, but the truck's bright headlights perfectly silhouetted the muscular frame pacing towards them. Chris stumbled out, clumsily ramming feet into his shoes. He fell on the ground with his fingers jammed behind his left heel. Hogtied by any definition, but a simple fool in this case. He quickly recovered. Matt reached the front corner of the Aztek and caught a glimpse of a young man with shoulder-length black hair caressing the taped taillights and shaking his head. Snickers refrained from barking and followed him with his eyes, panting heavily, tongue out.

"HEY! Get away from there. Yes, you!" Matt yelled.

The young man threw up his hands. "Sorry, mister. Your car seems hurt. Do you need help?"

"Maybe. Is there a town nearby?"

"Yes. Over the next two hills is the reservation center. My father runs a service station there." He pointed up the road.

"Reservation?"

The man put his hands down. "You are on Crow land, sir. Well, sort of. We do not own this road, just everything around it."

"Oh." Matt smiled.

"I have a tow strap. I can pull you there—to my pop's station, I mean. Can you steer? Do you have brakes?"

"Barely, yes."

"The young lady and the other man—"

"I'm her father." Chris interrupted.

"You both can ride with me if you like. My truck is warm."

Chris appeared apprehensive at first, then looked back towards Emily, shivering. It was a risk he'd have to take.

"Sure, thanks. Give us a moment."

The native drove around to the front of their car and backed close enough to fasten his tow strap. Chris and Emily gathered themselves and climbed into the man's toasty truck. The young man secured the tow strap and climbed back into the driver's seat. He checked on his passengers, smiled, and began to carefully accelerate away, building tension in the strap without jerking. Matt forced the steering wheel to follow in line, which became much easier at speed. Topping the next hill, the distant lights of Crow Agency flickered in Chris' and Emily's eyes.

"Dad, where are we going?"

"I'm not exactly sure Em, but I think this man is going to help us."

"Young lady, we are going to my father's service station just over there. In these parts, he is the only one to help."

Chris laughed. "So, he's something like a medicine man for cars?"

The young man grinned. "He may not appreciate the stereotype coming from *you* mister, but yes. We joke with him like that sometimes."

"Well, I hope he can help."

"Pop likes to think of himself as a modern healer. Maybe not so much with people or horses, but with cars and other machines."

"A noble way to present oneself, don't you think? Much more pleasant than 'mechanic'. By the way, my name is Chris, and this is Emily. We're from California, and I can't tell how much we appreciate this." Chris extended his hand.

With a firm grip, the young man said, "I am Twin Feathers. Uh, actually, my name is Abe, but my father is a traditionalist. Long story. Please do not use that name or Abraham in front of him. I think he hates it."

"Why?"

"He believes in the meanings of names. He won't allow me to use it until he is dead and I become a tribal leader, if so appointed. There's our shop," Abe pointed.

"He is a chief, then?"

"Officially he is Chairman, but his friends call him Chief in private. He is the leader of our nation."

Exiting the only offramp for miles in either direction, Twin Feathers chauffeured them to a partially renovated service station just on the other side of the underpass. The damaged Aztek squeaked to a rest under the fuel pumps' brightly lit canopy. Twin Feathers jumped out of his truck and disconnected the tow strap, tossing it into his truck's bed on his way back. Shielded by the overpass, the winds were wispy and peaceful, not at all brisk. Chris and Emily climbed out then regrouped with Matt as Twin Feathers disappeared inside the station. Moments later, a middle-aged man emerged wearing a pair of slacks and a long-sleeve mechanic's shirt with "River" embroidered on the left breast pocket. With folded arms, he passed in front of the group, giving them all a suspicious eye. Without saying a word, he circled the Pontiac, scrutinizing the damage and abuse. A thin, flat leather strap around his neck held a pouch about the size of a woman's small wristlet, which appeared to cover the end of his ponytail. Before completing the inspection of the car, he reached to pet Snickers, who was apprehensively acceptant and slightly whiney in anticipation of something. River surveyed the car's rear and then the dashboard area. Looking back across to the hopeful group, which now included Twin Feathers, River raised his head and closed his eyes briefly before speaking.

"You are in some sort of trouble?"

Matt, not sensing the context, was the first to respond. "The car died on us a few miles away. It has plenty of gas, so we're clueless."

"That is not what I inferred. The reason for your car being sick is a foregone conclusion. There is enough of Bonneville corroding her to have nothing left by morning. I meant the damage. The mirror. The rear. It speaks of trouble."

Bewildered by River's curt deduction, Chris attempted an evasive explanation. "We were in an accident this morning. A truck hit us, but it was still drivable and … we're trying to get across the country."

"I see." The old man answered with a sneer. "Please come inside; it is warmer there."

"Aren't you going to take a look at it?" Matt griped.

River ignored him and continued inside the station's front door.

Chris and Emily followed while Matt threw his arms up at Twin Feathers. The young man nodded. "You get used to that around here."

They both wearily stepped inside, Matt first. Turning around at the entrance, Twin Feathers whistled at the car. Snickers jumped out of the back window and trotted through the station's front door. Inside, Emily quickly reminded herself that she had not eaten in a while.

River noticed her ogling the shelves. "Young lady, if you are starving, the candy bars and chips are in the next row." He turned to Chris. "There is no lodging in this town. You will need a place to stay."

Matt interrupted. "You're not going to look at the car?"

"There is nothing I can do for your car tonight."

"Calm down, Matt. If he's right, there's no remedy at the moment."

Matt bit his lip and let the man continue.

"It is against my teachings to be inhospitable, so you are welcome to stay with us tonight."

"Are you sure?" Chris was in disbelief.

"Yes. I am interested in hearing your story."

"But father—" Twin Feathers intervened.

"Remember what you've been taught. It is our way."

"Yes, father."

River turned back to Chris and Emily. "Please gather your belongings. It is time to close, and we must leave." He then turned to Matt. "Twin Feathers, you will follow me with this man and his dog. I will take the others."

"Come on, Em." Chris said cautiously.

Emily found a bag of corn chips she liked and placed them on the counter. River looked down at her and smiled.

"Take those with you little one. We will eat more later." He grinned at Chris. "I will add those to your bill."

Chris and Emily walked to the car and waited. River turned off the Apsáalooke Auto station's lights and locked the main entrance. Matt and Twin Feathers climbed into their truck. Snickers instinctively jumped into the cab with them. Matt thrust his hand across and grabbed him by the collar.

"It's okay, sir. Animals are the same as people around here. He would get cold back there."

"Oh. Well, if it's okay with you. I'm sure the dog doesn't mind."

"What is his name?"

"Snickers," said Matt.

Twin Feathers smiled. "You must excuse me; I am embarrassed to say I don't remember yours."

"I never gave it to you. It's Matt, Matt Jacobson, and it was rude of me not to introduce myself. I'm not used to people being as friendly as you and your father."

"Him friendly? If you say so. I guess if you don't know him . . ." Twin Feathers laughed. "He is more open today than usual—even for him. Well, it is nice to meet you, Mister Jacobson. My real name is Abraham, but do not call me that in front of my father."

"So you said. Why is that?"

"He doesn't like it since it is not a Crow name."

"If you say so, Abe. You can call me Matt. It's okay."

"Mister Matt."

"No, it's just . . . never mind."

Twin Feathers tailed his father for several dusty miles along a washed-out valley on the east side of town, tracing a creek until it terminated at a small clearing by a dammed pond. At the water's edge was an old, wooden house with an extraordinarily large structure just on the other side of it.

"Dad, what is that?" Emily pointed towards a large, dark, conical mass on the other side of the house.

"Why, I think it's a—"

"A tipi?" Matt had also taken notice from the other vehicle.

"Yes." Twin Feathers smiled. "That's what I was trying to warn you about. He is a traditionalist. It is the only permanent one in town. The only other time there are tipis around here is during the fair, then there are hundreds. We have not slept in the house since I was little."

Twin Feathers rolled to a stop alongside his fathers' truck a few yards away from the tipi.

"A freakin' tipi?" Matt cackled in disbelief. "You've got to be kidding me!"

"We still keep a lot of the stuff in the old house. We do laundry there, take showers and cook meals, but he insists we sleep in the tipi. It is not as bad as it looks."

Matt exited the truck and laughed. "This is one for the books."

Snickers bounced out of the truck and bolted to the other side of the tipi, sniffing around. He spooked four grazing mustangs, and they neighed and galloped to the far edge of the pasture, well away from the pursuing Labrador. River tugged on a leather strap at the tipi's entrance, illuminating its interior. He then held the opening's covering flap, which was fashioned from oiled bison leather. "Please, come in."

One by one, they gazed in astonishment at the tipi's appointments. Instead of an empty interior with a dirt floor as they might have imagined, this one was peculiarly tamarack-planked in a circular fashion, surrounding an open fireplace masoned with river stones and a locally-improvised raw umber mortar. Four beds, each fabricated from large, lacquered fir tree logs surrounding a mattress on the floor, made a semicircle around the large fireplace. On the floor in front of each bed was a large bear pelt—two grizzlies and two blacks in total. One grizzly pelt kept the bear's head, signifying head of household. Emily squeaked upon its sight, as she had never seen anything as ferocious as the size of full-grown grizzly's head.

"That's AWESOME!" Matt shouted.

Chris gazed thirty feet upward where the supporting timbers converged. "Quite impressive."

River pointed towards the two of the beds on the far side. "You are welcome to those for the evening. I will prepare for dinner. Make yourselves comfortable. Twin Feathers, please get the oven started with enough for our guests."

The young man nodded.

On the other side of the tipi, Twin Feathers reached into a small cabinet and removed a large Dutch oven that most city-dwellers would consider a stylish antique. Stretching into another cabinet, he extracted several potatoes and some dried meat. Using a pitcher located to one side, he filled the oven halfway, then placed the meat, potatoes, and a few other garnishments inside. He placed the oven's lid on top and suspended the pot from a hook that was on an iron crossbar straddling the fireplace. Next, he fetched a stack of firewood, including some kindling. Using the smaller scraps and a squirt of starter fluid, a wooden match ignited the awaiting accelerants in a ball of fire. The inferno temporarily engulfed the oven until its flames slowly settled.

Emily sat at the edge of her bed's bear pelt and opened a small bag of chips. Munching away, she lost herself in the fire's dance upon the tipi's walls. Chris settled in, removing his jacket, and placing their luggage at the foot of the bed. He sat and watched Twin Feathers work. Matt stepped to the entrance, not as interested in the meal as he was the where-abouts of Snickers—last seen antagonizing the horses. Matt threw open the tipi's flap, and immediately, a golden blur flew past and started sniffing around—particularly interested in the bear pelts. Matt grew more curious about Twin Feathers' disposition.

"So, Abe, what's the story with your name?"

Twin Feathers stopped stirring and stared blankly into the fire. "He does not like it because it reminds him of my mother. She gave it to me."

"How do you mean?" Matt noticed Chris' sudden interest.

"She died after giving birth to me, and . . ."

"And what?" Chris asked.

"She was a white woman, who . . ."

"A white woman? How did that happen?"

A deeper voice cut in. "It was long ago, and it saddens my heart to tell the story."

River appeared at the entrance; his body animated by the flame's light. He was dressed in a light tribal suede garment with leather straps tying the front and cinching at the waist. Decoration was spared for casual wear—leather moccasins and long sleeves. The leather pouch was still strapped around his neck, cradling his ponytail.

"I met my bride in New England after participating in one of your government's skirmishes on a small island in the Caribbean."

"Grenada?" Matt asked. "So, you were a soldier."

"Marine. After that, I returned and was admitted to Harvard on a scholarship. That is where we met. She was Jewish and became pregnant. You might imagine the hardship—a Native American and a Jew. Alas, we were in love and blessed with a child. She named Abraham before his birth, but since the way I was treated in New England, even as an Ivy League graduate, I have yet to make peace with his name. This is why I returned to my reservation. Because of my education and principles, my people felt it natural to elect me Chairman. At first, I thought it shameful because I had not fully embraced my heritage. Now, I think it more important than ever. My people are underprivileged and directionless. The path is not as clear as it once was."

River stepped over to the Dutch oven, used a metal rod to open the lid, and stirred the contents with a wooden spoon.

"You graduated Harvard on a full scholarship? That's astounding!" said Matt.

Chris kept staring at the pouch attached to River's neck. "So, what do they call you around here, 'Chief River'?"

Puzzled, River remembered his shop uniform's nametag. "Formally, it is Chairman River. We no longer elect chiefs; that was a title conveyed only after successful leadership in battle—although, my colleagues believe the Grenada affair loosely qualifies. It is not my place to debate their honorable gesture. Just call me River. It is easier for everyone since it is the short version of my name. I do not care too much for titles."

River checked the oven. "I think we are ready. Twin Feathers, please distribute the bowls and spoons for our guests."

His son used an iron rod to grab the oven's handle and laid the steaming cauldron beside the fireplace on a wooden stand. Starting with Emily, they all took turns ladling the soup into their bowls. River invited them to sit in a circle surrounding the fire since it kept everyone comfortably warm.

As their bowls emptied, Chris motioned to River as he cleared a mouthful. "So, what's the long version of your name, if I may ask?"

"You may. It is Chairman Hair Flows Like River."

Matt uncontrollably chuckled, spitting a small chunk of potato back in his bowl. River chagrined. Emily suddenly stopped gazing into the fire, now interested in this strange man. His eyes were not dispirited in the wake of Matt's disrespect. The fire in them reflected contemplation of the ignorant. With a sigh, he brought his thumbs under the leather strap running around his neck, and then lifted it over his head to the front.

"When I was a child, my mother passed down the story of a legendary Crow who lived some 2,700 moons past. He was an ugly man and he kept ugly hair. He was not of an ugly mind, she said. One year, in his early adulthood, he was selected for marriage to a woman of higher peerage. She did not want the better-looking braves as her elders insisted. She instead selected the ugly man to spite them, and the elders could do nothing but accept her wish. The legend says that this woman, out of love, concocted a special treatment containing bear oil, berries, and other medicinal herbs, and then she spread it on his scalp. Soon after, his hair began to grow very long as did his confidence and powers of leadership. A face, once contorted by despair, became joyous and beautiful. My mother said, one day he abandoned her to seek a vision, and weeks later, he returned with special powers. This chief also fought in a war, but she did not say which. She never glorified killing. He led a lengthy and fulfilling life along with his wife of unmatched beauty. My mother told me I am descended from this chief, and that he should be honored. I never respected this until my wife passed."

River removed his banded hair from the pouch, and Chris' jaw hit the floor. Matt was speechless and Emily could only sit and stare. River stood and dropped the heavy ponytail to the ground. Taking three steps back, he revealed a length of at least twelve feet.

"Well, umm. As your name implies . . ." Matt said.

"Flows, indeed!" Chris added. "I have to ask about the river part. Is it because of the length or some other reason?"

"You have a keen sense of observation, my friend. You see, most of our people, the full-bloods that is, have *straight* hair. Without the banding to keep it straight, mine has waves. I suspect that my blood isn't as pure as my parents profess, but it is not my place to disrespect their words. If not for the teachings of your people, I would never know."

"How long—I mean, when did you start growing it?"

"The day Twin Feathers was born." River solemnly bowed his head as he turned to face the dying fire. "Son, please gather more wood for the evening."

Retrieving his seemingly interminable tress, River coiled most of it into the leather pouch and swung it back around his neck. Taking a seat at the edge of his grizzly bear rug, he carefully observed the others. Emily's post-meal yawns and blank staring at the hypnotic flames meant she was on the sleepy clock. Twin Feathers reemerged from outside with an armload of cut logs, two split and an all-nighter. Positioning the logs in the fire created a swirling mass of sparks ascending through the open top high above. One spark landed just in front of Emily, briefly startling her as it faded. As the fresh wood cooked, another round of its crackles annoyed Snickers enough to leave his rug, drift over to River, make three circles, and plop down with his head across the man's thigh.

"He likes you a lot," said Emily.

"Animals innately know good nature, young lady." River confidently scratched behind Snicker's ears.

He gazed into the fire for a few moments during the lull in conversation. Twin Feathers sat on his rug and warmed his hands with the building flames.

Looking down at an appreciative Snickers, River scratched more fervently, gaining a rise in the dog's head to match the warmth. "I have given you my family's truths. Would you tell me yours?"

Matt began to coach Chris before he could speak. Catching himself, Chris looked at Matt with an eye of reverence before continuing.

"Matthew and I are engineers for a semiconductor company in Silicon Valley."

"That explains your strange choice of conveyance." River smiled. "Please continue."

"Yeah, about that. Look, we don't want any more trouble than we're already in."

"Chris!" Matt shouted. "Oh man . . ."

River glanced at Matt with forgiving eyes before turning back to Chris. "You are in no trouble here."

The fire's sparks spiraled up a column of warm air, and Chris breathed a sigh before continuing. "I want to show you something that better explains our predicament."

Matt jumped. "No, Chris! Don't involve them."

Twin Feathers refocused from the fire to Matt as a possible threat. River motioned him to be calm and stay seated.

"Matt, these people have been nothing but forthright with us. They appear harmless to me."

"They don't need to know, Chris. They don't. There's no reason for this."

"I feel there is. We're stuck here, we don't have a functioning car, and frankly it will continue to corrode throughout the night. We can't use our phones and we don't have a lot of money."

Matt frowned. "What does the device have to do with them, huh? What?"

"I don't know—good rapport? Maybe they'll find it interesting, if not amusing. There is no reason to fear them, and there is nothing harmful about the laptop's abilities."

Matt slowly relaxed, realizing he was the only stressed person in the tipi. As he sat back, Chris turned around and grabbed the handle to his attaché case. He laid it down at his side, flipped it open, and reached in between his clothes to withdraw the slim computer. He held its power button, initiating the boot sequence.

"I must caution you, Mister Miller. I know little of computers. I leave such devices to the young. As much as I am a follower of certain achievements, it is my son that is more enamored with such things."

"Please, call me Chris. I don't exactly know what to call this device. It's no longer just a computer, but more of a portal. We were studying a way to utilize orphaned brain tissue as a memory container."

River raised an eyebrow for a moment until Twin Feathers explained. "He means they were going to use brains for computer memory, Pops."

"Don't call me that in front of them." River quipped. "Please go ahead, and ignore my son. He forgets that my schooling was not in the dark ages. We had computers, but they were huge beasts."

Chris smirked. "The reason for this is because our current technology will eventually run out of room for expansion. There are many of us who believe in the old maxim, 'art imitating life'. We knew the human brain held a near infinite amount of memory, but we didn't know how to unlock it. Or—we didn't know until now. This is a prototype housing module for a 'Soft Drive', and we managed to get a sample module working a few weeks ago. The achievement itself is monumental, if I might say so, but there's something else, and it is difficult to explain. Do you have any unwashed fabric lying around?"

River examined the tipi's interior. "Look around—almost the entire place except the bed sheets. We beat the bear skins once every other week. We oil the tipi's skins twice a year. There is not much else around here."

Twin Feathers laughed. "Father, you don't beat the bear's head!"

"This is true. I was told it would anger his spirit."

Chris walked over to River's bear pelt and sat next to its head. Carefully, he ejected the laptop's filter and held it under the bear's left ear. With his right hand, he tapped its floppy cartilage over the collection tray. Waiting a few moments for any unseen particles to make their way downward, he snapped the tray closed and placed the computer on his lap so both he and River could watch. Moments later, the recognition algorithm began counting identified particles. The machine rapidly enumerated over two hundred fragments containing varied information. As the data assimilated, Chris selected a random sample.

"Okay, this is what you need to see."

A series of bright white flashes appeared upon the laptop's screen. River squinted from the changing contrast. A scene slowly emerged from the static, as though it was taken from Twin Feather's eyes. He was embroiled in a heated argument over consistently poor school grades—a regular bone of contention after River decreed that Cs were the new Fs. "*What would your mother think of you?*"

Twin Feathers was not within view of the screen, but he instantly recognized his father's voice, the tone, and the fear it struck. His emotions wavered between simple curiosity and shameful embarrassment. The scene dissipated into a sea of white flashes and returned to the file selection prompt. Chris noticed River's near trance-like fixation on the screen. Slowly and tearfully, he raised his eyes to Chris'.

"Please continue, my friend."

Chris selected another fragment file. Again, the white flashes gave way to a scene partially obscured by the static. This time, the viewpoint was River's, who was flat on his bed looking into the exotic face of the woman on top of him, grinding and moaning. The scene quickly dissolved into the white flashes. River fell back against the logs of his bed with a troubled look. Chris did not know if he was overwhelmed, scared, or angry. The only thing he knew was that River wasn't saying anything.

"What is it, father?" Twin Feathers could not reach him. "POPS, who was *that*?"

River turned with a scowl, then back to Chris.

"I didn't believe this day would come."

"What do you mean?" Matt asked.

"Finally, and I am here to see it . . . to be a part of it." River delighted at some sparks disappearing through the top of the tipi.

"Father, I do not understand," said Twin Feathers.

Sighing, River could only mumble, "I don't suppose you would, *dáaka.*" He turned back to Chris. "You have finally done it!"

"Father!" Twin Feathers insisted.

With a wide grin, River continued. "That was your mother."

"What?" Matt said. "No, it wasn't. I saw it; you were old in that scene. You said she died just after giving birth to *him* (pointing to Twin Feathers)."

"You are correct, that was me. It is the truth. And that *was* her. That is also the truth. And that was what she looked like before she died many years ago."

"I don't understand." Matt rubbed his brow in frustration.

"I do." Chris put the computer down. "It was a dream."

"Yes."

"You were dreaming of sex with my mother?" Twin Feathers blurted.

"Quiet! I had forgotten this until it came upon the screen."

"How long ago was this?" Chris asked.

"I am not sure. Maybe last week."

"Pops!"

"I am not sorry. It shows I am human and that I still love her. I am getting old. Besides you, my memories are all I have left."

"River, I didn't mean to dredge up any ghosts. If I did, I apologize."

"An unfortunate choice of words Doctor Miller, but I know this is not in your control. Nothing is, when nature is factored. I will return in a few moments."

River opened the flap at the tipi's entrance, walked out, and closed it behind him. Chris powered down the laptop started to place it back in the case.

Matt grabbed him by the arm and whispered, "I don't think that was such a good idea, Chris."

"You may be right. I hadn't considered the possibility that it might display something controversial. It appears to be intrinsic to the soft drive somehow. I wonder if I ever should have built it in the first place." Chris stared into the white-hot coals at the bottom of the fire.

"Don't even think about it. Your device is probably the single most important discovery in the last thousand years, and you know it."

Twin Feathers felt uneasy with the strangers in his house, so he opened the flap of the tipi's entrance for some fresh air. River was just about to walk in with an armload of various items. Surprised by the timing, Twin Feathers stepped out of the way to let him pass, and then closed the tipi's flap behind him.

River placed the items around him as he lotused in front of the fireplace. Something wrapped in buckskin about the size of a rolling pin's cylinder, some small clay jars, and an old grey cloth containing a few handfuls of pine needles lay before him.

Matt laughed. "I think he's going medicine man on us."

River frowned and continued placing his curiosities in a neat arrangement. He purposely tucked his hair-stuffed pouch inside of the back of his collar and slowly removed his suede buckskin shirt. With only a trace of grey chest hair, his bare skin was a smooth, light brown hue. For a man of his age, his muscles were well toned from the rigorous daily mechanic's trade he and his son performed. River looked at his friends circled around the fire, settling on Chris and Emily with a confident leer. Twin Feathers returned to his rug and sat down, legs crossed, mimicking his father. Chris and Emily scooted closer, enjoying the fire's warmth while River continued preparing. Matt sat on the other side of the fire with Snickers. Its flames beat a silent rhythm across their faces. The trance-inducing calmness was interrupted a moment later by River.

"Doctor Miller. I say 'doctor' in appeal to your esteemed higher education from . . ."

"M.I.T." Chris said.

"What do you know about this world?"

"I thought I knew quite a lot. After this week? A mouse's dropping."

River opened one of his jars, scooped a small dollop of its contents into his left palm, and then passed the jar to his son. River worked the lotion over his hands until none remained. Twin Feathers did the same and passed the jar to his left. Chris stared awkwardly at the jar and smelled the contents, causing him to choke on its pungent odor.

"What is this stuff?"

"Beaver musk. Our ceremonial version of a hand sanitizer."

Chris poked a finger into the jar with a grimace and extracted a small amount. "Em, open your hand. Don't be afraid. It's just hand lotion like your mother used to have."

River looked at Chris, noticing his words. "Used to?"

After taking his own portion, Chris passed the jar along to Matt. Matt held the jar under Snicker's nose, causing the dog to immediately sneeze.

Salving his hands with the musk, Chris turned back to River. "We have something in common, I'm afraid."

"They have both taken the journey before us. I am sorry."

"You may be one of the few people uniquely qualified to understand, River."

Grasping a wad of pine needles in one hand, River cast them into the fire. The needles briefly suffocated the flames, producing a voluminous thick smoke. He rubbed his hands amongst the gently rising cloud. Twin Feathers also stuck his hands into the smoke and motioned Chris and Emily to do the same. Matt joined in before the needles heated to the point of combustion. A moment later, a ball of flame erupted. Broken glowing needle embers slowly spiraled upward on the column of immense heat, exiting through the lashed intersection of the 15 poles at the tipi's top. River reached down to grab the buckskin roll and carefully placed it in his lap. He untied its thin leather straps, unrolled the buckskin wrapper, and revealed another multi-layered roll of different colored cloths.

One by one, he peeled away the layers and revealed yet another buckskin wrapper. With caution, he untied its leather straps and slowly exposed the contents—a short lock of jet-black hair.

"More hair? That figures." Matt laughed.

"Shssh." Chris begged Matt to be respectful.

Ignoring them, River held up a few strands of the hair. "My mother bestowed these to me just before she passed. She said they belonged to a relative. It is said that they belonged to the chief I told you about earlier. Legend speaks that this hair has special powers. Powers to heal. Powers to compel. Powers to see. I dared not touch the hair until I knew how to use it properly. Many moons ago, when Twin Feathers was a small boy, I learned."

Closing his eyes and rubbing the small lock of hair with both hands, River began a ceremonial chant. The singing only lasted for a dozen or so seconds and then River cast the strands into the fire's edge. The hair burned with a bright violet color and plumed a dark green smoke. River leaned forward and partook of the smoke, gathering it with his hand until his nostrils were tinted. Taking on a deep breath, he held the smoke in his lungs for as long as he could before exhaling. Several moments passed as he kept his eyes closed in medi-tation. River erupted in another chant, lasting several minutes. Nobody said a word, not even Matt who could barely contain himself.

Folding his hands across each other, and then interlocking his fingers, River stared deep into Chris' eyes with pensiveness.

"I've been told repeatedly of your coming for over twenty years. And here you are in front of me now, all doubts removed."

"I don't understand."

"It is not expected that you would, Doctor Miller. I disregarded that part of the visions. Others had different agendas, but always contained clues to this, here, today. I asked you earlier what you knew of the world. If you cannot tell me, then please listen to what *I* know. I know you are in more trouble than you say."

Matt perked up. "Now wait a minute."

"Settle down, Matt."

"Am I wrong?" River asked.

After a long pause, Chris looked at everyone around the fire and then back to Matt, who was shaking his head negatively. Chris turned back to River, "Yes, but we don't know why."

"I do. At least, I do *now*." River said. "Constant condescension is a side effect of a free education at Harvard. There were others like me—the lowest rung of their caste—but I was more the rarity. It empowered me to focus on my heritage and on the reasons why the powerful must conquer—why the powerful must control. It is out of fear. Fear of equality. Fear of loss. The evil of entitlement. It is said that one time long ago, many people were at peace—most people. People were in balance with nature, too. In my heart, I feel we are all brothers, but somehow, the powerful feel it necessary to keep us apart and keep us in fear. The imbalance, you see. They operate under the fallacy that imbalance is necessary. They seek *you* now. Why? The answer is simple. You threaten the imbalance. You've unlocked a truth known and passed down through our people for countless generations."

"What do you mean—*our* people?" Matt asked.

"I mean our race and many of the mongoloids as well. We have not lost some of the ways of old. We have known how to commune with the spirits. We know how to flow with their bidding and how to communicate with our surroundings. We know how to guide our own dreams and, in those states, determine our purpose. The pale eyes lost their way long ago. It is referenced in many of the texts that keep your people divided to this day. Even though the teachings are primarily for the good of all, the division comes on the absurd notion of who gets the credit. Vanity, you call it. The division keeps you apart, to not act as one. The division keeps you occupied with the need to compete. The need to be better than the other one. And, in that competition, it means the destruction of many of us at peace. This is not a Native American phenomenon; this is everywhere to some degree. Have you ever stopped in your hectic lives to look around you? To notice that there is something in common with people like myself?"

"Just the Native Americans?"

"No, the entire race. We don't even get a classification by the official anthropology community. I mean us, the Eskimos, the Pacific Islanders, the Iroquois, the aboriginals, Sudanese and so forth. The people at peace in this world." River laughed. "It must drive many of you crazy that we are content with so little. That we do not need to 'progress', as you define it. At the same time, so many of you in your—what do you call them—hamster wheels, end up wanting to get away from it all and retire to simplicity. Isn't that natural? We are happy to have fewer things. We are happy to not desire your things. Well, maybe some things. I like the pickup trucks and some of your candies."

River returned to Chris. "Many visions tonight. I saw your house on fire. I saw people dying. I saw you falling from great heights. I saw the yellow eyes that torment your daughter. I see your journey's continuance, and I felt a warmth that I've not felt in a very long time—the warmth of a true love."

"You got all that from the hair?" Matt asked. "Why hasn't anybody documented this?"

River frowned again. "The power is not for everybody. Doctor Miller, you've discovered something through science that's been lost to your people for many centuries. The last time you practiced medicine as powerful as this, you were burned at the stake as witches and heretics. The powerful that divide us are after you again."

"Father, I heard this man tell him that the device was the most important discovery for a thousand years." Twin Feathers cleared his throat. "Is that true?"

"His box has unlocked a secret of this world. It is the secret that chains us together. The secret that reveals our destinies, communicates with the past, and charts our future. A seed of the universe. A fundamental truth. The secret that the powerful have worked for centuries to confiscate and control because with it, there *are* no secrets."

"Christ, I'm going to be sick." Matt trudged outside and gulped the cool, fresh air. He wasn't prepared.

Emily drifted off to sleep on her father's lap, too tired to keep up with the conversation. Chris gazed down at her and the glow of the fire flickering across her cheek.

"Enough for tonight," said River. "The mind can only absorb so much."

Chris nodded.

The stillness of the steamy meadow by the pond was disturbed by a bantam splake leaping for its breakfast. Emily awakened to the smell of coffee and bacon. As she stretched, her eyes focused on Twin Feathers taking an iron hook to a percolator dangling over the fireplace. Sitting up, she looked around and noticed the other men entering the tipi.

"Doctor Miller, your people have been in pain for so long. The spirits favor you, and I believe the creator has given you a purpose by this miracle. Use it for good. Show your people they are not lost. Show them they are not alone."

"That's one heck of a guilt trip, River. I don't know if I'm the right person for this. I don't even know where to begin."

"You will. And, I know your friend is here to protect you on your path. The pairing is obvious and natural. You must find the way."

They sat and sipped cautiously at the piping-hot brews.

"Doctor Miller, do you and Matthew believe in the concept of purpose?"

"Yes, but I do not subscribe to predetermination, if that's what you mean."

River turned to Matt, who shrugged. "I always felt that way, but never knew what it was, exactly. When I was a younger man, I hoped that the answer would come."

River grinned. "Hope? Hope is one of the most dangerous traps of men. It can be far worse than fear. When I lived in the east, I used to sit on a bench and watch the people walk back and forth in front of me. They were all busy going to whatever it was that they were doing next. Many of them didn't even know why, except that it was for the *hope* of making lots of money, doing something they maybe liked—or maybe not. I thought about those moments. Did these people know what they were meant to do? Did they know what their purpose was? I often asked that of myself, and for decades I knew it was to be a part of something bigger than myself. I didn't know what it was exactly, I just knew it was for a *reason*. That reason would be eventually revealed, and I think it is now—to help *you* find the path. Something so simple, yet infinitely potent."

"River, I don't know that helping us is such a grand idea. I appreciate your willingness, but considering everything, I don't know . . ." Chris savored his steamy cup.

"You must go east as your friend has instructed. You must find a way to use the machine for good. You must expose the truth and remove the fear and mystery from your lives."

"Chief?" Matt interrupted. "I too appreciate all of your kind words, but there's one huge problem to this plan."

River spun around to reiterate that he didn't prefer the chief title. He raised a finger and began to open his mouth, but wasn't quick enough to get it out before Matt continued.

"We don't have a car."

River sighed and lowered his hand. "I am aware of your needs, which is why I am giving you my son's truck."

"WHAT?" Twin Feathers jumped up, not believing his ears.

Chris looked at Twin Feathers in disbelief, as did Matt. *How could a father take away his son's ride?*

"River, we don't want to take his truck. I appreciate the offer, but it doesn't seem right for us to take something that belongs to him."

"It is not his to keep, and I should have used the word 'lend'. Whenever you get to your destination, call us and we will retrieve it."

"Oh!" Both Chris and Matt said in unison.

"But—" Twin Feathers tried to get in a word.

"Quiet! I'll have no more of this. Come with me outside."

River opened the flap to the tipi and held it until Twin Feathers exited. Outside, they continued a heated discussion for several minutes. River explained the inevitability of the truck's use by the strangers to his son. Eventually, he began to agree with his father's reasoning, and their voices became quieter. The entrance flap opened and in stepped Twin Feathers with his head hung low. With arms crossed, River followed him inside.

"My son would like to relay instructions for using the truck. Even though it is not that old, it seems to have acquired some personality."

Chris glanced at Twin Feathers. "Are you sure?"

With a tone of capitulation, the young man admitted, "Yeah."

Walking over to River and slapping him across the arm, Chris laughed. "Geez, River. You really *are* an Indian-giver!"

"He jokes, but he knows not what he says." River said, praying upward.

"Hey, I was just kidding!"

"Of course." River cracked a smile.

Matt walked over to the truck with Twin Feathers. Chris and River continued talking while watching them review it.

"Look, River. That car of ours . . ."

"I know. It does not belong to you."

"How do you know?"

"It does not fit your conformist, submissive personality."

Chris laughed. "I don't know how to take that, but it certainly sounded malicious!"

"Perhaps. We will take care of the car."

"How?"

River tapped his temple and pointed to Twin Feathers. "Internet. Parts auctions."

"River, I don't know how to thank you for all of this. Having us at your home, giving, er, lending us your truck. When this is over, I want to come back and visit. Maybe you and your son can come to California. I will compensate you for all of this."

"Doctor Miller, I do not see this as so much a favor to you, but as a favor to all of us. It is the least I can do in that regard. Now, it is getting time for *us* to make a journey."

"Emily?" Chris called to her inside the tipi. "Get your backpack ready; we're leaving."

Matt tested the truck's clutch pedal. "So, Abe. What did he say to you to make you give up this truck?"

Twin Feathers looked over his left shoulder through the rear window, making sure his father wasn't anywhere around. "He said I must learn to give first before receiving. He said I must learn to not make decisions so quickly or to curse what is beyond my control."

"But he's taking *your* truck, not his own!"

"Yes, that's right, but what he didn't tell you was that he is giving me *his* truck. He does this to me . . . always testing."

The young man sighed and stared at the floorboard. His failure of patience was a life lesson, and he knew it now.

Matt's smile widened. "He is a great father to you, Abe. He may jerk you around a bit, but it's teaching you to stay balanced and focused."

"I know, but it kills me every time he does it—like he wants to show me how superior he is or something."

"Well, next time he does that to you, just smile and say, 'Whatever you want to do, Dad. That's okay by me.' Watch what happens. The lack of satisfaction will eat him alive."

"Okay, I will try it."

"Great. Now what were you saying about the—what did you call it? The 'grandma gear'?"

"Granny . . . granny gear."

Emily packed her things and emerged from the tipi's entrance. Chris went inside to collect his attaché case and a bag of dirty clothes. Taking a last look around, he noticed a small plastic grocery bag on the kitchen table that was tied off at the top in a bow. Beside it was a foot-long, rectangular, buckskin leather pouch tied with thin leather straps.

River stood at the entrance of the tipi. "Those are for you."

Chris was curious of the gesture and the contents.

River chuckled. "Those are for your dog. Rawhides. He will like them."

Chris turned his attention to the rectangular pouch.

"Go ahead, take a look." River said.

Chris untied the leather straps and flipped open the pouch's lid. Inside was a beautifully handcrafted stainless blade about seven inches long with a carved antler handle.

"I don't know the first thing about knives, River, but this one's incredible. Did you make it yourself?"

"Yes. Around here, a man must have many hobbies."

River picked up the blade and bounced it in his hand. "You don't have to know much about knives, just when to use them."

With a lightning move, he grabbed the knife's blade with his right hand and flung it at a bench on the opposite side of the tipi. The knife penetrated the wood deeply, staying inserted into the backboard. Emily heard the knife striking the wood from outside and jumped. River walked over to the bench, wiggled the knife up and down to loosen it from the wood, and then polished the blade. Walking back over to the table, he brought his pouch of hair around to his front side and pulled out the end of his train. River looked up to Chris as he sliced off a short lock.

"Maybe like my ancestors, this will harvest something special for you."

River placed the small bundle of hair into the knife pouch, ran the blade's side along its outside skin for cleaning, and carefully placed the knife back inside. After tying the straps back around the pouch, he handed it to Chris.

"Let's go."

"River, I—"

"Please, we must get the truck serviced and fueled before you depart. You will follow us back to the station. It is almost time to open."

River emerged from the tipi and headed towards the trucks. Chris followed him, dumbfounded by his generosity. Taking Emily's hand, they walked over and climbed into Twin Feather's truck. The young man stepped out of the way as Matt slid into the driver's seat and flipped the ignition switch. The powerful V8 turned over with a low growl. Matt looked backward to see Snickers still on the ground, whining to come along. River whistled for him as he slapped the outside of his door. Without hesitation, Snickers jumped into the back of the truck and sat just behind the rear window, tongue dangling. Twin Feathers walked around and climbed into his father's truck.

"No, take the other side." River corrected his son as he attempted to enter the passenger side. "You drive your *own* truck."

He laughed as his son smiled and trotted to the driver's side. Twin Feathers fired up the engine, backed out, and headed for their service station. Matt followed close behind.

The morning air was crisp and dry. The intermittent roar of the interstate disrupted the town's quaint serenity. Twin Feathers climbed out of his truck and walked around to the orange disaster on the other side of the fuel pumps.

"Mister Jacobson, would you give me a hand to move this thing?"

Realizing his shoulder was in no condition for hard labor, he deferred to Chris. "I, uh, can't."

Chris hopped out and helped Twin Feathers push the wreck into one of the bays of the garage. Matt drove the truck next to the pumps, and Twin Feathers swiftly ran over to start servicing it.

Chris returned as River emerged from unlocking the station. "What's the matter with your friend?"

"When our laboratory was destroyed by gunmen, he saved my life. He received a nasty gash on his left shoulder helping me escape."

River went back into the store and returned after a few moments holding a small, clear glass jar that contained a maroon-colored paste. He walked over to Matt's side of the truck and handed the jar to him.

"What's this for?"

"Your shoulder. For pain and infection. Try it."

Matt looked back to Chris, embarrassed that he told him of the disability. Matt was at a loss, shrugging and clumsily thanking River.

The chief smiled. "What? I *am* the medicine man, you know."

Matt laughed. "You made this?"

"No. An old lady down the street made it. She makes me feel guilty if I don't sell them. Not to the tourists, though."

"Does it work?"

"You tell me. You will be the first to try it." River winked and strolled around to Chris' side of the truck while Twin Feathers finished filling the tank.

"River, please let me pay for the gas, at least."

River laughed. "Don't worry about the gas. We don't pay as much as you do. Reservation—no tax!"

"Well, I don't know what to say. You have been too kind."

"Just remember what I said. That is all I ask."

Chris shook his hand firmly and looked deeply into his eyes. "I will."

"Okay, Mister Jacobson, you're ready." Twin Feathers closed the truck's fuel door and returned to Matt's window.

Matt released Twin Feather's handshake and hit the ignition. "You remember what I said too, young man."

Waving as the group pulled away, River asked his son, "What did he say to you?"

"He said you were a good father."

"Intelligent man. Now go get your tools. We've got a *beautiful* pile of junk to shred."

"Beautiful?"

Matt brought the truck onto the interstate and continued their southward leg of I-90 towards Sheridan. "I don't believe it."

"What?" Chris asked.

"I don't recall anyone ever being that nice to me—ever. Well, besides my parents."

"I think that's an old western custom."

"What, being nice? Don't make me puke, it's too early in the day."

"Well, sort of. I don't know about the whole hospitality thing, but a long time ago, people used to give other people shelter—no questions asked. Weren't many hotels out here. I suppose folks were just glad to see another human. Anybody."

"Entertainment. I get it."

"That, and maybe good etiquette."

Emily realized that her seat was in front of 12V outlet and reached down to retrieve the music player from her backpack. Earbuds in place, she drifted away while leaning on her father's left side.

Matt noticed her and laughed. "Well, that didn't take very long."

Industrial Complexity

The Spanish-tiled floor drifted in and out of focus as her thumbs kneaded his spinal column. A voluptuous brunette worked each vertebra upward and outward each pass—beginning with the coccyx and ending at the top of his cervical curve—generating ancillary heat for both client *and* therapist. Reaching perhaps further than necessary when at the base of his neck, her breasts intentionally caressed his buttocks. He rolled his eyes. Signal games. These unadvertised technicians knew their colleagues considered such behavior unprofessional. That is, in the context of the overt profession. Jack Kattner never once complained about it. Just the opposite, in fact. He had become the regular subject of every masseuse's gossip because he frequented the establishment regularly and compensated well above average. The nature of this unadvertised facility kept its peculiar protocols to oral accounts only.

Numerous suggestive techniques were tested over the years: The nip tease, the accidental thigh climb, and the waterfall, which involved playful tickling using one's lengthy hair if their breasts weren't up to compartment specifications. Heated breath, sighing, and so many other tactics were also reliably utilized. Jack was not the submissive type; opening moves were typically his. When naked under a towel, belly-down on the massage table with his head on a foam ring, he was totally in command. At least, in *his* mind.

The masseuse finished Kattner's lumbar, then moved forward to work her vigorous digits on his right shoulder.

Occasionally, she toyed with playful aggression. It was enough to make him wince, but not enough to coerce a complaint. He knew and played along. She clamped down hard on his trapezius. Again, he flinched. No complaints. *How far can I push him?* She wondered. *Likes it that rough?* In fact, her puckish tortures were mere pinches on the arm of a man who needed reassurances that he wasn't in a dream—that he was actually at the center of the world's true power, in a secretive salon, being serviced by a woman who might just as well be gracing the center pages of magazines.

Kattner took full advantage of the lifestyle he had created within a boorish corporate sphere. Amerimem provided membership to the exclusive Las Bajos Country Club and, commensurate with the politics associated with the position, an inordinate expense account. His obscene compensation was predicated strictly on performance, and he acquired a penchant for consistently sourcing and developing the top talent in the field. His job eventually transitioned to a more social endeavor than managerial, and he mingled as he pleased. As long as the ideas, accolades, and advancements kept flowing, most of the board members looked the other way. The others may just as well have been alongside him at the clubs. Not that he minded; the lifestyle precluded any possibility for a traditional family. Jack succumbed to bachelorism in early adulthood, having never married or considered it in the first place. If he needed company or companionship, he knew where to find it. Anything further was an exercise in unnecessary encumbrances. He tied knots at his quinquennial employment contract renewals, and his workers provided enough emotional instability to mimic a traditional marriage of sorts. One major difference being that the divorces came easy and were always one-sided. The clos-est semblance to a life partner for Jack was his administrative assistant, and she was an impregnable fortress.

Rebecca Morningwood entered the company seventeen years ago as an intern to the branch CFO's administrative assistant. She soon discovered where all the company's discretionary funds channeled and, when promotion opportunities appeared, she based all her decisions with that specific knowledge in mind. Upon graduation, she settled into corporate life, marrying her career, same as Jack. Amerimem first employed her as a simple clerk, which she knew would entail regular audiences with the middle executives, whom she also knew would appreciate her concisely constructed appearance. They already considered Morningwood tall at 5'9", and she preferred further ostentation by wearing skyscraper pumps—the type that need an altimeter in the heel—pinstriped power suits that outlined her buxom chest, and split skirts to frame the longest legs. Rarer still, her naturally straight auburn hair descended three quarters the way down her back when not gathered in a ponytail. Morningwood was devastatingly beautiful. Worse, she knew it, as demonstrated by the pride whenever someone asked why three entries in the Wardrobe and Conduct sections of Amerimem's employee manual were the direct result of her gleeful indiscretions.

As to how Rebecca Morningwood ascended to Amerimem's top technical office, many of her colleagues would attribute her appearance. At least, that's what every high-level executive knew intrinsically, and what the envious staffers speculated. It was her tenacity that kept her around, however. While Jack made a habit of involving himself with anyone, and sometimes at the office, those breakups were often expeditious. Morningwood knew she was at the top, and to stay there meant not being conquered by him or anyone else at the company. And Jack's favorite pastime was defeating impossible challenges. After seventeen years, he occasionally made a half-hearted attempt, and when she brought him down gently, he could predictably be found soon after at a gentleman's club with an 18-year-old Macallan in one hand, and a 25-year-old blonde in the other.

Jack winced for the fourth time. "All right, that's a bit much. You new here?"

The masseuse tensed. "Well, yes, but they said if I—"

"Relax. I'm just rattling your cage. Go ahead and finish the left side; I've got a meeting in thirty minutes."

The bouncy brunette shuffled over to Kattner's left and rapidly started molding his deltoid like a potter.

"Slow down, honey. I'm not in *that* big of a hurry."

She reduced her oscillations, kneading her way down to the biceps and triceps—what little of them remained. Jack tried to stay fit, but his version of the country club lifestyle included the bar just as often as the sauna. Once finished with his left side, she returned to his lower back. A few seconds later, she walked over to a drawer, removed a tennis ball, and worked it vigorously into his left buttock. Needing more pressure, she bent down and drove the ball deep into Jack's less-than-fleshy posterior with her elbow.

"OW! Jesus, girl! What the hell?"

"I'm sorry Mister Kattner! They told me you like it this way."

"What way? Who said that?"

"Sarah told me you like a little pain."

Jack thought for a moment and conjured his best lie. "Sar— Oh, for God sakes. You take one girl out from here and everyone thinks you're a meal ticket."

"But she said—"

"Damn, that smarts!"

"I'm so sorry Mister Kattner. Is there *anything* I can do?"

Jack examined her deeply apologetic eyes, and her young, healthy body.

"No."

Pouting as if her entire career was in jeopardy, Jack let her continue while he dressed. As he walked out, he slapped her bottom hard, making her jump and squeal, yet just restrained enough to not attract attention.

"Don't cry, you deserved that. Give me your number and I'll call you after the meeting. What's your name, anyway?"

The young woman perked up, wiped away her sniffles, and gathered her lips in a smile. "Kim."

"The number?"

"Oh, yeah." Kim wrote her telephone number on a paper note and brought it back to the doorway Kattner was exiting.

"I'll pick you up this afternoon. And, I *don't* want to see any tennis balls!"

Kim dreamt of inking her signature on the bottom right-hand corner of a down-payment check. That barely-used white Mercedes convertible was just an evening away. Pursing her lips and nodding, the young doe-eyed brunette released her catch with a tingling sigh.

Jack slipped down the hall to the reception area on the western concourse, E Ring of the Pentagon. Waving to the receptionist, he continued to the elevators and his afternoon appointment on the fourth floor. He flashed his identification to the elevator guard. A bell rang and the door retracted. Jack donned his lanyard and walked inside.

He spoke at the surveillance camera in the upper left corner. "Fourth floor."

The doors converged and the fourth-floor button illuminated. Slowly, the old elevator rose to the topmost level. Exiting to the left, Kattner strode through several corridors and past dozens of doorways until finally reaching his destination. Two undecorated, armed guards manned each side of the room's double doorway. Kattner reached for his lanyard and presented it to one of them. After a close inspection and a careful assessment of Kattner's likeness, the guard swiped his own identification card, unlocking the entrance. Kattner entered a reception area just outside of the main conference room. A man dressed in a civilian suit was standing with his back turned to Kattner in front of a large wooden desk. He was receiving a phone call while a thickset trunk of a man sat behind in a darkened corner, sizing up Kattner. The man's face tried desperately to produce a smile, but his eyes were unwilling to cooperate. Kattner could not help but overhear the ongoing conversation.

"Yes, he's arrived. No, he does not. No, I do not believe so—no. Yes."

While on the line, the man turned around to Kattner, uttering one more sentence before hanging up.

"As you wish."

The man hung the phone's handset back on its base, keeping eye contact with Kattner.

"Mister Kattner?"

Kattner answered slowly with a scrutinizing leer. "Yes."

"You are likely not aware of the events yesterday, no?"

Kattner glanced off to his right briefly before answering."

"Evidently, not. What's the problem? I have a presentation in three minutes."

"I am afraid this is not going to be possible."

Kattner's brow furled. If there was one thing he intensely loathed, it was a change in schedule, or worse, a complete waste of his time by cancellation.

"There better be a very good explanation."

The silent man behind Kattner reached into his pocket and pulled out a cigarette case. Opening it, he slid one carefully out of the elastic binder and tapped its golden filter several times on the case. Reaching into his trousers' pocket, he retrieved an ornate silver lighter, flipped open its small cover, and ignited a tiny, magenta-flamed torch.

As much as Kattner would normally be quick to caution someone about egregious violations of Pentagon policy, he knew there were certain personnel to whom some rules simply did not apply, and he belonged to that class. Still, that wasn't so much what was bothering him at the moment as the realization he was conversing with people atypical of the usual Pentagon sort.

Slowly, the man previously on the phone walked over to the solid doors of the conference room. Twisting both knobs at once, he swung them wide open. Inside the room was a large, rectangular conference table made of stainless steel and striped with a walnut veneer. Seated around the table were three highly decorated Air Force officers: A three-star general, a colonel, and a female brigadier general. A third civilian-suited man stood behind her holding a thin, black stiletto tightly against her neck, just over the jugular. The knife penetrated her skin enough to produce a small trail of blood, staining her jacket's collar down to the lapel. Behind her was a skirted aide, lying prone on the floor in a fresh pool of blood. The officers' mouths were gagged, and their arms had been tied behind their lavish leather chairs. The general seated left attempted to warn Kattner, but his gag was too tight to make any sense of the mumbling.

One of Kattner's most attributable executive traits was a rapid deductive assessment of any given corporate scenario. Stunned by the scene, he nonetheless noticed that all of the officers' bindings came from their trousers—a fact verified by the unused scraps scattered about the floor underneath the table. The chairs and table were large enough to mask their naked legs, but not their feet.

Kattner suddenly felt a burning sensation from a pointed blade's ingress through his suit and into the few top layers of dermis at the lower back of his spinal column. For a moment, he calculated himself as expendable. *Wrong place, wrong time. No, he'd be dead already. Why the show?*

"Mister Kattner. I do not wish to instruct this man to end your life—as much as he would enjoy it."

"What have you done?" Kattner started to hyperventilate.

"Please, you must try to relax. We do not need another mistake, now do we?" He pointed to the corpse on the floor.

Kattner felt the blade sink one more millimeter into his flesh. The heat and numbness spread, and any flinch meant permanent paralysis or death.

"It is not what we have done, but more what *you* have done." The man said.

Kattner struggled. "And what is that?"

"You were to give a demonstration of a device today. I believe you were expecting to have it delivered while you were golfing in Canouan, yet it is not here."

"Well if it's not here, then I don't know what happened."

Kattner looked towards the two gagged officers as their wide-open eyes underscored their desperate expressions.

"Neither did we until one moment ago." The man rounded the large table to face Kattner from the other side. "It would seem that two of your scientists interrupted an operation yesterday morning at your laboratory. Your lab was destroyed, including one of the devices. We have no further information other than the existence of a second device."

Kattner continued to stare at the gagged men, and while he did, the general exaggeratedly blinked once. Understanding the message, Kattner said nothing more.

"I did not think it necessary to inform you that we will exhaust every option. Your comrades give us trouble." The man pointed again to the dead secretary on the floor. "Eventually they were made to comply, as will you."

The man motioned to his associate holding the pointed blade at the female general's neck. He snapped his fingers and pointed to the other side of the table. The woman felt the blade withdraw. Her persecutor dashed to the other end of the table. The man with the stiletto took position just behind the colonel and gazed wildly at the back of his head. He glanced up to his leader who nodded once. Without inhaling, he thrust his blade deeply and angrily into the colonel's neck at the base, instantly paralyzing him in a flash of agonizing death. Horrified, the gagged brigadier at the other end of the table started squealing and jostling about in her bindings. The other general closed his eyes before coldly glaring at the assailing provocateur and his dripping dagger. The assassin merely paused to wipe his blade on the dead colonel's slumped shoulders, then winked at the general in defiance.

Kattner cowered, biting his hand at the grave injustice. The assassin took position behind the commanding general and awaited his instructions.

"Mister Kattner, the deceased people in this room will be on my conscience regardless of my profession. This general's death will be on yours if you do not tell me what I need to know."

Kattner's eyes darted about the room in shock of the situation. Looking at the female general sobbing uncontrollably on his right, then left to the murderer standing behind the general, his pupils dilated wide in anticipation of the consequences.

"Yes . . . there is another."

"Where is it?"

The gagged general's eyes went the ceiling in disgust. His face turned tomato red and his screams of "NO!" were easily intelligible through his gag. He stopped as soon as he felt the sting of the blade's tip piercing the bottom of his neck. Kattner averted the general's glares, turning away as he stumbled for answers

"Umm . . ." He coughed. "I don't really know."

The leader nodded to the man behind the general. Kattner tried desperately to stave him off.

"No, NO! WAIT!" The assassin stopped just before plunging the knife into the general's upper vertebrae.

The leader lowered his hand. "Please continue, Mister Kattner."

"I really don't know where it is . . . not exactly. I'm told one of my engineers took it home without authorization, but I didn't do anything because our engineers take their work home all the—"

"Enough. And where are they *now*?"

"I told you. I really don't know. This is the first I heard about an operation at the lab."

The leader snapped his fingers at the smoking man behind Kattner. Instantly, the sharp burn of his blade refocused Jack's attention.

"You will come with us. There will be no trouble. You attempt anything and he will sever your spinal column as efficiently as the colonel's."

Kattner was speechless from the agonizing burn as his torturer led him back to the reception area. The leader looked back to the assassin and signaled, ordering the general's instant execution. In the same manner as before, the murderer crisply thrust his blade, ending the general without so much as a tremble. Again, he wiped his blade on the victim's shoulders, and then moved briskly to the other side of the table, behind the female brigadier and her muffled squeaks.

"Do not kill her! It is better we leave our enemy in the hands of crying women." The leader laughed as he exited the doorway of the conference room.

On his way out, the assassin looked back to at the general and blew her a kiss, to which she convulsed. He bolted the conference room doors behind him and joined his leader and their third associate, whose knife was still firmly plugged into Kattner's lower back.

"We are going to open the door now, Mister Kattner. Remember, they are only one step behind you. I will be in front, and we will walk silently past the sentries—down the hall and into the elevator on the left. Understand?"

Kattner nodded. The door opened and all four men walked purposely by the guards, down the hall and into the elevator as described.

"H-how did you guys get in here?" Kattner asked.

The doors closed behind them, and the leader looked up to the camera above the control console.

"Ground floor," he said with a perfect southern drawl.

The G button lit, and the elevator slowly descended.

"Pardon, Mister Kattner?"

"How did you get past security?"

"Part of your American arrogance, Mister Kattner. You assume we are not already here."

The elevator stopped. The men exited towards a corridor leading to the Pentagon's E-Ring and to one of its main exits. Colonel Osterhoudt did not take notice of these men on his way inside, coincidentally checking his watch in confirmation of his tardiness to Amerimem's presentation as they passed. He picked up his pace towards the other direction. Outside, the group entered a large SUV waiting at the northwestern valet. The leader climbed into the front passenger seat while the other assassins sandwiched Kattner in the rear.

"Where are we going?" Kattner demanded.

The leader snapped his fingers. The man to Kattner's right gagged him tightly and stretched a long black stocking cap over his head. Kattner struggled for air as the wool covering his mouth became moist.

"Relax or you will most certainly hyperventilate."

The sentries standing outside of the office suite briefly pondered the faint and regular poundings emanating from behind the door they guarded. Colonel Osterhoudt, now waiting impatiently before them, interrupted their debate.

"Ten-hut!"

The guards came to attention but did nothing else. Osterhoudt was further annoyed. "What's the matter with you two? Open the door!"

The sentry on the right swiped his card and unlocked the door. Upon opening, Osterhoudt immediately heard the pounding on the inner conference room doors and stench of cigarettes that permeated the office. Rushing to the doors, he flung them open, revealing Brigadier General Tomlinson attached to her chair—gagged and on the floor with her bound feet pointing towards the doorway. Inspecting the other end of the large conference table, Osterhoudt marked two dead officers, including the general responsible for his current assignment. Behind Tomlinson was the secretary's carcass, her blood pool now encircling her entire body.

Osterhoudt jumped behind Tomlinson and untied her gag, then her hands. She struggled for fresh air. The guards ran to their aid and paused upon seeing the carnage.

"Call it in, now!" One of them yelled, which triggered an emergency lockdown.

Osterhoudt held the recovering general in his arms, her neck slowly bleeding on his sleeve. "Who did this?"

"I don't know." She said with an agitated rasp.

"Appearance?"

"Men dressed in civvies. Three of them. One had a slight accent. If I didn't know any better, I'd say Eastern European, maybe Russian."

"Russian? To hell, you say!"

"I said maybe. They couldn't possibly get in here if they were."

"You're mistaken, General. Yes, they can and yes, they have. It's classified—happened once before in the '60s."

"WHAT?"

"Yes. One man infiltrated. They called him "The Leopard", and they captured him eventually, but the damage was done.

The Pentagon doesn't talk about its embarrassments. Need to know . . ."

"Get me up; I need to make a call."

Osterhoudt reached behind and brought Tomlinson to her feet. Tomlinson straightened her uniform and held a napkin across her neck.

"Did you see Jack Kattner on your way in?" She asked.

"Who?"

"Jack Kattner. Amerimem. He was supposed to brief us on the device, but it never arrived. We thought he had it on him . . . the other one."

"Strike Two." Osterhoudt mumbled.

"They took him out of here just before you walked in, sir," said one of the guards.

Osterhoudt checked his watch again. "How long ago?"

"No more than five minutes, sir."

Osterhoudt vaguely remembered the men just before he checked his watch. *Them!*

"General, they will interrogate him, you know, but he only has strategic value."

"The leader asked Kattner about the other device—a second. Colonel, *is* there in fact another device?"

"Yes, which I tried unsuccessfully to retrieve this morning in Utah."

Tomlinson held her neck trying desperately not to faint. "Why wasn't I briefed about this operation?"

"Classified." Osterhoudt looked back over towards the other end of the table. "Although it appears *you* are now Boxwood's commanding officer."

● ● ●

Apsáalooke Auto now three hours behind them, Chris' thoughts drifted upon River's abilities and their parallels with his mystified soft drive device.

"I don't mean to interrupt your one man show over there, but I think we have some company." Matt said.

Chris' eyes danced around the surrounding landscape. "What? Where?"

"Don't turn your head around, adjust the rearview mirror. The white van about four cars back on the left side—see it?"

"No. Oh, wait—yes."

"They've not changed position in the past hour no matter what speed I go."

"Well, what should I do?"

"I don't know. Where are we?"

Chris picked up a map and studied the northeastern part of I-90 in Wyoming. "Moorcroft. We're just outside some little town called Moorcroft. Why?"

"I want to test if they are following us. That's why! Look, is there a detour we can use to get back on the interstate a few miles down?"

Chris rechecked the map. "Yes. Take Highway 14. Head north. It looks like it returns to I-90 after twenty or so miles."

Matt made the exit leading to the alternate route. He glanced in the rearview and the van didn't follow.

"You may think I am being paranoid, but it's better to err on the side of caution, don't you think?"

"I've had my fill of white vans."

Several minutes passed and Chris returned to his previous thoughts. "You haven't commented much on this. What do you make of it all?"

"Make of what?"

"Well, you know—the soft drive, the scenes, and the spirit visions. The whole thing."

"I really haven't had too much time to absorb it, to tell you the truth. On the one hand, it fascinates me that these little memory blips are all running around attached to particles, and on the other, it depresses me that, at one point, we all knew how to decode them. Well, *we* forgot. Some of these *other* people haven't. I feel like we've been living some sort of illusion—that what we're doing is somehow important, when in fact, we're just running around in one gigantic vivarium for someone else's research or amusement. Who are the real spectators and why should I care? It doesn't seem so important to me as, well, simple happiness."

Chris gazed across the landscape. "I think it means something. It's important."

"How?"

"It exposes a huge lie. People are living with a big lie, that's what."

"Maybe, but you can't assume people want to hear the truth. Think they need it? I'm not exactly sure, which might possibly explain why there are people after us. What's worse—the truth or the lie?"

"If anything, proving the link between the device and ancient aboriginal communication customs could be interesting."

"What? The hair snorting?"

"Well, yeah." Chris lamented. "It sounds like something I caught in the news some time ago about Keith Richards."

"What about him?"

"Didn't he snort the ashes of his father or something?"

"EWWW!" Emily shouted.

"What?"

"Yeah." Matt chuckled. "It was on the news. He said he snorted the ashes of his father, saying it would bring him knowledge and long life or something."

"That's insanity. He denied it later, didn't he? Said it was a hoax?"

"Yeah, but in another interview, he said he actually did it. I don't know what to believe anymore."

"EWW! Dad!"

"What, Emily?"

"That's disgusting!"

"Then put your binky—I mean, your music on."

"The battery's dead."

"Look." Chris turned around. "There's a plug-in right down there. Charge it."

Emily plugged in her adapter, and Matt felt compelled to continue antagonizing her. "Probably wouldn't hurt him much."

"What?" Chris asked.

"The ashes. After everything he's done? I mean, look at him!"

"Dad!"

"I wouldn't make any assumptions. We won't live to see him gone."

"That's not funny."

"DAD!"

Chris hushed her with a finger. "Can we change the subject?"

Matt pursed his lips. "Okay, but he's already dead! He's just extremely adept at making everyone think otherwise."

"Look, there's the interstate." Chris pointed.

White Line

Two lulling hours of road noise elapsed before Matt switched on the truck's radio. A talk show was the first place he landed. He suddenly slammed both feet on the brake pedal. The antilock brakes' oscillations buffeted the truck wildly, jarring everyone awake and sending Snickers yelping to the floorboard. Matt stopped in the emergency lane, killed the engine, and increased the radio's volume.

"Jesus, Matt! What the —" Chris held the back of his head, which had just been whiplashed against his headrest.

"Shh! We need to hear this."

> . . . Repeating the evening outlook for the Greater Minneapolis/St. Paul area . . . Clear this evening, lows in the lower 50s with some light fog developing after 11.
>
> Thanks Alan.
>
> And in other news, two men died yesterday in an apparent tipi fire. Local authorities say they were killed when their tipi ignited on a reservation in southern Montana. Their identities are not yet known as the investigation continues.
>
> Did you say a *tipi*, Phil?
>
> Yes, Alan. My producers are informing me that it was the only permanent tipi on the reservation, but there are reportedly hundreds of them during their yearly festival around—
>
> [click]

Matt slowly rotated the radio's volume knob. "God, no!" he whispered.

Chris and Emily's grogginess disappeared in shock.

"Matt, that was *them*. It had to be them. Oh please, no!"

"Daddy, what's the matter?"

"Em." Chris kept a snug arm around her. "The people we stayed with last night—River, Twin Feathers . . ."

"They're gone, Emily." Matt gulped.

"Gone?"

Matt pounded the steering wheel. "Murdered. Killed. Gone," he shouted. "They didn't have any accident. They were killed because of us!"

Emily's tears erupted, and a slow, droning mewl underneath them was Snickers' empathy. Matt restarted the truck and merged back into traffic.

"Dude, take it easy; you're upsetting her."

"Well, I'm upset! Aren't you?"

"Yes, but I can't think about that right now."

"We have to get off this road," said Matt.

"Why?"

"If they got to them, then there's no doubt they know what we're driving *and* our probable route."

"You think they talked?" Chris asked.

"It doesn't matter what I think, assume they did."

"We'll need another vehicle. Can't you steal another? Your ignition trick?"

"You see a parking lot anywhere around here? Besides, that will generate another report, and they'll put two and two together if they find this truck in the same town."

"Okay, what about a new license plate?"

Matt pointed to a roadside billboard. "There's an exit coming up with a shopping center."

"Well, there's your parking lot."

"Not in the mood, Doc. I like your plate idea better."

"Em?" Chris tugged at her arm, but she was still sobbing from the news. "Come here."

She scooted closer and leaned against her father, weeping. In a low and calming voice, Chris consoled her.

"It's okay. I'm sorry—we didn't want to upset you. Sweetie, we're several hundred miles away from there. They don't know where we are, and in a few minutes, it will be extremely difficult to find us." He combed his fingers through her hair and hugged her tightly.

Matt took the next exit and found a home improvement store with an abundantly full parking lot.

"Perfect." Chris said.

"Yeah. Sometimes, you just get lucky—again." Matt hopped out and started to walk inside.

"What are you doing? I thought we were only stealing a tag?"

"I'll be right back."

Chris appeared frustrated at the lack of information, having no choice but to sit patiently. It was a short wait. Matt soon emerged at a brisk pace from the store's exit carrying two bags. He threw them into the back with Snickers, opened the driver's side door, and reached under his seat. He retrieved a small toolkit, opened it, and picked out a screwdriver. He closed the kit and placed it back under his seat before climbing back into the truck.

"Here Emily, hold on to this."

Driving next door to a crowded strip mall, he spotted a similar truck.

"Bingo!"

"What?" Chris asked.

"Same truck. Perfect. Emily, I need that screwdriver now."

Matt jumped out and made quick work of removing the other truck's license plate. Climbing back in, he handed the plate and screwdriver to Emily.

"Where are we going to do this?" Chris asked.

"The old airport across the street. See it? There are some hangars we'll park behind and be out of the way."

Matt brought the truck over to the other side of the road and into the compound. There was no notable activity. The airport's light beacon was at rest, and no cars were parked at the main office. Dead. Matt found a hiding place on the back-side of a hangar and parked under some leafy ash trees. Both he and Chris immediately bounced out and got busy. Chris grabbed the stolen license plate along with the screwdriver.

"Hold on for a minute, Chris. I need you to help me tape things off first."

"Tape?"

Matt took one of the bags from the back of the truck and pulled out two rolls of painter's tape along with some sales flyers. He tossed one roll to Chris and began taping the edges around the windshield.

"Painting?"

"Yes. Come on—tape the paper around the back glass."

"Why are we painting when we just stole a plate? Isn't that enough?"

Matt stopped. "Look, I have to assume they know the tag number, the make, the model, and the color. We can switch tags all day long, but we're still two guys, a girl, and a dog in a white pickup truck."

"Oh." Chris fervently started taping the back glass.

Matt grinned. "Change the color and they're not going to give us a second thought, let alone run the tag."

"Then why steal the tag?"

"Cameras, which will trace it back to here as a stolen plate, nothing else."

"Ah, brilliant."

Chris stretched the clingy paper tape around the truck window's borders. Before long, both he and Matt had all the windows, mirrors, chromed bits and lights papered. Matt produced the first of eight cans of midnight blue spray paint and started shaking it vigorously.

Chris picked up another can and did the same. "You do that so well," he said.

"Jesus." Matt glanced to the heavens. "Forgive me Abe, I hope you like blue."

The canisters periodically rattled from the tiny metal pellets inside them as the men slowly sprayed their way around the vehicle. Using all but one of the paint cans, they evenly applied enough to make it passable as a blue pickup, although the shade was slightly lighter than they had envisioned due to the white undercoat. They found time to kill, waiting for the paint to dry enough for roadworthiness. Matt picked up a stick that fell from one of the nearby trees and played fetch with Snickers. Emily stretched her legs while listening to music. Chris stared at the airport's beacon, counting the timing between white and green flashes.

Twenty minutes dragged by. Matt walked back to the truck's driver side door and depressed his right index finger into the fresh coat of paint just over his door's handle. It did not feel tacky, nor did it leave any residue upon inspection, not even a fingerprint. He rubbed along the door. Nothing.

"Time to go," he said. "Let's get this tape off."

Tape removed, Chris went to the driver's side. Matt was already halfway into his seat.

"What are you doing?" Matt asked.

"I assumed it was my time to drive."

"Assumed? We've got another six hours to Chicago. I can manage it. You can take over there and make the entire run to DC. It's another ten to twelve hours, not including stops. We could arrive by tomorrow late afternoon with a little luck. I need you rested."

"I thought it was already late and you've been at it since early this morning in Montana."

"Trust me, I'm okay. Besides. I've got my eyes on a particular pizza place that stays open late."

"Oh?"

"Daddy?" Emily held up her hand.

Both men simultaneously shouted, "You're hungry!"

Emily shrugged with a slight grin. Snickers jumped into the seat with her and plopped his head across her thighs.

Chris stuffed himself alongside him and shut the door. "Let's get a snack. Something light, though. Chicago isn't that far away."

"Please, God, no sandwiches! I'm sick to death of sandwiches!" Matt barked.

Emily spontaneously hugged him. "My new best friend, Daddy."

Disappointed with the local selection, they ventured to a nearby mall. Matt drove around its entire perimeter scouting for lighter fare, finding none. "Wow," he said dryly.

"The sign said 'Mall'. This is not a mall; it's another strip center. How can they . . . never mind. Look, there's a Chinese take-out."

Chris pointed to a slot near the end of the building—a solitary storefront lit brightly with assorted flickering neon.

"I will take care of Snickers." Matt said. "You guys go ahead."

"Do you want anything in particular?"

"Something light? Maybe just some soup."

"Which?"

"Wonton."

Matt whipped out a water bottle and got to work. Chris and Emily returned with two sacks several minutes later.

Chris handed Matt a container of soup, some dry noodles, a spoon, and some napkins. "You're going to be disappointed."

"That bad?"

"Let's just say the Bay Area has a tendency to spoil in this regard."

"I completely understand."

Chris quaffed his two eggrolls and leashed Snickers for a trot in an adjoining field. Matt tried desperately to be as expedient, but his steaming hot soup was proving a problematic exercise in masochism.

"Oh, man. I'm not going to be able to taste a thing when we get to Chicago. Arggg!"

Emily giggled. "Mister Matt thought he was going to be the smarty!"

"Oh, I see your sense of humor is coming around. You'll have to tell me how the pizza tastes later."

Emily kept laughing. "Dad tells me it's like the best. Like, the best on the whole planet, right?"

"It is. Well, it is for *Chicago* pizza. What are you eating now?"

"Fried rice. It's not very good."

Chris returned from the walk with Snickers. "Let's get rolling. I'm not comfortable mulling around here with that tag."

"What about my soup?"

Chris gulped his drink down and gave the large empty foam cup and a straw to Matt. "Here you go."

Matt looked at the cup for a moment and laughed. "I should've thought about this years ago."

"As long as the straw doesn't melt. Is it hot?

"Don't ask."

Emily cackled again. "Mister Matt said I'm going to have to tell him how the pizza tastes because he burned his tongue."

"Aww, what a pity!"

Matt would have his revenge, even if it meant his own inclusion in the suffering. Less than an hour down the road, they were running for the restrooms.

"Well, you'll be hungry in Chicago." Matt held his sour stomach.

"Not funny." Emily held her belly too.

"Dear God." Chris belched. "I hate being the object of a cliché."

Jacobson was preoccupied with his injurious soup as he guided the pickup eastward, deep into Wisconsin's dells before heading south-southeast past Madison and finally the drop towards Chicago. The large pinkish glow appeared on the horizon as they reached its exurbs. He continued into downtown and onto Wells Street. Stopping in front of a hotel across from his lauded pizza joint, Matt examined the situation. Chris was clearing his head from a long nap, and Emily seemed dreary-eyed and only mildly interested so late after her normal bedtime. Still, it was bustling Chicago, and they were in the middle of one of its trendier neighborhoods.

Chris couldn't believe his eyes after checking his watch. "You've got to be kidding me. There's a line half a block back!"

Matt slid out and closed his door. "Hang out for a few minutes, I'll be right back."

Chris looked on as Matt walked the opposite direction of the pizzeria and into the hotel. A couple minutes later, he reappeared clutching a small white card in his hand. He held it up to Chris as he walked across the street and straight in the front door of the restaurant, much to the astonishment of those queued.

Chris waited patiently while calming Snickers' anxieties. Loud barking was not something normally heard in chic areas, let alone from the bed of a spray-painted pickup truck. *Clodhoppers in Chicago?* The line abruptly became an unstylish drudgery of soaked armpits and skyward noses.

With a bounce in his step, Matt triumphantly pranced across the street with a steaming flat box and a bag with paper plates, forks, and napkins. Some in the queue were scratching their heads; others shouted complaints. Matt opened the driver's side truck door, handed the package across, and climbed inside. Chris was naturally curious.

"How did you—"

"It's nothing, really. I used to be a regular. The hotel has an agreement: Guests can skip straight to the takeout counter. The night deskie doesn't know or care who's checked in or out during the day. They're too lazy to cross the registry. I've been doing this off and on for years—you just say you're a guest of a room number and ask for the coupon—works every time."

"Perfect."

Without further delay, Matt sliced the container's seal and began divvying the pie. "You should wait a moment; it looks piping hot."

"Voice of experience." Chris said, making Emily giggle.

"Well, Miss Emily, how do you like the pizza?"

Emily looked up to Matt with some semblance of a furled brow. "That's not pizza!"

"Sure it is."

"No it's not. This looks like a cheese pie. I can't pick this up with my hand."

"You're right. It's Chicago pizza, which does resemble a pie. That's why they call it a pizza pie. Isn't it delicious?"

Emily nodded after devouring a forkful of stringy mozzarella, unable to speak . . . or breathe.

Chris paused between bites. "Matt, this is outstanding. Thanks."

"Thank you, Mister Jacobson." Emily added.

He smiled. "You're both very welcome."

Licking his paper plate down to the very last red stain, Matt asked, "You ready to switch?"

"I suppose, but I'll need assistance with the navigation."

"No problem. Just remain on this street through downtown and across the river."

They traded seats and settled in for the last long leg ahead. Matt guided Chris through Chicago's downtown and back onto the interstate.

"We should hit Indy in two hours, then another nine or ten to DC. Accounting for fuel and eats, our ETA lands around noon tomorrow. I need to call my friend and give him a heads-up before we arrive, though. About an hour outside of town, okay?"

"On what phone?" Chris asked.

Skirting around the bottom of Lake Michigan, Chris grabbed I-65 southbound to Indianapolis. Stopping to refuel and hit the restrooms, the group readied for another four-hour run.

Chris discovered new ways to keep himself alert without disturbing anyone. He observed the passing traffic, noting the characteristics of each vehicle. It was his equivalent of bikini ogling—something that used to drive Suzanne insane. He counted the time between expansion gaps in the concrete to estimate his speed without use of a gauge. He reflected on his life as a top developer for the world's foremost semiconductor manufacturer. He replayed scenes from his personal best moments. He discounted the flashes of anger fighting to occupy the happy spaces. He methodically sought answers to the hardest questions. It was his nature as an engineer.

"Dao." Chris subconsciously mumbled, not realizing the volume was enough to wake anyone.

"What?" Matt asked.

Chris glanced over to see Matt waking. "I'm sorry?"

"What? You said something. What was it?"

"I didn't say anything."

"Yes you did, I heard it."

"I was thinking about something, but I don't think I said anything."

"Well you did and I heard it, but didn't know what you said. What was it?"

"Dao."

"Doctor Ming? Ha! I *knew* you liked her."

"Well, yes I like her, but—no, not—never mind."

Chris checked to ensure Emily remained asleep. "Look, when we get to your friend's place, I need to contact her. She may be in danger and besides, if anything were to happen to the soft drive, she's the sole adjuvant necessary to manufacture a new one. I can't do it alone."

"Huh? Whatever. You just keep doing what you're doing to stay awake. I'd be thinking about her too if I were in your shoes."

"No, that's not the point. Ugh! Never mind."

Matt repositioned himself, searching for comfort. "Where are we, anyway?"

"East side of Columbus. We'll arrive at your first objective in another four hours."

"That sounds just about right. Goodnight!"

Matt rolled his eyelids and promptly reestablished a rhythmic snore.

Unsaving Graces

With all his services and accomplishments to Spada Sacra, Monsignor Trovarto had only two known weaknesses. The first of which was occasional hints of compassion for his foes—a trait His Eminence found admirable, although undesirable given certain circumstances. The second was air travel. Trovarto loved to fly, yet his secret battle with Ménière's disease consistently drove him to the condition of near hospitalization. His affliction begat a legendary talent for alternative rationalization. The long descent to Reagan National proved no exception, and Bishop Esposito showed no mercy. Noticing the Monsignor wincing at each wisp of turbulence, his grin became devilishly wide and pointed.

"My dear Monsignor, whatever is the matter?"

"I am-a not so confident our dinner's vintage was up to expectations, Your Grace."

"Are you sure? I selected that label myself, and I am not in the slightest indisposed condition, nor is anyone else."

"Forgive my palate, Your Grace." Trovarto said, ruining the bishop's facial expression.

Trovarto suddenly felt the intense heat of his communicator's silent invitation, tucked away deep inside his cassock. He covered his mouth, stood up, and headed to the privacy of the jet's restroom. The bishop's wry slit for a mouth cocked in assumed triumph, blessing the meek in his own special way.

Locked away inside the spartan lavatory, Trovarto retrieved the small rectangular device and held his finger over its flashing green square. He lifted it to his ear and a message played.

> *Brother Trovarto, collect Doctor Miller and his companions, then proceed to Charlie Alpha India, Terminal 4. Good Luck.*

Trovarto carefully buried the device inside the folds of his cassock while contemplating the implications of the directives. His years with Spada Sacra were at an end. This surely must have been the moment he spent his entire career working for—"the mission", as his director often mentioned. He dismissed the sickness in his right ear and paid more attention to the growing metamorphosis in his stomach. Looking flusher than when he went into the restroom, he returned to his seat opposite the bishop.

Narciso could not help himself. "My, my."

Trovarto would have none of it, however. "At my temporary expense, I am-a blessed to report a parting with your selection, Your Grace."

Discerning the faces of the curious attending brothers, Esposito could not decipher whether their smiles were for the Monsignor or for him. *Better let it go and embrace the latter,* he thought.

The jet's tires barked upon touchdown on Runway 33 at DC's Reagan National. After taxiing to the corporate terminal at the end of the airstrip, the cabin's forward stairs articulated down towards the two black Cadillac Escalades idling below. The drivers and their seconds were dressed in black cassocks, dark wire-framed sunglasses, and tucked pectorales as the prelacy mandated. There were partially-concealed, translucent, coiled wires appearing along their necks and disappearing into their left ears. Every inch of them was as businesslike as the United States' Secret Service. Esposito and his two guards climbed into the back seat of the first SUV, while Trovarto and his entourage took the second. The doors closed and they sped off to a relatively diminutive cathedral complex on 10th Street.

Arriving at an iron gate on its north perimeter, the aggregation exited their vehicles and entered an enclave of hand-carved stone buildings. Trovarto and Esposito were ushered down a short flight of stairs and into a lower lobby lit with natural gas-powered sconces along its granite walls. At the end of a vaulted hallway, they gathered in a large conference room appointed with plush velour chairs, chalices of iced water, and formal notepads. Two other clergymen seated at the table stood up quickly, while a third man between them rose slowly.

"Your Grace, Bishop Esposito. Monsignor Trovarto," the priest introduced himself. "I am Father—"

Esposito interrupted, "I am to understand there have been developments during our flight. Begin your presentation; time is short!"

The priest's expression changed to surprise with a hint of seething annoyance. "Direct your attention to the screen behind me, Your Grace. Our network determined the identity of the Swiss imposters as mercenaries for the American military. Likely Air Force subsidized, per normale."

The large projector screen behind the presenter flipped to a shot of the crushed bodies being removed from the docks in San Francisco. "These two picked up our pursuit shortly after the incident at the laboratory and were disrupted by one of their own—an operator who's either rogue or compromised by another entity. We understand the Americans made another unsuccessful attempt at the Bonneville Salt Flats yesterday morning, local time."

Monsignor Trovarto cleared his throat. "It would-a appear that this infiltrator who helps Doctor Miller is perhaps more formidable than anticipated." *Or, divinely fortunate.*

"Insolence!" Narciso Esposito reclined with a sneer. "Your estimation forgoes the obvious alternative that they were confronted by the inept. They will be properly administered in due time. Tojagić, continue."

Esposito slyly directed his next question to the presenting priest, while glancing at Trovarto. "And, what exactly do we know about this American infiltrator?"

The presenter paused momentarily, looked at an associate whose face hid behind the screen of a laptop on the table, and waited for an accompanying dossier to occupy the projector's screen. "His name is Lieutenant Commander Matthew Jacobson—a Special Forces inductee after serving honorably in Mogadishu. He is currently assigned to a general by the name of Tutlow."

There were a few mumbles after the mention of that name. "As far as we know, Jacobson was sent to observe the operation under the guise of an audio specialist assigned to Amerimem's Chief Technical Officer, Jack Kattner."

Trovarto chimed in. "Will he a-listen to this Kattner?"

"This is now an academic matter, Monsignor. Just as you were arriving, our people at the Pentagon reported an infiltration at Tutlow's classified conference on the device. He and his second were casualized . . ."

Esposito raised a brow.

"Killed, Your Grace," said Tojagić.

"I see."

The presenter bowed. "His third, a woman, was left alive. Kattner was taken hostage."

"By whom?" Esposito asked.

"Unknown."

The bishop abruptly stood. "I must contact His Eminence at once!"

An intense flash of heat from deep within Trovarto's cassock briefly distracted him, inviting a glare from Esposito.

"Apologies, Your Grace." Trovarto struggled to clear his throat. "I must be excused."

Esposito quickly dismissed the priest with a wave of his hand and turned back to the presenter with the gaze of annoyance.

The presenter offered to escort the bishop as the rest of the table came to their feet. "There is a phone in my office, Your Grace."

Cardinal Tagliabue was an elderly priest, not easily rousted in the sixth hour of light, let alone darkness. The time spent on hold waiting for His Eminence put a damper on Esposito's zeal.

"Good afternoon, Narciso. I have been briefed by the local consulate. You will make inquiries into the Pentagon raiders. Seek contact with them and develop a rapport. They are after the same items as us. Kattner will be leveraged, naturally; he serves no other purpose. I came across a piece of intelligence that may interest you concerning the operative, Jacobson. I need to speak to you privately concerning him."

"Yes, Your Eminence. *Un momento.*"

Esposito muted the telephone's mouthpiece with his hands and motioned the others out of the office. Once the last person vacated, he continued his conversation with Vasco Tagliabue.

"How peculiar. I bet he didn't know either. Yes, Your Eminence. I will work on this right away. God be with you."

The bishop hung up and stared blankly through an office window as the first drops of rain bounced on its sill. His fiendish grin slowly returned, spreading his already thin, well-manicured pencil mustache as wide as it would ever stretch. Esposito twisted one hand around a large, dark, violet crystal adorning the top of his gilded cane, and strutted out to the conference room with sickening confidence.

* * *

Matt's eyes struggled open as the steady rumble of the truck's V8 slowed to idle at the end of an off-ramp. Sticky and caked from a rough sleep, he squinted to make out a road sign. "Maryland?"

"Panhandle, about seventy miles outside DC, so I'm looking for your payphone." Chris made a turn at the end of the ramp and entered a small town.

"Perfect," said Matt.

After intersecting the town's center without spotting a phone booth, Chris stopped in front of an elderly man whittling a foot-long chunk of maple on his front porch.

"Excuse me, sir. Do you know where we can find a payphone?"

The old man, replete in his rumpled suspenders, leaned forward in his creaky rocking chair, cupping an ear to better understand Chris' words. When he repeated the question, the man leaned back and continued rocking.

"Only one in these parts, if it's still there. You might try the airport across the river in Virginia. They used to have a public phone. You can use mine if you got an emergency, though. Are ya in trouble, young man?"

Chris smiled as if he were conversing with an unframed Norman Rockwell painting. "No sir, just want to find a payphone to call my girlfriend back home. Which way is the airport?"

Looking somewhat slighted, as if he suddenly became unimportant to the world again, the old man pointed down the street towards the south. Chris thanked him, rolled up his window, and pulled away. Both he and Matt remained silent as the truck progressed through its gears, reflecting on the last hospitable people.

Crossing the Potomac, Chris guided them around the end of a runway and over to a cropping of several small hangars surrounding the airport's FBO. The metal building's entrance was flanked by a soda machine and, more importantly, a payphone.

Matt turned to Chris. "Okay, looks like we're in business."

"I need to stretch." Chris opened his door. "Do you want anything to drink? Em?"

"Yeah, I'll take one." Matt replied.

Emily shook her head side to side and curled up into the middle of the front seat to continue sleeping. Snickers leaped out of the truck's bed and climbed in front of Chris, whining.

"Looks like I'm taking this one for a walk."

He stepped over to the soda machine and reached into his pocket, bucketing a large pile of change he had collected from various purchases made along the way. He handed Matt a soda and walked back to the truck to place his and Emily's drinks on the front seat. Chris then gathered Snickers and made for the adjacent meadow.

Matt slipped a quarter into the payphone, but an internal guard in the coin slot blocked its pathway. At first, he fiddled around with the refund lever, trying to break the blockage free somehow. After pounding the phone's casing in frustration, a tall man appeared from the office with a straightened clothes hanger in his hand. Without a word, he motioned Matt to step aside. Flipping open the slot with the refund lever, he jammed the hanger wire down the opening, releasing three quarters into the coin return trough at the bottom of the unit. Reaching into it, the man retrieved the damaged quarter and handed Matt the remaining two. He then held up the damaged coin for Matt's inspection.

"Happens all the time. Sorry about that. People think any coin will do."

"Thanks." Matt said.

Without another word, the man returned to the sleepy airport office, leaving Matt to attempt his call.

Come on, answer damnit! Two rings passed without any response.

After the third ring, a familiar voice finally answered. "Hello?"

"Drill? Hey, it's me."

The voice on the other end suddenly raised its pitch by several magnitudes. "Matthew? Oh my God! Are you in town? Please tell me you're in town."

"Calm down, silly. No. At least, not yet."

"What a pity. Same 'ole, same 'ole. Wait . . . you said 'not yet?' So, you *are* coming?"

"Look, we're in sort of a bind here. I need to see you immediately."

"Well, okay. Hold on—*we*?" Matt's friend quickly surveyed his house to make sure it was ready for visitors. "There are others? What's the emergency?"

"Um, I'll tell you about that when we get there, okay?"

"Sure, I guess. How many, so I'll know what to expect."

"Me, two others, and a dog."

"A dog? Oh, this should be interesting. How long have I got?"

"We should be there in an hour."

"Uh, how typical! Well, in any case, I can't wait to see your pretty face."

Matt said his goodbyes and hung up. He sipped his soda can and walked over to the truck where Snickers was lapping ice-cold water from Chris' cupped hands.

"I'll take us in from here. Grab a short nap."

Drill's

Chris marveled at northwestern Maryland's lush greenery and its stark contrast with his California dream—a dream that was. *Just a few acres in Glen Ellen would have been nice . . .* He drifted for miles.

Matt eventually blazed their tired hunk of spray paint to an unassumingly quaint and mature neighborhood just on the outskirts of Washington. The wisps of fresh-cut lawns fronting the white and brick colonial revival homes in Herdman's Park spoke to its tradition of unabashed conformity, yet pockets of esoteric rebellion appeared sporadically if one looked deeper. In this unique enclave, rampant civil disobedience took the form of eccentric doorbells and their impractical switches. Matt had forgotten about these affronts until the precise moment he arrived at his friend's front door. Before he rang the doorbell, he signaled Chris to join him. Emily remained behind with Snickers, who wasted no time in investigating a tall hedge on the opposite side of the truck.

Matt grinned widely as Chris climbed five brick-accented concrete steps to the front porch. Immediately, Chris' attention focused on a piece of metallic art to the side of the door—a painted cast iron male figurine, roughly the size of a shoebox, was fashioned in a post-ragtime top hat and tails, blushing, and looking back over his shoulder with one gloved hand covering his mouth. Chris' brow furled slightly.

"Go ahead." Matt chuckled. "Ring him."

Chris inspected it hastily. "Where?"

"Press on the coattails."

He gently depressed the hinged casting. Instantly, some egregiously loud chimes—probably located just on the other side of the door—began hammering out the melody for "Puttin' on the Ritz".

"Dear God, you must be kidding!"

"That's the neighborhood in a nutshell." Matt laughed. "Everything looks so nice and quiet. Perfect houses, perfect lawns, and seemingly perfect people. Very Stepford, well, except the doorbells. Everyone has something either goofy or macabre."

He pointed across the street. "There's a family over there with a dinosaur, and next door, the guy has snakes. They make different hissing sounds. Very strange."

Chris pointed upwards. "And this isn't?"

The door swung wide revealing a muscular, tall man wearing a black kimono-style robe over some wrinkled dungarees. The shine of a brass and crystal light fixture reflected off the top of his closely-shaven dome.

"Matthew!" He shouted with a slightly effeminate drawl. "Please come in. Come in, both of you!"

He held open the glass storm door and stepped aside, allowing Matt and Chris to walk past.

"And who do we have here?"

Matt turned back around. "Oh, sorry for my rudeness. This is my lab supervisor, Doctor Christopher Miller. Chris, this is my dearest old friend, Adriel 'Drill' Friedman."

They shook hands, but Chris' grip was somewhat diminished upon hearing the inflection. Paying no attention, Adriel completed his sincerest handshake and then held his arms wide open wide to receive his old friend.

Nonchalantly, Matt walked into Adriel's embrace and planted a firm kiss on his right cheek. From years of practicing the unwritten etiquette of contextual modesty, he chose not to make an obvious display.

Chris could not help noticing. At times, it served him well to answer even the most mundane questions. At others, a hot bath ensued for his lack of sensitivity.

"You two—"

"SHH!" Matt loudly hissed while continuing to hug Adriel.

Chris held his arms open and shrugged. "Ahh, not that there's anything wrong with that."

"Oh, Matt, I like him. He's funny! Nothing like a gift for arcane trivia." Adriel turned to Chris. "I loved that episode."

I bet, Chris thought. He turned back towards the front door, pointing down to the truck. "Adriel, my daughter is down there with our Lab assistant, can we—"

"Cute!" Adriel jumped. "Yes, of course, bring them right in. I'm dying to meet you all. Matt shared some funny stories already, especially those body bunny suits or whatever you call them. Oh, and friends call me Drill."

I . . . don't want to know why. Chris hopped down the stairs and over to Emily on the other side of the truck.

"Come on, sweetie. We're going inside." He grabbed Snicker's leash, then bent down to whisper in Emily's ear. "Remember those people we saw in the park a few days ago? You know—the two guys that were making out?"

Emily's eyes widened and she nodded slowly.

"Well, as it turns out, Mister Matt and his friend share the same, um, well . . . Just don't say anything about it, okay? It's not nice, no matter what you think."

Emily started giggling.

"Shssh." He glanced back up to the doorway to make sure they weren't looking.

"You know Mister Matt's a good guy. He saved us. And his friend is offering us a place to stay. Let's just keep questions to ourselves, okay?"

"I guess." Emily shared the disappointment of many young women upon discovery that an exceedingly dashing prince was off-limits and completely immune to one's persuasion.

They climbed the concrete steps and through the front door while Adriel held it open. Snickers tested the end of his leash, thoroughly examining Drill's scent, top to bottom. The rest of the house would soon follow.

Adriel bent down to greet Emily. "My, what a gorgeous animal you have there, and the dog's cute too!" He gave her a sincere hug, and Emily's eyes were bulging. "What is your name, little princess?"

"Emily," she said guardedly.

"That's beautiful, Emily. My grandmother had the same name so it will be easy to remember. And who's your curious friend here?"

"Snickers."

"Sweet!" He shouted into the house at Matt. "Ooh, I like it." Adriel turned to pet the dog, stooping to scratch behind both ears. "He's—oh goodness—he's adorable."

Standing up, he wiped his hands free of Snickers' omnipresent fur. He then assessed the entire road-weary group now occupying his living room.

"Aren't you guys famished? I took a liberty and ordered Chinese. It was delivered a few moments ago and sitting on the kitchen table if you like."

"We had that yesterday," said Emily, frowning.

"Oh, mercy. That's what I get for not asking."

Matt was quick to cut in. "No—it's not a problem, Drill. It *has* to be better than the slop we ate last night in Minnesota."

"To be sure." Adriel relaxed.

"You have a nice friend here, Matt, and we are of course grateful." Chris said. "I can't thank you enough, Drill."

"Follow me, please." Adriel looked down at Snickers as he struggled with the slick hardwood floor. "Someone could use a pedicure!"

Table conversation was scarce at first. The group slowly emptied the cartons of fried rice and vegetables. The small cloth-covered cherry table was a cozy and inviting setting in which Emily felt comfortable. Every detail in the kitchen's decoration showed extra attention, and it reminded her of a dollhouse with which she played with her mother some years ago. *This was certainly not a typical man's house,* she thought.

Snickers sat patiently at their feet, anticipating scraps. Chris' curiosity intervened again, stumbling over another awkward question. "Where, um, how did you two meet?"

Matt had just taken in a heaping forkful of rice and motioned to Adriel, who was clearing his throat to answer.

"Saudi Arabia during Desert Shield, just before the invasion. We were stationed at Al Karhj, south of Riyadh. I retired a few years later as a contractor; Matt stayed in. The distances and odd schedules, not to mention the protocols, made it tough, but we've remained in touch over the years."

Matt nodded while scarfing more rice. Adriel disapproved of Matt's table manners with a brief smirk, which was exaggerated by his walrus mustache.

He continued, "Skipping ahead a dozen years, the second Iraq tour was pretty arduous, I should say. We were assisting some water project just outside Baghdad and lost a truck to an IED. Always an IED. Me and three others made it out. The rest of my friends were paraded in town—heads only."

Emily momentarily dropped her fork.

"I found out later that Matt's squadron was the outfit that got us out of there. What a coincidence, huh? I lost some good friends on that one. No—great friends. I told my C.O. the hazard pay wasn't worth it and retired. That was '05. I made enough to invest off that and, well, still collect some other consulting business that keeps me local." He smiled at Matt. "But they set me up in *Leave It to Beaver* hell after the real estate market collapsed."

Chris laughed before choking down his last forkful. "Wow. That's about as real as it gets."

Adriel's smile slowly disappeared. "So, what can I do for you gents? Matt says you're in a bind."

Matt pointed towards Chris. "Well, first, he needs to use your phone to call long distance. I will pay you for the call."

"Geez, Matthew, how '90s of you! What happened to your cell?"

"We ditched our phones, and this call's to China."

"China? Whatever for?" Adriel's voice climbed, revealing an unplanned falsetto. "You know it'll get pinged by Homeland. You're going to get me Patriot Acted!"

"Look, it's *real* important. I'll explain everything to you while he makes the call. Believe me, there is quite a lot. Is this okay?"

"Yeah. There's a phone in a cradle next to the living room sofa. But tell him not to take all night. I don't have free calling to China, and I don't want to see a $500 bill. Had enough of those with you!"

"Go ahead Chris. As he says, though. Keep it short."

Chris wiped his face and headed towards the phone. "Thanks Drill."

Emily followed him since Snickers nearly dragged her under the table when he got up. Her earphone wires tangled. She heard nothing of her father's comments. He stood up and proceeded into the living room where he sat down on the end of the sofa, pulled out his wallet's telephone directory and picked up the handset. Carefully, he dialed the international code for China, then the number for the desk of Dao Ming. After three rings, her voice mail message answered. The first part of the message was in Mandarin, the second part was the same repeated in English.

> THIS IS THE VOICEMAIL OF DAO MING. I AM
> EITHER OUT OF THE OFFICE OR UNAVAILABLE. IF
> YOU HAVE EMERGENCY, DIAL 00-3760-0231190
> EXTENSION 424. LEAVE A MESSAGE, PLEASE.

Chris hung up and dialed her emergency number. He looked at Adriel's wall clock and realized the time difference. In her part of China, it was considerably early in the morning. After the seventh abbreviated ring, a nervous female voice finally materialized on the other end of the line.

"*Wèi.*"

"Dao? Is that you?" A few seconds of silence passed before getting his answer.

"Doctor Miller?"

"Yes, Dao. It's me. I'm so sorry to awaken you, but I desperately need to talk."

"Christopher, please listen to me. Do not worry; I am already awake. A man is here who wants to speak with you. You must listen. What he has to say is important. I must put him on the line now."

"Dao? Are you all right?"

"Yes, Christopher. Listen to him. Please."

Before Chris could ask anything else, another voice spoke with a slight French accent. "Doctor Miller, we were hoping you would make this contact."

"Who are you? Please put Dao back on!"

"I understand your frustration, Doctor Miller. I assure you, Doctor Ming is unharmed. We are aware of your current situation and warn that you and your family are in severe danger. As well, you are not alone, monsieur. Doctor Ming just discovered that her safety has also been compromised. I am instructed to have you both come to Cairo, immediately."

Chris couldn't believe his ears. "Cairo? Look sir, I don't even know—"

"There is a private jet waiting for you and your assistant at Reagan National, General Aviation Hangar 5A. Additional information will be explained upon your arrival. I will return the phone to Doctor Ming now."

"SIR!" Chris shouted into the mouthpiece.

"Hangar 5A."

"Even if I decide to go, I'm not leaving my daughter."

"Christopher," Dao took the phone. "He said it is optimal for her to stay behind. These people are here to help. Are you and Emily all right?"

Chris was dumbstruck at the whole prospect of leaving the country under such conditions.

"Emily? Wait. You're asking me to leave her too? Come on, Dao, I can't do that. No way. You wouldn't do it to *your* daughter. Oh—sorry, Dao. I didn't mean it that way."

For a moment, Chris had forgotten one of the most controversial Chinese laws. He looked down at Emily, who appeared oblivious to the conversation, shaking her head to some unknown song. Chris was unaware that she had in fact been eavesdropping and attempted to hide her emotions the best she could by looking the other way.

"I know, Christopher. I am not offended. What they are saying—there is not much time, you must understand. Does she have a passport?"

"Well, no, but—" Chris' flash negotiation tactics, or lack thereof, served little purpose. He was a person steeped in logic, and even though the situation appeared to contain logical chasms, emotions overcame him.

"Christopher, please. This is important. You must attend. Please."

Chris looked up to see Adriel and Matt hovering over him. "Dao, I don't know . . . I have to go. Let me call you back."

"I want—" Dao tried to console him further, but Chris slowly replaced the handset into its cradle, and faced his friends.

Adriel was the first to say something. "Chris, Matt told me everything, and I overheard the last part of your call. I don't know exactly what you guys are mixed up in, but my services are at your disposal. I owe Matthew that much. Your daughter and the dog are welcome to stay as long as they like. My house is theirs."

"Do they realize what they're asking me to do?" Chris angrily stared at both of the men standing over him. "Do *you*? No, I don't suppose you do."

"Daddy, don't leave me!"

Snickers barked twice. Emily scooted over to hold her father tightly. Chris ran his fingers slowly through her hair. The heat of her scalp, and the moisture in her eyes. It was unbearable.

Chris looked at Adriel and Matt with complete uncertainty. "I would *really* like a shower to think this over,"

Adriel turned back to Matt, squinting an eye. "It's down the hall, first door on the left—clean towels in the closet."

When Chris stood up to walk down the hallway, Emily began sobbing heavily. It was enough that he recognized her anxieties, especially in these moments. She was fiercely independent, but only to a point. When she reached that point, the hearts of weeping angels melted. Chris wrestled with inevitability. His destiny appeared to lie somewhere on the other side of the planet, yet his parental duties must supersede. His only outlet was anger, and with no outlet for that form of release, he opted for the seclusion of a scalding hot shower. As much as its walls repelled water, it absorbed everything else.

Matt and Adriel consoled the young girl. "Miss Emily," said Matt. "We've been through a lot already, haven't we?"

Emily nodded slowly as the unceasing fountain of tears continued beading down her cheeks. "Uh-huh."

"Your father and I have something very important to do. We will only be gone for a few short days, I promise."

Matt's consolation had little effect on Emily's cries. Snickers let out a yawn with a high-pitched whine—his eyes empathized Emily's.

"Miss Emily, it just so happens that I have the week off and need someone to go with me to Six Flags," said Adriel.

She continued sobbing.

Matt threw his arm around her. "Come'on kid, it will be okay." He looked up to Adriel. "She's been through an awful lot the past three days."

"You told me, but I still can't imagine it. Alcatraz?" Adriel reached to wipe her tears. "You poor girl."

Chris let the hot water race down the back of his spine. The noise drowned his inner monologue. The water's blistering heat took focus away from the parental crime he must commit, yet it wasn't enough to keep his teeth from grinding. Any other time, this constituted a non-issue. He believed he was in control, but choice was an illusion. He had no other option. He must face the danger and see it through. He made a promise to River, and Christopher Miller didn't break promises.

The shower's control knob squeaked, and the warm water around his feet gave way to dry, cool air. He opened the glass door and retrieved a towel. An exhaust fan removed the steam, but not the heat. Chris was indifferent to his surrounddings. The towel removed any residual emotions. Replacing his glasses, he took one long, last look in the mirror and saw nothing.

He returned to the living room, dried and dressed. "Matt, I'm ready when you are."

Emily couldn't bear looking in his direction, feeling betrayed by everyone except Snickers. Matt leaned forward to get up.

"I'm a little on the ripe side. If you guys don't mind, I think I'd like a shower too before going 'round the world."

"You *do* stink." Emily sniffled.

Matt turned around and checked under his arms. "Thanks."

Adriel bent down to Emily and held his nose—making her giggle slightly. Matt trotted down the hallway and ran through the standard two-minute shower drill. Amongst the clothes he just swiped from Adriel's closet, he remembered the jar given to him by River. Curious, he opened the container and convulsed at its freakishly pungent odor. Undeterred, he slathered a thin layer across his stitches, redressed the wound, and dressed comfortably for the trip.

"You're a kind man, Adriel. I don't know what to say." Chris looked down at Emily. "I can't believe I'm leaving my daughter with someone I don't know."

"Oh, please. You did the same thing when you dropped her off on the first morning of school."

"You're right. Funny, isn't it?"

"She'll have a great time. If you know Matt, you know me."

"Honestly?" Chris laughed. "I've only known Matt for a short time."

"Right. Well, just promise me you'll be back soon. My floors won't survive with *this* one around." Adriel pointed down to Snickers' claw marks.

Chris sat next to Emily. "Look, Adriel—"

"Drill."

"When this is over, I will be in your debt. I don't know how I can repay you."

"If what Matt tells me is true, this is far more important than my little role in the matter. If anything, I haven't felt this useful in quite some time. Besides, I needed to get outside. This is a great excuse."

Chris broke a tear, sniffling as he rubbed his hands up and down Emily's arms. Letting go of her was the singular toughest moment he had felt since his wife's burial. All the same emotions were present, the foremost being fear of the unknown. Upon standing up, he retrieved the cash from his pockets and handed all of it to Emily. "I have a feeling I won't be needing this. You take it. Make sure Mister Friedman doesn't pay for everything, okay?"

Emily took the money and said nothing. For her, it was a cold moment.

"I'll be back in a couple of days." He sniffled again before wiping his eyes and replacing his glasses to refocus. "Come on, Matt."

Matt shrugged and opened his arms for Adriel. Brief encounters seemed to be a standard operation between them— a fact both recognized long ago. Adriel embraced him and looked down to Emily before planting a solid kiss to Matt's right cheek.

"Do be careful."

"Nothin' but!"

Chris hugged his daughter one last time. "I won't be long."

Levels

Matt resumed command of their faux-midnight truck, glistening apparent in the late dawn's light. Chris climbed into the passenger side and turned sideways to hug his little girl one last time before abandoning her. At least, that's how he saw it. *How could a father do such a thing?*

"Why do you have to go?" Emily tearfully asked.

Chris leaned closer to caress her cheek.

"I don't really know, Em. They say it's important. A lot of people are depending on me, and well, I made a promise to Chief River. You know I don't break my promises."

"Promise me you'll come back!" Emily cried.

He kissed her softly on her forehead and looked deeply into her eyes, pausing to wipe a tear.

"I promise."

He closed the pickup's door and rolled down the window as Matt hit the ignition.

"I have your number and I'll call as soon as we touch down. It will probably be early in the morning, so don't miss me!"

He knew she probably wouldn't sleep well awaiting his call. Expectation anxiety ran in the family.

Chris turned to Adriel with a searing flash of utmost sincerity. "Take care of my little girl, Drill."

"No worries."

Adriel took Emily's warm hand and waved goodbye while Matt backed down the driveway and into the street below. In a moment, they were distant, then gone. Emily sniffled and did not move, staring down the street well after the truck disappeared.

"It's okay, Emily," said Adriel in a spritely southern whisp. "My friend won't let any harm come to your father. He's one of the best in the entire country."

She let go of his hand and turned around, nodding.

"Six Flags?"

Taking 16th Street through downtown, across the National Mall and over the Potomac, Matt and Chris found their way to the main entrance of Reagan National. Crossing over and looping back under Smith Boulevard, they slowly crept through the parking lot towards Hangar 5A and the mystery that awaited. A muscular man in a plain black suit caught their attention as he pointed towards a parking space adjacent the hangar's entrance. Two additional men, also wearing black suits, ties, and dark sunglasses, ushered them into the space. As they rolled to a stop, the man closest to Chris' side of the truck motioned for them to raise their hands. Chris quickly complied, but Matt was hesitant and suspicious, prompting a second request. He reluctantly surrendered a moment after he caught a glimpse of a shoulder-holstered pistol underneath the man's jacket as he started to reach for it. Under any other circumstances, he would have blown him into the river, but Matt cautiously placed his hands on the steering wheel while the agent opened the door, reached into Matt's jacket, and examined both sides of it. Nothing. Another man opened Chris' door and performed the same search of him, then inspected the truck's interior.

"Please excuse the precautions, Doctor Miller. You may lower your hands now. Will you and Commander Jacobson please follow me?"

Chris reached back into the truck and retrieved his attaché case. Matt hopped out and circled the front of the truck to join Chris by the hangar's office entrance. One of the agents opened the door and allowed everyone to enter, with the first agent leading. After passing two offices and a restroom area, the men entered a vast, open hangar with a coruscating ultramodern private jet parked on the far side. Two agents waited at the bottom of its stairway—one in the same black on black outfit, and another was wearing a clergyman's cassock.

"HALT!" Came from an agent behind them.

They froze.

"Not you, Doctor Miller. You may continue. This man must wait."

"I'm not going anywhere without him!"

"Please continue to the aircraft, Doctor Miller." The man gently nudged Chris forward.

Matt lunged towards the suited man. "Hey, you can't—"

One of the larger agents jumped in front of him. "Commander Jacobson, please, it is unnecessary!"

Making his way around the port wing, Chris eventually confronted the men waiting by the jet's airstairs. A clergyman extended his right hand and spoke in a thick Italian accent.

"Doctor Miller. It is-a my great pleasure to finally make your acquaintance."

Chris hesitantly shook his hand and turned back around to discover Matt being relieved of the pistol he had tucked in his rear beltline. He displayed the disgusted look of a duped criminal while the search concluded at the bottom of his right pants leg.

"You must-a excuse us. You know that aircraft such as-a these do not withstand bullets very well."

"Clear." One the inspecting agents declared. "You may join Doctor Miller and the Monsignor, Commander. Apologies for the inconvenience."

Matt squinted briefly, displeased with the loss of his weapon, and then joined the men at the jet.

The clergyman shook his hand vigorously.

"Ah, Commander Jacobson. I am-a to understand your services have been indispensable. My name is Trovarto. Monsignor Trovarto. Gentlemen, please come. We have-a long flight ahead of us."

The priest climbed the airstairs and into the lushly appointted cabin. Matt looked the aircraft over at the top of the stairs.

"I didn't know any of these had been delivered yet."

"Ah, yes. It is-a new one, I am told, and it will complete the trip to Cairo non-stop—eleven hours, according to our captain. As close to the speed of sound as possible, and we have a seventy-five-knot tailwind. Someone is-a looking over us tonight! Please be seated over here; we depart immediately."

Chris and Matt looked down the length of the cabin's seating, noticing that they weren't traveling alone. Several others occupied the aft recliners, and only a few of them were curious about the newcomers; the others glanced once and continued chatting amongst themselves.

A diesel tug pulled the glistening Gulfstream out of the hangar as its engines ignited, the sound of which was barely audible inside the cabin. Neither were the hydraulic actuators when the jet's control surfaces were tested. Taxiing to Runway 15, the captain briefly waited on a landing jumbo before queuing for takeoff. Once the tower signaled, its Rolls-Royce turbofans surged with a tremendous thrust, testing the thicknesses of their supple leather recliners. The automated avionics departure route eventually rocketed them to a cruising altitude of 43,000 feet, then leveled off at best efficient speed for the long voyage across the Atlantic and Mediterranean.

Lieutenant Colonel Ninel Zabroskov could not believe his ears. His upbringing taught him never to trust an enemy, yet mandated the most equitable route when confronted with difficulties. His father torturously professed Sun Tzu's pacifisms every morning at breakfast chess as if a religion, but Tzu's ancient strategies were often vague concepts to him. Zabroskov preferred the teachings of mechanized field commanders such as Rommel or Guderian, but when it came to the chessboard, Botvinnik became his undisputed master. While none of his military mentors could foresee and overcome every scenario, Zabroskov always felt he had options. There were always options. Perhaps later, but not at the moment. *These are complicated times,* he thought. He stared at Jack Kattner's gagged face, contemplating his strategic importance. *En passant, you poor bastard.*

A high-pitched squawk in Zabroskov's ear unnerved him, realizing that there were depths of vileness even he found detestable. This was simply another tournament for his calculation, and a telephone call was one of those insufferable sacrifices.

"Let me be absolutely succinct, Comrade Colonel. You assist us with this matter and the rewards will be greater than you can imagine."

"I have a fantastic imagination," laughed Zabroskov.

"We may use this as a basis for a continued relationship, Colonel—one that you may find gloriously equitable once consummated. I believe our terms are fair considering what you possess. More than fair if you acknowledge our reach. What is your decision?"

A cigarette with a small golden filter tapped against its silver case, packing the leaves more tightly. As he brought it to his lips, the crackle of ignition from his tiny torch engulfed the tip in purple. The burn was slow and the flavor rich. His iced grey eyes slowly lifted to meet those of the colonel, and he whispered smoke in repeating one of Zabroskov's own maxims.

"Never a lever shall you gift." *Never a lever . . .*

Zabroskov lifted his hand from the mouthpiece. "My associate will provide the instructions . . . ."

● ● ●

Brigadier General Tomlinson's assistant took notice of the tall, blonde officer standing before her desk. His vivid blue eyes, penetrative to her subconscious desires, concealed his calculative coldness. She stared at him compulsively since arriving moments earlier, there for a briefing with the general in her section of the Pentagon. That was two floors below where she had been bound and gagged a just few hours earlier.

The general worked diligently behind her office's glass door. She continued to experience momentary tremors but remained focused—a trait that helped her promotion to the office in the first place. The door swung open. Osterhoudt entered and walked around to the front of her desk next to a chair and saluted. She concluded reading the last page of an intelligence report before paying him any attention. That moment stretched to uncomfortable excessiveness. Peering above the top rim of her glasses, she never returned his salute.

"Afternoon, Colonel. Please have a seat."

She slid a copy of the report across her desk to him.

"The infiltrators have no intention of returning, of course. Facial detection at the lobby identified all of their aliases. They need to update that system for automatic recognition and alarm. The dinosaur that it is—well, I bet it's already on everyone's radar by now. Have a look at the third photo. Nothing appeared on INTERPOL with the exception of *this* man. He was arrested in a Project Millennium sweep twenty-two years ago. Fourteen tons of hash and more currency than any bank in Minsk. He dispatched four of their best before purportedly entering retirement. Does he serve any prison time? Nope!"

Colonel Osterhoudt examined the headshots of the subject in question. His mind recounted the scene of rescuing Tomlinson earlier in the conference room. He remembered a conspicuous odor and the out-of-place cigarette butt smashed on the floor. At the time, he paid it little attention. Brass bent the rules often in a boorish display of seniority. Now, the sketchy intelligence myths he overheard—mere rumors from watercooler lore—seemed to rematerialize. His jaws began a slow oscillation, grinding his capped molars.

"The French ALAT were the first to rumor this man," said Osterhoudt. "'Le Brochette' they call him. He and his operatives skewer their enemies. No deviation."

The traumatic demise of her colleagues brought a fresh shiver down Tomlinson's spine.

Osterhoudt continued. "Many of the Bratva are ex-KGB or otherwise *outstanding* in their fields. This operation isn't like them at all, frankly. They always stuck to drugs, oil, weapons, and other commodities. Why this?"

"The understanding from State Department intel is that they've grown to the point where they intend to extort upper-echelon organizations."

Tomlinson pointed to the ceiling.

Osterhoudt looked confused. "General, I am at a loss."

"This isn't written in any field manual or in many of the history books for that matter. Nonetheless, it is what this office facilitates, and it's a ghost."

"You mean classified."

"I meant what I said. It's neither classified nor unclassified. It's off the books. It doesn't exist, and yet it does."

Osterhoudt straightened himself in his chair.

"I already know what you are about to utter, General."

"Well, I am going to say it anyway, because I think you need to hear it from me. Colonel, we ensure the continuance of our existence through the propagation of our craft. We foment global conflicts, we sell weapons to one side, the Russians, Chinese, or someone else happily supplies the other. We create jobs, and our employees keep their enchanted lives. We're no different from any other self-perpetuating need fulfillment organization. General Tutlow explained this thoroughly to me and it is absolutely logical."

"I don't care about all this second-level nonsense, General. What is your point?"

Osterhoudt's trenchant reaction irritated Tomlinson enough to make her stand.

"Well, you should. We would be back to pre-World War II levels if not for this regiment. Vulnerable, and you'd probably be on the street!"

"Jesus, would you please get to the bottom line?"

Tomlinson sat back down as Osterhoudt released his temples to see over his hands.

"What I am trying to tell you is that they, the Bratva, have evolved to the point of extorting the largest organizations."

Osterhoudt straightened his neck. "You mean the church."

"I mean the Catholic Church and its one billion members."

"Ridiculous. How in the world did you put that together?"

"The church's susceptibilities began years ago when it was unable to make its certain internal problems disappear. Leave an open door and people will march through it. So, it's a simple deduction for me. Who else would want the device and the scientists that developed the technology? And, who do you think pulled the job in Santa Clara?"

"I thought that was *us*. Just because there were Swiss weapons doesn't mean—"

Tomlinson interrupted him by slinging another page of information in his face.

"And just yesterday, an Italian-registered jet from a fictitiously-registered Italian leasing agency landed and is still hangared just down the street at DCA. Customs records have it as clergy—the diplomatically immune variety. I see no coincidence, Colonel. When the mission folded in Bonneville, did you know where those people were headed? Personally, I guessed that they were coming here—right here."

Tomlinson rose out of her chair once again, banging her right index finger on the table. Her intercom light flashed. She sat back down before getting a conclusion past her scarlet lips and pressed the lighted button on the intercom.

"Yes?"

"Pardon the interruption, General. You wanted to be advised of any diplomatic flights departing Reagan National?"

"Yes."

"One just took off with a flight plan for the Eastern Mediterranean."

"Hold it!" Osterhoudt intervened.

"Yes, Colonel?" Tomlinson asked.

"What the jet's type?"

The intercom crackled. "Its prefix returns as a Gulfstream prototype, sir. Originated from Savannah."

"Thank you, Nancy. That will be all," said Tomlinson.

Osterhoudt scratched at his cheek. "No matter. Likely a factory test leg. And, General—your mystery bird from Italy. It's a Dassault, is it not?"

Tomlinson scrambled to find and verify the information on the report.

"Yes it is."

"Well there you have it; they're still here."

General Tomlinson depressed the intercom button again, deactivating the system. She scribbled a name on a small scrap of paper and handed it to Osterhoudt.

"This man is CIA and liaises our department when warranted. His office will have information on the whereabouts of those infiltrators. Find them. Find those sons of bitches that murdered our people. I am going to send them all back to Minsk on a pole."

Osterhoudt smirked. "I like your style, General. What about the device?"

The Crescent Passage

Monsignor Trovarto returned the communicator to the folds of his cassock and settled at the table next to a fidgety young man seated across from Matt and Chris. He savored the contents of an artful porcelain cup for a few moments, checking the windows for any signs of dawn before steaming his nostrils with it.

"Commander Jacobson, do you-a find it acceptable?"

"The tea? It's certainly not panda poop. No complaints."

"Complaints?" laughed Trovarto. "It is-a one of the finest in the world according to the owner of this aircraft, but I suppose it is a question of a-blissful ignorance. All subjects are a matter of education, are they not, Doctor Miller?"

Chris massaged the handle of his teacup, blankly staring down at the sparkling service.

Trovarto continued. "I can see there is-a element of trust I must earn." The Monsignor lowered his head, peering directly into Chris' eyes with determination. "Very well."

The priest nodded to the young man on his right—a freckled adolescent wearing a light windbreaker, a spiked red haircut, and ghostly complexion common to northwestern Europeans who the sun seldom saw. He casually bit into his apple while conspicuously focusing on Matt's teacup. In an instant, the cup slid to the edge of the table, but not over it. Matt's split-second reaction threw his hand just underneath the edge of the table in anticipation. Chris nearly fumbled his tea. Matt's eyes glared across the table, but the young man was coldly unemotional. In fact, he kept chewing his slice of apple with a slight smirk. There was a peculiar tinge—an odor of something burnt as if from lightning-produced ozone—that quickly disappeared into the jet's ventilation system.

"Okay, Trovarto," said Chris. "You have my attention."

"Commander Jacobson, Doctor Miller, this is-a Patrick." Trovarto carried the tone of pride, and Patrick smiled with confidence. "You may have read about the fantasy of telekinesis at-a some point in your lives. He is—how do you say it?—the genuine article."

"Could be a gimmick." Matt folded his arms. "Magnets under the table or something."

"Commander, I assure you, there are no gimmicks."

"Yeah?" Matt placed his right palm flat on the table. "Well, have him move my hand."

"I cannot!" Patrick shrugged. "I mean—"

"There, you see! He can't."

Patrick leaned forward, swallowing the last bite of his apple. "No sir, you don't understand. I cannot move anything of the flesh, only inanimate objects. If I try to budge your hand it would be extremely painful."

Matt looked at Chris and then turned back to Patrick. "Prove it!"

"Patrick, NO!"

Trovarto tried to stop the young man, but he had already concentrated on Matt's hand for a second longer than necessary.

"JESUS, H!" Matt screamed, yanking his hand from the table and burying it under his left armpit. Again, there was a faint odor.

"Are you injured, Commander?" Trovarto asked.

Matt flicked his fingers several times, wincing. "No, father. Sorry for the blasphemy, I meant—"

"It's all right. Better you call-a for Him instead of-a someone else."

Chris inspected Matt's hand and found no lacerations, abrasions, bruising or any abnormality. "How bad?"

"Felt like someone stuck my fingers in a clothes dryer power socket!"

"I warned ya, didn't I?" Patrick rolled his eyes.

"That's enough; I think-a he knows," said Trovarto.

Chris gave Matt's hand back and focused on the monsignor. "So, who are *you*?"

"Are you wanting to know about me in particular or-a something else, Doctor."

"Of course, I am intrigued by Patrick, you—this—but I mean, who are all of you?"

"Ah, yes—directly to the most important question. I should-a have anticipated nothing else from such a mind."

Matt cautiously tapped his finger on the table. "Well, you're obviously well-funded or well-connected. This jet ain't exactly cheap by my estimations, nor available. What gives?"

Trovarto laughed. "I wish it were mine to use. Much work could be accomplished with a vessel of-a this kind. Alas, it is on loan from a friend. It *is-a* nice, isn't it?"

"Yes of course, but why are we here, exactly?" Chris' frustration mounted.

"This part may be difficult to swallow. If-a you can believe that someone such as Patrick exists, perhaps you might entertain the possibility that there are-a many, many more the same as him. Variations, to be sure, but the fundamentals of the existence are common. I am but-a one member of a larger organization. We call ourselves *La Fratellanza di Verità*—The Brotherhood of Truth. We dedicate our very lives to just that principle. You see, for millennia, there have been nefarious animals that wish to hide, stall, or systematically destroy a truth to sustain their livelihood. These livelihoods manifest under false pretenses. And, to make matters worse, there are now other organizations whose sole purpose is-a the extortion of the largest organizations. Evil begets evil, *una propagazione di serpenti.* For centuries, we fight this evil. We have only a surgical force with limited resources, and for those centuries, we have maintained our anonymity by remaining modest. True power is a matter of-a resources."

Chris leaned forward. "That's over now, isn't it?"

"I am afraid so, but it is-a our destined evolutionary process. We are now healthy enough—secure enough—to come forward. At least, we thought so."

Matt laughed. "Evolutionary? I didn't know that word was in *your* vocabulary?"

"Did you notice the men seated behind you, Commander? They are returning from a conference. Nothing out of the ordinary, you see. They belong to a Jewish fundamentalist movement seeking neutrality and common ground with other faiths. Last year, they met with consortium of Iranian imam and ulama, and before that, they exchanged knowledge in-a several Asian religious centers—Hindus, Buddhists, Sikhs, Jains, Confucians, Shintoists (someone clapped once in the back of the jet when Trovarto said it, causing a glance from the others), and-a . . . Taoists. I hope I am not forgetting anyone."

Matt couldn't help himself. "I'm trying to put this together, father. Are you blaming the major religions around the world for all the wars, all the positioning, the posturing, and for scientific suppression? It appears that you are walking hypocrisy's tightrope to me. You are a man of the cloth! What about that?"

"Not at all. The leadership of the world's major religions is purposely *not* aware of organizations within their own ranks for reasons of plausible deniability." Trovarto's irritation became slightly apparent. He took his hat off and placed it on the table.

"The ulterior parasites are the ones responsible for abstinence of-a the truth and manipulation of the well-meaning. Their intimidation tactics went underground as far back as the Inquisition, although a number of us agree that it goes further back than the years of our Christ. The church doesn't investigate as-a long as their influence grows. They are operating with ignorance of-a the truth, both purposeful and perpetual.

"Wait. Are you trying to tell me that you deny your own religion now?" Matt asked.

"No, no, no." The Monsignor sighed. "You have it all-a wrong. My faith, *our* faiths are forever resolute. All of us believe in the same supremacy in-a one form or another, the same omnipotent power that we all share in this creation. We all believe in the positive messages in the teachings of the major faiths. What harm comes from this? Sure, there are many unbelievable, unsustainable, or worse, wrongly inter-preted anecdotes in each doctrine. This is-a part of the human condition. My former history and science teachings alone dis-count some of the anecdotes of our Holy Bible, and there are more undeniable anthropological fallacies in the other script-ures. This does not preclude the good intentions—the message —of each, nor the metaphorical intentions of the authors. We all believe in 'The Way' even if we do not label it as such. The malevolent powerful seek to keep us, the powerless, ignorant, and divided to necessitate their existence in the name of-a peace. Peace!" The priest laughed. "The historical power enigma is-a that they all talk of peace. Lying bastards, I tell you. They want the peace so long as there is a piece in it for them! We seek something more universal."

Trovarto paused for a few moments and sipped his tea. He then turned to Chris.

"Doctor Miller, as a human being, I implore you to search-a your heart. You may think that all things may one day be explained by science. This may be true; I cannot deny this fact. And coming from a man of God, it is-a not intrinsic. Science, however, is no different from any other faith. Until it provides all of the answers, faith in-a heaven above provides the comfort we need. La Fratellanza believes that science must embrace religion because they do not have all the answers. *Parimenti*, religion must also embrace the science. We are *all* neighbors. How can we function if-a we break our own commandments, eh?"

"And, this is why you came to find me."

"Yes."

"For the device."

"Not just the device, Doctor. You, your friend, your colleagues. We had to collect—pardon me, that is-a very poor choice of words—*find* you before they did.

"They. Just who are *they?*"

Trovarto tucked his lower lip, and his eyes fell away.

"Many-a organizations have-a come and gone over the centuries. Several have managed to remain at-a the top, while others were swallowed and digested. Crime lords in East Asia, military industrialists, Cosa Nostra, monarchies, fascist dictatorships, and religious separatists. We know of-a six major concerns actively practicing extortion of some form. First, there is-a the Bratva. Russian mafia and eastern European syndicate. They leverage others for money and other valuable commodities. The New Inquisitors—remnants of the Salian Franco or Merovingian, representing old-world western European corporate interests. The Asian underworld—various and loosely affiliated crime syndicates. Too many names for-a my memory. There is-a also Al-Ghaiz—an Islamist protectorate of several Middle Eastern governments, given to extremism and distortion. The military-industrial complexes you probably know—global conglomerates facilitating conflict for profit and expansion of corporate interests in natural resources and government consolidation. It is imperialism at-a its worst. Finally, a group that will-a soon, if not already, sanction my annihilation—the Spada Sacra.

"Why?" Chris removed his glasses and wiped the lenses with a damp napkin.

"Because less than an hour before we stepped onto this aircraft, I was imbedded with them and had been in a top-level position for over eight years. Spada Sacra covertly ensures the continuation of an institution representing over one billion faithful. They are also responsible for some of the most egregious proscriptions of scientific discovery and invention. Only now, through the free access to information and-a La Fratellanza's interventions, they are losing their grip. Man will excel faster than he ever dreamed possible. Man will also regain his vanquished memory."

Trovarto shouted towards the Jewish congregation a few rows aft. "Yusef! Let me borrow your case, please."

A rabbi seated three places down, unbuckled his seatbelt, and walked towards the table with an old wooden case. Monsignor Trovarto removed his hat from the table, allowing the cleric to set the case on it directly in front of Matt and Chris. Turning the front around to face them, he unlatched the case and opened its lid, revealing a tarnished toy wooden bird of about a foot in length.

"A glider? Cute. Does it fly?" Matt reached for the model. The rabbi abruptly pulled the case away.

"No! You must not touch!"

"It doesn't fly?" Matt laughed with a degree of superciliousness.

Trovarto explained. "We believe it could, but that is-a not so much the point, Commander."

"What is, then?" Chris asked. "I see that it's a wooden bird that looks very much like a glider, but why is it significant?"

"What if I told you it is over 2,200 years old?"

Chris' jaw dropped. "I would have a difficult time believing that."

"It was unearthed in an Egyptian tomb close to Saqqara by an archeologist named Doctor Kahlil Messiha over a century ago and 'lost' for almost seventy years in an old museum."

Chris studied the model further. "Are you sure it's not just a carving of a bird?"

"That was the standard explanation for-a many years, even at the insistence that, if it were a bird, the tail would not be a vertical fin. We believe the tail may be missing the equivalent of an elevator, but it cannot be proven. Nobody is about to loft it from a balcony, you see. A man once constructed a replica of it, and it did not fly well. Again, that is not the real point. It could have been made for any number of reasons; it is the fundamentals what matter. It is-a an aerodynamic craft like no other."

Matt puzzled over the model, and then looked around the cabin. "I'm more interested in these organizations, Father. May I call you Father?"

"Of-a course. What would you like to know?"

"If you are following all those groups, you knew of the attack on our laboratory. Am I right?"

"Yes. Remember, I was embedded with the Spada Sacra at the moment of the operation. We were monitoring the laboratory experiments for your Project Tumor. Those mercenaries were not of the usual variety and acted carelessly in my opinion."

Trovarto glanced to a man sitting behind Matt.

"Then who?" Jacobson asked.

"Why Commander, don't you know?" Matt felt the breath of a man just behind him holding his pistol.

Chris abruptly turned around to see the man pointing the pistol at Matt's head. "NO! You're making a big mistake. This man saved my life. He saved my daughter. He brought me here! I thought you knew all of this!"

"Yes, but what he didn't tell you was that he is an observer for an Air Force general named Tutlow. We know of this general. One of several in bed with the industrial complex. Am *I* right, Commander?

"Matt *told* me he was a plant! Listen to what I am telling you! He is a good man!" Chris squirmed to maneuver in his recliner, but the table quelled any thoughts of speedy movement.

"Well, Commander?" Trovarto asked patiently.

Matt slumped as he felt the cold tip of the pistol's barrel on the base of his skull "I will not lie to you, Father. Just like I didn't lie to Chris. Yes, I no longer feel compelled to do their dirty work after I got to know Chris, after I got to know his daughter, and especially after the soft drive's little secret popped out on the screen. I assume you saw it. It changed me. I woke up. Then the lab was hit. I panicked. If someone could get away with that . . . they don't care about me. Expendable, right? So we ran. Saw some things I can't explain along the way, too. Then they found us. If you were monitoring, you'd know about Bonneville."

Trovarto placed his hat back on the table. "Who was it? A soldier named Osterhoudt? A friend of yours, he is-a not?"

"I thought so until he shot at me!"

"Orders are orders, but I am lost on one thing. You are a commander, but-a you work for the Air Force, and they do not have commanders."

"I don't exactly work for the Air Force. Boxwood is a multi-agency affair. We keep our ranks from our original branches. I was part of a SEAL team for twelve years before a CIA man approached me."

"Interesting." Trovarto signaled the agent behind Matt.

He slowly withdrew the weapon, walked around to Matt's side, and presented it to him.

Matt picked up the weapon and pointed it at Trovarto. "I thought you didn't like guns on planes, *Father*?"

"It is not loaded, Commander." Trovarto handed its clip across the table. "Please be careful."

Chris breathed a huge sigh of relief. "Did you *have* to do that?"

"Put yourself in-a our situation, Doctor."

Matt loaded the clip but did not chamber a round. "Can't blame him, Chris. I would have done the same."

"Okay, Commander. No hard feelings, no? You mentioned seeing some things. I am-a curious."

"The device. Technically, it decodes and displays scenes derived from memory fragments embedded in airborne particles. Miniscule electrical charges on common lint and dust generated from humans and animals."

"Yes, we witnessed your Iraq battle scene in the lab. Anything else?"

"It didn't end there. It replayed old thoughts and dreams, Doctor Miller's wife's memories." Matt paused. "That was just the device. There were also those rituals with a Crow chief in Montana. He did sort of the same thing, but with smoke and hair."

Monsignor Trovarto laughed. "Yes! We know of such rituals. Well, maybe not of *your* exact episodes, but of the ancient knowledge. Your device bridges a gap between modern technology and the knowledge of-a the old. Patrick's abilities, for example. He is not the only one. There have been many others throughout the centuries. If they were not persecuted as freaks, destroyed for heresy, or clandestinely vaulted away by powers that sought their secrets, they were relegated to reclusion, if not complete isolation. They hid in constant fear of destruction. Patrick's abilities were discounted when his validators insisted on testing in nearly sterile conditions. Only when we tested him in the contaminated air, did he triumph. In fact, the dirtier the air, the stronger his powers of manipulation. It's-a very fascinating, but you see the correlation, no?"

Matt nodded slowly and Chris offered the same sentiment. "Absolutely. So, he's learned to manipulate the energy contained in the particles. The same particles that contain information—memory."

"Doctor Miller," Patrick cleared his throat. "You said 'learned'. I don't recall teaching myself anything. I've had the ability ever since I can remember."

Trovarto continued. "That is correct. It is an innate talent blessed randomly by God. That is-a of course until science provides an answer. Your device contains a key to this mystery."

"River was right." Chris mumbled.

"River?" Trovarto asked.

"The Crow chief. He gave his life to help us. He showed us his ability—his inheritable ability—to commune with his elders. I believe the ritual is a crude variant of our device."

"I know of the natives in which you speak and apologize that I was powerless to intervene. You must know they were victims of Spada Sacra's interrogators, a fact revealed to me just before my own escape. I am saddened by the loss of such noble people, Doctor Miller. The device, is it in your attaché?" Trovarto rubbed his forehead. "Perhaps you would entertain us with a demonstration?"

Chris tilted his head to meet Trovarto's eyes, wondering what could possibly appear on screen. "One moment."

He reached down to retrieve the attaché case leaning against the inner cabin wall next to his right leg. The assistant that previously held the pistol to Matt's neck removed the spent tea service to make room next to the Saqqara Bird's case. Chris set the attaché down, flicked both latches open, and retrieved the laptop from under some loose articles of clothing. He stared into the case for another moment and decided to also remove the buckskin pouch given to him by River. Closing the case and placing it back on the floor, Chris unfolded the computer flat in the middle of the table. Everyone at the table had an unobstructed view of the screen. The machine initiated its booting sequence and soon displayed its main menu. Chris executed the particle reading application and waited for its interface to appear. Once open, he navigated the cursor to the eject icon and tapped the screen. The collection tray popped from the side of the unit and automatically closed on its own.

"That's odd . . ."

Chris fumbled with the touch pad, but the program became nonresponsive. A grey, staticky screen briefly appeared before abruptly changing to a short series of bright white flashes. A close-up of Xeno's ominous face slowly materialized; his eyes clearly glared in Chris' direction. He laughed hideously. "Did you forget something?"

Patrick, closest to the unit, was mortified. Trovarto jumped away from the table. Xeno grinned wide and his pupils shrank as the staticky white flashes consumed him once more. The capricious string of clown messages puzzled Chris immensely.

"I have a feeling this was not the demonstration you had in mind, Doctor Miller. What *was* that?"

"My apologies, Father. It is a recurring dream my daughter had one evening. I sampled a stuffed toy she won long ago at a fair—a church festival, ironically—and it's probably an anomaly with the collection system. Some particles carry stronger residual traces than others, apparently. I'd swear though that this *dream* carries some degree of lucidity."

"Intriguing."

Chris toggled the tray ejection mechanism once more. It remained open this time. He glanced down at the buckskin pouch next to the laptop. "Monsignor, I am wondering if you would mind a minor indulgence for this demonstration."

Trovarto tucked his upper lip. "Are you sure? What do you have in-a mind?"

Matt leaned back in his chair as the jet's fuselage quavered ever so slightly from a rogue air pocket. "If he's doing what I think he's going to do, this could be quite interesting."

"I'd like to test something River insinuated during our encounter. Matt mentioned smoke and hair to you earlier. River brought forth messages from a long-deceased elder in a fire ritual. I want to see if the soft drive can emulate the same."

"By all means."

"He presented this to me just before sending us off."

Chris untied the leather straps and unraveled the buckskin pouch. He reached inside and retrieved the lock of River's hair. Carefully, he extracted one strand and placed it in the collection tray. After rebundling the lock of hair, he tucked it back inside the pouch along with the knife, rolled the flap back around, and tied its leather straps taut. He snapped the collection tray closed and waited. After a few moments in anticipation, only one fragment file appeared on the screen.

"That's a lot lower than normal. Dozens if not hundreds usually appear, Father." Chris noted the fragment's details. "Nonetheless, the file appears quite robust."

"Are you going to play it or keep talking about it?" Matt quipped.

Chris stared him down with a smile, at the same time he tapped the execution command. Bright white flashes gave way to an image of River's tipi fireplace, roaring with many of its sparks disappearing into the rising column of heated and smoke-filled air. Chris and Emily were barely visible as they slept behind the dancing flames. River's profound voice echoed from the laptop.

"We all have a purpose. The spirits blessed my son and me after many, many moons—our purpose determined, our promises kept. We are at peace, my friends. May your paths be so fortunate. I will always be here for you."

The image disappeared behind a series of white flashes, and then the screen returned to the player prompt. Chris' eyes were watery and red behind his glasses. He wiped a tear. The faint roar of the jet's turbofans fluctuated slightly as another bump of turbulence nudged the cabin.

Trovarto stood up. "Let-a there be no doubt why we are all here, gentlemen. Doctor Miller? *Magnifico!* Absolutely magnificent presentation."

Matt was speechless as he slouched in his plush recliner. Chris stared at him again, shutting down the laptop and placing it back in the attaché case along with the buckskin pouch. The flight's captain gave a short announcement detailing a climb of few thousand feet to avoid some oncoming rough air, and to update the ETA as a result.

Trovarto sat reclined, allowing the headrest to engulf him. "We have a few hours before reaching Cairo. You may wish to get-a some rest, no?"

Patrick did just that. They were accustomed to frequent long-distance jet travel, and notions of lag disappeared from their conversation.

Chris searched around his seat's armrests and found the position actuator. Matt studied the others. Discussions were ongoing towards the back of the jet. A few had also begun resting. He stood up to make his way down the aisle to the rear lavatory. "I have to hit the head."

Closing the facility's door, he proceeded to take his seat. The nagging itch from his stitched shoulder became painfully intense. Scratching softly through his shirt offered little relief. He expedited his business, stood back up, and stripped off his shirt. He reached around with his right hand to softly scratch the stitches and felt something quite peculiar. The stitches were still intact, but the wound felt completely closed. He turned around, exposing his back to the mirror. There was nothing left but the stitches themselves. No inflammation and no scabbing—not even a scar. He couldn't believe his eyes.

"Son of a bitch." He laughed. "Some granny!"

Pinching the stitches' small knots, he slowly pried them from his flesh, one by one. He wiped a drop of blood from the last puncture and threw his shirt back on, shocked in astonishment. He finished cleaning up and went back to his seat towards the front of the aircraft.

"You won't believe what—" Matt tapped Chris' shoulder, but he had already shaken hands with the sandman.

Pyramid Schemers

An authoritative, yet alluring female voice charmed the intercom.

"This is your captain. Our descent into the Nile River basin will begin in one moment. Please raise your seatbacks, secure loose items, and prepare for landing. *Merci beaucoup, messieurs.*"

Chris felt Matt's nudge on his left arm. He turned, and a shaft of morning sunlight blazed through one of the portside windows, immediately blinding him. He squinted, rubbing beneath his glasses. Matt grinned but said nothing. The small jet buffeted through turbulent changes as it passed from the cooler Mediterranean to the scorching sands on the outskirts of the delta. To the left, the sun glistened over green, lush farmlands of the Nile's estuary. To the right, the tan abyss of the Sahara stretched into a darkened horizon. Several minutes later, the intercom's distinctive twinkle tones interrupted Chris' blissful view of the landscape beyond his portal.

The captain followed, "We are instructed to land on Runway 5-Left. This will provide a unique view of the Giza Plateau from the starboard windows within a few moments for those of you who are interested. We will be landing in less than five minutes. I hope you enjoyed our flight as much as I. *Merci.*"

"I always wanted to see them in person." Chris mumbled. He checked if Matt was enjoying the sights, only to find him paying no attention whatsoever. "I suppose you've had enough of the desert."

"Yup." Matt replied with a flat tone. "Don't care much for the sand. I am also wondering where the priest ran off to."

Patrick overheard the conversation and turned around. "He's a terrible inner-ear disease, you know. Fatal to some, from what I understand. Buggers him completely on descents. He's taken ill back there in the toilet, I'll wager."

"Is it serious?" Chris asked.

Matt tapped him on the arm and whispered, "Chris, he said it causes fatalities. What do *you* think?"

"Sorry. Some people, including myself, mean that expression figuratively."

Patrick became fidgety. "I imagine that it is rather serious if you can't control the fluids in your ear. Guaranteed nausea and most debilitating, they say. This is the fifth trip I've been on with the Father. Terrible, if I should say so."

The captain aligned the jet on a long final for 5-Left. Tens of thousands of conjoined grey rooftops blurred underneath its fuselage, then the Nile River, and soon afterward, the airspace over Cairo's most sacred mosques. Electric motors actuated the landing gear doors, and a rush of swirling air slightly raised the noise level inside the cabin. The starboard windows filled with Cairo International's latest additions to its new terminal—structures that escaped the mêlées of Arab Spring. Trovarto's passengers bobbed as the jet's main rubber contacted the pavement. The tires chirped twice then moaned from the bouncy traverse across cracked, exhausted concrete. The runways were reportedly next on Cairo International's renovation list, but they had become a long-running joke in the international pilot community. A gradual turn onto a taxiway heading the opposite direction placed them on the path to the lesser-publicized Terminal 4, where most of the business elite kept themselves from envious eyes. Rolling to a stop in front of the terminal's entrance, the passengers unclasped their seatbelts and prepared to debark.

Emerging from the rear of the aircraft, Monsignor Trovarto uncovered his mouth briefly to give instructions.

"Doctor Miller, Commander Jacobson, my apologies. Please remain seated while my associates prepare for our arrival. I have visited this city on several occasions without incident. Lately, I am-a told it has become more difficult for certain foreign travelers."

"Monsignor, I need to make a call to my daughter and let her know we arrived safely."

"That would be a security concern, I am afraid."

Patrick stepped forward. "Here, use my cell."

"Are you a-sure? Because, you know they have the monitors for the international communications." Trovarto straightened his cassock to ventilate.

"Of course I'm sure, Father. We've got it bouncing three continents through a police kiosk in Tokyo. Good luck sniffin' that one out, I tell ya."

Patrick handed Chris his phone. He dialed Adriel's land-line, but nobody picked up after eight rings.

The monsignor put his hand on Chris' shoulder. "It is a six-hour difference, Doctor Miller. They should be asleep, no? Best you try again in a few hours."

Chris didn't say anything and handed the phone back to Patrick. Trovarto followed his four, well-detailed agents down the jet's airstairs and onto the ramp.

Two late-model, white passenger vans with dark-tinted windows parked alongside the aircraft. Additional agents jumped out of each vehicle and crisply walked around to unite with Trovarto and his entourage. They briefed him over the impending commute and its potential hazards before he climbed inside one of the vans. A taller agent returned, motioning the remaining passengers to vacate the aircraft. Patrick rolled out of his seat, grabbed his backpack, and shuffled forward with the exit queue. Yusuf, shielding the Saqqara Bird's case, signaled Matt and Chris to exit before his group. They inched up the aisle with the others, past the galley, and finally down the stairs.

Land! Chris' legs were suddenly aware.

Once down on the scorching concrete they were ushered to sit with Trovarto, Patrick, and the two best-trained agents in the security detail. Yusuf and the others exited and climbed into the other van without delay.

With purposeful intent, the vans beat a path through the swelter of the awakening city's interior—its streets not yet clogged. Their drivers whisked them past Cairo's most ancient mosques, across the Nile, through several miles of densely populated housing, and finally through Palace Mena's colossal, gated entrance.

Situated less than half a kilometer from the Giza Necropolis, the facility captivated Chris and Matt in a state of complete awe. Once host to sultans, prime ministers and presidents, the Palace had evolved into one of Africa's top resort and convention facilities. And, while the continent's most magisterial tradesmen cavorted their wares at the resort's extramural markets, those organizations requiring insular accommodations convened at a less conspicuous concourse located inside a quietly guarded corner of the compound.

Trovarto's diligent chauffeurs eschewed the Palace's main entrance for a narrow vine-canopied stone path along the northern border of the compound. On the other side of a large garden, a discreet, yet opulent traditional Egyptian edifice appeared. The vans slowed to a halt at the facility's entrance. Immediately, two men from the security details of each van exited and secured the building's arched doorway. Yusuf and the fundamentalist Jewish contingency exited the first van, then Patrick, Monsignor Trovarto, Chris, and Matt exited from the second. The detail led them inside the facility's doorway, then down a rococo and wood-carved hallway that featured a ceiling in excess of nine meters high. Chris had difficulty maintaining a direct path along with the others, his eyes wandered and wondered.

Towards the end of the hallway on the far left, another arched entryway displayed massive, hand-carved ebony double doors. A suited detail guarded each side of the entrance, and one of those agents was a towering monolith of a man—at least 350 pounds and chiseled. It normally took two men of any variety to open the room's elephantine doors, but he handled the task efficiently one-handed, and gave a confident smile while doing so. The jet's congregation finally reached its nirvana, and Chris knew it within the first glimpse through the doorway.

He broke the entrance's threshold into the fascination of hundreds of hushed attendees in a vast conference room. Yet another agent greeted him and, although his dialect was barely intelligible due to his thick Arabic accent, he instructed Chris to stay close behind him en route to the podium area on the far side of the room.

The whispers at first were deafening, but soon drowned in the commentaries of those he passed. The oohs. The aahs. And then the clapping started—louder and louder until the room erupted in spontaneous standing ovation. Chris and Matt were overwhelmed trying to interpret these people encircling the dozens of large, round tables. Their faces were locked in wide smiles of adoration, and Chris wanted to return those smiles, but he was shocked and puzzled. He didn't know what to make of it all. His mind exploded with hypotheses.

"What is this?" Matt finally shouted.

An agent tapped Matt's shoulder and motioned him to follow Chris. He reluctantly stumbled forward in the same incredulous state as Chris', but instead felt like prodded cattle, paraded before a salivating banquet.

The Monsignor caught up with him and shouted into his ear. "It is-a for you too, Commander. Do not be intimidated!"

A rectangular stage waited at the far end of the convention hall. Upon it were a few long tables covered with decorative cloths, leather chairs with high seatbacks, and a dominating projector screen on the back wall that displayed the La Fratellanza logo featuring animated primary geometrical shapes nested within other primary geometrical shapes—a circle, a square, and an equilateral triangle rotating in opposite directions until stopping with the triangle pointing down. Chris' eyes slowly began to focus on individual people as they cheered. He recognized a few from various scientific journals he read and consulted with over the years. A couple he regarded as colleagues.

"Why are they clapping?" Chris asked Trovarto, having to climb above the crowd noise.

"*You*, Doctor. Your presence, your safety, and the most important discovery since electricity, maybe even-a fire—that is why!"

"I don't understand!"

The cheering slowly abated as the attendees furthest away from them began taking their seats. Chris and Matt suddenly found themselves surrounded by a small throng of admirers and felt uncomfortably claustrophobic because of them. He was squirming to escape the multitude of congratulatory handshakes, questions, and pats on the back. After another few moments, he became numb from it. The noise, the jet lag. It was enough for anyone to fall faint. Then he heard a voice that jolted him into crystal consciousness.

"Christopher?" The voice resonated a second time as he desperately prairie-dogged over the scrum. Some acutely perceptive revelers recognized his attempts to make contact and cleared a path to the origin of the voice. Chris' knees weakened with relief, feeling a sense of something familiar and something he could hold onto. And, hold onto her he did when Dao Ming zigzagged her way through the crowd to embrace him in the midst of chaos. Their hug was tight and genuine, lasting for several moments until the two wondered if their show of affection was slightly more than cordial. Dao felt like home, and she held him as tightly as he held her. The mutual admiration and affection were indeed real. No more platitudinal flirting; they were in each other's arms, and Chris wasn't about to be first to let go. Dao's eyes shimmered with happiness. She was not about to let go either. The room approved.

"Oh God, Dao. I'm so glad you're here."

"I feel the same! I worried about you. They told me of the attempts on your life. I am glad you are here. I cannot believe it. It is unreal to me."

Chris felt the tap of inevitability on his shoulder. Monsignor Trovarto, Patrick, and the security detail behind them, helped clear the way to a small group of individuals conversing just in front of the stage. An elderly gentleman came into view first—curly haired and wearing a sport coat over a buttoned shirt with wool trousers. Chris identified him as the 1992 Nobel Psychology Laureate, Dr. Edgar Beckmann. *He doesn't look a day older.* They exchanged greetings briefly and were next introduced to a robed Tibetan Gelugpa monk named Jet Sun. He bowed deeply with praying hands, then smiled and congratulated them on their treacherous escape.

Behind the monk stood another individual Chris recognized—famed Egyptologist Dr. Amid Harwaziz. His genuine charm and positive nature captivated Chris as they spoke.

"Welcome to Giza, my friends. Welcome! Welcome! We have so much to share, but for now, there are more introductions."

Yusuf broke from the crowd behind Chris and handed the Saqqara Bird right away to Dr. Harwaziz.

"He was extremely useful to us, Doctor H, but blessed, I am glad he is back home where he belongs."

Harwaziz thanked him and then turned to introduce Chris to the last people of the group—a young man and a young woman, both in their mid-twenties, and a man in his late fifties who was wearing a black shirt and tie, large, black, square-framed glasses with thick rims, black trousers, and a camelhair blazer.

"Glad you made it, Chris," said the man. "That you are here safely is important . . . to all of us."

Chris turned towards him and squinted. "I don't feel safe. Someone is after us—after me and my family. They killed our friends! Until they are caught . . ."

"You are in very good hands now."

Chris uncharacteristically paused when shaking his hand. "Do I know you?"

"Not formally, Doctor Miller." The man replied with a playful grin. "Allow me to introduce my family. This is my son, Rocco, and my daughter, Anastasia."

"My friends call me Tulip," said the young woman. "Father told us much about you."

Chris scoured his mind, knowing that he met her father somewhere before. The names. He knew those names!

"Oh dear, but—no! It can't be! The Monkey Man? From the church fair? But that was—"

"A mere five years ago. What an extraordinary memory. I have been keeping my eyes on you for much longer Doctor Miller, and I am very sorry about Suzanne."

"*This* is Rocco and Tulip? I thought you were talking about your dogs!"

Anastasia poked the man in the side and said, "Gee, thanks Papa."

"They are my adopted family, Doctor Miller. I found Rocco just before the Austrian Child Services gathered him in Salzburg. Anastasia's mother abandoned her in Prague. At least, that is the official record. Both of my children possess, well, remarkable abilities."

Matt felt something tugging at his mind as Anastasia peered into his eyes.

"This one is mistrustful and wants to know your name, Papa."

Matt scoffed at the notion. The Monkey Man offered his apology and a slight laugh.

"You'll have to excuse my daughter gentlemen. She has a botheration with privacy. Sometimes, however, her talents are quite advantageous, and I apologize for my lethargic manners. I am Anund Harwin Hammett, the Third—current chairman of The Brotherhood. Or, if you prefer, Monkey Man will do. Please join me on the stage; we have a presentation to make. Many of our people convened hours before the break of dawn in anticipation of your arrival, and they are quite anxious as you can imagine. Commander Jacobson, please do my children the honor of gracing their table with your presence."

Without further formality, Harwin Hammett, Trovarto, Beckmann, Harwaziz, and Jet Sun made their way towards the stage's staircase.

Trovarto turned back to Chris and Dao. "Please join us. You are the primary reason we have assembled in-a the first place!"

As the group took their places behind the tables on either side of the dais, enthusiastic cheering spontaneously re-erupted and boisterously continued until Anund Hammett lured the crowd to eventual quiescence.

"My esteemed colleagues. Ladies and Gentlemen. Welcome to the First International Convention of La Fratellanza di Verità!"

The audience of over three hundred again exploded in a standing ovation.

"Please. Please. *S'il vous plait. Qí. Bitte.*" Hammett smiled, feeling the overwhelming optimism that swept the room. "It is my deepest pleasure to be in the company of so many that I have come to know and endear over the decades, as well as the new friends who endeavored to be with us today."

Another round of cheering blossomed in recognition of Chris, Dao, and Matt.

"Our society has struggled for its very existence since the times of the Medieval Inquisition, and they almost extinguished The Brotherhood some 350 years ago, but we survived, fighting to carry on the tradition of our moniker. For over a thousand years, the truth—the *veritatum purus*—was suppressed by *inherited* corruption and greed, passed down by progressive fallacies. This cyclical disease has been an unbreakable ring of falsehood, that is, unbreakable until now."

Again, the entire room came to their feet, cheering wildly and releasing a millennium of angered futility.

"Fellow members, we are here today because our struggles' end is in sight. The link between the spiritual and scientific worlds is forever bonded—not that *we* did not know it."

Hammett attracted a short round of laughter throughout the room. "The truth, my brothers, the truth is at hand, and for the first time in hundreds of years, the light of world peace and the prosperity for humankind is now aflame!"

For the fourth time, everyone stood and cheered, whistled, yelled "bravo!", or quietly clasped their hands in prayer. The exception this time was that some people were looking directly at Chris, and such adoration he found overwhelming. Sure, he had given many presentations in front of many people before, and in several instances, to more people than currently attending this convention. Still, those presentations were for middle-career colleagues and various other devoted underlings—nowhere near the illustrious attendees now adoring him.

Oh, but how selfish am I. Chris turned and hugged Dao, insisting those same people would recognize her contributions, not that it was necessary; they *knew.*

Monsignor Trovarto sat next to Chris, nudged him, and whispered in his ear. "You are to make a small demonstration of the device, now. They want to see it for themselves."

Chris felt a little uneasy by the lack of any warning. Nonetheless, he had another problem. "A demonstration using what sample material, Father?"

"Not to worry." Trovarto whispered while taking the podium. "Ladies and-a Gentlemen, I give you Doctor Christopher Miller and a demonstration of his extraordinary device."

Chris entertained the clamorous hurrahs by being politely humble. No waiving or anything of the sort, he simply smiled, stepped over to the podium, and stood alongside Hammett and Trovarto. The auspicious chairman winked an eye, then reached down into the podium's lower storage and produced a stuffed toy—the very same blue monkey from the fair several years ago.

Hammett handed the toy to Chris and said, "I'm sure you'll collect a colossal number of samples from this one."

Chris could only sigh at the continued ride down memory lane. Hammett showed him the projector's input cable, a communications link, and a compatible power supply lead for the laptop. He then instructed a production engineer to initiate the presentation equipment's booting.

"Okay, Doctor Miller. It's all yours." Hammett stood aside and turned around to view the large screen on the wall behind them. Chris connected the computer and executed its startup sequence.

"Good morning . . ."

He began his introduction of the device and waited for the spontaneous clapping to subside.

"After years of research and utilization of fantastic, cutting-edge nano technologies in partnership with Doctor Ming's research team, a new paradigm for digital memorization—ironically, through analogue matter—has been accomplished, or so we thought. A few days ago, we discovered that this device not only dawns a new era of memory capacitance, but also recaptures residual analog memories stored on the cellular level of particulate matter. In essence, it is measurable self-capacitance on the picofarad scale. Tiny, ubiquitous—the proverbial snake in front of us all. You all seem quite aware of this device; I will now initiate demonstration of it."

During another round of resounding cheers, Chris pointed the laptop's cursor over the program's executable icon and tapped once, waiting for the collection tray to eject. Abruptly, the cheering dissolved into hushed gasps as the audience pointed at the screen in horror.

"Bishop Esposito!" Trovarto yelled. "But how—?"

Chris refocused his eyes from the massive projector screen on the wall just behind him to his device's display. A robed man holding a jewel-topped cane appeared as if he was looking directly in Chris' direction. It was indeed Narciso Esposito, and there were other robed men standing behind him. Intermixed were several well-dressed and heavily-armed agents, but two of them sat towards the rear of the room, puffing on cigarettes and looking mildly disinterested. It wasn't these people that drew the wind from the crowded Egyptian meeting hall, but the gagged and blindfolded victim wallowing just beside Esposito and his cane.

"Jack!" Chris gulped.

Monsignor Trovarto repositioned himself beside Chris. Hammett jumped up and whispered in Chris' ear. "Let Trovarto handle this man."

Chris turned around to face him. "Who is he?"

"He is Bishop Narciso Esposito, second in command of the Spada Sacra—our oldest and most powerful foe."

"Ahh, the delightful Monsignor." Esposito sarcastically chaffed. "I see you have aligned yourself with an illustrious collection of banal misfits. How predictable. I had an itch about you, but His Eminence, no surprise, would not let me scratch it."

Trovarto cursed himself for not fully examining the laptop before the presentation. He inspected its surface and found a pinhole camera lens in the upper-right corner of the frame.

Esposito continued, poking his cane into Jack Kattner's ribs. "It is a little late for that now, my dear Monsignor. You see, our friends made more use of this executive than we originally conceived. Trust is a foolish notion, and it appears this man had none for his friends. Intelligent, this one . . . installed GPS tracking and video into that device without any of his engineers the wiser. At least, not the ones that mattered. What a pity, all this deceitfulness. Maybe he is not so intelligent after all. Difficult to believe in his present state. Look at him. Just another helpless piece of meat. Nonetheless, all of you are senseless to believe a pathetic band of hapless eccentrics measure against the longest-running network of power on this earth."

"That is where you are mistaken, *Your Grace*." Trovarto barked with utter contempt. "Long before your kind, peace and prosperity existed for-a thousand years. You are but a momentary illness in human history. A cough. One that will soon be vanquished forever."

"Spare me your illusions of utopia, Trovarto. Just what do you plan to do? Run to His Holiness with the news? Email it to the media? How do you know your first contact outside of that room would not be one of us? Of course you know. You tried countless times throughout the centuries and—what happened? The same thing that is going to happen when you bring Doctor Miller, Dao Ming, and this device to me immediately."

"Not a chance."

"But of course. The Monsignor needs motivation!"

Before Trovarto was able to offer his own brand of acerbity, Esposito produced a jewel-topped cane. A pulsing amethyst light became visible from within its crystal top just before the bishop pounded it against Kattner's nape. A flash of intense violet blanked the convention's projector screen. Shock and horror overtook the attendees as they gasped in fright. Jack Kattner, longtime contributor to the world of computer science and beloved division conductor, collapsed motionless to the floor. La Fratellanza cried in revulsion.

Chris picked up the laptop and looked directly into the camera's pinhole. "How can you call yourself someone of the cloth when you just murdered a good man?"

Trovarto made the sign of the cross and prayed as Esposito's face filled the screen.

"But Doctor Miller, your friend is not dead. He is—how should I put this—permanently incapacitated. A minor inconvenience; no commandments have been broken, God be praised."

"Except the last one. Guess you neglected to read the entire manual, you evil sick and twisted man." Chris shouted. "Jack Kattner didn't deserve this! I will never come to you, understand? NEVER!"

Esposito yawned and snapped his fingers to someone off-screen. "I suppose we all lack imagination sometimes."

Chris' pupils dilated to the most open blackness, reflecting his most intimate horror. A horror that now stood before him on the screen. *Oh no.*

"Daddy?"

Acknowledgements

My wonderful bride, translator, and part-time editor, Maria.
Never to be underestimated or thankless.
Te Quiero Mucho, Mi Amor.

To my parents' steadfast encouragement.
(It never hurts to have a couple highly-educated educators
nearby!)

My close family and friends
Jessica and Reesee

To my literary professors at the University of South Florida for
encouragement and inspiration.

Special Thanks to the freely available reference websites, their
providers, and donors:

Google.com, Google Earth, Dictionary.com, Wikipedia
(expertly filtered), Encyclopedia.com, Bablefish (2008), and
Aaron Spence's Panedia (c2009).

NEXT!